Dahlia Cassidy

Dahlia

Dahlia Cassidy

Anne Cameron

HARBOUR PUBLISHING

Published by
HARBOUR PUBLISHING
P.O. BOX 219
Madeira Park, BC
Canada VON 2H0
www.harbourpublishing.com

Edited by Mary Schendlinger
Cover design by Peter Read
Interior design by Jason Dewinetz
Cover photo © Getty Images
Printed and bound in Canada

Harbour Publishing acknowledges
financial support from the Government
of Canada through the Book Publishing
Industry Development Program and the
Canada Council for the Arts, and from the
Province of British Columbia
through the British Columbia Arts
Council and the Book Publisher's
Tax Credit through the Ministry of
Provincial Revenue.

Canada Council   Conseil des Arts
for the Arts   du Canada

BRITISH COLUMBIA
ARTS COUNCIL

*Library and Archives of Canada
Cataloguing in Publication:*

Cameron, Anne, 1938-
    Dahlia Cassidy / Anne Cameron

ISBN 1-55017-344-8

    I. Title.

PS8555.A5187D33 2004
C813'.54   C2004-903010-8

Acknowledgements:

With sincere thanks to Mary Schendlinger,
my editor, who always goes above and
beyond the call of duty.

And for Eleanor, as ever.

For my children, and their children, with love.

One

Dahlia Cassidy drove back to Nanaimo from Tofino in her '57 Chev in a foul and bitter mood. She figured she was just about ready to swear off sex forever. Not only was she in a great deal of pain, she was bored. The preliminaries weren't all that bad. At least when they were in rut you could get them to dance, although few of them did that very well. It seemed they had to be mostly drunk before their inhibitions loosened enough to get their feet moving. But once the dancing was finished—and let's face it, she could dance by herself or with one or two or three of the kids—it was the same old thing.

Even the few tentative attempts at foreplay were tiresomely similar. Dahlia had decided that the men she met up with just weren't interested in foreplay at all. For them it was something a guy had to endure in order to get down to the nitty-gritty. For years she had clung to the hope that she had simply been fishing in the wrong bay and that if she moved around often enough, sooner or later she'd happen upon a few men who had more in mind than some friction. But so far, in spite of more miles and moves than she could bother trying to remember, she had missed the turnoff.

The men she encountered would kiss a bit, usually too vigorously, their teeth pushing against her lips as if crushing was as much the object of the exercise as arousal. Then, totally fixated on their goal of penetration for its own sake, they would push their tongues into her mouth as a shortcut. She never enjoyed it. Did they? Or did they just think tongue-kissing was daring? Then there would be nipping, and you had to slow them down on that one or you could get hurt. They'd move from that to some fumbling at her boobs, as if they'd learned their techniques watching their mothers knead bread dough. Dahlia didn't know how to tell them that a day-old infant did a better job of breast arousal, and could be depended on to hang in for at least a half-hour. Then, disgustingly quickly, before the tingling in her nipples could establish itself and grow to something more, it was the old push 'n' shove, push 'n' shove. She imagined a phalanx of male cheerleaders precision marching around the perimeter of the bed. Gimme a *P*, gimme a *U*, gimme an *S* and an *H*, yeaaaaa, *PUSH!*

Once in a while a truly adventurous one—or, to be more precise, one who thought himself truly adventurous—would dare to foray into oral sex. That's when she had to be careful, because whisker burn in that most precious of places is one of the things no female in her right mind will volunteer for, the others being a dose and an unwanted pregnancy. For a dose, they've got antibiotics. Pregnancy, well, after the swelling and discomfort are gone and your ankles are back to their regular size and shape, at least you get a delicious little jigger to cuddle. But whisker burn on the dear bird is straight hell, and all the worse if he's laced himself with Old Spice or Mennen After Shave.

Dahlia was so angry with herself that if she weren't so busy driving the Chev, she'd boot herself in the arse with both feet. Everyone knows that Frenchmen talk with their hands, fight with their feet and fuck with their faces. That's like rises in the east, sets in the west, one of the laws of creation and the universe. But everyone makes mistakes, and usually they're based on flawed presuppositions.

So she'd gone to Tofino, almost a three-hour drive, purportedly to see Long Beach, an excuse nobody from the coast would believe because all there is at Long Beach now is a stretch of dead sand and some big waves crashing on rocks still discoloured by the oil spilled by the Yanks. The razor clams are all dead, the butter clams too, and what was once an enormous pantry has become Mother Hubbard's bare cupboard. But she said she was going to see Long Beach, and the babysitter had grinned. What did she care? She was getting paid whether Dahlia got laid or not.

Dal had met the Frenchman in Toby's, where she had a gig playing violin and guitar. He kept buying her drinks and asking if she could play "When the White Lilacs Bloom Again." He didn't know the name of the song in English—for all she knew he didn't even know it in French—but he hummed it and had the first nine notes close enough to pitch that she recognized what he was trying to convey. She played the song five times that night. Thank God the crowd at Toby's kept changing or someone might have chucked something at her. She actually only sipped at one of the beers the guy bought her, but she got the money for the others. The bartender kept track for her. At three bucks a shot, she did all right with that song.

⌁

The Frenchman wanted to take her home, but she refused. She had her own car and had learned a long time ago never to let them know where you really live. He was back the next night and the next, and finally, because she figured anyone who could remember the first nine notes of anything might actually have some artistry hidden in them somewhere, she agreed to go back to his hotel room "for a drink."

She had a beer, and they talked a bit. She noticed that he didn't seem to use his hands for conversation any more than anyone else. Maybe it was only true when they were speaking French, and in English their hands became paralyzed. He was at least couth enough not to try to bounce on her bones right then and there. Instead, he invited her to Long Beach. Well, why not. She couldn't manage the entire weekend—she worked on Friday and Saturday nights—but Sunday morning saw her heading off in the Chev, honking goodbyes to her pack of kids. They waved briefly and then turned their attention back to the potato chip bribes.

The Frenchman was waiting outside his hotel with a mile-wide grin on his face and a small sports bag in one hand. He was undoubtedly a total hunk, one of the hunkiest Dal had ever met. He hinted that he'd do the driving, but Dal wasn't having any of that. From what she'd seen, putting men behind the wheel made them think they were in control. You had to practically kiss their arses to get them to pull in at Peepeeville, as if emptying your bladder was a privilege that they and they alone were bestowing on you. She supposed it had something to do with the scrotum. You watch them driving, and by God they have *got* to pass if the car ahead of them is driven by a woman. At risk of life and limb, their own and everyone else's, they have double-damn got to pass. And if that woman is in front of them because halfway up the hill she pulled into the passing lane and went sailing by in a worn-out old bazoo that is performing like a brand-new Maserati, you can be sure they'll do anything at all to get back in front, even if it means duelling with death. Dal figured a man's scrotum tightened as soon as he felt the wheel in the palms of his hands, and then, each time a woman passed him or happened to be driving in front of him, the tightened scrotum cramped, and the squished knackers hurt so bad that the right leg jerked and sent the gas pedal to the floor.

Dahlia stopped at the gas station at Cameron Lake and filled the tank, then visited the Ladies and emptied her own. She bought half a dozen ginger ale and a big bag of salted pretzels and waited for the Frenchman to come back from the Men's. She wondered why it was that the women had to go to the Ladies but the guys used the Men's. Ladies should be balanced by Gentlemen, or at least Gents. Men is balanced by Women. Not Ladies and Men. The Frenchman had a couple of bottles of whiskey in his little sports bag. He offered to mix some of it into her can of ginger ale.

"I'm driving, darlin'," Dal grinned at him, "and you just proved you've never been on the road we're about to take. The only people who drank liquor and then tried to drive to Tofino are dead and buried long ago."

There followed a good 15 minutes of "Great Roads I Have Travelled," all delivered in a heavily accented rumble. Dal began to wonder if there was a road in the entire province of Quebec that wasn't a total disaster, or a driver there who wasn't blind drunk.

The Frenchman checked them into the motel. "I've got dis," he said grandly, pulling out his MasterCard with all the panache of a Musketeer hauling out his sword. Dal left him to it and busied herself at the postcard rack, trying to find a different one for each of the kids because otherwise there was sure to be an uproar. Sometimes the kids chose which one they wanted by starting with the oldest, and working their way down to the youngest, sometimes it was the other way around. Sometimes Dal started them in the middle and went alter-step until each had chosen, and sometimes she just hucked 'em on the sofa and let the kids scramble.

The motel room was like any other motel room—nothing to write home about. The Frenchman hauled out the whiskey bottles first thing. With the road behind her, Dal could indulge. She managed three swallows before the one who had been nipping steadily through the entire two-and-a-half-hour trip was swarming all over her, grinning and seeming to believe she was every bit as hot as he was, and just praying for some of the push 'n' shove. There hadn't been any opportunity to see if he fought at all, let alone with his huge feet, and his hands had been either still or holding a whiskey bottle while he fractured the English language, but Dal was hopeful that at least part of the widely known truth would be proved.

Unfortunately the guy was heavily into hickeys—in more intimate spots than the neck—and got carried away with the momentum of the festivities. Dal yelped. It was sheer and total reflex action made her legs jerk. Her knees connected with his broad shoulders, and he was knocked back off the end of the bed to the floor. He stared at her with the same expression on his face as a two-year-old whose juice has just spilled. Except, of course, his hadn't. And didn't. Dal had more on her mind than satisfying his little itch.

The rest of Sunday and some of Monday, Dal hurt so badly she felt sick to her stomach. There isn't anything much more frustrating than being in the Lone Cone Motel in Tofino with a twat so sore you can barely stand, can't sit so driving home is out of the question, and can't eat because of a pain that goes right up to the bellybutton. There she was, practically next door to one of the finest seafood restaurants on the face of the globe, and too nauseated by pain to hobble over for a meal. It's a helluva note when your sore snap keeps you from the grilled snapper. And for this she had hired a babysitter?

The Frenchman sulked so badly you'd have thought he was the one with the huge and throbbing blood blister on his clit. All Dal could do was lie on the bed, drink beer and whiskey, watch TV and try not to hork. The very nerve pathways designed by Mother Nature to take clit sensation and magnify it until it culminates in glorious orgasm were, instead, taking the equivalent of a kick to the balls, roiling it around, turning it in on itself, spiralling it and intensifying it into just about the most goddamn horrible pain in the entire gut she had ever felt. Bearing-down pains were zip-all compared to this!

Finally, desperate and more than a bit woozy, she filled the tub. She lowered herself into the water with trepidation, but the hot water did more for her than all the futile fumbling attentions and ministrations of her clumsy companion. She lay back, sighed and thought there was a small off chance she might one day feel human again. The warmth eased the horrible cramps and put a stop to the stabbing pain.

She sipped her beer and thought of seven good methods for revenge.

1 Kick him in the nuts.
2 Kick him in the nuts and then hit his woodie with the heel of his own boot.
3 Kick him in the nuts, hit his woodie with the heel of his boot, then twist an elastic band tight around the shaft of his pride and joy.
4 Nail his scrotum to a black-pitch log, then set the log on fire at both ends, and leave him a sharp knife so he can make his choice to hack 'em off or burn to death.
5 Take away the knife.
6 Use the knife and *then* set the log on fire.
7 All of the above.

The hot water not only eased the terrible pain, it did what hot water always does to anything that is swollen—the blood blister softened, then broke. Blood stained the bathwater, and Dal came as close to passing out as a person can come and not actually do it. She managed to get out of the tub and sit on the toilet, the blood still flowing. She hoped she wasn't going to bleed to death. After all, the poor little place was known to be a mass of blood vessels. What if the Frenchman's clumsiness had broken the wall of a vital artery or something?

She dabbed at herself, and sat a while longer. Her list of vengeful acts went from seven to 10. Finally, she used a clean face cloth in place of a sanitary pad, pulled on clean underpants, and left the dinky little bathroom. She even got a few hours sleep. Alone. Wrapped like a mummy in the spare blanket. On the floor. When she woke up, the Frenchman was sprawled on the bed belly down, snoring in a cloud of whiskey fumes.

Dal got dressed, put on her jacket, packed her few things into her drawstring bag, grabbed her car keys and left. She had no idea how the Frenchman got out of Tofino. He might have caught the once-a-day bus, he might have hitchhiked, for all she knew or cared he might spend the rest of his life in the Lone Cone Motel, apologizing. She imagined him finally waving his damn hands and insisting it was only that she was so gorgeous, so passionate, so beautiful, so *je ne sais quoi* that he'd done too much, gone too far. Oh, well, it's always someone else's fault, thought Dal.

Dal ignored the knowing grin on the face of the babysitter and focussed on the smiles, cuddles, and smooches she got from the pack. She handed out the postcards and distributed the T-shirts she had bought in Coombs—damn if she was having her kids trooping around wearing Tofino T-shirt reminders of the time she'd nearly lost her little old woman in the canoe! Nothing awful had ever happened to her in Coombs, and she'd enjoyed more than one first-rate hamburger in the coffee shop next to the store with the goats on the roof. She paid the babysitter and sent out for pizza to feed the kids. She just didn't feel up to trying to cope with the making of supper, and the kids didn't feel short-changed in any way. Dal figured she could keep them calm through an earthquake if only she had plenty of pizza on hand.

She had another nice long warm soak, and steadfastly ignored the increasingly blood-tinged bathwater. She wondered if the rest of her life would be tainted by a dripping clit. When she tried to lean forward and examine the damage, she nearly passed out with horror. What had always been delicate pearly pink was bruised dark blue, and on the little old woman's hood was a slit at least a half-inch long. And that was amazing because the little old woman, in normal times, wasn't, Dal was sure, that long! In her agony, the poor thing was standing up as straight as she could, and her girth had grown. In fact, if she got any bigger around, there was apt to be more than one slit in her hood. The present one was leaking steadily—not a lot, but it wasn't supposed to bleed at all. Dal knew she ought to do something. But what? Hoof 'er up to the emergency ward and casually ask if someone could stitch her slit clit shut? She could imagine the look on her physician's face, and her question: "Dal, how in hell did this happen?" She couldn't imagine any answer. Had the guy bitten her, or just taken it into his mind that it was a good time to bring on the grandmother of all hickeys? Dal wasn't sure herself.

When she finally got out of the tub and dried herself, she fashioned a little doughnut-shaped piece of cotton batting to go around the poor little old woman, then realized there was no way to hold it in place. It's not exactly where a person puts a Band-Aid. She got the tube of antiseptic ointment and greased 'er up liberally, put the tiny doughnut in place, pulled on her panties and got a clean sanitary pad. She hoped the little doughnut would stick to the ointment and keep the old woman's throbbing head from pressing on the pad, or the underwear. The logistics of it all were at least equal to those needed for the Normandy Invasion. By the time she left the bathroom she was feeling decidedly better. Maybe the leaking had relieved the pressure. Maybe she'd spend the next who knows how long soaking in a warm tub so she could leak out the excess blood. She figured she could make it to at least 12 vengeful acts before she went to bed that night.

The pack hadn't managed to devour every scrap of the two large pizzas—there was actually enough left that Dal could satisfy the hunger pangs she was starting to feel now that her snap wasn't snarling at her. She had two cups of tea, and then had to start getting ready for work. She hoped her sister wouldn't be late. Dal had already spent more on a sitter than she should have.

Pansy arrived with a load of schoolbooks and 15 minutes to spare. The kids swarmed around her, all talking at once.

"You're looking a little bit pale there, old thing." Pansy picked up the Pipsqueak and set her on her hip. "You're not dieting or something dumb like that, are you?"

"No, just a bit under the weather, is all. I'll be okay."

"How was Tofino?"

"Miserable." Dal didn't elaborate, and Pansy didn't seem surprised or even interested in explanation.

"Okay if I sleep over tonight? I'm proving a bloody point. Again." Pansy frowned and gave her head a little shake. "One of these days, so help me..."

Pansy was in that demilitarized zone, the emotional wasteland between moving in with and moving out on yet another boyfriend. Dal wasn't sure she could even remember what this one's name was. One of them had been a Fred, but she wasn't sure if he was recent or relegated to the as-good-as-forgotten heap. Maybe this one was a Kevin—the world seemed to swarm with Kevins. And Shawns too. Bradleys, Dustins... Wasn't anybody called Bill any more?

Dal got her violin and guitar, kissed Pansy and the pack and headed out to the Chev. She prayed the entire way to Toby's. The last thing she needed, the last thing she could handle right now, would be to have the Frenchman show up wanting to talk things over. All too often the men she'd known had wanted to talk things over. The problem was that their idea of talking things over was to jab their finger in the air as if they had to make a hole in the fabric of the universe in order to make her hear their words. When the jabbing finger didn't get them what they wanted, they raised their voices. They seemed to think the only reason a woman might not agree with them was that she was too damn deaf to hear what they said. From raised voice they went to red face, then the veins in the neck swelled and they started to shout. She didn't need the Frenchman shouting and flapping his damn hands. Whether he shouted and flapped or not, she didn't need him.

He didn't show. Dal was so relieved she actually managed to smile, something she hadn't been sure she'd ever be able to do again. She wasn't relieved enough, however, to be able to bring herself to sing, no matter how many requests she got. She just shook her head, as if regretful, tapped at her throat and shook her head again. West Coasters usually take this to mean the raw wind has brought on another sore throat. It was only part of a lie, it wasn't the raw wind at all, but her clit did hurt so much that even the roof of her mouth felt sore. Besides, over half the requests were for "I Fall to Pieces," and Dal was afraid that was next on her agenda.

She didn't support her pack solely on what she made playing at Toby's. In fact Toby's didn't figure much in her financial stability. Most of Dal's money came from either planting trees or picking mushrooms, usually chanterelles or pines, but magics as well, given half a chance. The chanterelles and pines she sold to the mushroom buyer who had a stand on the side of the highway just south of town. The magics she wholesaled to an aging hippy longhair who happily paid prime price for them once she'd dried them in her food dehydrator. Dal didn't call herself a mushroom picker, though. If anyone asked her, she said she was a fungus plucker. Sometimes she transposed the beginnings of the two words, but only if she had reason to suspect the person wasn't a townie or, worse, was an import.

When the local fungi were plucked over Dal loaded the kids into the old school bus and headed for the outlands. For years she had made damn good money, but the pickings were getting slim. More and more people with no idea what they were doing were going out and trampling all over the moss, stumbling flat-footedly around and wrecking far more than they ever found. Some of the dumb buggers even took rakes with them, although most of the experienced pickers Dal knew had their own way of dealing with those ninnies. Take the rake and use it on the raker. Some of them even trashed the rakers' cars or pickups and one enterprising hillbilly not only beat the hell out of the out-of-towner, he took the mushrooms too.

The litter was good at finding mushers, maybe because they were closer to the ground. Even the smallest could be counted on to spot one or two white nubs peeking shyly through the moss. And the nubs were the very least of the mushrooms. Some of them, when properly removed, with the veils intact, were worth an amazing amount of money.

She didn't take the kids when she was going tree planting—it just wasn't safe for them. Dal didn't plant alongside the road or near a park or playground. She planted where the good money was, on the West Coast of Vancouver Island. The terrain is treacherous and harsh, and the living conditions worse—probably bad enough to be decried by Amnesty International. Not to mention the weather. There were times the wind blew so hard a person could be forgiven for wondering whether her feet were going to part company with the ground. No, it wasn't a safe place for her kids.

The kids stayed with Pansy while Dal planted trees. Pansy didn't like tree planting, said she would rather look after a thousand kids than plant a hundred trees. Dal considered it another of God's conveniences that Pansy felt so strongly on the subject. It meant all she had to do was head off, plant like hell and send her cheques out on the now-and-again-once-in-a-while mail runs. Pansy took the cheques, deposited them in Dal's account, and looked after everything while Dal was gone.

Dal usually got home from tree planting just as summer was ready to go into full swing. No use planting trees if the heat of the blazing sun is just going to fry the poor little things. Some crews did it anyway, especially after the government got out of the planting business and turned it over to private enterprise. Dal's crew had heard that thousands of trees never got planted at all, but were dumped into gullies and crevices. The workers got paid by the number of pieces planted, so it was in everyone's interest not to squeal to the dozers who were supposed to be supervising. After a few days' rest, Dal would go down to Toby's and let them know she was back. That gave her walking-around money until the autumn rains began and the mycelium began to react, and then she and the kids would head off to pluck fungi.

That night she played, she smiled, she even made a few jokes and exchanged some pleasantries, but by 10:30 she was uncomfortable. She took a break and went to the jane to check on the injured old woman. Sure enough, she was all swollen up again. Of course there's no privacy in a public washroom, so Dal couldn't give the old girl a warm soaking and she wasn't too keen on dipping a wad of toilet paper into the cold water in the bowl. She changed her pad, promised the old woman it wouldn't be too much longer, then went to the bar and had a good swift shot of raw gin.

"Jeez, Dal, never saw you drink booze before." The bartender tried to hide his amazement. "You're more of a beer type, I thought."

"Well, you know how it is—you just never know, right?"

"You okay? Nothin' wrong with the kids or anything?"

"Kids are fine. Hey, it's not a federal thing, okay? One little sip of gin. I'll be fine."

One little sip of gin didn't seem to do bugger nothing. The discomfort grew, and Dal found it hard to concentrate on what it was she was doing. She was beginning to be afraid she was playing horribly, but then the manager came up smiling from ear to ear to tell her she was really spot-on, never better. Dal wondered what the gap was between the things she saw and the things other people saw. Or at least said they saw. She was glad to leave Toby's and take her instruments home. Creation must have heard her prayers because Pansy was in bed, sound asleep, with a couple of the kids cuddled in with her. Dal left them where they were.

She filled the tub and did the old soak-the-parrot trip. This time she actually dared touch herself gently with a well-soaped face cloth, lifting the small bit of congealed blood from the aching slit. She dabbed again and then jerked her hand and the facecloth away, feeling a spurt of fear. Blood wasn't oozing or trickling, it was flowing. But after that first jerk of fear, after the first sting as the hot water touched raw places that had been covered by dried blood, it felt good to have the pressure relieved. She smeared on antibiotic ointment again, put on a clean pad, went to bed and waited to go to sleep. Half an hour later, more awake than she'd been when she climbed between the sheets, she went down to the medicine chest and hunted for something, anything, that might make her at least drowsy.

Mouthwash. The anti-plaque kind, it was a pale bluish colour and smelled like peppermint. She wondered why none of the mouthwash people had caught on to bubble gum flavour—they'd have every kid in the country happily rinsing before and after brushing. Some aspirin. Well, if that turned out to be all there was, maybe she'd take some. Band-Aids, with the Little Mermaid printed on them. Razor blades, and not a razor in the house. Who had put them in there, anyway? She left them where they were, though, because surely they hadn't put themselves on the shelf. Besides, they weren't taking up much room. Maybe Pansy needed them for something. Maybe she had the razor part hidden where the kids wouldn't find it.

On the top shelf, behind a cardboard rectangle containing five suppositories, she found the small bottle of prescription-strength codeine tablets. Of course, where else? The kids were never in a million years going to go anywhere near the suppositories, in case they wound up getting one inserted. They dreaded the thought, even those who had never had to endure the experience. The doctor had prescribed anti-nausea suppositories for Button once, when everyone had got tired of being horked on when she got carsick. The things were practically magic. After the kid had encountered the first one, that was it for the carsickness.

"Right in my bum!" she had complained dramatically to anyone who would listen. "Just 'cause I puked. Right in my bum. And that's not nice."

"It's not very nice to puke down the back of the driver, either," Dal answered. "I told you often enough, use the plastic bags. And did you? No, you didn't. You just leaned forward and *hork,* and it went in my hair and all over my clothes and the car stank for days."

"But in my *bum*? Is that nice?"

"In my *hair*? Is that nice?"

"I didn't mean to puke in your hair."

"Then why did you ignore the plastic bags and lean forward and let heave on me? You meant it, Button. You know you did. You didn't want to ride in the back seat."

"I hate the back seat!"

"You were in the back seat because when you rode in the front seat you puked all over everything, even into the glove box and you got it all over the road maps."

"In my *bum*?"

"The road maps weren't in your bum, they were in the glove box. So from now on, every time you ride in the car, you'll get that medicine before we even leave the house."

"What if I don't puke?"

"Well, if you don't puke you don't need the medicine, right?"

After that, Button would rather die than puke in the car, or anywhere else. Dal expected that at some point yet to come, Button would announce to the world that her therapist had told her the reason she was getting her head shrunk was that she hadn't been allowed to puke in her mother's hair when she was a child. But Dal had it all figured out. If Button started emoting and dramatizing all over everyone else's life, Dal was going to go for the suppositories. That would put an end to everything, even clinical depression. But Button's increasingly graphic description of what happens when an anti-nausea suppository is inserted had so appalled and horrified the rest of the bunch that Dal could have stashed just about anything, up to and including Halloween candy, behind the box and not one small hand would have gone anywhere near it.

She popped two of the codeine and sat in the big chair in the living room, her feet tucked up on the seat, an afghan snugged around her legs. Her box hurt, and the cramping pain from injury to navel was starting to worry her. But still, the idea of going to her doctor and trying to display her wound and describe how she got it was enough to give her a new understanding of Button's reaction to the jellied bombs. And what could the doctor do? Probably just charge the medical insurance company for telling Dal that she should soak the wound regularly and keep a clean dressing on it. Surely to all the Elder Gods nobody was going to try to stitch it shut! And if they did, how would the leakage drain out? And if it didn't drain out the whole thing would swell even more and it was already too damn sore and swollen.

Pansy padded into the living room and stopped by the big chair long enough to give Dal a good hug.

"You okay?"

"I guess."

"You don't seem okay, Dal. You don't seem yourself at all."

"Jesus, there's a fright! If I'm not myself who am I?"

"Well, you look like Morgue-Anna, if you want to know the truth."

"When did anybody ever want to know the truth, Pan? Do you want to know the truth? What part of it should I start to tell you?"

"You're very pale."

"Wouldn't you feel pail when hit by a bucket?"

"Stop doing that."

"Doing what?"

"Making those sick jokes. I hate it when you make those sick jokes."

"I only make sick jokes when I'm not feeling well."

"So what's wrong that you don't feel well?" Pansy's face brightened and a look of such open hope came over it that Dal felt as if her heart was about to crack right down the middle. "Are you pregnant?"

The idea was so far from the truth that Dal nearly laughed, but the look on Pansy's face stopped her. Pansy had been designed by nature to be the epitome of the much-loved and doting aunt. All Pansy had ever wanted to be in life was a mother. From the time she was two or three years old she had fashioned her future around a tribe of kids. School passed Pansy without so much as a ripple. She did math only so she didn't have to drop home ec to take remedial math. She took gym only so she'd know the rules of all the games and thus be able to play with her kids. If she brought in above-average grades it was only, she said, so that when the time came she could help her kids with their homework. She had a list of names she particularly liked, and added to it from time to time. She read the birth announcements to see what names other people had found or invented. She read the death announcements to see what names had once been popular. Pansy wanted the best names in the world for her kids when they began to arrive.

She started fucking when she was 13 and let it be known that she had no intention at all of using birth control. "After all," she reasoned, "I'm only going to get it on with the very nicest boys who ask me. It's not as if I'm going to get pregnant by some pimply-faced snaggletooth whose kids might turn out to be the same."

She didn't get pregnant by anybody. Not at 13, or 15, or any time afterward. Nobody talked about it. Nobody asked questions. Everybody knew that Pansy had been to the doctor, had even been referred to a specialist, but there was no use talking about it if the experts couldn't do anything about it.

If Pansy's heart was broken, she kept it to herself. Dal supposed a shrink would call it sublimation or something, but she figured it was just another case of "Make the best of a bad thing." Pansy would not only babysit every time she was asked, she was as apt as not to show up with movie tickets and practically shove Dal out the door. Pansy remembered everyone's birthday, and she showed up with incredible birthday cakes. She was there to make Halloween costumes, carve pumpkins, take kids Christmas shopping, lace up skates and smear on sunblock. Pansy was always there, making the best of it, loving the kids incredibly, and ensuring that Dal could find ways to bring in enough money to feed and clothe the whole pack.

"No." Dal tried to be gentle, but there's no way when you're poking a hole in someone's balloon of hope. "Not pregnant, Pan."

"Well, shit!" Pansy got off the sofa and stomped off to get the tobacco can and rolling papers. Dal rolled two cigarettes and handed one to her.

"A person would think you'd learn to roll your own."

"A person would think you wouldn't mind rolling one for a person now and again."

"What person is this, anyway?"

"Some damn fool!" they chimed, and laughed together in that way sisters do when either or both of them are nursing bruised hearts. Or birds.

"So what are you, on the pill or something dangerous?" Pansy wasn't going to let go of it. The bulldog part of her had found something to grip onto and chew into submission.

"No, I've been winning at Vatican roulette," Dal answered. "If my luck holds, maybe I'll try lottery tickets too."

"Really?"

"No, not really. I'm just a bit busy, Pan, that's all."

"Too busy to get pregnant? What, you're going to tell me it takes a long time?"

If it had been anybody else poking into her private business, Dal would have probably snapped back something along the line of "Well it must take a long time, you've been trying for a dozen years and haven't managed…" But it wasn't anybody else, and maybe it wasn't even none of Pan's business. After all, what are sisters for?

"It's going to take a while," Dal answered, finally. She then told Pansy about the Frenchman.

"Let me see!" Pansy demanded.

"Whoa, hang on there, Pan, we're not talking my thumb, you know."

"Let me see. Jesus, Dal, it isn't like you've got something unique there, okay?"

Dal felt like a damn fool, but in the hope that Pansy would have an idea how to make the nauseating pain go away, she showed her the wound. Pansy stared, her breathing getting deeper and deeper until she was almost snorting.

"That fuckin' Frenchman!" she breathed. "People who do things like that to things like that ought to be whipped." She stalked off into the kitchen to get one of Auntie Pansy's practically copyrighted poultice plasters together. She insisted she'd learned about it in home ec, but Dal had taken home ec and had never even heard of it.

Pansy took a package of Quaker instant oatmeal, the plain kind, and poured on some boiling water. Then she put a glup-loaded tablespoonful of it on a gauze square and tested the heat on the inside of her wrist. She waved it a bit, blew on it some, then tested it again.

"Okay, lie on your back on the sofa with a pillow under your bum. Now pretend I'm your doctor, okay? Just spread your legs a bit."

The compress might not have felt hot on the skin of Pan's inner wrist, but it felt like bloody fire on Dal's wounded twat. It hurt so much she couldn't even say anything. Pansy took the gasp and the silence that followed it to mean the compress was working, soothing the pain, easing the discomfort.

While Dal lay there feeling as if she was about to pass out cold, Pansy went to the kitchen and used the rest of the boiling water to make tea. Dal could only thank whatever gods or goddesses were still alive and functioning that she'd had the foresight to take two codeine pills before Pansy even woke up and came downstairs.

Pansy came in with the teapot and two mugs. "Feeling better?" she asked brightly, with a loving smile.

"Pan, darling, I have to tell you, I have never in all my fuckin' life felt quite like I do now," Dal managed. "And that," she added, "is the first part of that truth we were discussing earlier on."

"Yeah." Pansy poured tea, and added sugar to it. "I love you too, Dal. I just wish you'd have another baby. Pipsqueak's going to be out from underfoot real soon. A couple more years and she'll be for Christ's own sweet sake in kindergarten. Then what are we going to do? Watch TV?"

Dal managed to get off the couch and into her bed before tumbling into a deep codeine-assisted sleep. When she finally climbed up out of the no-place place and opened her eyes again, the sun was shining and she could hear Pansy singing in the kitchen.

She could also hear most of the pack singing along. The sound chased the cobwebs from her mind and nudged her out of bed. She stood up and was immediately aware of something bulky, cold and clammy lodged firmly where Pansy had put it the night before. Walking like someone with a dried corncob rammed you-know-where, Dal went to the bathroom and started the tub.

The poultice came off without much discomfort. Dal had been afraid it would have to be jackhammered off, bringing much too much of her with it. Cold oatmeal, however, is not the same as dried oatmeal. It lifted off with a sucking sound that made her think of invertebrates clinging to beach rocks.

There was blood stuck to it, a thick jelly-like clot of dark red, and something else, something yellowish, but not thick like pus. And no sooner had she sat down and slurped off the compress than her poor old woman released another two or three ounces of discharge. She didn't see any scalded- skin or traces of burnt-to-a-crisp labia on the poultice, so she carefully wrapped it in toilet paper and deposited it in the wastebasket.

Even Dal had to admit that she was feeling much better. And for some reason, feeling better made her feel like sitting on the jane and having a good down-home bawling session. But in Dal's experience, all you got out of that was swollen eyes, a runny nose and a blinding headache, so she didn't bother weeping, she just got into the tub.

When she bent forward for a good look, the old woman seemed almost normal again. There was still bruising and swelling, but at least she was there, and no longer buried in a damaged hood. Mind you, she was one hell of a colour. Dal didn't dare try anything that might be misinterpreted. She just dabbed gingerly with a soapy cloth, then carefully rinsed off the suds, patted it dry and smeared on the ointment.

She decided against going downstairs in her housecoat. The singing suggested some kind of activity and she wasn't about to be thrust into it in an old bathrobe. She went back to her bedroom and got dressed, being very careful with the positioning of the pad.

It wasn't Saturday, so why were all the kids in the kitchen? Had the school caught fire? Had they all been expelled?

"Pro-D day," Pansy explained.

"What's that?"

"*Pro* for professional, D for development. It's like homework for the teachers."

"When you gonna have the new baby?" Pape asked, cuddling Dal's leg and rubbing his cheek against her. "Is it a boy baby or a girl baby?"

"I'm not having a baby." Dal glared at Pansy, who paid no notice to either the hard look or the half-hearted denial. Dal didn't think the denial was half-hearted, but obviously Pansy chose to think it was.

"Well, when you do, can you have twins?" Button asked. "That could save a lot of time, you know."

"Boy twins, though." Skipper had been in school too long and he was starting to believe some of the BS and heifer dust that infected the place. "Boys are better," he explained grandly.

"Boys are bums," Twink said, breaking her traditional silence. "They're all bums."

"What would you know about it?" Skipper wasn't intimidated by the unexpected sound of Twink's voice.

"More than you do, you bum," Twink answered. Skipper wanted to argue about it but Twink had gone back into her usual non-communicative state. Dal often wondered if Twink was quiet because she wanted to be or if some part of her brain actually did hop from this dimension to another. Entire days went by without so much as a whisper from Twink. In fact you could ask Twink a question and never know whether or not she'd heard you. Dal had taken Twink for hearing tests at least four times, but the audiologist insisted her ears worked fine. The school had tested Twink so often she could almost recite the questions on the idiot sheets. What seemed to confuse the educators the most was that even if there was no sign of any kind that there was anyone home, Twink always got high marks on the written tests. Dal hadn't entirely given up going to the meetings with the teachers, counsellors, or principal at the school— she didn't want them to think she didn't give a damn or think that maybe Twink wasn't her kid but some kind of foster or found-in. She had just given up trying to explain that Twink just didn't always feel like talking. They seemed to take it all as some kind of personal affront. "I spoke directly to her," was a common complaint, "and she didn't even *look* at me."

"I know the feeling," Dal reassured them each time. "It's frustrating but I guess there's no law says she *has* to talk. At least when she does she's polite. That's more than can be said for most of the kids going to this school—my own included."

Polite didn't seem to cut much ice, though. Obviously, they would rather Twink talked nothing but cheek, sass and nastiness than have her quiet.

"How can we *help* her if she won't tell us what's *bothering* her?"

"Maybe the only thing bothering her is that you're all making a great big fuss out of things. Maybe all that's bothering her is that nobody is willing to respect her choice to be quiet."

Skipper was so frustrated by Twink's return to silence that he almost made the mistake of giving her a shove or a poke. He started to, and Pansy reached out, faster than a speeding bullet, and gently took his ear between her thumb and pointy-finger. "No," she said softly, "I don't want you to behave that way."

"I love you, Twink," Dal said, and her day was improved and blessed by the lovely wide smile Twink sent her. A smile from Twink was as good as winning at Bingo, and happened almost as often too. Well, her father had a nice smile, although Dal hadn't really seen it in years. Just as well. She had the feeling he'd have been as sticky as fir pitch if he'd known there was a kid of his in the picture. They don't seem to want to do any of the work, they sure don't seem willing to pick up any of the tab, but they do like to be able to claim ownership and brag. He'd been hard enough to off-load without knowing about the pregnancy. She'd never be rid of him if he ever caught on.

Dal supposed one of the reasons she'd never won at the lottery was she had used up so much of her luck in other ways. Twink's hair, for example. Twink's dad had a mop of blue-black hair that grew thick and straight, which he wore long and pulled back into a ponytail. Everyone in his family had the same kind of hair. Dal had worried that Twink would come out easily identifiable and that he would see her on the street or in a playground and show up at the front door hammering and pounding and insisting he be allowed to see what was obviously his kid. Bought and paid for, by God! But Twink came out with a head full of Dal's hair—dark red—the same colour as old arbutus bark just before it peels off to make room for the smooth new green stuff. She even had some curl to her hair. It marked her as a goddamn Cassidy, and nobody was going to come raising hell to claim any part of that. Thank you, God.

"We're makin' cookies," Pape said unnecessarily. "You want some?"

"Maybe after I have my toast and marma-jam, okay?"

"Kay." Pape was so easygoing and good-natured that if Dal had been the kind to have favourites, he'd have been it. He had hair so blond it seemed white, and if he stood in the bright sunlight, his hair seemed to disappear, leaving him looking bald. At least he had a nicely shaped little head. Dal didn't know if Pape's dad had been the same when he was young. She wasn't even sure she could say with certainty which of three candidates was Pape's dad. And she wasn't interested anyway. She had Pape and that was good enough for her.

Dal knew that a lot of people—practically an entire town full of people, maybe even more than that—thought it was just outrageous that Dal had so many children and no sign of a husband. What she didn't know was why any of them thought it was any of their business.

"Jimmy Scoggins says we're bastards," Button said conversationally. "Are we?"

"Of course," Dal answered easily. "So's he."

"What's a bastard?"

"Depends. It's a word like 'cat.' A cat is an animal, right? But a person who says snide things is a cat too."

"I don't say bad things. I'm not a snide. Why'd he say I was?"

"He didn't say you were a snide cat. He said you were a bastard."

"Oh."

"We all are. The world is full of them."

"Is it bad?"

"Are you bad?"

"No!" Button was indignant, her green eyes flashing fire.

"Then there you have it. You're a darling. You're a smooch. You're mine, mine, mine, mine, mine!"

"But..." Button wasn't about to be flarched or kissed out of her mood.

"Jimmy Scoggins," Pansy put in, "is a little boy with a lot on his plate. Okay? You all know what it's like for him."

"His dad drinks all the time," Skipper agreed.

"Right. And when he drinks he gets owly, okay? So Jimmy's real sad a lot of the time. And when people feel bad, sometimes they try to make other people feel bad too. They think that way they won't feel so different. So if Jimmy yammers at you, well, just try to remember why. You just smile at him and say, 'That's okay, Jim, I still like you.' And maybe after a while he'll stop trying to be as owly as his dad is."

"But I don't like him," Button snapped. "I don't like him one little bit."

"Then just say, 'Sure, Jim, sure, whatever you say,' and walk away."

"I'd rather just punch his nose."

"Oh, that'd be great. You're half his size. You punch him and he'll clean your clock for you."

"*I'm* not fightin' with him, Button," Skipper said hurriedly. "I'm not stickin' up for you if you punch his nose."

"No punchin'," Pape said agreeably. "No hittin'."

Pansy picked up a glob of dough, patted it and formed it into a bunny shape. Dal was, as happened so often, amazed. She could hear the words and see the body language, and she still didn't know how Pansy did it. A few like her in the UN, and the firefights and terrorist attacks might stop.

"Jimmy Scoggins says," Button pressed on, determined to air all her grievances at once, "that Skipper is a dog's name." Skipper bristled, but however insulted he was, he wasn't dumb enough to go up against Jimmy, who was two years older and much, much bigger.

"If you think about it, he's right." Pansy sounded so agreeable you'd have thought young master Scoggins had been handing out compliments. "It'd be a great name for a dog. One of those terrier kinds, like Mrs. Pelter has. You know how it's always tucking up one of its hind legs and skidder-hoppin' along the sidewalk."

"Yeah," Pape agreed, fumbling in the dough, "hop hop like a bunny."

"Right. Besides, lots of names are good for animals. Horses get called Tony and Bess. Cats are always being named Maggy Mae or Mary Kathleen or even Jasmine."

"Yeah," Pape said, agreeing with everything as usual. "Charlie's pig is called Norma."

At times like this, Dal knew, with no feeling of guilt or inadequacy, that Pansy was a far better mother than Dal would ever be. Pansy could hear past the surface questions to the real ones underneath, the ones too scary to put into words.

"Kiss you better?" Pape smiled at her, his little hands still daubed with dough.

"Oh, yes, please." Dal leaned forward and Pape put his arms around her neck, squeezed as hard as he could and peppered her face with wet kisses.

"You better?" he asked.

"I think I need a bit more." She could have sat like this all day, but Pape was a busy guy and had scads of things to do. He smeared more kisses on her face, then moved back to the dough. He seemed to be building a pyramid, but she hesitated to say so in case it was something totally different.

Dal left the cookie makers busy with their baking and went outside to pull chickweed from the flower beds. She didn't fuss much with her flowers. She got the soil ready, planted bulbs and seeds, and after that they were pretty much on their own. She felt the same way about people. She could hardly bear to watch any of the daytime TV talk shows because of all the dipshits who sat up there in front of who knows how many people and whined about the unfairness of things. Mass murderers who were upset because they weren't allowed a day pass so they could compete in the international snooker competition, and serial rapists who thought it grossly unfair they weren't let out of the pen to enter bodybuilding or weightlifting competitions. Dal thought they should consider themselves lucky they were even allowed to continue breathing.

She knew some of the neighbours thought it was funny that she filled her flower beds with dahlias. Dal herself didn't see the humour of it. After all, she wasn't the one had registered herself as Dahlia. It was her parents' stupid obsession—Dahlia, Pansy, Timothy, Ivy, Rosie and Forrest, who for reasons nobody could explain got called Boo. If the parents hadn't split up, maybe they'd have wound up with kids called Nutmeg and Chrysanthemum. But both had gone on to other relationships with people who had different ideas. Other kids were born, with names like Joe and Carol, Mary and Henry. Milly and Nancy had been the last contributions from her mother, but the old man continued undeterred by age, finances or the ravages of substance abuse. Dal knew for a fact that she had at least three half-sibs on the reserve, though she didn't know their names. Maybe one day she'd try to find out who they were, just to complete the list of people she didn't know, didn't want to know and preferred to pretend didn't exist at all.

The vegetable garden was waiting for her. She could almost hear it calling, "Dal! Dal, get your arse over here!" What she didn't lavish on the flowers she put into the vegetables, not because she was in competition with any of the neighbours—although if there was a competition she'd probably win—but because she wanted to know what her kids were putting into their bellies. Besides, the taste was so much better when the lettuce was only a few minutes old and hadn't travelled in a train car from California or Mexico or even South America.

She had beans until hell itself wouldn't have held them. Beans grew up poles set teepee style in the ground, beans grew up netting along the fence, beans grew on short bushes. Yellow beans, green beans, even burgundy-coloured beans. The kids loved them the most because they changed colour as they cooked. You put in purplish ones and *presto chango*—you had bright green ones. The only problem she could see with her bean patch was that she wore out her knees picking, picking, picking.

Tomatoes, which the kids called tommy-toes, grew in wire cones. The cones were supposed to help hold up the plants, but the fruit was so big and so heavy that Dal had to cut thick sticks and pound them into the ground, then tie the cones to the sticks to keep them from toppling sideways. She had onions as big as teapots, she had shallots and she had more cucumbers than she knew what to do with. Then there were the corn patches—three kinds of sweet corn as well as a big patch of blue corn, which she dried and then ground into meal. She even grew artichokes, although they were there mainly for the fun of it. Dal liked them best when the heads opened and the neon blue flowers showed. Bees went mad for them. She had almost convinced the kids that the bees came from 50 miles away, until Twink piped up and said that bees were restricted to an area of about a mile and a half, and after that they had to eat something or they ran out of energy, fell to the ground and died. Dal had no idea whether any of this was true, but Twink didn't usually say anything unless she knew what she was talking about. Maybe that's why Twink was so quiet. Maybe if more people knew what they were talking about, there would be less damn chitchat-chatter.

Dal took a box of beans into the house, then went outside with another cardboard box and dug beets, spuds and a few carrots. She cut two heads of lettuce, pulled some green onions and lugged it all into the kitchen.

"Beet greens, beet greens, we're gonna have beet greens," Pape chanted, feeding a freshly baked cookie to Pipsqueak, one bite at a time.

"Twink, darlin', can you get the greens off the beets for us, please? Skip, maybe you could sort the stuff. Button will help, I'm sure."

Every day the garden harvest was divided. Enough was kept for that day's meals, then two-thirds of what was left over got canned, jarred or frozen and the other third went to the food bank. Pansy was convinced that if enough people had the chance to taste fresh backyard garden food, they'd realize they could grow stuff themselves and not go broke buying stale wilted crap in the supermarket. Given even the hint of some kind of encouragement, Pansy would hold forth on how even people who live in slum apartments could turn the boulevards into vegetable patches. The road allowance, she insisted, would grow enough good food to keep the entire town nourished.

Dal scrubbed the garden earth off her hands and picked it out from under her short fingernails, changed from her earth-stained jeans to a clean pair of shorts, then went to the kitchen and got the box of food bank stuff. "Anybody want to come?" she asked, grabbing her car keys from the top of the fridge.

"We're goin' swimmin'," Pape chimed. "You take us?"

"Course I will. You got your swimsuit? Your towel? Got your life jacket? Flippers?"

Skipper carried the cooler with the jugs of cold juice and Kool-Aid, Twink had the sandwiches, Button had the potato salad and Pansy carried Pipsqueak and the desserts. Dal had the food bank veggies and Pape's extras, and he had his towel and the diaper bag with Pipsqueak's bottle and the sunblock. Pape dragged his towel behind him. He thought he had it tucked under his arm like the big kids, and, actually, he did. But his arms were much closer to the ground and he hadn't really learned how to roll the thing yet. They all trooped out to the Chev and got the stuff stashed in the trunk and themselves organized in the car.

Dal was able to back the car right under a huge maple tree so they could unload their stuff directly into the shade. The kids made sure everything was where it was supposed to be, and then they raced for the water, yodelling, screeching and hollering. Pipsqueak was already as good as asleep, so Pansy laid her down in the shade and handed her a plastic bottle of apple juice. Three sucks on the nipple and Pip was in dreamland.

Dal drove to the food bank and managed to find a parking space among the litter in the lot. Didn't anyone know how to use a broom? Most of the vehicles parked on the lot looked as if they were made out of rusting lace, held together with untidy strips of Bondo and fibreglass. Her well-kept Chev looked totally out of place, which made her feel weird. These were her kind of people. These were the kind of rusting hulks of cars, parked all over the weeds and clay of backyards and even front yards, that she'd grown up with.

She carried the heavy box inside and waited for someone to take it from her. Two men and a woman sat behind a table with metal legs.

"Excuse me," Dal managed, but nobody so much as turned to look at her. She wondered if they were in the middle of an emergency meeting of some kind. This wasn't the usual crew. Had there been some kind of emergency? Or maybe some kind of job politics were at work. She wanted to ask but it was none of her buttinsky business, and they would tell her so. The woman looked as if it had been a hard night, and the two men were yammering at her about something.

Dal tried again, a bit louder. "Pardon me, but where do you want me to put this?"

What had the new crew done with the table?

One of the men, built like the Michelin Tire man, had greasy hair —what was left of it—and a bald, glistening dome. He hadn't shaved in days, and he was smoking a tailor-made cigarette, his fingers stained yellow from tip to bottom knuckle. The other guy was small, skinny to the point of looking anorexic, and was smoking a Colt cigarillo.

The damn box was heavy and getting heavier. Dal walked over to put it on the table where they were sitting, but the fat guy held up his hand and shook his head.

"Pardon me!" Dal knew they had heard her that time. "Where do you want me to put this box? It's full, and it's heavy."

"What's in it?" At least the woman could speak, even if she did sound as if she was primed for a damn good fight.

"Fresh garden vegetables."

"Are they washed?"

"They're washed."

"Are they weighed and packaged?"

"No, they aren't."

"That's a lot of trouble for us, you know," the fat guy said, glaring at her.

"Where do you want me to put it?" Dal repeated.

"Oh, anywhere'll do, I guess."

"Sure." Dal smiled and let go of the box. It tipped and fell, scattering beets, spuds, beans, lettuce and carrots on the dirty floor. "Have a great day."

Two

The lake was glorious, the water sparkling in the sunlight. The droplets sent into the air by the splashing kids were like diamonds, catching the sunlight and breaking it into beads of colour, living liquid rainbows. Dal sat against the trunk of the maple tree and drank a full glass of chilled lemonade, then took off her shoes and socks and walked to the edge of the water. The sand was dark grey, cooler where the water soaked it. She skrinched her toes in it, the grit making a strange soft sound, the sound of the air passing between the finger feathers of a raven's wing as she flies overhead.

Pansy had Pip, holding her by the armpits, swishing her legs back and forth, back and forth in the water, a bit deeper each time until suddenly Pip was in up to her waist. Pip's eyes opened wide, and so did her mouth. She got all set to yell, but already Pansy was lifting her, swinging her, and the yell changed to a gurgle of sheer enjoyment. Before Pip could forget that she was having a wonderful time, she was back in the water up to her chest, then up in the air again. Pape swam energetically, his legs kicking, his arms thrashing, the bright red life jacket holding him up. Dal was amazed at how nonchalant her kids had been about wearing safety gear. When she was their age, a person would have died rather than wear water wings or a life jacket. The lake had been as segregated as a far-south lunch counter then. Babies and non-swimmers kept to the little cove where the water was shallow. The swimmers had the rest of the lake and the really good swimmers had the log raft with the somewhat unstable diving tower. You had to be able to swim out to the raft by yourself before your presence was tolerated. No cheating, either, and no inner tubes. The biggest, toughest boys were the raft cops, and their word was law.

Now it looked as if anyone who could make it out there was allowed. Twink was practising her back flip from the tower. She still wasn't very good at it but by summer's end she'd be ready for the local diving team. Except Twink was almost guaranteed to refuse to go out for anything like the swimming team, diving team or gymnastics team. Anything that involved any compulsory camaraderie was sure to be ignored by the Twink. Button wasn't ready for the tower. She was diving off the decking, her dives sloppy and off-balance. Skip kept yelling at her to straighten up, keep her legs stiff, point her toes, do it his way, which he was convinced was the right way. Button ignored him. Pape just kept swimming, his eye on the raft. He'd probably make it out there in time to clamber onto the deck and slump there, worn to a nub. About the time he had caught his breath it would be time for the whole bunch to head back to shore, and Pape would be lucky if he got even one clumsy attempt at learning to dive. Probably he'd have to just cannonball in and start the long swim back to shore.

Dal walked in until the water covered her boobs, then lay forward gently and started to swim. The kids were so intent on their diving pursuits that they didn't see her coming. She could have offered to take Pip and give Pansy a break, and she also knew that if Pip stayed a toddler forever and Pansy lived that long, it still wouldn't be enough time for Pansy to spend with Pip. She didn't want a break from any of the kids. She would gladly hole up with them for the rest of her life. It was Dal who insisted on paying a sitter on the weekends, and the only way she got Pansy to agree to it was to finesse her verbally.

"And just suppose I'm away and something happens to you."

"Like what?"

"Like anything! Appendicitis, maybe, or an impacted wisdom tooth. And you have to get a sitter, but the kids have never been with one so they all kick up a huge uproar and take hysterics and drive everyone crazy."

The kids had accepted the sitter easily the first time, and from this Pansy had seemed to conclude that they never needed another all the days of their lives. But Dal had stood firm, or as firm as Dal could stand when nose to nose with her beloved Pansy.

Dal caught up to Pape and swam beside him. He tried to smile at her but he was working too hard with his arms and legs and couldn't spare the energy or the attention.

"I'm right here, Pape," she said softly. She wanted to help him, put one hand on his round little butt and shove him forward, but that kind of help can prove to be a hindrance. Pape had his eyes set on a goal, and he ought to be allowed to give 'er his best shot. If he needed help, he was smart enough to holler.

He didn't need help. He made it to the edge of the raft, grabbed at it and hung on, his breathing heavy, his smile wide.

"C'mon up." Skip reached down, grabbed a wrist and hauled his baby brother out of the water.

"I made it," Pape managed.

"Yeah. You did okay."

Those three words, "you did okay," coming from his big brother, did more for Pape than a hero badge. He sat with his skinny little legs dangling over the edge of the raft, his baby feet paddling gently in the water, and heaved in huge gulps of air. Dal hung on to the edge of the raft and grinned at Pape. He grinned back at her.

"C'mon up," he invited.

"I have to catch my breath first," she lied.

"I'll help."

"In a minute. I'm way lots older than you are, eh, and it's a long swim for an old broad."

Pape accepted that. Why not? What did the Pape know about old or not old? He had hardly been here long enough to be young. He patted Dal's arm and lay on his side, pulling his legs up onto the sun-warmed wood of the raft. He shivered a few times and then was sound asleep. The other kids stepped over him as they made their way to the diving tower. Nobody mentioned his fatigue, nobody said anything about the distance being a challenge for him, and his only bit of praise had been "you did okay" from his big brother.

Dal heaved herself onto the raft, climbed the frame of the diving tower and launched herself. She made no attempt to shallow her dive, she let herself go down, down, down into the lake, down into the dark water. Local legend had it that one guy had gone down so deep he'd grabbed a handful of mud and gravel from the bottom and taken it back up with him. Dal had never tried that. She just enjoyed the sudden change in temperature and enjoyed even more the sensations when she turned and headed back up again. The light shafted down from above, the raft seemed to be hanging in mid-air, the water warmed with each kick up and she awaited that wonderful moment when she thought she was out of the water but she wasn't. If you sucked in air then, when the water was as bright as the air, you'd choke. The trick was to hang on until you felt the breeze on your skin.

She saw it then, under the raft. She kicked like hell, made it to the surface, gulped air, then wakened Pape as gently as she could.

"Everyone back to shore," she said quietly.

"Huh? Why?"

"C'mon. The word is emergency, okay?"

"Emergency," was all she said to Pan and it was enough. Dal raced for the car, got the keys out of the ashtray, and was off. She didn't have far to drive. At the mini-mart less than a quarter of a mile from the lake, she gasped, "Telephone, I need to use your telephone."

Dal was back at the blanket and parked out of the way when the first cop car arrived. The ambulance was right behind it. The kids sat on the blanket eating sandwiches and potato salad, watching everything with wide eyes. Dal had suggested that Pansy drive them home, but their response to that was so intense that she relented, not feeling up to open rebellion at the moment. They had been promised a picnic, and by God they were determined to have one.

The second cop car pulled up and a diver got out, walked to the water, pulled on his flippers and his mouthpiece, and in moments was swimming rapidly toward the raft. It took a half-hour to bring out the body, because there was a procedure they had to follow. The diver took pictures with his underwater camera while a rowboat was put in place, ready with the rubberized body bag. Dal wanted to tell her kids to turn away, to close their eyes, not to look, but she said nothing. Silently they watched as the body bag was loaded in the ambulance, and listened as Dal told the cop what she had seen. He asked her a few questions and then they were gone, the diver, the cops, the ambulance attendants and the body.

Only then did the kids speak.

Even Twink. "Was it a kid, Mom?" she asked, her voice shaking.

"A guy." Dal winced when she saw the look of sheer relief on her children's faces. "I guess he was, oh, I don't know—older, though."

They looked away and nodded. Dal wanted to grab them up, hold them forever, keep them safe, especially safe from the relief and the fear that had preceded it. What was the world like for them, that their first thought would be that the body was a kid? No kid would be swimming or jackassing around here all by itself. A kid would be part of a group. No group of kids would bugger off home leaving one of the bunch missing. They were tribal, and the tribe had to be together before it moved off to somewhere else. Dead kids, especially to other kids, were murdered kids. In their way, they knew how defenceless they were, how easily one of them could have been the body under the raft. They must have been transfixed by the fear that it was a kid they knew.

The fun had gone out of the day. The lake still looked gorgeous, in the soft late-afternoon stillness that precedes the lavender and pink glory of sunset and the lilac gleam of twilight. This was the best time for swimming, the lake flat and still. But they had all heard the gurgle of water in the body bag. Lake water.

Wordlessly they packed their stuff and loaded it in the trunk. Only Pip wasn't riding a mammoth bummer. Dal tried desperately to think of something, anything, that could dispel the mood. But nothing would. The best place for them to deal with everything was at home.

"Is there heaven?" Pape asked suddenly. Dal nearly took the Chev into a ditch. She had never talked about heaven or hell with her kids. Where did they pick up this stuff?

"Sure there is," Skipper said reassuringly. "It's where Santa Claus and the Easter bunny live."

"And the tooth fairy," Twink added. "And the Great Pumpkin too."

"That's silly." Button nearly let the cat out of the bag. "You know—"

"You know it isn't nice to tease a little kid."

"I'n big," Pape insisted, "I swam to the raf', okay?"

"Okay, Pape," they agreed.

"A grown-up, you think, Mom?"

"A grown-up," she reassured them all.

The construction crew was still hard at work on the subdivision going in where Bob Thomas's farm had been. All the grass was gone. They had cut it in strips, rolled the strips into big bundles and hauled them off piled like logs on the back of a flatbed truck. The topsoil had been dug up by a backhoe and loaded into enormous earth movers. Dal supposed that the people who bought the new houses would have the chance to buy back, at premium prices, the dirt that had once been where their ugly front yards were now. The orchard looked naked, and some of the trees were obviously not going to survive—the rumble of trucks and track machines, the digging and lugging away, the bumping and banging had sent them into root shock. The only thing on the entire 60 acres that didn't look ravaged and raw was an enormous sign with a picture of a blossoming orchard in a painted oval frame, beneath which was written "Apple Blossom Meadow." Three blocks away, a similar assault had resulted in Hazelnut Place, and the lone surviving hazelnut tree stood guard in front of a four-foot high concrete wall. The developer insisted that the wall was a sound barrier to protect the residents from the noise of passing traffic. Hazelnut Place looked like a detention camp and the kids called it "Cracked Nut Hollow" and "Nutward." They were all very angry because the hazelnut orchard had been chainsawed, the roots dug out and hauled off to be burned. They had thought of it as their own nut patch, a place they could go and vie with the Steller's jays and ravens, gathering nuts, stuffing their pockets or filling their lunch pails and backpacks, bringing the booty home and spreading the nuts on top of the hot-water tank or on the floor registers, drying them and saving them for Christmas. What to some of the kids was a lifetime of tradition had been hacked, gouged and made to vanish in less than one day.

When Dal had come out of the bush almost fourteen years ago, with her first season's tree-planting pay in her pocket and the blob of cells that became Twink securely lodged behind her navel, the entire place had been next best thing to the outback. She had put her tree-planting money into the house, a substantial down payment on what was then a 12,000-dollar carpenter's special. She got a job with a country-and-western band and that paid the mortgage and gave her walking-around and eating money until mushroom season. By the time Twink was born, the worst financial burden of home ownership was off Dal's shoulders and she could breathe without feeling as if something was sitting on her chest.

She came out of the bush long enough to have Twink and take a week to rest up, and then she and Twink headed back. Her boss nearly had a fit, but he needed all the experienced help he could find. With Twink in a Snugli, Dal planted trees hour after hour after hour, stopping only to breastfeed the baby and change her diapers, which she stuffed into her bag of seedlings to take back to camp with her.

She washed the diapers by hand in water heated in the cookshack, and the cook let her hang them near the big woodburner. At night she and Twink slept in their own tent, and by the time the season was over, Dal had enough money saved that she could write postdated cheques for the next year's mortgage payments. What she made with her music kept them fed and dressed, and her shroom money paid for the repairs and renovations on the admittedly rundown big box of a house.

Now the farms were going, the orchards as good as gone, and a real estate agent had offered her three times as much for her house as she had paid. Dal wasn't even tempted—yet. She knew she would be when the last farm was chopped up and covered by row after row of townhouse developments and condo complexes. She figured she had maybe two years at the most before it would be time to sort and reject, then pack the surviving stuff and move. She had no idea where.

◌

The Frenchman walked into Toby's halfway through her second shift, and she knew from the way he looked at her that one way or the other, he was going to talk to her. She decided she'd rather he did

it on her break, over a drink, in a quiet voice, than the alternative. She didn't smile at him and she had no intention of giving him any reason to think she was at all well-inclined toward him. He grinned at her and waggled his hand. She nodded, then flicked her gaze down to her fingers, as if she needed to see her strings before she could play "Malaguena." She stalled as long as she could but finally took her break and went directly to the bar. She sat on the end stool, leaving the Frenchman with only one place to sit, and ensuring that nobody was going to sit on the other side and have the chance to eavesdrop. The bartender had her 7-Up in front of her before the Frenchman made it from his table to the stool next to Dal. He put his drink on the bar and slid his gorgeous tight butt onto the stool.
"How you doing?" he asked, smiling as if his life depended on it.

"Just fine." She didn't ask how he was doing.

"I mean...you know..."

"I know. And you know is recovering."

"Would it do any good to apologize?"

"Wouldn't change anything."

"I never done sometin' like dat before."

"I never had sometin' like dat done to me."

"So, would you go out wit' me again?"

She just shook her head, as gently as she could. He sighed and pulled a face, then drained his glass and waved the empty to attract the bartender's attention. He lit a cigarette and waited until he had his fresh drink in his hand.

"Is dat fair?" He looked as mournful as a spaniel puppy who has just been weaned.

"I think so."

"I don' t'ink so." He wasn't smiling. "I t'ink anyone entitle' to a second chance."

"I think it's up to me who I go out with and who I don't. And I don't think I owe anyone the right to go out with me."

"Dat's not fair."

"Fair? Jesus! When did fair have anything to do with anything else?" Dal was willing to bet 10 dollars the guy thought they were having an in-depth relationship discussion, the kind all gentle, sensitive new-age guys are supposed to be learning how to have.

"You should give me a chance to apologize and make up for my mistake."

"You should give me enough respect to not natter at me."

"I'm not nattering. I jus' want to go out wit' you and show you dat I'm not a bad guy."

"I know you're not a bad guy. If I thought you were a bad guy I wouldn't even be talking to you."

"But you won' go out wit' me again?"

"No. I'm not interested in going out with anybody." She almost grinned, but she didn't want to make him think she was thawing.

"Dat's not fair."

"Hey, stop telling me that's not fair, that's not fair. Of course it's not fair. If going out with me depended on some kind of fairness, I'd have had to go chronologically and go out with guys I've known most of my life before I got around to going out with you."

"So dat's it, huh? It's because I'm not from aroun' here?"

"No, you didn't listen to what I said."

"Yeah, I did. You just scared, is all."

"Oh, and I have no reason to be, right?" She laughed bitterly. "I'll be lucky if it doesn't dry up and fall off, the shape you left it in."

"See, you *are* mad!" he said triumphantly.

Dal couldn't remember saying she wasn't. She stood up and forced a small, polite and very distant smile. "Would you excuse me, please." She didn't wait to hear if he said yes or no, and headed for the jane.

She stayed there as long as she could, took her time doctoring the old woman, then went back to the bar, where the dejected Frenchman was sitting with yet another drink. The ice had melted in her 7-Up and she signalled the waiter for a fresh one. "I have to get back for the next set. Excuse me, please."

"I want to talk to you."

"I'm going back to work now. My break is over."

"Nex' break then."

"I don't think so."

"After your shif' is finish."

"No."

She fiddled for most of the next set—it was easier to ignore someone when you had a fiddle tucked under your chin. A group of line dancers took over the square of uncarpeted flooring set aside for the twinkletoes. Dal knew what they wanted, and if she gave it to them she could change the tone of the crowd, maybe even make sure there was too much laughing and bopping for the Frenchman to collar her and repeat his litany. She winked at a guy in a bright yellow satin shirt with red roses and went right into good old boring sick-to-death-of-hearing-it "Achy Breaky Heart." If only she could take the guy who had written the damn thing and stake him out naked and covered with maple syrup on the very tip-top of a five-foot anthill. Dee dee dee dee *dum* dee dee dee dee *dum*—my dear lord in heaven please intercede on my behalf. Or my bewhole if possible.

When next she looked around Toby's, the Frenchman was gone. There were more people on the dance floor than had been there all week, and the manager was grinning from ear to ear. The more people dance, the more they sweat. And the more they sweat, the more they drink. The more they drink, the happier everyone is. It's a joyous world, after all.

Pansy was still awake when Dal got home. They made a pot of tea and got out the last of the potato salad and sandwiches.

"Kids settle down okay?"

"They're fine. I think they're waiting to see if it's anybody we know. All Pape talked about was the great ride back he had from the raft and how when his legs get longer he's going to be able to kick the way you do. They'll be okay."

"Makes you wonder how anyone managed to get under there in the first place. I mean even if you came up under there by mistake, it doesn't take an IQ in the high triple digits to feel your way out, even in the black of night."

"Maybe he bumped his head. Maybe he was drunk. Maybe..." Pansy shrugged. As if the shrug was the signal, the front door began to shake and the sound of hammering made them both jump. Without thinking, Pansy was off her chair and over to the door, opening it. Dal had a mouthful of sandwich to swallow so her warning, "Don't, Pan!" came too late. Pansy's as-good-as-ex shoved his way into the living room.

Dal was so angry with her sister for having forgotten all the words of caution she had given her nieces and nephews that she had almost no energy left to be angry with the intruder. Pansy knew better than to just go open the door! Maybe there had been a time when it was safe to leave the door unlocked, to feel safe in your own house, but if so, that time was long gone. And she'd not only gone over to open the door, she'd done it at top speed because she didn't want the noise to rouse the kids.

"What do you want?" Pansy demanded.

"When the hell you comin' home?" His demand was louder than hers — he'd had more time to work himself into a full sweat.

"Stop shouting."

"Shouting? You think this is shouting? You want to hear shouting? I'll give you some shouting!"

"You start shouting..." Dal said, her voice pleasant, her smile gorgeous, her left eye just a touch narrower than her right. If Chummy had any sense at all he'd back down, because the narrower that eye got, the closer Dal was to going into orbit. "You start shouting and I'll have the cops come over and quiet you."

"You fuckin' try! Go ahead! Phone them if you can." He grabbed the phone off the end table near the sofa and yanked. The cord snapped, and as triumphant as if he'd just crossed the Alps with elephants, he threw the phone the length of the living room. It slammed into the middle of the TV screen. The screen imploded and Dal sighed.

"Now look what you've done," Pansy scolded. "That's going to cost you. Why don't you just calm down and sit down on the sofa. Or better yet, leave."

"Cost me? What's it gonna cost me? You think I'm payin' for that lousy relic of a TV? You got another think comin', lady. You never mind telling me to sit on the sofa and calm down. I'm doin' the tellin' around here, and I'm tellin' you to get your goddamn coat and get your ass into the car because I'm takin' you home, right now."

"No." Pansy sat down.

"You dare tell me no? Who are you to tell me no? You been here long enough! Get your shit and get yourself back where you belong. I'm sick of this, you hear me?"

"If you'd sit down and stop shouting we could discuss it."

"I'm not interested in discussing any goddamn thing at all." But he did sit down on the sofa next to her. "You just get yourself home."

"I'll be over tomorrow afternoon," Pansy soothed.

"Tomorrow afternoon my achin' arse!"

"I thought about one in the afternoon would be a good time."

"Now, damn it."

"No, I'm not going now. If I go now you'll think you won something. And you'll think you've got every right in the world to expect me to go to bed with you. And none of that is true, and none of that is going to happen. I'll go over at about one tomorrow. It'll take me that long to arrange for a rental trailer. I'll pick up my stuff and bring it back here. You've got until the end of the month to find another place for yourself."

"Why'n hell should I move?"

"Well, it *is* my apartment. My name is on the lease. I've been paying the rent. If you want to stay there, talk to the landlady. And pay the rent."

"Bullshit!"

"So I'll be over tomorrow."

"I'll be at work at one in the afternoon!"

"I know," Pansy smiled. "I think that'll work out best all round, don't you?"

"I never agreed to you moving out!"

"You don't have to agree. My moving has nothing to do with you. You look after you, I look after me. If you want to move, you move, and if I want to move, I move. It's called individuality and autonomy, okay?"

"Don't give me any of that horseshit! You're goin' home now, with me."

"I am home now. I live here. I just have to go and get my stuff, is all."

"Pansy, stop arguing with me or I'll lift you a good one on the side of the goddamn head!" He was off the sofa and winding up to pitch a full and total fit. "Stop yammering and get your tubby little arse out into that car, you hear? You're going with me!"

"No shoutin'." Pape came into the living room lugging his Teddy by one arm. "You're not s'posed'a yell. You woke me up."

"G'wan back to bed." Chummy waved his arm, as if shooing away a fly. "G'wan, now, do what you're told."

"No shoutin'," Pape repeated. "It's not nice."

Chummy whirled as if ready to rip arms and legs from torsos. Pansy had no idea where Dal was. She seemed to have vanished, and just as well, because if she'd seen Chummy waving his arm so close to Pape's head, or seen the look on Chummy's face, it would have taken more than Pansy to stop the blood from flowing, even if some of the blood was Dal's. Chummy stared at Pape and his Teddy and a dark red flush came up in his neck and worked its way up until his face and ears were the colour of a ripe beefsteak tomato. Pape was obviously frightened. And, just as obviously, he had no intention of going back to bed and pretending that nothing was going on in the living room.

"Didn't I tell you to go to bed?"

"You're not my dad," Pape quavered. "You're not my mom. You're not no boss."

"You think I'm not the boss? I'll show you if I'm the damn boss or not, little boy! I'll warm your ass for you is what I'll do."

Pape started to cry and clutched his Teddy even tighter. Pansy wished with all her heart that the bear would jump out of Pape's arms, turn itself into a snarling grizzly and clean house for her.

"Look at you! Big brave man! So tough you can make a little teeny boy cry with fear! My goodness, Brian, don't you think you've proved what a big strong tough job of work you are? Don't you think you can go away now? You've got the four-year-old scared stiff, isn't that enough?" Pansy hunkered down and pulled Pape to her, wiping his tears and whispering to him.

"Cheeky little bastard," Chummy grumbled. "Someone should teach him some manners."

"You want to teach my kid manners?" Dal appeared, her eye so slitted it was almost shut. "Well, you'd have to learn a few yourself before you could teach them to anybody else. And in the interests of having a well-educated child, I've arranged for these nice guys to teach you some manners so that you can turn around later on and teach some to the kid."

Two RCMP officers walked into the house behind Dal. Chummy sagged, Pansy stood up and Pape walked over to one of the Mounties and looked up at him with tear-filled eyes.

"He shouted," Pape managed. "And he don't live here."

The Mountie looked down at Pape, who came up to his knee. "Who'd he shout at?"

"My auntie. And me. Gonna hit me, he said. Warm my ass, he said."

"Oh, did he indeed?" The officer had his little notebook out and was making notes. "And what's your name?"

"You gonna put me in jail?" Pape started to cry again. The cop looked as if his uniform had evaporated, leaving him stark naked in the middle of a crowd. He bent over, picked up the sobbing child and patted him awkwardly on the back.

"No, you're not going to jail. You're a good boy. Look, even Teddy is upset now. Look at him—he's going to cry too. Poor Teddy."

"Give him here." Dal reached out and took Pape from the cop. "Hey, Pape, it's okay. These guys will take Chummy away and you can go back to sleep. Nothing's coming down on you. You're fine. Teddy's fine, Auntie Pansy's fine, Momma's fine, even the cops are fine. Everything's fine."

Pape snuggled his face into the curve of his mother's neck. Tears and snot glistened on her skin. She walked slowly, crooning to Pape about all the things that were fine in the world. Pape calmed down, his eyelids fluttered and without even a yawn he was asleep again, wrapped in his mother's arms and the sound of her voice.

Even while they were snapping cuffs onto Chummy's wrists, the cops were watching Dal. She was still in her work clothes, blue jeans tighter than skin on her full, rich body. Her white cowboy shirt had blue roses embroidered down the sleeve of her right arm, but it wasn't the roses or the delicacy of the hand embroidery that had the cops staring. The common legend is that breastfeeding causes the breasts to sag and hang like empty balloons. Not Dal. Even with Pape held up in front of her, his weight pressing on her, there was no doubt that Dal could fill a 38-c and have plenty left over for cleavage. There was also Dal's hair. She wore it just below her shoulders, swept back—or as much back as she could manage. Her hair had a mind of its own. It did what it wanted, and right now what it wanted was to look like the mane of an enraged lion. Pansy would have bet 10 dollars both those cops were wishing any number of things not covered by the Queen's Rules and Regulations.

"How can you do this to me, Pansy?" Chummy whined. "How can you do this to me? How can you be so mean, baby? Come on, tell 'em to let me go."

"Good idea," Pansy agreed. She smiled at the police. "Could he go? Straight to jail and right now?"

"Yes ma'am," they agreed.

Dal watched Pansy work her magic on the RCMP, knowing that the best thing she could do was keep her mouth shut. Nobody knew better than Dal Cassidy just how much trouble her mouth could get her into. If she started talking she'd vent all her fear and anger, and that might inspire the cops to put the cuffs on her too. But Pansy just turned those huge blue eyes in their direction and gave them her 10,000-watt smile, and the arm of the law was as good as eating out of her hand. Dal knew she was tall and well built. She knew how men responded to her. But she knew too that Pansy had her beat all to hell. Pansy was shorter, and her body was softer. Where Dal roused feelings of awe, Pansy roused feelings of protectiveness. Men saw Dal and lusted. They saw Pansy and lusted too, but they only wanted to fuck Dal—they wanted to be with Pansy.

By the time the kids got out of bed and came down for breakfast, they knew what was going on. Pape had clued them in. He was still very upset, which made the other kids, except for Pip, who didn't understand any of it, very angry. They weren't the least bit inclined to forgive and forget, and they sure weren't of a mind to wait and see what might happen.

"Scarin' a little kid!" Twink's contempt was so big it defied expression. "Big deal. It doesn't take much guts to scare a little kid." They were all for heading out right then and there, but Dal very much needed several cups of good strong coffee. She felt as if she was trapped in some kind of brutal counting game. Finished work at two, eating sandwiches at three, invaded at four, Pape and cops at five, bed at six and up again at eight. She tried to tell herself that she'd get it all back when she was 80. Usually that thought consoled her and saw her through a bad spot. After all, people who are 80 don't have a lot of things to do and don't seem to need much sleep, so however tired she was now, when she was 80 it would probably all even out.

The coffee didn't exactly wake her up but it did make it possible for her to be mobile. She was subdued enough, however, that she let the guy at the rental place attach the trailer for her. They got some boxes from the liquor store and some more from the supermarket, then parked with the trailer facing the big back doors of Pansy's apartment building. Pansy seemed very quiet, and Dal hoped that didn't mean Pan's heart was breaking. She hoped all it meant was that Pan was tired too.

The kids went through the living room like scavengers. They wrapped each and every little thing in newspapers as carefully as if it was priceless European porcelain. All Dal had to do was carry boxes to the elevator, then ride down with them and pack them into the trailer. The burly guys from the moving company arrived to get the heavy stuff just as Dal and the kids were putting the last of the small stuff into the rental trailer. Pansy let them into the apartment and waved her arm wearily. "Not the sound system," she told them. "It stays." One of the moving guys grinned and nodded. He knew what was happening as clearly as if someone had written him a book about it. Someone was hoofin 'er off, and someone else was apt to wind up sleeping on the floor tonight.

They carried the boxes in from the trailer and stored them in the spare room off the living room. It wasn't big enough to warrant being called a bedroom, and wasn't small enough to get away with calling it a closet. With the boxes out of the way they cleared a path for the furniture. Dal felt a twinge of dismay when the truck arrived and the movers started hauling furniture into the house. Pansy had as much stuff for one person as Dal had for herself and the kids. Dal liked to have some space in the house, and leaned toward only the most basic of furniture with an absolute minimum of knick-knacks, bric-a-brac and folderol. Pansy liked space filled and surfaces covered.

The installing of the furniture would have gone a lot quicker if Chummy had not arrived. But he did, and the presence of the movers had less effect on him than the presence of the Mounties had. He wailed and ranted, raved and shouted, as if noise would convince everyone that he was right. Pansy was worried at first. She knew he wouldn't hesitate to throw a few punches and she was embarrassed—would someone think that she had known he was a total drip when she moved in with him? She had an urge to grab people by the arm and explain that his drippiness was why she was moving out.

"What in hell am I supposed to sleep on?" he raved. "And what am I supposed to keep my clothes in? You've taken the bed, you've taken the dressers, you've taken every damn thing we had."

"I've only taken what I had before I met you." Pansy tried to keep her voice even. "If you want a bed, buy one. If you want dressers, buy some."

"Easy for you to say! Damn easy for you to say!" He moved toward her, as if the closer he was the louder he would seem and the more convincing he would be. "I don't even have a goddamn blanket to keep me warm! You took them all!"

"They were mine to start with!" Pansy yelled back. "Try getting your own stuff. Go buy a blanket. Buy two."

"With what?"

"That's your problem. You've got a job, it pays money. Use some of it. Just leave me alone."

Pansy walked past him and up the steps, through the front door and into the living room. Already it was starting to look like her home. She was mentally rearranging the furniture when Chummy marched in.

"Out!" Dal yelled. "Get out of my house!"

"You shut up!" he snarled, "I'm talking to my girlfriend, not to you!"

Dal blew. Pansy never once said anything about it but she did deeply regret the loss of the lamp Dal threw. She'd got it for 50 cents at the Goodwill and had been very fond of it. You don't find many lamps where Elvis has the bulb in the neck of his guitar. Elvis shattered against Chummy's chest. Chummy stumbled backward, hooked his heel on the doorsill and landed flat on his back on the porch. Quick as a pack of feral cats, the kids were on him. They rolled him off the porch and down the steps. Chummy lurched to his feet and headed back up the steps. One of the movers gave him a slight nudge with the headboard of Pan's waterbed. "Excuse me," the burly guy said, "but you're in the way."

"I'll sue!" Chummy promised. Nobody paid him any attention so he sat on the steps, a bluish egg-shaped lump forming on his forehead where the headboard had connected. The kids arranged themselves on the guardrail of the porch, watching Chummy, ready to yelp and yodel if he showed any sign of getting up and heading for the front door.

He glared at them. "What you starin' at?"

"I guess it's still a free country," Skipper remarked, to nobody in particular. "I guess I can sit on the rail of my own porch if I want to."

"Yeah," Button agreed.

"Yeah," Pape echoed. He didn't trust Chummy at all. Pape didn't remember what had happened the night before and almost thought of it all as a bad dream. But if it was a bad dream, this was the Booger Man sitting on the steps. And you don't trust the Booger Man.

Pansy paid the movers and they drove off in their big truck. Chummy lingered on the porch, mourning. But at least he was mourning in silence. Pansy collared the kids, took them into the house with her and put them to work lugging boxes. Dal swept up the remains of Elvis, then took Pip with her for a nap. Pip was asleep almost immediately. Dal took longer. She lay on her bed wishing she had someone to talk to, someone she could really talk to. Not Pansy. Much as Dal loved Pan this was something she couldn't discuss with her. How many times had Dal suggested Pansy move into the house? How many times had she said, "Well, after all, Pan, you're here a big chunk of time, anyway, why not just take over the third floor? Or you can have the second floor and we'll shift the kids to the third." And how many times had Pansy smiled vaguely, as if she couldn't quite envision the first floor, let alone the second or third? How many times had she said, "Well, it's something to think about, all right," and then done nothing at all? She wouldn't move in with Dal and the kids, but she'd move because of Chummy. Dal had the feeling Pansy would have checked herself into the SPCA and taken up residence in one of the cages if that was the only way to put space between herself and the dreary lump now sodding on the steps. Dal's feelings were hurt. You'd think your own sister would move in because of you, not because of some scratch-face virtual stranger.

Pip snuggled closer and the warmth from the tiny body coaxed Dal's thoughts away from her own hurt feelings. She yawned, and the next thing she knew she was in bed all by herself. The light in the room had changed, her mouth felt as if it had been used as the bottom of a parrot cage, and her head was threatening to ache. She got up feeling as if she'd been poisoned.

She could hear the kids in the kitchen and she could smell Pansy's blistering spaghetti sauce. She realized she was hungry enough to eat the pasta without any sauce. She went to the bathroom and glared at her reflection in the mirror. She looked like someone who would chuck Elvis at some jerk. She figured she almost looked like Elvis. She wanted a good long soak in the tub, but she also wanted something to eat and she could hear the clatter of plates as the kids set the table. She rinsed her face with cold water, brushed her teeth, flapped her hands at her unruly hair and went downstairs for supper. She half-expected to see Chummy sitting at the table, a loaf of fresh bread in front of him, smiling and waiting for someone to fill his plate. She had made up her mind that if he was there, he was going to eat every scrap of the Elvis lamp.

He wasn't there. His absence cheered her. She went to the stove and hugged Pansy from behind, silently apologizing for her own sullen disappointment at Pansy's motives. "You spoil me," she said softly. "God, it's nice to have you here."

"You spoil *me*," Pansy answered. "Who else would let me cook spaghetti sauce all over their kitchen?"

It was true. When Pansy cooked, she cooked all over the house. The kids were used to it, though, and had long ago decided they'd clean up after her in return for the food she put in front of them. They insisted Pan's sloppy joes were the best in the world and told all their friends it was Pansy had taught Ronnie McD how to cook hamburgers. Their friends believed them.

There was time after supper to go outside and catch up on the yard work. Dal cut some roses and took them inside, filled a mason jar with water, stuffed the roses in and set them on the table.

"Momma," Twink sighed, "you should arrange them so they show up."

"What, you can't see them? I can see them. They're gorgeous."

"Oh, Momma," Twink sighed again and shook her head. "Really."

Dal hid her smile. At the rate Twink was going, she would soon be 96 years old. She went back outside knowing that Twink would arrange the roses and turn a bunch into a bouquet.

When she went around to the front of the house to check on the big purple and white dahlias, Chummy was still sitting on the steps. "Can I talk to Pansy?" he asked mournfully.

"Go home," she snapped.

"I've got no home. Pansy was my home and now she's evicted me."

"Get off my steps. Get out of my yard. Move, or I'll have you arrested for trespassing."

"I'm not doing anything wrong."

"You're breathing. Move it."

For a moment he looked as if he was going to stand up, tell her to go to hell and smoke her a good one. But he just sighed and mumphed his way down the steps, along the walk and out the gate. He stood there looking mournful and misunderstood and trying to tug on the heartstrings of the world. The world ignored him as thoroughly as Pansy was doing. He scuffed off down the street. Now she had two of them to try to comb out of her hair. Chummy and the damn Frenchman! What did they do, split down the middle like amoebae? One day you've got one pain in the toosh, the next day you have two. By the end of the week how many would you have? And why?

Three

Saturday night in Toby's was as close as Dal ever wanted to get to outright pandemonium. All the guys who worked in camp had come into town and were vying with the townies for the attentions and, they hoped, the favours of the single or pretending-to-be girls and women. They also seemed to be locked in an unspoken competition to see who could get the drunkest, and still stay upright. Within each group were any number of stalwarts trying hard to qualify for the boozy equivalent of MVP and more than a few who were well into their attempts to achieve a Personal Best. Or Worst, depending on your point of view.

The dance floor was so packed she couldn't even see it. When she looked out, she saw hair, and lots of it. She saw brightly coloured clothes. She saw shoulders, cleavage and chest hair. But she couldn't see the floor itself for the strutting, gliding, bopping mass of celebrants. She played some jazz, she played some c&w, she played mouldy oldies and she played Top-10. She played until her fingertips were starting to feel tender and then she played some more. The rumour was that Toby's was going to get a karaoke machine. Dal didn't know whether to grieve or cheer. The machine might put her out of a part-time job. On the other hand, it might give all these people something to do other than drink, drink, drink, and get loud,

loud, louder. Besides, summer was winding down. Soon it would rain, then the mushrooms would sprout and she'd be gone. And Toby's wasn't the only place in town.

Some of the crowd seemed to think the karaoke machine had already been installed and it was Dal. It wasn't too bad when they just stood on the dance floor and crooned with the music, but it got awkward when they decided they were plenty good enough to share the spotlight and got up on stage with her. You get one and the next thing you know you've got another, trying to outdo the first. Once you have two, you've got more. Dal didn't know how she was supposed to get rid of them without making them so angry they left the place and went to spend their money somewhere else. Toby didn't want that. But Toby also didn't want anybody putting a drunken foot through the speakers. The sound system, such as it was, was his, and in Toby's mind it had cost an arm and a leg. Dal didn't want to hurt his feelings by telling him the truth—the system was lousy.

Some young woman who was probably using her older sister's ID seemed determined to prove that she had all the same bits, pieces and morsels as Tanya Tucker. She didn't sing anywhere near as well, but she certainly could gyrate. The crowd loved her. Dal worried that the young woman would lose her balance and pitch herself off the stage. If she did, her chest alone could cause serious injury. When the balding guy with the expanding waistline got up and started to holler "Rock'n'roll, gang, rock'n'roll!" Dal gave up completely. Smiling as if this was one of the happiest, most memorable nights of her life, she backed off the stage, violin in one hand, guitar in the other. The sea of drunks parted as if she was Moses, and she made it to the bar. Toby smiled at her, took the instrument cases and put them safely under the bar, then got her a beer.

"Busy night," he said, smiling. Sometimes Dal wondered if Toby had gotten his face carved into a permanent smile by a cosmetic surgeon. Nothing wiped it off his face. When there was a bad fight, the smile might start to fade, but you could see it, waiting in the wings, impatient and eager to get back to where it belonged.

"Noisy night." Dal drank thirstily. "Ah, I might live. My throat was starting to feel gritty."

"Lotsa happy people out there."

"Lotsa drunks out there, Tobe. If anybody gets out of line, this could be the next best thing to a riot. The fire marshal will shit bricks if he sees this."

"I know." Toby didn't seem worried. "Hot night like this, we had to open the back and side doors to get a good flow of fresh air, and they're coming in from all directions."

"You're losing out on the cover charge."

"Yeah. But making it up on bar sales." He reached under the bar and turned on the stereo. The music blared, the crowd roared happily and more bodies tried to squeeze onto the dance floor. Dal sipped her beer and watched. She didn't see how a karaoke machine was going to work out here. Nobody was listening. The ones at the tables were all busy trying to talk, to have their jokes heard, to put the tap on someone else. The ones on the dance floor were sweating, shouting and swaying. Toby said something to her but she couldn't hear it. She had no idea how the bartenders could hear the orders shouted by the table waiters, or, for that matter, how the waiters could understand what the rowdy drunks were saying. Maybe after a certain point any kind of booze poured over ice cubes would satisfy them.

She was supposed to play until 2:30, but by half past midnight it was obvious she might just as well go home. Even if she could make herself heard over the uproar, she couldn't push her way through the crowd to get to her mike. Besides, some bozo had it clutched in a death grip and was singing "The Frozen Logger." The crowd loved it and half of them sang along. Except "The Frozen Logger" has an estimated 42 verses—more if you count the disgustingly filthy ones—and everyone seemed willing to sing a different one at the same time. About the only words they seemed to agree on were, "Nobody but a logger stirs his coffee with his thumb."

She took her instruments and squeezed through the access door behind the bar, past the stacked cases of booze, through the cooler room and out the "Deliveries Only" door. Even out on the parking lot people were singing and dancing. But at least nobody was imitating the Canada goose and honking into the potted plants.

The house was dark when Dal got home. She parked, got her instruments from the back seat, locked the car and headed for the front steps, holding her keys so they poked out between her fingers. You just never know, and why take chances? She nearly stepped on Chummy, who was lying on the porch, sound asleep in front of the door. Dal leaned over him to unlock the door, stepped over him, went inside and then turned on the big lamp to get a good look at Chummy. He was lying on his side, his mouth half-open. If she grabbed him and rolled him down the steps, he'd bash his head, suffer brain damage, sue her and maybe successfully sue them to be allowed to stay in the house, paralyzed and needing constant care. She closed the door and locked it. She wanted to go to bed and leave him out there for the mosquitoes to feast on but she wasn't too clear about English common law. There was one that said if you let people use a path or roadway or shortcut across your property and never posted signs, put up a fence or in some other way closed it off, it became public access and anybody could waltz past at any time. Maybe front porches were the same. Maybe if you let someone sleep there, that gave him the right to live there. Then maybe that gave him the right to expect all the privileges of a rent-paying tenant—heat, light, something to cook on. They might hit you for maintaining an unlawful rental suite and take your house away as punishment. Then you'd be the one out looking for a porch to sleep on. It was safer to just phone the police. Dal would have preferred to phone the garbage collectors, but they don't work at night.

The police came and hauled Chummy to his feet. He gave Dal a reproachful look that didn't faze her one little bit. "I wasn't doing you any harm," he whined.

"Go home. Stay away from here. And be quiet, or you'll wake up the kids."

"Oh, God, the kids." He shuddered.

The cops walked him to their car, shoved him into the back seat and drove off. Dal wondered how many nights Chummy would have to spend in jail before he got the message. She hoped Pansy didn't relent. She didn't want Pansy moving into a place of her own and there was no way in hell she would let Chummy move into the house. She ate some cold spaghetti, drank a big glass of milk, then checked to make sure all the doors and windows were securely locked. Satisfied that they were temporarily safe from invasion, she brushed her teeth and went to bed.

Dal was the first one awake in the morning. When she opened the front door to let the cat in, there was Chummy, lying across the doorway. Dal could only thank all the known gods and goddesses he wasn't one of those stalkers who carry loaded weapons and kick in doors and smash windows and blast the occupants to smithereens. What the hell was the matter with the cops, anyway? Had they just driven him as far as the fish'n'chips shop and turned him loose, or what? Well, she would handle things herself. She made a pot of coffee and took a cup of it and a cigarette outside, by way of the back door. She went to the side of the house, turned on the tap, picked up the hose and calmly aimed the jet of cold water at the front porch. Chummy shrieked and stumbled to his feet. "Jesus Christ!" he roared. "You outta your mind?" Dal just kept spraying, as she smoked and took sips of coffee. Chummy lurched down the steps and headed for the front gate. Dal directed water at him until he was moving off down the street, his clothes streaming water.

"What was all that about?" Pansy yawned from the front door. "You always wash the porch at this hour of the morning?"

"Chummy was using it as a bedroom."

"We told him to eff off last night!" Pansy frowned. "What's a body got to do, anyway?"

"Maybe we should buy some gas and matches."

"The police took him away about 10:00 last night."

"They took him away again at one, when I got home."

"You got off work early."

"It was a zoo. An absolute zoo."

"Maybe that's why the cops let him go. Maybe they needed the cell."

"If he was taken at 10 and again at midnight, he didn't even see a cell. For this we pay taxes?"

"Now don't you get started!" Pansy said. "And don't phone them again or we'll be visiting *you* in a cell."

Dal made breakfast. The kids rightly understood this to mean that they were having a party. During summer holidays they were usually on their own, and it was cereal and toast. To waken to the smell of frying bacon and braunschweiger sausage could only mean it was a party. Dal cooked enough bacon for an army, then began cracking eggs into a bowl. She started off counting—one for Pip, one for

Pape, two for Button—but somewhere between there and Skipper she lost count, so she just cracked away until it looked as if there might be enough to fuel them up until lunchtime. When the bacon and braunschweiger was done, she took it from the pan, drained off most of the fat, then carefully poured in the bowl of eggs. She didn't care who wanted theirs sunny-side-up and who wanted them once-over-easy. They could eat whatever came their way.

Dal filled the bathtub and got into it before the kids started in on the dishes. Otherwise she knew she'd have to wait until well after they had finished. Somehow they used an entire tank of hot water, whether they were cleaning up after a big supper for the whole family or rinsing out dishes from a little mid-morning snack. She'd yammered at them, yapped at them, lectured and nagged, and for all the good it did she might as well have saved her breath.

She soaked herself until the water cooled, then soaped a cloth and gingerly swabbed at the old woman. No blood. She bent forward, blowing the suds and bubbles out of the way. There was a thin line of darker-coloured skin, but no scab. It looked as if the hood had been ripped to the very edge. It also looked as if not all the rip was healing. In fact, if she'd been of a mind to talk to anyone about it, she would have said it looked as if she had been moderately circumcised. Certainly there seemed to be more of the old woman showing now than had shown before the clumsy nitwit as good as inhaled her most tender portion.

"You taken up full-time residence in there?" Pansy called. "There's only one toilet in the house, you know, and I've been drinking coffee!"

"Coming," Dal sighed. One day. One day she'd have a bathroom all to herself. She'd be able to lie in the tub and, if she wanted, eat maraschino cherries and read *Gone with the Wind* from cover to cover without someone evicting her.

Pinch and Duck arrived home just before suppertime. Dal was so glad to see them she could only hang on and cuddle fiercely. "I love you," she said again and again. "I missed you."

"Missed you too, Mom." Pinch squeezed Dal in a bear hug. She was tanned the colour of hazelnut shells, her eyes so green they seemed to jump out of her face and leap across the room. She had the same Cassidy hair as Twink and Dal—people turned to watch her when she passed them on the street. Ducky had inherited Pansy's black, black, black hair, and curly too, as thick as Dal's and almost as hard to manage. Duck had Pansy's eyes as well—big, blue and fringed by long, thick lashes. For the past three summers they had gone out with their dad on his fish boat, and each of those summers, for Dal, had been painful. Not only did she not have them with her, they were out there on the heaving chuck, and it was no comfort to know their dad was a fanatic about survival suits, no comfort to know that they could both swim like seals. Even in summertime the chuck is so cold a person will succumb to hypothermia in a terrifyingly short time. Even with survival suits, danger rides on every wave.

Their dad was one of the nicest men Dal had ever met. She was glad of that, glad that she had an example. Whenever any of her kids asked about the paternal absence in their lives, Dal talked about Pinch and Duck's dad. She didn't tell the others it wasn't their particular dad she was describing, so each one of them thought their dad was a prince among men. In the case of Duck and Pinch, it was true. Dal knew there were plenty of people, even her sisters, who thought she was right out of her mind when she not only didn't marry him, she didn't stick with him at all. She had begun to wonder recently whether, if she had met him later on, she would have been quite so independent. If she met him now, for example, would she still recoil from commitment? And wasn't that a hoot. Recoil from commitment? She was up to her eyeballs in commitment, and not just for five or 10 or 20 years. She was to her hairline in lifetime commitments.

He was the only guy who had taken more than a proprietary interest in the unborn. When he found out Dal was pregnant, he showed up in his best jeans and T-shirt with a bag of fresh-baked cinnamon buns, and knocked on her door politely but firmly.

"Dahlia," he had said, "I do believe I helped you get pregnant."

"Well, yes," she admitted unwillingly.

"I would like to talk to you about it, please."

"Talk? What talk?"

"I want to know what you want to do."

"Do? What's to do?"

"I'd like to talk to you about that."

So she let him in and they sat in the kitchen with coffee and cin-namon buns and talked.

"I'd like to know what *you* have in mind first." Dal had felt much less threatened once she was in her own rented kitchen.

"Okay. What I have in mind is this: if you want to get married, I'd be real happy. It's what I wanted pretty much from the start anyway. If you want to sign it off for adoption, then I'd like to be the one who adopts it. I've talked to my sister and she'd look after it when I was away."

"I'm not giving any baby away! I'm keeping this baby. It's mine!"

"Do you want to marry me?"

"No. I don't want to marry anybody."

"Live together?"

"No."

"Then I'd like to be involved. It's mine too, Dal. Ours."

"What's your idea of being involved?"

"Oh, hey, you know me. I'd prefer to be on tap 24 hours a day, seven days a week, 52 weeks a year for the next couple of decades." He laughed, and Dal relaxed. "But you've already nixed that so I want as much as I can get without being a pain in the face."

Dal had expected it would be a case of out of sight, out of mind, but it wasn't. Not only did he show up on weekends to see Pinch and Duck, but time proved that he was willing to take some or all of the other kids with him to the circus, the pizza house or wherever he was taking his own girls. And he not only contributed money for Pinch and Duck's care, he set up bank accounts for them and deposited money regularly for future education, or whatever. He had even had a will drawn up to ensure that they were protected if something happened to him. He was married now and had other kids, but his wife had known from the start what the situation was. Dal knew some people refused to believe it was possible, but there wasn't any jealousy or discord. Or if there was, neither she nor the girls had ever known about it.

"Did you make lotsa money?" Pape asked hopefully.

"Yeah." Duck picked Pape up and twirled him around. "Why, what do you want? A fire truck, maybe?"

"Nah. Jus' wondered."

"You comin' out with us when you're big enough? We'll have our own boat by then, Pape, and you can be the cook."

"I'm glad you're home." He grabbed her around the neck and squeezed as hard as he could without hurting her. "You were gone a long time."

The twosome had arrived home just before school started. They filled the long weekend with shopping trips to the mall for clothes and school supplies. There were sneakers to buy, and not just one pair each. Each of the kids needed one pair to wear to school, another pair for use on the expensive wood floor in the gym and a third pair for when gym class was held outside. Those kids who were going to play soccer had to have shoes for that, and once those were bought and paid for, the problem of waterproof boots presented itself. By this time, Dal was used to the assault on her finances.

Pansy insisted that Pipsqueak should start preschool and Pape should go to full-time kindergarten. "They need the socialization experience," she said.

"Socialization? They aren't even old enough to—"

"I've read up on this, Dahlia. It's very important that they are introduced to a structured fun environment before they have to get used to a structured school environment. Otherwise—"

"But Pan, you're the one didn't even want a babysitter, and now—"

"Well, they aren't babysitters, are they? They're educators."

Dal wanted to argue but felt that much of the decision had been taken from her simply because the shrooms would soon be rising from the moss and she'd be off picking, with much of the home-and-hearth stuff resting on Pansy's shoulders. Besides, Pansy was heading back to full-time classes and obviously, sooner or later, something would have to be done. Might as well do it sooner, before everything was full and they had to fall back on the second line, the do-it-at-homers, not all of whom did it the way Dal and Pansy wanted it done. Pansy arranged to take Pip and Pape with her in the morning and pick them up on her way home. Dal pretended that was just fine with her, and made jokes about actually having some quiet time to herself.

On Tuesday they all went to school for a couple of hours to register and be assigned their lockers. Wednesday they went for the full day. Dal felt as if the house had suddenly grown to six times its size. Everything echoed. When she walked down the hall, it sounded as if she was wearing huge, heavy boots. The vacuum cleaner didn't hum or buzz—it roared. She filled the tub and climbed in, then couldn't relax. Even though she knew nobody was going to hammer on the door or yell at her, her body strained, listening and waiting for what wasn't there.

Dal decided that if she couldn't relax, she'd work it off—whatever *it* was. She started in the kitchen, with the fridge. That was guaranteed to make a mess and take hours. Little bits of this and that, a dab at a time, each with its own saucer or butter plate. Science experiments, perhaps. Three jars of pickles, each with a few in the bottom, two different quarter-filled jars of hot salsa. Something, God in heaven alone knew what, lurked in a bowl, covered with a thin blue film. She turfed it all into the compost bucket and emptied the vinegar down the sink. The smell of it hung in the kitchen long after she had taken the compost to the box outside. She scrubbed the inside of the fridge, put the shelves back and replaced what she hadn't tossed out. It was a fraction of what she had removed. After the fridge, she did the oven. With that done, it was all-out assault—cupboards, shelves, woodwork, counters and, finally, the floor. When she was finished, she felt as if it wasn't even her kitchen. It seemed so clean, so alien, so uninviting. She headed upstairs and took on the kids' bedrooms. More science experiments and enough socks to start her own store. Jeans she hadn't seen in weeks. T-shirts in corners, blankets twisted behind the bed, trapped between mattress and wall. Dal went bed by bed, room by room until the laundry basket was overflowing with clothes that ought to have been done weeks earlier, and the vacuum bag was so full it had to be replaced. Then she took a break. She lugged the laundry downstairs and started putting it through the washer. While that was turning and churning, she went into the next-best-thing-to-sterile kitchen and made herself a pot of tea and a toasted tomato sandwich. Except for the mutter and chunter from the washing machine, it was so quiet in the house she could hear her own jaws working as she chewed.

When the kids came home from school, Dal had supper started in a house so clean they gaped, then looked at each other and went quietly to their rooms to stare in awe and a measure of dismay at accommodations they no longer recognized.

"Are we movin'?" Button asked.

"She does it every year." Duck tried to sound reassuring. "It doesn't mean anything."

"Pretty creepy," Pape decided.

Summer hung on with the determination of a wood tick. The days were clear and warm, and the kids went swimming in the lake until well past the middle of September. No rain fell, and the shrooms stayed in the earth. Dal busied herself as best she could with the garden, putting it to bed for the winter that might never arrive. She canned until she was sick of the sight of glass jars, and she made packages of vegetables and froze them until it looked as if she was going to have to buy a second freezer. She made chutney, she made pickles, she made salsa and then she made more of each. And every night she took her instruments and headed off to Toby's to play for the crowds.

In the third week of October, while she was mowing the lawn, she noticed ripe blackberries on the vines that twisted along the back fence. The neighbours often made cracks about Dal's blackberries. They fought theirs constantly—digging the roots, spraying and daubing on all manner of herbicides, even going at them with pro-pane torches and trying to burn them to death. Dal pruned hers and harvested the berries. She had enough jam and jelly to keep even her family going for a good two years. The neighbours struggled to keep their raspberries, loganberries, may berries, marion berries and tayberries alive, while Dal stood like a lion tamer with whip and chair, fending off her blackberries and being rewarded by ice-cream bucket loads of gleaming treasure. But she had never had berries this late in October.

The rain finally came on the 7th of November. For three days the wind howled and the ditches filled. On the 11th, when proper people were putting on their best clothes and heading to the cenotaph to pay their respects to those who had died because of war, Dal was out in the bush, wearing drybacks and knee-high rubber boots, picking chanterelles and pines. She made $500 the first day.

Dal wanted to take Pip and Pape out shrooming with her, as she'd taken the other kids when they were that age. But Pansy didn't have a good thing to say about the idea and plenty of criticism, which she considered constructive. "Pip needs the preschool experience," she said firmly. "She has to learn to relate to kids her own age."

"Pip's nearly buried in kids. She—"

"They're all older than she is, and they all treat her like the baby."

"Well, jeez, Pan, she is the baby."

"Exactly. She needs to be encouraged to act her age."

"She doesn't?"

"No. She acts like a baby. She thinks all she has to do is look at something and it's hers. She thinks everyone else in the world was born for no reason but to get her drinks of water and juice. She can't even get her shoes on her feet, let alone get them on the right ones."

"Oh."

"And Pape needs a break from her. He also needs the kindergarten experience."

"And what experience is that?"

"Being by himself."

"How can anyone be by himself in a room with 25 other kids?"

"Those 25 other kids aren't his siblings. They don't have him slotted. He can develop his own personality, not the one the other kids have decided is his. And he can learn how to be a little boy without having to be a little boy who trudges around doing things for a bossy little baby."

"I took the other kids shrooming." Even to Dal it sounded almost like a wail. "And they've been going to preschool and kindergarten for weeks already. They could miss a few days. It didn't hurt the others when I took them."

"You can take these ones too, but on the weekends. Besides, you know full well you can pick more and better if you don't have to keep one eye on the kids. Remember the time you turned around and the kids were playing in the shrooms? I bet *that* cost you a bundle. And Pip is such a sucky baby, she'll cry and want to come home after the first hour."

Dal wanted to say that Pip would only do that until she realized it wasn't doing her any good, but she knew she was fighting a losing battle. Preschool and kindergarten *experiences*, for crying out loud. Wasn't everything an experience? What had the shrooming experience done to harm the others? She almost said shrooming was more fun with the kids along, but she knew what Pansy would say to that. Dal tried to pretend that she didn't feel something very important had vanished from her life.

Life shifted gears again. She was up in the pitch dark, filling one thermos with hot soup, the other with coffee, stuffing her sandwiches in her backpack and heading out to logging roads and skidder trails, revisiting places she had been shrooming for years. Sometimes she deliberately parked her Chev, which all the pickers knew was hers, near the most miserable blowdown and swamp she could find, knowing that behind her a dozen others were cursing and muttering, slipping off logs and into heaps of slash, thrashing up to their armpits in windfall, exhausting themselves in their attempts to follow her and find her picking spots. When she figured they were all confused or bogged down, she doubled back, got in her car and raced to the real mushroom bed as fast as the road or skid trail allowed. There she would pull right off the road, bounce and shudder in behind a screen of elderberry or young alder to one of the parking places only she knew about, then turn off the engine and have a quiet cigarette, waiting to see if anyone had followed her. Only when she knew she was alone would she head off to fill her baskets. She picked steadily until the light began to fade, then hurried to her car, trying to get to it before the early dark folded down on her, and she got lost in the heavy black of the nighttime bush. At the buyer station, other pickers glared at her with envy and resentment and made bitter jokes about greedy people who hogged things to themselves. Some asked her outright where she picked. Dal just grinned. The only reason she had good picking sites was that she had never told anyone, not even Pansy, where she went.

Once she had sold her day's take, she rushed home, got into a hot bath to thaw herself, caught something to eat, then rushed off to Toby's. When that stint was done, she went back to the home she was hardly seeing these days. It took her a good hour to unwind enough to get to sleep. A few hours of sleep and the alarm was shrilling. She wanted to grab it and fire it out the window, but she reminded herself it wasn't only telling her to get up out of bed, it was promising money, money, money, and she needed about as much of that as she could get her hands on. One thing a person could count on is that the good times wouldn't last long. On the weekends, when the kids wanted to go with her, Dal woke them up early, filled their bellies and headed off, but not to her special places. Kids talk. Kids brag. Kids don't mean to let cats out of bags, but they do. She drove up known logging roads and headed into the bush with the kids, and there were shrooms for them all but never the kind of numbers she got on her own. "Don't break the veils," she told them, over and over and over again. "Break the veil and the price goes down with a thump."

She would have eaten ground-glass sandwiches before she admitted to Pansy that without the short-legs to distract and amuse her, she picked probably twice as many mushrooms. Even she was amazed at how much money she made, all of it cash money—unrecorded, unreported and untaxed.

Shroom season ended with a week of heavy frost at the end of November. The only good thing about the unusually short season was that prices were higher than they had been in several years and Dal had done well. Very well—her best year ever. She had four days to rest her back, and then the contractor called. It was time to phone Toby and drop the news on him so he could find a replacement, pack her tree-planting gear in her duffel bag, oil the very devil out of her bush boots, kiss the kids repeatedly and take a cab to town to hook up with the other tree planters who were taking the bus with her. She was off to wade through knee-deep snow, planting hardened-off and dormant seedlings on the steep sides of slopes that had been clear-cut and slash-burned down to the very rock.

Three weeks of it, and not a day off in all that time. They slept in down-filled sleeping bags inside tents that were designed for Arctic expeditions. They paid 30 dollars a day in "camp costs," which, Dal supposed, since she had provided the tent and sleeping bag herself, were meant to cover the costs of the food and the cook. It didn't cost her 30 dollars a day to feed herself at home, so she could only suppose that the cook was making a very good wage indeed. She didn't bother writing letters. They wouldn't get home much earlier than she would, and anyway, what is there to write about? Up in the dark, dress in the cold, rush to the big tent, grab coffee and a plate of pancakes, eat quickly, pick up the packed lunch and a thermos of coffee, then go get the seedlings and stuff them in the special bag. Into the crummy and rattle and bounce off to the slope, then hour after hour after hour after hour of the same thing, the world shrinking until all she could see was the ground immediately in front of her, and her planting tool hacking through snow and rock, hacking at the frozen earth, making a little hole into which to drop the seedling. Then her boot, pressing the earth down around the ball of roots, and on, measuring distance by her own strides, planting what they all tried to pretend would one day be a forest like the one that had been strip-mined and squandered.

Out for Christmas, she told herself. It will all be worth it—out for Christmas. All day, planting, striding, hacking with the digging tool, over and over, she promised herself, out for Christmas, out for Christmas. They were almost at the bottom of the slope and every morning they moved farther down, away from the increasing load of white that came down the mountain. She was starting to worry about the snow load up there. It didn't take much for the damn stuff to shift. The hillsides were eroded, and deep gullies cut down like ravines in some places. Entire new canyons had been cut by runoff because the roads had been built improperly, in the wrong places. Sometimes she had waking nightmares about dislodging the one rock holding everything in place. It was ridiculous, to be out here, planting seedlings in ground already frozen. What chance did they have? But if the forestry experts were willing to go along with the sham, who was she to spit in the eye of the one paying her? So much per seedling, and if the seedlings froze to death, well, whose business was that? At least she wasn't dumping entire boxes of baby trees into gullies or behind rocks and claiming that they'd been planted.

Pansy and the kids had the Christmas tree up and decorated when Dal stepped into the house, put her gear on the floor and started getting hugged, smooched and welcomed home.

"Come see the tree," they urged. "You'll love it! Come see."

Dal supposed it was fatigue and the hint of pain in her back that made her think the tree looked like every other tree they'd ever had. But she smiled and agreed with them that it was indeed the best one ever. The house smelled like Christmas, and no sooner had she plopped her butt on the sofa than the kids were plying her with short-bread and mincemeat tarts, fruitcake and butter tarts. Pip climbed on her knee and cuddled close, her thumb in her mouth, her eyes blinking drowsily. Pape sat beside her, pressed against her, his little hand on her leg. He'd been chewing his nails again, and the tips of his fingers looked sore. Button and Skipper fussed over her, Twink smiled, and Pinch and Duck interrupted each other as they tried to fill her in on everything that had happened in the three weeks she'd been gone. Dal tried to give each of them her attention, tried to spread herself around so nobody would feel left out or slighted, but it didn't take much more than an hour for her to feel that she'd had as much of it as she could handle. She felt overloaded and impatient, and she hated herself for it. Why couldn't she just come home and wallow in all the love and attention? Surely other people did that. Why not her?

Twink looked at the clock and grunted with surprise. "We have to hurry!" she blurted. "Come on!"

"Come on where?"

"The concert! We have to get there!"

The rush was classic. Only Pansy seemed to have any idea where anybody might find socks, T-shirts, jeans. She stayed calm and kept saying, "In your drawer, dear. In your drawer." Dal would have been roaring at them to stop yammering and go look in the damn drawer for a change. But either Pansy was unflappable or she gave a real good imitation of it. Did Pansy ever feel that if one more high-pitched voice grizzled on about nothing at all, she'd be over the edge and into some ugly physical violence? Did Pansy ever feel that what she'd like to do is put a row of strong brass coat hooks on the wall beside the furnace and hang the kids there until they had grown big enough and old enough to figure out how to climb down and behave like responsible adults?

Dal wanted a long, hot soak in the tub. But she only got to wash her hands and face, then had to go look in her own drawer for some clean clothes. Somehow, with no help from her, it all pulled itself together. There were ironed white shirts for the boys and Pape found a tie. Skipper had one too, but he refused to wear it or even carry it folded in his pocket. "If they don't like it," he shrugged, "I just won't go out and sing, is all." Pape wore his as if it was a badge of honour. Dal couldn't remember ever buying any ties for the boys, and wondered where these ones had come from.

The concert, like all Christmas concerts, was a total success in the indulgent eyes of the rellies in the audience. Pansy sniffed and snuffed a bit, as she always did. It was almost guaranteed that she'd bubble over at a parade too. One look at the little girls in their majorette costumes and Pansy was snuffling. Tonight it was the preschooler who came out first, dressed as the angel of something and piping "Peace on Earth." Pansy made a dive for her pocket and hauled out a whack of tissues.

"Oh God," she wept in a whisper that could be heard at least five rows away, "there isn't a drop of peace anywhere, and people in this country are getting rich selling the ingredients for napalm to other people who want to burn up the children of still other people."

"Sssshhhh," Dal hissed. "You want to ruin this for everyone?"

"I'm sorry." Pansy blew her nose noisily, then shushed before anyone else had to tell her to shut up about the state of world affairs.

Pipsqueak stood on her chair and pointed at the stage, yelling as loud as she could. "Skipper! Look! That's Skipper!" The kids on stage were supposed to keep their eyes front and centre, hang on to as much dignity as they could muster and focus all their attention on singing, "Hark! The Herald Angels Sing." Instead, Skip grinned widely, waved his hand and winked.

"He *sees* me!" Pip screeched. A young woman in the row ahead turned, smiling, and handed Pip a small candy cane. Pip plopped onto her chair, immediately forgot about her brother onstage and busied herself with the noisy wrapper on the candy. That one little white stick with green and red mint stripes on it kept her quiet for the rest of the concert. In fact, halfway through "Good King Wenceslas," Pip fell asleep, her head on Dal's lap. But at least she got to see Pape being the page, treading in the footsteps of the good king himself. Dal wasn't sure the page was supposed to be wearing a tie—after all, Skipper the King wasn't—but Pape looked gorgeous.

The concert ended shortly after nine and they were home by 10:00. By then, Dal could have slept on the pointed end of a rusty nail. She didn't even bother thinking about a bath, she just tucked in kids, kissed kids, assured kids she loved them, then lurched to bed. She took off her jeans and underpants and crawled into bed in her shirt and socks.

She came awake slowly, with no idea where she was. Bit by bit the pieces began to make sense. Ah, yes—her own bed, her bedroom, the smell of coffee and beef sausages, the sound of two kids, probably Skip and Button, debating shrilly over which one was supposed to do something. Home! The evening before she had yearned to wallow, and that morning she did. She wallowed like a sow, indulging herself in the smooching attention she got from Pansy and the kids. She felt so relaxed that she thought she might need a shoelace to tie up her jaw. She drank the coffee they poured into her mug, she ate the sausages they put on her plate, she enjoyed every bite of her Scotch eggs and would have eaten more of Pansy's baking powder biscuits if she'd had the room for them. She even considered going back to bed. God, it was so good to be here with them, loving and being loved, able to love and accept love. But there were things to do, and nobody could do them but herself. Going back to bed would have to wait.

The malls were jammed and the first half-hour of Christmas shopping was a real test of her maternal love. She had been so far from any of this for so long—off prowling in search of shrooms, then racing over the bottoms of slopes, jamming as many seedlings as possible into the mess they kept insisting was "ground" before the snow got too deep. She'd been by herself much of the time, and while other planters worked to the tunes coming from their portable tape players, Dal preferred the chitter of overwintering wrens, the sound of the high winds moving like rivers in the clouds far above her head. Suddenly thrust into the push and shove of the mall, with every store's sound system blaring a different carol, she felt as if her next move would be to fall to her knees and yard out chunks of her own hair.

And then it passed. The feeling she and Pansy had always called "discombooberation" was gone. The tinsel sparkled, the people smiled, she had money in the bank and a raft of kids to spend it on and it was solstice. They'd have a huge supper tonight, light candles and put up cedar boughs and holly. There would be jokes and teasing, and they would promise each other that the days were going to start getting longer. They had rounded the corner and were heading steadily toward the snowdrops and daffodils, hyacinths and dandelions. Dal had a wonderful time. Twice she had to go back to the car to stash her loot in the trunk and return to the noise and clamour for yet another assault, in the name of another kid or two.

She met up with Pansy at the hot dog stand in the mall and they compared notes, ate chili dogs and drank a hot brown liquid that purported to be coffee. Then the kids began to trail up, and for a while it was hectic behind the counter—this one wanted raw onions, that one wanted cooked, another didn't want any at all. This one wanted cheese, the next wanted pizza sauce and then they all wanted another. When the snacks were devoured, the drinks consumed and the mustard wiped from mouths, Dal hauled out her wallet. She paid the tab, then handed each kid some money. "One hour," she warned.

They scattered, except for Pip, who was showing every sign of fading. Dal got a shopping cart and sat the droopy-lidded bubbah in the carry seat.

"What have you got left to do?" Pansy asked, studying her scribbled list.

"Groceries. You?"

"Meet you at the deli in 10, 15 minutes?"

"Do we need a turkey?"

"No, we have to go pick ours up at the farm. Should probably do it today, if we've got time."

"Four days to go," Dal reminded her.

"I know, but those who get theirs first get the pick, right? It'll be fine in the fridge. Hell, the ones in the supermarket probably hung somewhere for a week before they got frozen. It's not going to go bad, Dal. Trust me."

Dal knew she could phone Toby and there would be a spot for her that night, and not just because Toby lived in hope of bouncing on her frame. She'd been good for business, the customers liked her and she could just slide in between sets, not taking anything away from whoever had replaced her while she was gone. But she just didn't feel like it. She wasn't exactly physically tired, although she'd be glad to get off her feet and maybe even catch a nap while the kids were getting the greenery. It was something else, and she wasn't sure exactly what.

They took their parcels to their rooms and hid them from each other, then changed from go-to-town clothes to bushwhackers and headed off up into the hills behind the lake to gather cedar and salal for the decorating party. On their way back, with the trunk half-full of greenery, they stopped at the farm to choose the turkey.

The slaughter was still underway, and the kids were fascinated. In a pen near the converted trailer at least four dozen turkeys paraded and strutted. While the kids watched, a teenager in gore-stiffened jeans and mac, with gumboots that were covered with feathers stuck in the dried blood, reached over the fence, grabbed a bird and lifted it up, flapping and shrieking. The boy looked bored, or perhaps overloaded, and he moved with a precision of motion Dal recognized in her own muscles and tendons—the energy-saving movement of someone who has done the same brutally hard job time after time after time.

Several big galvanized cones were fastened to deep-set posts, and the youth stuck the bird, head down, into one of them. The feet stuck out the top and the head appeared through the hole at the bottom of the cone. "Stand back," he said quietly. He waited until the kids moved. Then, with one quick slash of a strong-bladed knife, he cut off the head, instantly stepping aside to avoid as much as possible of the pulsing blood. The kids gasped. The youth tossed the head onto a pile of others, moved back to the enclosure, leaned over and grabbed another bird.

"I wouldn't like that job," Skipper said quietly.

"Someone has to do it if people want to have turkey dinner," said Dal.

"Oh, that part doesn't bother me. I mean we can't all grab a gun and go out hunting our own. It's just that I wouldn't like to have to do something like that hour after hour, just the same thing, over and over. I'd go bugs."

"You know that this is where I'm supposed to give you the lecture on school, and marks, and grades, and higher education and the age of technology and all that good stuff, eh?"

"I hear you. Damn, he's going to go get another one."

When all the cones were full, the teenager went back to the first bird, lifted it and took it to a riggins on the wall. He slid one leg into a slot, grabbed a lever, and pulled it down. Something in the leg snapped and he moved the carcass aside, letting the severed shank and foot fall to the floor. He snapped off the other shank and placed the turkey in something that looked very much like an oversized stainless steel washing machine. There was room in the feather machine for 12 big turkeys. When they were in, the kid pressed a button. With an incredible roar the feather machine began to revolve, and in an amazingly short period of time the birds were naked, the feathers removed by rows of what looked like little rubber fingers. The boy turned off the machine, removed the birds and slid them along a stainless steel tabletop where a man, a woman and another youth were busily cutting open the carcasses and removing the innards.

"Which one is ours?" Button asked

"You see that room over there?" The boy was wiping his hands on a surprisingly clean towel. "You can go in there and have a look. Pick the best one you can find. Then there you are, all set for Chrissy prez day."

What with the smell of blood and wet feathers and the heap of amputated feet and shins, Dal felt as if she'd rather have the young woman at the hot dog stand deliver five dozen chili dogs for Christmas dinner. But the kids seemed more eager than ever, and nothing would do but to trudge into the cold room and look at all the birds encased in their plastic bags on the frosted metal shelves.

"How big?" Duck asked, peering at the weights marked on the bags.

"Not too big or you'll be eating leftovers for a week. And soup until Easter."

"I don't mind the soup part."

"Yeah, but you have to admit that after three days the leftovers start to look like punishment. What about 20 pounds?"

"That's not very big." Pinch shook her head. "Look, there's two shelves of them bigger than 20 pounds."

"If it's just big you want, maybe we should phone the zoo and see if they've got a spare elephant. Don't forget, we have to get this sucker in the oven."

They settled on a 22-pound bird. The kids all thanked the young man and headed back to the car with tail feathers as souvenirs. But Dal and Pansy didn't get off that easy. Halfway back to the car, Pape saw the kittens. He dropped his tail feathers and darted over to the litter.

"No," Dal said firmly. "Abso-tively posi-lutely no."

"I know," Pape smiled at her, "but I could pick one up for just one little cuddle, couldn't I?"

"No!" Dal would have grabbed Pape and pushed him into the back seat, but her arms were full of turkey. By the time she had the trunk open and the bird in with the evergreens, Pape was holding a silvery-grey and black striped kitten with white chest and feet. The kitten was purring loudly. Pape looked at her, his huge green eyes sparkling, his dear little face serious.

"All my life," he said clearly, "I wanted a striped cat with white feet that I could call Socks. All my whole life."

Dal would have given $500 for the strength to say no. But even if it was only a half-dozen quickly passing years to her, it was Pape's whole entire life. And that's a long, long time to nurse a dream.

"Oh, Pape," she managed. He nodded and turned to put the kitten back on the ground with the rest of the litter. When he headed for the car he was trying so hard not to cry that Dal felt she might do it for him.

"How much?" she asked.

"For a kitten?" The youth grinned from ear to ear. "Hey, it's a Chrissy prez. From us to you. And from you to me too, because I'm the one got told to pop 'em off tonight. If we kept them all we'd be up to our ear holes in cats. You have fun with that kitty, okay?"

Pape carried Socks into the house, Duck carried the new plastic dish and Twink carried the bag of kitty litter. Dal took the turkey, Pansy carried Pip and the other kids unloaded the boughs and lugged them up the stairs. Socks didn't hide under the sofa or try to race up the tree, and he didn't sit in the middle of the kitchen and yowl. Maybe he knew that he'd been saved from a sudden and premature end. He curled up in the box Pape had prepared for him on the layer of outgrown sweaters, and purred loudly while contemplating his snowy white toes. By the time supper was ready the kitten was sound asleep, still purring.

Meat-and-potato pie. To Dal, it was another way to spell "home." She and Pansy had different approaches to the making of it. Dal grated her onion and mixed it in with the ground beef as if she was making meatloaf, but Pansy spread a layer of ground beef on the bottom crust, then added a layer of sliced onion as in scalloped spuds. Either way would do. A layer of sliced potato, some frozen peas and carrots, more meat, and so it went, building carefully until the deep dish was full and there was nothing else to do but add the top crust to keep everything from sliding off. Supper was fun and Dal was glad to be home, with time to spend with the people she loved. She didn't have to rush off to Toby's and she didn't have to go to bed early in order to face another gruelling day with a pack of seedlings weighing her down. She could just wallow in the life she had chosen.

For dessert they had what they all called "Pan's Indulgence." One day a few years ago, when Pansy had been making butter tarts, she had suddenly got sick and tired of all those ditzy little tart shells. Totally fed up, she had made two big pies instead of the small bite-sized ones. She hadn't made butter tarts since. "Only one slice each, now," she warned, "or you'll all wake up tomorrow with more zits than brains."

"I don't get zits," Twink said calmly.

"Rotten teeth, then."

"Don't have them, either."

"You wait," Pansy warned.

As if that had been a signal, someone knocked at the front door. Skipper slid off his chair and peered out the front window to see who was standing on the porch.

"It's okay," he yelled.

Seconds later, he returned with his Auntie Iris and both of her kids. Which to Dahlia did not seem to be anything remotely okay. In fact she didn't know whether to screech and race out the back door or moan and fall under the table. She stared at her sister.

"Jeez, Iris," Pansy said mildly, "you look like you got hit by a logging truck."

"Not the truck, the driver," Iris said. Her lips were so swollen it was hard to believe that she could still make them work.

Dal had so many questions she didn't bother asking any of them. She got off her chair and took Iris by the arm, urging her with gentle pressure to sit down before she fell on what was left of her face.

Iris plunked onto the chair with a settled finality that suggested a very long visit. The two kids, John and Rick, looked as if they hadn't slept in days. Their faces were pinched and pallid, with big blue half moons under their eyes. Button had looked like that after her bout with the measles, but only for a day or two. These kids looked as if their spectral appearance was usual for them.

Dal's kids were on the move, clearing plates, making room, getting more plates, pouring milk into clean glasses, getting the skinny little boys set up for supper. Iris just shook her head wearily. "I'm not hungry," she sighed. "Anyway, m'damn mouth is too sore. But if you've got a cup of tea..."

"No problem," Pansy assured her. "If you start to feel hungry let me know and I'll make you some soup."

No problem? For Dahlia it was a problem. At the very best of times she had all she could do not to go nose-to-nose with her older sister and yell, "Wake up!" The only reason she didn't was that all it did was invite Iris to whine. The litany usually started off with "Easy for you to say" and went through "You don't have any idea" and wound up at "All I ever wanted was..." If Dahlia suggested that Iris could do what millions of other people did every day and get a job, Iris would trot out two dozen reasons why she couldn't.

Iris had the same kind of hair and eyes as Pansy and had, at one time, had Pansy's soft, round body shape. The eyes and hair were still there, but the shape had burgeoned. What had once been voluptuous was now porky.

You'd think a woman who had waited so many years before marrying would at least have hooked herself up with someone who made the whole thing worthwhile. But no. Iris, who could have married Bob Gayner or Ted Wilson, had to dump both of them and a few others as well, and marry Dwayne Morgan. Mothers, Dal growled to herself, never name your sons Dwayne or Bradley—therein lies nothing but horror. Curses are attached to those names. No matter where you are, if there are kids raising hell and mothers hollering at them, the two names that will ring the loudest the most often are Dwayne and Bradley.

The Morgans had one thing going for them—they were all gorgeous. There probably hadn't been a plain, let alone homely, Morgan since before the brothers left Wales all those generations ago. And, unfortunately, they all had tempers like tinderboxes. They also had hard fists and weak heads and no stomach at all for booze, which they insisted on consuming. The Morgan women usually calmed down by the time they hit their mid-20s, but the Morgan men just kept at it, in spite of societal disapproval, the police and even the courts. Give them a 200-dollar fine and they laughed. Toss them in the crowbar hotel for 30 days and they went damn near hysterical at the comedy of it all. And too many of their wives had too often looked exactly the way Iris did now. Dal found nothing the least bit funny about that.

"You kids want some dessert?" she asked gently. Johnny nodded and tried to smile. Ricky stared up at her as if she was the angel on the top of the tree. Damn, damn, damn, but it was hard to think that in a few years they could easily wind up just as bitched around as their father! Dal could remember Dwayne Morgan when he was a kid, with his scabby knees showing through the vents in his worn-out jeans. He'd been the best soccer player in a town that regularly produced champion teams, and people said he could probably go on to bigger and better things if he wanted. What they hadn't said out loud was, "if he wasn't a Morgan." The only family that came anywhere near the Morgans for such weary disapproval were the Cassidys. When Iris and Dwayne had gone down to the courthouse, paid their money, got their licence and then, a week later, got married, Dahlia wasn't the only person who cringed. Gas and matches, people said. Just trouble waiting for the time to happen.

"So where's Dipshit?" Dal asked, reaching for the teapot.

"In jail. The neighbours phoned the cops."

"You've got stitches in your eyebrow so you must have seen a doctor."

"And on my head. See?" Iris tilted her head slightly and lifted her hair. "He hit me with the steam iron."

"You should phone the women's centre and get some counselling," Pansy said quietly. "This isn't the first time he's done this. Maybe you need to find out why you keep standing in line for more of it."

"He said he wouldn't do it again." Iris blinked and tears dribbled. She had probably already cried so much she didn't have enough fluid left in her for the tears to flow. "He promised."

"Jeez, Iris, how many times has he promised, and how many times have you been sucked in?"

"I love him."

"Love?" Dal exploded. "Tell you what, I'll go out to the woodshed and get a big chunk of alder, come in and pound you senseless. Then will you love me too?"

"Now, Dal, you aren't doing any good talking to her like that," Pansy protested.

"Any good? Nothing does any good!"

"I don't want to go back," Ricky said clearly.

"See? The eight-year-old has better sense!"

"Can I stay with you, Auntie Dal?"

"Darlin', I wish to God you could."

Dal patted her knee and Ricky was off his chair and climbing onto her lap. He snuggled against her and she could feel his body trembling. All her anger and frustration with Iris was buried under a welling up of emotion for the kids. "Hey, if you've finished your supper you can help us with the solstice decs." She gave him a little hug, afraid to scoop him into the kind she gave her own kids. He might freak out, thinking it was a threat. "And look—Pape got a kitten. Cute, eh?"

"My dad killed my cat." John sounded so calm and so matter-of-fact that Dal wanted to screech. "He just picked him up and threw him against the wall."

"Well, nobody here is going to do that to this kitten." She looked at John and smiled. "Or to you for that matter."

Dal couldn't bear what was happening at the table. She lifted Ricky and carried him into the living room. John followed close behind her. The kids had the cedar and fir boughs separated into piles, the salal and Oregon grape in boxes.

"You know how it's done." She put Ricky on the floor. "All around the doors and windows, and when it's in place, we'll put some icicles on, and some tinsel if there's any left. And when the room is ready...tree time!"

"But the tree is already up," John puzzled.

"Oh, it's up, and it's decorated, but it isn't finished. You'll see."

Dal headed upstairs to her room. She closed and locked her door, hauled all the presents from their hiding places and re-sorted the piles. A toy originally intended for Pip, a sweater bought for Skipper, another she had thought would look good on Twink, a bubble bath she had been going to use as a stocking stuffer—bit by bit she swiped enough loot to make the two little additions feel that they hadn't been left out or forgotten. She could always whip out to the mall the next day and replace it.

Dal didn't buy wrapping paper. She saved the comics from the newspaper. The kids saw nothing odd in this. She had explained to them that what it cost for the fancy paper, ribbons and bows added up to enough that they could buy a couple of boxes of chocolates instead. "And anyway, it all gets ripped to shreds in no time flat." She wrapped quickly and was finished just before the kids started yelling, "It's time, it's time!" She took the big box of loot down with her and the kids all cheered when they saw her coming. "Okay, you know the rules. Nobody touches anything with his or her own name on it, okay?"

They would, of course. They would sneak in, find their parcels, lift them, shake them, try to determine whether anything was rattling and if so, what. But for now they were happy putting everyone else's packages under the tree. Dal wished she could look at them and feel the same joy she'd been feeling before Iris and her bruises arrived. Talk about the Ghost of Christmas Too Often Seen! To give the devil his due, there had been years when one thing or another had held off until after the great day. But there hadn't been one year when some damn thing or other hadn't dumped on her before the New Year was rung in and the ham in the oven.

No sooner were the comics-wrapped presents under the tree than the sound of knuckles against the door was reverberating through the house. Iris went dead white under her bruises. "If that's Dwayne, we're not here," she hissed, grabbing her sons' hands and hurrying them to the kitchen. Ricky began to shake and his face became so pinched that he looked like an old man. Twink answered the door.

Chummy stepped in as boldly as if he hadn't been lugged off the porch several times already. "I'd like to see Pansy," he announced from behind an armload of gaily wrapped packages.

"I don't see how you can see anything," Twink answered. "You're out of sight behind that stuff."

"What do you want?" Dal demanded.

"I want to see Pansy."

"You've seen me," Pansy answered. "And now if you don't mind—or even if you do mind—I think you should leave."

Chummy ignored her. He made his way to the tree, hunkered down and put his load of parcels on the floor. Then he stood up, defiant and obviously determined. "Merry Christmas."

Dal wanted to Merry Christmas him a good one but this was Pansy's business, not hers. She wasn't, however, so hospitable as to leave Chummy and Pansy the living room, and move herself and the kids into the kitchen with Iris and the boys. She figured the majority not only ruled, it got to choose where.

"It's okay," she called to Iris and the kids. "C'mon back. You," she said coldly to the latest arrival, "can talk in the kitchen."

"No need," Pansy said flatly. "I've said what I've got to say."

"Pansy, you're being very unreasonable." Chummy sounded so sane, so calm and so rational that for a moment Dal wondered if it was his cousin had showed up and not him.

"You want to know unreasonable? Look in the mirror. This has been going on for months!"

"And I've really learned a lot. Really." He turned and gazed at Dal and the kids. "Do you think we could get some privacy here?"

"Tell you what." Dal was fed up, all the way. "You buy a house of your own and you can have all the privacy you want. However, in this case I am the one who bought the house, and I am the one who is going to sit on the sofa, and I am the one who is, after all, in her own place, and you are the one who has been told to leave."

"And I am the one," Pansy said, sitting on the sofa beside Dal, "who told you to leave."

"Pansy, I've had lots of time to think things over." He seemed to have given up on the idea of privacy and was willing to spill his guts in front of the assembling family. "I've changed. I really have. I want you back again, and this time I won't be the same as I was before, I promise. If you want to go to school, fine. If you want to babysit your sister's kids, fine. If you want," he waved his arm in what he obviously hoped was a convincing gesture, "to fly to the moon, fine. I won't stand in your way. Just come back, give us another chance, let me prove to you how much I've changed."

"Jeez, that's real white of you." Pansy was angry, dangerously angry. "It is so nice of you to condescend to allow me to have a life of my own. That's just so super of you. I hardly know what to say. Except no. I am not moving back in with you, I am *not* interested in 'another chance,' and I am not convinced anything at all has changed except that you've learned that yelling at me won't get you anywhere so instead of doing that, you're doing this other humble shit."

"What do you want from me?" He tried not to shout, but his voice was getting very loud.

"Absence. I want you to go. I want you to go and leave me alone. I want you to build your own life without me. And I want you to take all those presents with you when you leave."

He didn't. He refused to take any of them. He almost refused to leave, but when Button turned on the TV and turned up the sound, Chummy realized he wasn't winning anything and was only making things worse for himself.

"Pansy," he tried one last time before the door shut in his face. "I love you."

"Go away," she told him, and closed the door. She turned and leaned against it. "Now what do I do?" she gritted, glaring at the gaily wrapped parcels.

"Take them to the Salvation Army," Dal suggested.

"Keep 'em," Pape grinned. "There might be somethin' good."

"Give them to me," Iris said. "Be better than the last half-dozen Christmases have been."

Button turned off the TV. "You gonna play for us, Momma?" she wheedled. "Please?"

It was fun. Dal's fingers were a bit stiff at first—she'd been lugging a heavy sack and swinging her planting tool, and she hadn't played a lick—but after the first few songs her hand became more limber and she could move from slow carols to some real music. The kids sang and some of them danced. Pansy forced herself to at least look as if she was having a good time, and Iris actually seemed to relax a bit. Who knows how long the music might have lasted, but Chummy came back and hammered on the door, yelling his side of things from the porch when nobody would let him into the house. Dal put away the violin and the kids yelled back for Chummy to go away, take a long walk on a short pier, take a hint, take a hike, buzz off and get lost. Eventually he did. By then it was time to stuff the little ones into their pyjamas and send the older ones off to brush teeth and get ready for bed.

"Happy solstice," Pansy sighed.

"Yeah. Well, it started out okay. Maybe it'll improve again?"

"Sure, maybe."

Four

Dal started packing her tree-planting gear again in mid-March, getting ready to head off into the burned slash to get paid for pretending she was actually reforesting. She wasn't looking forward to it, but she knew it was time to start bringing in some decent money. She'd been playing six nights a week with a small band, and that paid better than doing her stint at Toby's, but it was really only enough to pay the hydro, cable, phone and milk bills. The rest of what it took to keep the family going had come out of her savings account. Dal didn't mind being the only one bringing in any money, but it did pick at her that it was so hard to get anything into savings, and so easy to let it out.

There were a few moments of tension as Dal was getting ready to leave. She had made it to the goodbye hugs, and as she held Pansy, Dal said quietly, "And can we remember, please, you are the only person who drives the Chev?" Pansy nodded, but Iris got herself in a snit.

"What is that supposed to mean?"

"It means that Pansy is the only one who drives the Chev, that's all."

"It means that I am not allowed to drive your ratty old wreck!"

"Right."

"Well, isn't that nice? I don't think."

"Iris, let's not go into orbit on this one, okay? You couldn't drive shit through a siphon, especially not if you had to use a gear shift to do it."

"I could learn."

"You could. But not in my car. Pansy is the only one who drives it."

"Why are you being such a bitch?" Iris hollered.

"Why? Because if I'm not, and if there isn't a real clear understanding of how things are supposed to be, you'll take the car and then Chummy will wind up driving it, and he isn't driving anything of mine unless he promises to drive himself to hell in it, okay? Pansy is the only one with permission to drive the Chev."

Iris glared, but she stopped arguing. That in itself was a blessing. Iris had been known to keep feeding the same argument for up to a week, repeating the same accusations as if she was water and, given time, could eat holes in stones. The kids didn't say anything, but Dal knew they had heard every word and knew exactly why she was being hard-nosed. She was certain they would feel free to jump up and raise the roof if Iris even hinted that she might want to, just this once, use the car. Having the kids as backup was almost as good as having a pit bull.

Dal smiled at Pinch and Duck and gathered them in her arms. She whispered to each of them, kissed them, then reached for Twink. Pip cried and Pape tried hard not to, but his eyes glittered with tears and he hung onto her with the next best thing to a death grip.

"I'll be back, darling," she said. "You know I wouldn't go if I didn't have to."

She took a cab to the bus depot because she didn't want another goodbye scene. Better to say goodbye in the living room, where kids could head off to their rooms to weep, sulk, pout or cheer, depending on their moods. And she could hold it together, because who needs to freak out the cab driver?

The rest of the crew was already waiting, with more damn gear than it made any sense for a group of people to have. It had all been easier when the government ran the show. You didn't need to take your own tent back then—they had big ones, probably hand-me-downs from the Army or something. Males in this one, females in that one, and the cookshack in another. They'd had little folding cots too, and you could spread out your sleeping bag, climb in and sleep up off the ground. Now, even with the bubble-pack groundsheet, even with the insul-foam strip, you were on the cold earth and it seemed as if no matter how fussy you were about levelling things off, smoothing them out, tamping and flattening, there would be at least one unyielding lump, usually in exactly the place your hip bone landed when you rolled over, trying to get comfortable and managing to get less so. Back then, in what were rapidly becoming the "Good Old Days," Dal had gone tree-planting with her guitar. Now it was just too difficult—there was too much other stuff needing to be lugged and stored. She felt naked, and she knew she would miss her instruments almost as much as she missed her kids.

She could smell the off-putting pungent reek of stinkweed and knew from the loose and easy grins on the faces of the rest of the crew that they were the ones had been toking. She was glad she had arrived almost late. It made her uncomfortable—not because she was wedded to obeying the law, not because she was convinced the stuff would lead you down the fast slippery slope to total drug dependency with tracks marring the insides of your arms and strange viruses teeming in your blood, but because she was such an easy contact high. All she had to do was be in the same room with someone who was lighting up and she got light-headed. Which, in itself, wasn't bad. It certainly meant that she could save a lot of money. The problem was she got carsick when she was stoned, even if her stone wasn't really a stone at all but some twist in her imagination. And she wasn't interested in getting sick all over her own camping gear.

The driver finally finished her coffee and decided to put in an appearance. Dal took the first seat on what in a car would have been the passenger side, right behind the steps coming up from the door. The window came lower down here, and she had excellent visibility through the windshield. Best of all there wasn't any seat in front of her, the tall back of it hemming her in and blocking her view, making her feel as if she had been crammed, unwilling and uncomfortable, into the shell of an oversized egg.

She knew most of the others on the crew, but there were some new faces, all of them younger. A couple of them looked as if they ought to still be in high school. She knew what that meant. The old faces, the ones replaced by these babies, had thought long and hard and carefully about things and had decided to pull the plug. The people who had been part of the crew when she herself had first joined, the people who had at one time looked at her and probably thought she was someone who ought to go back to school, had packed it in. The work was just too damn hard. And that probably meant that before very long she herself would be saying thanks but no thanks.

She'd have died on the rack before she admitted to the fact she sometimes thought the job was easier on men than on women. Something to do with pelvic structure, maybe. Her mother had said often enough that each baby cost the mother a tooth because it drained the body's reserves. Maybe that was part of it too. Still, there was that up and down hormone thing and let's not forget the monthly inconveniences or the fact that menopause was clicking in at an earlier age all the time and they were finding out more and more about the loss of bone mass and muscle tissue that comes with it. She knew there had been a time no more than 10 years ago when she could have kept up with or beaten any man on the crew and then gone dancing. She had, on more than one occasion, swallowed a few pints of beer and joined the c'mon-I-dare-ya wrist-twisting competition. She hadn't always lost, either. She even had a cheap medallion from the loggers' sports day saying she was the women's wrist-twisting champion, heavyweight division. But that was then and she'd had three kids in the interim.

Life, she supposed, had a way of moving on, and in the moving on, it was apt to do the most goddamnable things. Not just slowing a person down or making the ground seem as if it was farther away every year, but stupid things. Things that sort of snuck up on you. Like Dwayne Morgan, the dumb tick, getting out of the crowbar hotel and checking himself into the alcohol treatment program, doing his six weeks and then asking to sign on for a second go-round because he didn't feel he was quite ready to face the outside world. He'd be out in another couple of weeks, and in any TV movie of the week would walk, sober and steady, up the front steps, ring Dal's doorbell, and be greeted by his ever-loving little woman and his daddy-I-love-you overjoyed kids. Except it wasn't going to be like that, and Dal didn't regret that she wouldn't be there to see the look on his face when he found out Iris wasn't even at Dal's place. She was pretty sure he'd be just as flabbergasted as she had been when the dime dropped and she realized a few things.

Pansy had arranged for a babysitter one Saturday night and headed off with a guy who was taking the same courses she was. Dal personally thought he looked about as much fun as a bowl of custard, but Pansy seemed to like him, and who knows, he might have hidden assets. Dal was so used to dipping into her pocket and paying the tab that she hadn't thought to ask why she was paying for a babysitter to look after her kids and Iris's kids when Iris herself could surely see that Pip got her pyjama bottoms where they belonged. She came home after work, paid the babysitter and drove her home, then went back to the house and got herself ready for bed. She didn't even realize Iris wasn't there. In the morning the kids got their own breakfasts, and when Dal crawled out of bed and went down to make coffee, Iris was definitely home, still in bed, snoring so loud that Dal could hear her through the closed bedroom door.

Sunday Dal took all the kids to the rec centre and they swam in the chlorine-reeking pool until their eyes were too sore for any more fun. Half an hour later, still smelling faintly of chlorine, they were in the car and off to the Dairy Queen for burgers and ice cream. Iris was just getting up when they got home. Dal hadn't said anything—things were at the point where everything went better in direct proportion to how little verbal exchange there was between her and her older sister. They watched a video and played Monopoly until they were all bored with it, and then it was late supper, early bath and check the homework. That's when Chummy arrived. The one Dal thought of as Pansy's Chummy.

"Is Iris ready?" he asked, smiling happily.

"Pardon me?" she gaped, her brain spinning.

"Iris," Chummy repeated. "Is she ready?"

"Iris?" Dal couldn't make things find their slots and slip into place.

"Hey, Aunt Iris, the loser is here!" Skipper yelled.

"Skipper, you stop that or I'll box your ears a good one for you!" Iris yelled, coming down the stairs all dolled up and glowing. "It's time you learned a few manners and if your mother won't teach them to you, I'm apt to."

"Hi, Iris." Chummy stared at Iris as if he had never seen anything so delicious in his life, exactly the way he had once stared at Pansy.

"Hi." Iris blushed. And so she bloody well might!

Of course, nothing Dal said the next day made any difference at all. Even Pansy seemed to think Dal was overreacting.

"Why would I care?" she shrugged, "I don't want anything to do with him. If Iris wants to play games with my castoffs, well, that's up to Iris." She grinned, even chuckled. "He's not much, but he's at least a couple of miles ahead of Duh-Wayne Duh-Pain."

"It's the next best thing to incest, Pan, and you know it!"

"No." Pansy wasn't grinning any more. "I don't know any such thing. I reached into a grab bag and hauled out something I decided I didn't want, and I put it back into the bag and now Iris has reached in and got the same thing and decided she does want it. And that's all there is to that."

But for Dal, that wasn't all there was to it at all. Why couldn't she just shrug and accept it? She knew why Pansy didn't care. There was the future social worker with his tweed jacket, well-pressed wool pants and almost expensive loafers. Pansy said she could actually talk to him. Dal couldn't even imagine what kind of conversation a person could have with a guy in a tweed jacket and black loafers. Pansy said the guy was gentle and sensitive, and he understood her. Well, there you go, he could understand her, which certainly put him in a minority because few people had ever understood Pansy Cassidy.

Dal knew why Chummy was so eager. Iris would never, ever, not in a million years, drive Chummy crazy with her independence. He wouldn't have to bitch about Iris being gone so much because Iris wouldn't take two steps along the sidewalk without either having him in tow or getting his permission to go alone. Iris was in no danger of heading off to finish her high school, then mount a frontal assault on college. And she certainly wasn't going to get a job that involved shift work. In fact, there wasn't any threat of her getting any kind of job at all. She also wasn't going to point out quietly that it was, after all, her apartment, leased in her name, and he could stay and accept the way things were, or leave. Iris didn't even seem to care that not only was Dal horrified at the situation, John and Rick detested Chummy. Dal would have worried if she'd been getting herself heavily involved with someone her kids hated, but then Dal wasn't one to get heavily involved. Pregnant, maybe, but not heavily involved. And pregnant was something she was willing to bet Iris would be before very much longer.

Chummy wouldn't come right out and say that it was the one thing that would be sure to hurt Pansy, the one weapon he had that might make Pansy feel at least regret, if not downright sorrow. Maybe he wouldn't even realize what he was doing. But Dal suspected that he would want at least one and probably several kids. He'd talk about how deeply it would bond them, how it would allow them to be a real family, and he'd be sure to say he had always wanted a raft of kids. And Iris, well, she'd swallowed that line when it was Duh-Whine coming out with it, so why wouldn't she believe Chummy? Mind you, if Duh-Whine walked up the front steps, knocked on the door and saw Chummy standing protectively beside Iris, he was apt to fire a couple of boots that might fix Chummy so he could never be a father.

They were talking about getting their own place. Dal hoped they got it about four miles to the west of Timbuktu, because there was a small chance Dwayne wouldn't be able to track them that far. Of course, whether it was Timbuktu, Ladysmith, Cedar or even Campbell River, the boys had already loudly proclaimed they weren't going.

"Oh, of course you are." Iris had tried to dismiss their protests with a wave of her soft white hand.

"I'll live with Dad first," John threatened.

"Don't be silly, you can't live with your father!"

"Why not?"

Iris shook her head and made a tsk-tsk sound with her tongue against her teeth. "Don't be silly."

"I don't like that guy," John said, although Chummy was standing right there. "He's nothing to me. I'm not living with him."

"He's bossy." Rick went and stood beside John. "I won't go. I'll stay here, with Auntie Pansy."

"You can't stay with Auntie Pansy!"

"Why not?"

"Come on, guys." Chummy put on a heartiness that even Pip knew was phony. "Don't give your mom a rough time about this, okay?"

"Butt out," John said casually.

"Hey, watch it, buddy." Chummy didn't sound the least bit casual. "Come on now, just drop it."

"Butt the hell out, asshole!" John's calm exploded. "Mind your own damn business."

"This *is* my business." Chummy reached to grab John by the arm.

"Don't touch him," Pansy said quietly. Chummy whirled, glaring. "If you touch him he'll tell his dad, and if he does that, I can guarantee you the shit will definitely hit the fan."

"I'm not afraid of him!"

"No? You're either braver than I am or a lot stupider, because I'd be afraid of Dwayne Morgan if I was standing where you're standing. Iris has sense enough to be scared of Dwayne. I bet there's times even Dwayne is afraid of Dwayne!"

"But they're *mine*." Iris had lost it then. Up against the cold hard facts of reality, Iris always lost it. She didn't take hysterics, she didn't grab the phone and call a lawyer, she just stood with tears trickling down her face, looking so helpless even Dal wanted to step in and solve the problems for her. The problems, however, had seen their mother doing this too many times to be anything other than certain that they had just won the debate.

"You live with him if you want," John shouted. "I'm not going to!"

It hadn't ended there, of course, but the boys were probably two miles ahead of Iris and Chummy in the race toward whatever they thought the prize was going to be. And Dal was willing to bet that Dwayne Morgan might agree to let Pansy look after his sons, but he'd convert to Catholicism before he'd let Iris and Chummy have them. If, that is, he didn't blow his cool, cripple Chummy and drag Iris off by the hair.

Dal was glad she was on the bus, even though they were travelling through the increasingly awful mess that lined the highway to Parksville on both sides. It could have been such a pretty town. At one time it had been beautiful, with the sea lapping on one side and the mountains rising on the other. Now you couldn't see the ocean for the strip of tacky tourist traps, engine overhaul and repair shops, and more bad fast-food outlets than a person would ever need. Neon signs, billboards, parking lots and junkyards, and sometimes it was hard to tell which was which.

Someone toward the back of the tree planters' bus turned on some music, not loud enough to annoy the driver but loud enough to fill the silences between the few words some people were exchanging. Nobody was exactly keyed up. The trip in was always like this— everyone subdued, already feeling the weight of separation. During one trip, a few years ago, someone had suddenly stood up and pulled the cord, and when the bus pulled over, the guy got off, yelling for the driver to unlock the bay doors and let him get his gear. She'd felt envious. How nice to be able to just say, "No thank you, not me, not this time." What a privilege to have the choice. Even before, there had been so many loving mouths to feed, that kind of choice had been a stranger. For as long as Dal could remember she'd grabbed at just about any job she could find.

Her first job, when she was seven and a half, was yardwork. Her father had teased her about it and called her a yardbird. At first the old bugger had seemed amused, but as the weeks passed and Dal continued heading off after school, his amusement had turned to something else. She hadn't known what, and she still didn't know what it was about a little kid with a trowel that had threatened him so much. Eventually his amusement had evaporated and he began making growling comments about how some people don't seem to have enough pride to know when they're being given charity. But it wasn't charity that Dal got for trimming the hedge and weeding the flower beds. It was music lessons. She'd have licked the soles of Mrs. Dunsmuir's shoes clean if that had been what it took.

Sylvia Dunsmuir was unlike any other woman in the world as far as Dahlia Cassidy was concerned. For one thing, Sylvia lived alone. Dal didn't know anybody, male or female, who lived alone. Sylvia owned her own house too—another first. It was a smallish house, square, with stucco siding and a cedar shake roof. In the backyard Sylvia's vegetable garden was laid out with raised beds and bordered with nasturtiums, marigolds and chrysanthemums, and the beans grew up what looked like teepee poles. The walkway was made with flat, irregularly shaped stones, and between them something aromatic was planted so that when you walked the perfume drifted up from your feet. The rose bushes along the front of the house were so old that the stems had become trunks. Dahlia had been attracted by the flowers, and hooked by the sounds. Sylvia gave music lessons. Cars would pull up and kids would get out, every half-hour another kid, and after a while Dahlia knew who took violin, who took piano. It was easy to tell—the violin kids brought their instruments, the piano kids had only their music sheets or books.

Of course, it didn't take long for Sylvia Dunsmuir to catch on that the grubby brat was doing more than just sitting on the fire hydrant. She might not have any kids, but she knew how to relate to them. At first it was just a nod, then a nod and a smile, and finally, a brief spoken word. Then one day she asked Dahlia why she spent so much time sitting on the plug.

"I like to listen," Dahlia mumbled.

"What do you like the best?"

"The fiddle."

"Do you have one?"

"My grandpa had one but nobody plays it."

And so, not long after, there was Dahlia taking the old boy's pride and joy with her and trudging off for her first lesson. Which she paid for by weeding the vegetable garden. When she got older, there were other chores. The garden shed needed cleaned, the basement tidied and swept. Eventually, when the boy who mowed the lawn left school and got a full-time job, Dahlia inherited the push lawn mower and the grass became her responsibility. Later, because of those chores and the lessons, and Grandpa's violin and Sylvia Dunsmuir's kindness, Dahlia began to get jobs playing music. She was 16 when she bought her first guitar and a book on how to play it. By then, Sylvia Dunsmuir was dead of cancer and buried in the cemetery at the top of the hill. The house was sold and relatives who had never come to visit Sylvia when she was alive pocketed the money—or what there was of it after the lawyer took his bite. Dahlia had been flabbergasted when that same lawyer told her Sylvia had left her violins to Dal.

By then Dahlia had moved out of home and into a room in the basement of the house her brother and his wife rented, and she had a job pumping gas and running the little corner store where the pumps ruled. And wasn't that a job! All you needed to do it was a second set of arms and legs.

To be able just to decide you didn't want to spend a couple of months away from home after all, making damn good money! And then actually to do something like stopping the bus and getting off at the side of the highway.

They stopped at the roadside toilets just before Union Bay. Dahlia was the first one off the bus after the driver, so that she could pee first, then catch a fast smoke while the others waited. A woman with brown hair cut in the next best thing to a crew cut came and leaned against the side of the bus beside Dahlia. Dal smiled and nodded. The woman returned the smile, lit a cigarette and stared past the biffies at the heaving sea. She sighed and yawned. "Buses," she said quietly, "do it to me every time. I could sleep the rest of my life away if they just put me on a bus and left me there. You got any idea how much longer we'll be?"

"Oh, another couple of hours. Then we get to off-load our gear and stack it in a four-by truck. And we, lucky sods, get to climb in with it and bounce like corn in a popper for another God alone knows how long."

"Great, and we haven't made five cents so far."

"Ah, but you know we aren't doing this for the money, it's our highly developed sense of civic responsibility has us doing this. Giving a helping hand to Mother Nature, healing the scars. All that good stuff."

"I'm Maggy Wallace."

"Dahlia Cassidy."

"Dahlia as in the flower?"

"You've got it."

"What colour?"

"What colour what?"

"Your Dahlia."

"Oh. Red, I guess."

"Is that hair real?"

"My hair? Yeah."

"Colour and all?"

"Been this way all my life."

"Some people have all the luck. Next you'll tell me you're happily married with not a care in the world. And then I'll probably shoot you."

"Put your gun away, no need. I'm not married, happily or otherwise, and I have more goddamn cares than I want."

"But you've still got that hair and those eyes. It's still not fair."

The driver finished her smoke. "Sorry," she called. "I'd love the chance to spend the next couple of days here, but tempus fugits and so should we." They crushed out their cigarettes and climbed back into the stale-smelling bus. Dahlia swung into her seat and Maggy slid in beside her. "I won't be here long," she said, "but I want the others to sort themselves out first. I was trapped." She grinned. "Surrounded by testosterone, and if I have to hear one more bit-by-bit description of 'How I Cleaned the Carb'."

"I don't clean carbs. I don't even change air filters. You?"

"I wouldn't know where to find either. The best I can do is slide change into the collection box on a city bus."

Just before they got to Fanny Bay, the bus slowed and stopped. Ahead of them the line of cars stretched out of sight. A young woman with a flagger's sign stood on the side of the road, a little black box held to her ear. She looked tired, as if she'd already spent too much time today listening to other people's opinions of the wretched state of highway construction and the unbearable inconvenience all this was causing them. She put the little black riggins in her pocket, then came over to the bus to talk to the driver.

"Boy, have I got some news for you," the driver called to them in a voice that said it all.

"How long?" someone called from the back.

"They don't have any idea how long. Make yourselves comfortable."

Almost an hour later, the long string of traffic began to creep forward. The driver honked her horn and the smokers, who had been standing outside in the thin spring sunshine, discarded their butts and hurried back into the bus. Slowly they inched their way forward without seeing any sign of the reason for the delay. Bit by bit their speed increased, until finally the bus was moving along at a normal speed.

"So what was the holdup?" Maggy asked. "I don't see a thing."

"Well, they've had time to build the road and take their bulldozers home to wash them."

Just before Campbell River they had to stop again. This time they could see all too clearly the reason for the delay. A propane tanker truck lay on its side half in the ditch, half on the road. Blocking the other lane was what was left of a fifth-wheel that had tried to pass the tanker, and the pop truck that hadn't been able to avoid the idiot who was in such a rush to start his holiday that he'd smeared himself and two passengers all over the road. A bright red crash truck was spraying foam over everything, and two cops were waving frantically for the traffic to back up in either direction, away from the gas truck. Except the road behind them was jammed and there wasn't any place to back up to, unless the driver wanted to flatten a few hatchbacks and station wagons.

Two hours later the emergency crews had the gas truck winched back onto its wheels and dragged off, the wreckage moved off the road enough to open one lane of traffic. Then it only took another three-quarters of an hour for the bus to get past the flashing lights and overworked cops. The driver stopped at the bus depot in Campbell River and went in search of a phone.

"Hey, how long we going to be here?" Maggy called. The driver shrugged. "Well, at least I can get some coffee. Want some?"

Already more than three hours late, and with the daylight fading fast, they went into what passed for a bus depot in Campbell River. They got coffee out of a machine, and Dahlia's paper cup leaked. One taste of the stuff and she didn't care if the whole mess leaked onto the floor. She shook her head and tossed it into a garbage can. "I'm not brave enough," she admitted. "I have this hang-up about stuff that doesn't taste like it should."

"I didn't know you were a coward." Maggy shook her head and pretended to be bitterly disappointed. "Here I had this image of you as being an Amazon, afraid of nothing, so spit-in-their-eyes that you'd even drink machine brew and eat those botulism special egg salad sandwiches over there."

They waited while the driver tried to get in touch with the contractor. Dahlia went outside for a quick cigarette then came back into the warmth of the waiting room. She sat on a scarred bench and tried to make herself relax, tried to tell herself it didn't matter if they were a bit behind schedule. After all, even if it was pitch black when they arrived they could always sleep in the cook tent and get themselves settled in tomorrow. She also tried to tell herself that this turmoil was impatience, and the kind of unsettling stress that caused ulcers. She tried to nap, but the bench was hard and people kept tripping over her feet.

When the driver finally returned, she looked like someone who had just gone through a marital dispute and wasn't sure if she'd survived. "He says we're to keep going," she said, pretending to be calm. "He'll arrange a place for us to stay over, probably at Kelsey Bay."

"There isn't a place to stay over in Kelsey Bay," one of the young men grumbled. "Hell, there's hardly even any Kelsey Bay."

They climbed back into the bus and arranged themselves as comfortably as they could. Dahlia wasn't in the mood for company, even if it was good company, and Maggy seemed to sense the mood. She took the seat behind Dal, rolled her jacket in a ball and stuffed it between her head and the outside window. Dal did the same, but swung her legs up, her feet dangling over the edge, hanging out into the aisle. Maybe she had listened to the lecture she had given herself. The unsettled feeling was fading, and she had begun to believe that all she had to do was relax and go along for the ride.

She slept, but not soundly. She was peripherally aware that she was in the bus and she even heard the motor change in tone each time the driver switched gears, but some part of her was definitely clicked off and resting, like an old lab who seems to be sound asleep at the foot of the driveway but springs up, alert and barking, at the first hint of a newcomer. She opened her eyes, her back stiff and beginning to growl protest.

"Where are we?" she asked.

"On the road to Kelsey Bay." The driver sounded as if she was grinning. "More than that, I couldn't say."

"That sounds like the opening line of a somebody-done-somebody-wrong song. You always talk in rhymes?"

"Not always. Only on my better days."

They didn't get to sleep over anywhere in Kelsey Bay. They didn't even get to the town itself. The contractor flagged down the bus a couple of miles before the outskirts, and they got to unload the bus bays and transfer their gear to the back of a pickup truck. But at least they didn't have to bounce in the back with their duffel bags and camping gear—there was a 15-passenger van for them.

"You think to bring any sandwiches or anything?" someone asked. The contractor didn't answer.

"Coffee?" the questioner asked. The contractor turned away and

Dahlia repressed the urge to give him such a kick up the arse his brains would rattle.

"I'm sure not paying any 30 dollars camp costs for today!" she said loudly. When the contractor whirled to see who had spoken, Dal was busy tying her bootlace. When nobody said anything else the contractor shook his head and walked over to the pickup truck, knowing the comment had taken root in each member of the crew. He also knew that by saving the price of some sandwiches and a couple of thermoses of coffee he had just cost himself nearly $500.

The driver of the van wore the sullen look of someone who, like themselves, had missed a couple of meals. He also looked like someone who was here only because it was the first job to come down the pike in a long, long time. He glared at the pickup truck sitting in front of him, its engine running and huge plumes of exhaust showing pale in the headlights. "There'll be soup when we get there," he said, his voice husky and grating, the sound of someone who has had too many cigarettes and not enough sleep. Dal could have kissed him. Instead she smiled and nodded. He seemed surprised to find there were still people in the world who could at least try to be pleasant. "I don't care if you smoke in the van," he added. "Non-smokers can open a window or something, I guess."

Dal sat next to a window and cracked it. Her eyes felt as if half the sand on the beach had been jammed in there, and she wasn't feeling happy about bouncing over some old and untended mess of a logging road in the dead of night, on her way to some place she didn't even know for sure existed.

"How long?"

"Oh, Jesus," the driver sighed deeply. "It could be anywhere from three hours to three days. The road is a total bitch in the daytime, and I personally think we're all crazier'n shithouse rats to try it at night."

"That's what I like to hear—enthusiasm."

"Yeah, well, you know how it is. Life's a bitch and then you're dead. And the poor fuckin' Buddhists have to come back and do 'er again."

Uphill, things weren't too bad. The four-wheel drive could have handled worse with ease. Downhill, even the heavy tread tires could do little but toboggan in skids that were nearly out of control. The road looked as if someone had taken huge gouges out of it, then stirred the deep ruts and washouts with a stick, turning what had been frozen dirt into a grim slurry of mud. Where the washouts were particularly bad, the headlights picked up large boulders, some of them teetering on the edge of the road, just waiting for the excuse to plunge down through 500 feet of nothing at all to crash on the slope below and set off a rock slide.

"Well," Dal said loudly, "what do I care? My insurance premiums are paid up!"

"Yeah, but they might decide anyone who agreed to take this trip was actually committing suicide and refuse to pay."

"Is anyone else in here scared, or is it just me?"

"It isn't just you." The driver began to laugh. "I've been scared shit-less since about six this morning, when he told me I was going to drive this fuckin' coffin. One thing about it, though, it's about half as scary at night as it was this afternoon, because now I can't see what's over the lip and this afternoon it was all I could see! By me, they can give this whole stinkin' mess back to the Indians."

A woman's voice, until now unheard, came from the half-darkness behind Dal. "What in hell makes you think we want it? We're hol-din' out for something worthwhile, like the city of Vancouver, or the beach frontage. You guys made this mess, you can have it."

"See, there you go, racial discrimination on every side." It was Maggy, her voice teasing, laughter bubbling under her words. "All this, and on an empty stomach too."

Dal figured it was just as well they hadn't eaten. Anything she'd put down her throat before the trip started wouldn't have stayed even this long. She could feel a thin line of sweat dribbling down the middle of her back, and a knot in her gut so tight it hurt.

Her watch said 10 minutes to three when they finally pulled up beside a large army surplus tent. There were lights inside, and the canvas seemed almost transparent. A hunk of stovepipe stuck out the side, smoke pluming, and she could see the shadow outline of the wood stove, and of tables, with what were undeniably baskets of bread buns waiting. They piled out of the van and stumbled to the cook tent. Inside it was warm, and ripe with the smell of soup and something else that Dal hoped was spaghetti sauce. She supposed she really ought to wash her hands, but she couldn't see anything that looked like a basin or a towel. Besides, the cook was already ladling soup into bowls, and people were lining up.

"Thank you," she said, forcing a tired smile. The cook, who was called Cook—no one seemed to know her name—grinned at her and Dal could have kissed her. She looked like everybody's efficient auntie.

The buns were still warm and the soup was thick, with plenty of barley and fresh vegetables. "I might live," Dal said. "I really might."

"At least until we have to drive back out over that damn blister of a road." It was the Native woman, sitting across from her.

"I'm Dal." She reached across the table.

"Nancy." The hand that gripped hers was strong, the palm slick and hard, the hand of someone who had chopped more than one cord of wood in her lifetime.

"Did anyone see the pickup truck with the gear?" Maggy asked. They looked at each other, but nobody answered.

They ate until they couldn't eat any more, then helped Cook with cleanup. And still no sign of the pickup. Dal had the uncharitable thought that if she'd known then what she knew now, she'd have hung on to her sleeping bag. But it was warm by the stove, and she was the first one to think of lying on the floor, fully dressed, with her arm under her head. She was asleep before Nancy lay down beside her.

When she finally woke up, Cook was starting breakfast, stepping carefully around the sleepers. The four women were sleeping in one group, the guys in another, with a good six feet of space between the two. Dal sat up, feeling almost as tired as she had been when she lay down. The cook smiled at her and waved her hand to indicate a pot of fresh coffee.

The pickup truck arrived at noon. One door was creased and a fender crumpled, and the contractor looked as if he'd taken one helluva rap on the side of the face. His eye was swollen, his eyebrow was slit and there were flakes of dried blood in his hair.

"Couldn't come and look for us or anything," he accused.

"Come look for you?" The van driver looked blank. "Hey, if we didn't see you last night, why would we see you today?"

"We came within three inches of gettin' ourselves smeared!" the pickup driver yelled, "and you dumb bastards went right on by, never noticed a thing."

"Oh, yeah, sure we did," Nancy answered him, her tone sarcastic. "We just thought we'd leave you there. Took a vote on it and everything."

"Jesus Christ! We go off the road, we blow out two tires on the boulders, you guys go by like we aren't even there and then we get to change tires and struggle back on the fuckin' road by ourselves! And you don't even come to see why we're late?"

"How were we to know you were late before we got here and found out you weren't here?" the driver asked.

"You I could leave forever," Dal cracked, "but if I'd known my sleeping bag was sitting on the side of the road, I'd'a made him stop for sure!"

"And the damn jack doesn't work properly."

"Well, cheap-shit on the equipment and that's what you get."

He glared at her but had no reply.

Cook stopped the argument by hollering out the door that she had breakfast ready for the latecomers and lunch for the rest of them. Breakfast and lunch turned out to be the same, and before it was over, the argument was forgotten and the hard feelings gone. By two in the afternoon, Dal had her gear unloaded, her tent set up and her stuff laid out in neat piles inside. It was wonderful to peel off the clothes she had been wearing for almost two days and climb into fresh. No sooner did she have clean wool socks on her feet than they began to feel warm. She didn't know if it was physical or psychological, but she always took clean socks with her when she went out on the slope and changed when she stopped for lunch. By then her toes were feeling numb and no matter what anybody said about it being all in her head, she was convinced fresh socks were the remedy.

The contractor, given his own way, would have had them all out with their bags of seedlings that afternoon, but he wasn't getting any cooperation. The best they'd get was an hour of planting, and that wasn't even worth the effort of climbing into the truck. Dal used the time to crawl into her sleeping bag, and she stayed there until she heard Cook hollering that supper was ready. Moments after her belly was stuffed, she was back in the sleeping bag. This time she stayed there, sound asleep, until her travel alarm sounded.

They walked from the cookhouse in the dark, picked up their bags, stuffed them tight with seedlings, then sat in the back of the pickup and bounced off to the site. The darkness was just starting to fade when they clambered out of the pickup and headed off with their heavy bags and digging tools.

The rhythm was slow to take hold that first day. Dal's muscles had to adjust once again to the weight of the bag, the heft of the digging tool. She stopped often to ease the crick under her right shoulder blade, and when she stopped to eat her sandwiches and drink her thermos coffee, she found a boulder and sat with her back against it, trying to ease the tight ache near the base of her spine. She wished she had been able to appreciate her own strength and fitness in the days when she first started planting, the days when she could walk hour after hour across the uneven misery of ground and never feel stiff, never have an ache or pain. She'd thought then that it would always be just like that. God, how stupid could a person be!

She could, of course, always light up a joint and ease her aches and pains with the stinkweed. Some of the planters stayed high all day, actually enjoying the monotony. Probably because with a few lungfuls, time became fluid—a full day of hard work could seem like nothing at all. But Dal knew that if she started toking now she'd spend day after day depending on the stuff, living someplace other than where she really was. She'd seen what happened when people did that, they thought they were working like crazy and doing well. There was no sense in trying to pass the time of day with them, let alone have any kind of conversation. They could say what they liked. To Dal there was no difference between the people who spent their lives in a cloud of smoke and the ones she'd grown up in spite of, the ones who swam in gallons of cheap booze. She'd spent her life running from the one and she wasn't about to volunteer to be caught in the other. She knew just how susceptible she would be because of how easy it was for her to get a contact high.

If a contractor had sense enough to haul in some kind of bathtub and set up a solar heater, he could probably add 10 bucks a day to the camp costs and nobody would complain. Right now, for example, Dal would pay twice that just to be able to look forward to a good hot soak once the day's work was done.

By the time the second week was half over, Dahlia's muscles were toned again and her average daily number of trees was almost as high as it had ever been. One afternoon she walked off her section of the slope and stood waiting for her ride. After a half-hour or so, she got tired of standing and sat down with her empty seedling bags under her backside and a first-growth stump at her back. She took her small tin of tobacco from her shirt pocket and rolled a cigarette. Her daily consumption was down to a fraction of what it was when she was at home. In the time it would take her to roll and smoke a cigarette she could plant two dozen seedlings, and each one planted was money. Besides, they didn't taste the same outdoors as they did when she was sitting and watching TV or taking a break at Toby's. She wondered if her stress level was bottoming out as well. She finished the cigarette and was shredding the butt, scattering the tobacco to the wind, when the pickup finally came bumping and clattering down the road. Dal waved at Cook, who was driving, and scrambled in. She put her bags on the floor and sat on them. They weren't much by way of padding, but they were better than nothing at all.

"How come Cook's driving?" she asked.

"Jimmy got hurt." Maggy cupped her hands around her Bic and leaned forward to light her cigarette. "Says he tripped and got his foot jammed between two rocks, then one of them shifted and he fell sideways."

"You see it?"

"No. Poor bugger had to try to crawl back up to the access road. Lucky for him he was first one to be picked up. Kid just loaded him into the van and took off for town."

"Jesus, I don't envy him the ride out. Over that road? Sixty miles of gravel and washout? With a bad leg?"

"No damn reason for it," Nancy blurted angrily. "If the boss wasn't such a cheap shit he could have radiophoned for a helicopter."

At supper the planters sat together with a good-sized space between themselves and the contractor. He tried hard to ignore them, but it was like trying to ignore an iceberg sitting in the living room, chilling the entire house.

"What?!" he finally yelled, glaring at them. Nobody answered. "Say it or bury it!"

"How come you're here?" Nancy asked. "How come you didn't call in a chopper and go out to the hospital with him? You're the boss."

"Someone has to keep tally."

"Shit, you saying we're all too stupid to figure out how many seedlings to a box, how many boxes per day? You figure we can't tell which of us took how many? It's not exactly brain surgery. You're his boss, you shoulda gone in with him. You don't just drop somebody over the side like a bucketload of fish guts."

"You like your job?"

"Like my job?" she said with a laugh, "No, I hate my job. But I do it, and I do it well. Why? You going to fire me?"

"I could."

"Sure you could. And I'd put in a grievance. And then I'd call out my cousins, second cousins, shirttail cousins and neighbours and put a land claim blockade around this place and shut it down tight."

"You wouldn't."

"No, I wouldn't, because you're not going to fire me. We're just jokin', right?"

"Not much to joke about."

"You're right. It's nothing to joke about when a guy's bouncing over that damn road with a bad-hurt leg. They're probably only halfway there. How'd you like another couple of hours of jiggling if *you* had a broken leg?"

The boss sat glaring at the tabletop for a while, then got up suddenly and left the cook tent. They didn't see him again that night. But less than an hour later they heard the *hunga-hunga-hunga* of a helicopter, and before bedtime the van came back. The Kid looked white-faced and slammed the door of the van as if it was to blame for everything.

"You okay?" Georgie asked.

"I was never so glad in my life to see anything as to see that big thing hanging over the road directly in front of me." The Kid accepted a cup of coffee from Cook. His hands were shaking. "They sent a guy in a bright orange suit down on the end of a rope and lowered a stretcher thing that looked like some kind of aluminum baby cradle.

We got Jimmy on it and strapped him in so he couldn't move, and then they just hoisted him up slicker'n hell."

"How bad was he?"

"He'd been screamin' for 10 minutes by the time we stopped." He sat down suddenly, the muddy earth making squelching, slurping sounds around his skinny backside. "Jesus Christ." He began to cry. "I didn't know whether to shit or go blind. It was awful. Road's worse'n it was when we came in. I'm in second gear all the time and the washboard is shaking me so bad I though my teeth'd fall out. And Jimmy's nearly going nuts. All's I could do was keep driving, and every bump he got worse."

Nobody spoke. Maggy reached down and took The Kid by the arm. She tugged gently and he got to his feet, still sobbing. The crew walked with him to the cook tent where there was food, and hot coffee, and lamplight and warmth from the big stove. Cook poured coffee and they each took a mug. The Kid continued to sob, his hands shaking. And still nobody said anything. They just let him cry, sitting all around him, cradling their warm mugs in their cold hands. Finally, the heartbroken sobbing subsided, and The Kid began to hiccough and sniff. Cook handed him a roll of yanky-hanky and he ripped off a piece and blew his nose. He opened his mouth and then closed it, unable to think of anything to say. The warm, companionable silence stretched, and finally they rose, one at a time, washed and dried their mugs and left for their tents.

Nobody talked about it at breakfast the next day. They all tried hard to pretend that the only thing going on was sausages and eggs. And then The Kid stood up and hollered, and nobody could pretend that it hadn't happened. "If I didn't need this job so bad I'd fuckin' quit!" he shouted, his voice cracking. "I'm sick of being nothing!" He seemed to take comfort from their silence and sat back down again, speared a sausage and cut it into pieces.

"T'hell with it," another planter agreed, chewing his toast. "Come the first chance I get, I'm going into town. I'm gonna get myself a motel room. I'm gonna buy me a new pair of jeans and a new T-shirt. I'm gonna have a bath that takes me at least an hour in hot, hot, hot water as close to my chin as I can manage without flooding out the bathroom. And when I'm warm and clean and wearin' m'new clothes,

I'm goin' to sprawl me out on a bed and stare at the TV, and I don't care what is on it as long as it doesn't look like 200 acres of burned-over slash and bare-rock clear-cut."

"Make room for me," Cook called. "I'll buy the damn bubble bath and the soap that smells like lily of the valley."

"Save me the water." Nancy said. "But I'm not watchin' any TV. I'm going to a real movie house and I'm going to eat so damn much popcorn it'll set a new world record."

They didn't get the chance until the end of the month. The shipment of seedlings didn't come on time, and when the boss phoned about it, he got told something he didn't much like. He cursed a bit and stomped around as if his big boots would solve his problem, and then he announced that he had to go into town and might not be back for a couple of days.

"And what are we supposed to do?" Nancy asked. "There aren't any seedlings to plant."

Before the boss could think up some time-wasting thing for them to do, they were grabbing their backpacks, tying shut the tent flaps and heading for the vehicles.

"There isn't going to be room!" the boss insisted. "I'm takin' the pickup and it'll be full on the way back."

"That's okay. The Kid knows how to drive the van," Cook said calmly, reaching for the door handle.

The boss looked as if he was going to complain about the cost of the gas it would take to go out and come back in. But he said nothing. Dal couldn't understand why it was such a pain in the face to have them go into town. Maybe he was afraid they wouldn't come back and he'd have to get off his duff and actually plant something himself.

"Hell," she called to him, "it's not as if we're going to walk off and leave our tents and sleeping bags behind. That gear costs money, eh."

The trip out seemed to take forever, and by the time they got to a motel it was black night and the town seemed zipped shut. All the stores were closed and only a few kids clustered around the pool hall. The motel manager was glad to see them but embarrassed about the lack of rooms. "Got some Yank tourists showed up," he explained, "and I've only got four units left."

Of course, the boss had to have one all to himself. Dahlia held out her credit card to claim one of the remaining rooms.

"I'll split it with you," Nancy said quickly.

The room wasn't very big but it had two double beds in it. Dahlia and Maggy took one of them, Cook and Nancy the other.

"Jeez, we're a mess," Nancy said. They looked at each other and then started to laugh. They hadn't seen their own faces under electric lights for a month. They were tanned by wind and sun, and had left camp without scrubbing the dust and grime of the slope off their faces.

"My hair," Dal moaned. "What a mess."

"Oh, sure." Maggy gave Dal a gentle shove. "I wish to God when I was a mess I was a mess like you're a mess."

"Yeah," Nancy agreed. "Even when I'm not a mess I don't have hair like you do when you are a mess."

They decided that since Dahlia's credit card had got them the room, it was only fair that she have the first bath. She didn't argue with them.

She stripped off her dusty slope clothes and piled them in a corner of the bathroom. She had dirt between her toes and fine particles of dust trapped in the skin of her ankles. Where the tops of her boots began there was an anklet of dirt. She imagined herself shaking out her clothes, shaking out her socks, enough soil piling up to be able to plant two seedlings right here in the bathroom. Dal would have liked to lie back and soak until breakfast, but each of the others must be feeling the same. She soaped and scrubbed with the face cloth, then scrubbed some more. After she had pulled the plug, she shut the shower curtains and turned on the spray. One last fast shampoo, and a good, thorough rinse, and she was ready to give someone else her turn.

She was towel-drying her hair, as naked as the day she was born, when the bathroom door opened a crack. "You shy?" Maggy asked. "Or can a body get in here and start the tub?"

"I'm not shy, and the tub is washed clean and ready for the next filthy slob."

Maggy came into the bathroom, put in the plug and started the water. Then she very calmly started stripping off her dusty clothes, tossing them in the corner on top of Dal's. She gave every indication of having been raised in a large, easygoing family, or having spent time in a girls' dormitory. She didn't try to cover herself at all. Dal couldn't help noticing that Maggy was built very differently than she was. Maggy's breasts were small, her waist didn't dip in as far, her hips didn't curve out the same. In fact, though she was slender and in top physical shape, there wasn't all that much of what those who mould public taste would call shape. Her short hair had grown in and lay straight and flat on her head, except for the line just above her ears from her peaked cotton hat. Her shoulders were wide, the muscles of her arms clearly defined, and one look at her legs and anyone would know she spent 10 or 12 hours a day walking over rough ground with a heavy load.

Dal wrapped her damp towel around her and left the bathroom. She rummaged around in her pack for a roomy clean T-shirt. She pulled it on, stepped into a fresh pair of underpants and hauled on clean jeans. "I'm going to go over to the office and see if I can score some more towels."

"I'll go," Nancy said. "Your hair's wet. You go out and you're apt to catch cold."

"I'm too tired to even chase cold, let alone catch it."

But Nancy insisted. She came back with a stack of towels and tossed a dry one to Dal, who was stretched out on the bed, staring at the TV. Jodie Foster was falling in love with a guy who looked exactly like her husband but was really an impostor. Maggy came in naked from the bathroom and sat on the side of the bed with her pack, searching in it for clean clothes. "Tomorrow it's laundromat time. A person would think none of this stuff had been washed in a month. How does that happen? I know for a fact I've washed all this. So much for the good old days and cleanliness next to godliness."

Dal could feel herself losing the thread of the Jodie Foster story. She would have liked something to eat but was too tired to go looking for it. Probably wouldn't be any place open at this time of night anyway. Hell, if they delivered it to the door of the motel she was too tired to open her mouth to bite into it. She stood long enough to pull down the covers on her side of the bed, then slipped off her jeans and crawled in.

"Lift your head," Maggy said softly, and she slid two neatly folded towels on top of Dal's pillow. "There, that might keep you from a soaking wet pillow. Put your head down now."

Dal did. She heard water running in the bathroom, she heard the door open and close, heard it open and close again, then heard the soft murmur of voices and the pop-hiss of cans of pop being opened. She fell asleep and dreamed of a sky full of pink-tinged clouds and a Ferris wheel suspended between heaven and earth. All the people she loved were riding the wheel, talking and laughing and having a wonderful time. She was glad they were enjoying themselves, but why wasn't she in the dream? She couldn't find herself anywhere—not on the clouds and not in the gondolas that moved dreamily around the central mechanism of the machine.

Five

Dahlia half-wakened hours later. She was lying on her back and wanted to roll to her belly but her right leg wouldn't move. She was so groggy she thought that she was the one who had fallen, not Jimmy, and that her leg was weighed down by a heavy cast. But as she fought through the fog and began to wake up, she realized her leg was held down by Maggy's leg. She slid it out carefully, and as she turned to her side she became aware of sounds from the other bed. Clearly, whatever else was happening in that bed, neither of them was sleeping. Dal rolled to her belly and lay with her face turned away from the other bed, away from Maggy. She didn't know how she felt about the sounds, didn't know what she thought about them. She supposed it wasn't any of her damn business anyway. Into each life some sun must shine. God, we can't live in a constant rainfall from cradle to crematorium. The pink clouds were forming again, but there wasn't any Ferris wheel this time, nor could she see anybody. Just the clouds, and the sensation of drifting slowly through them. Not falling, just drifting. The mattress cradled her, the bed was warm, and sleepy as she was, she knew that much of that warmth came from the sleeping body beside her. She was almost asleep when that warm body moved and an arm slid across her back, the fingers curling naturally around the curve of Dal's shoulder.

When she woke up again she was lying on her side, spooned around Maggy's sleeping form. Dal raised her head. In the next bed, Cook and Nancy were snuggled close, Cook lying on her back, Nancy pressed against her with her head on Cook's shoulder. The blankets were every which way and the counterpane puddled on the floor. From outside she could hear the first sounds of morning traffic. Someone shouted and a car door slammed shut. Dal wanted to slip back into sleep but her bladder was so full that it was painful. She eased away from Maggy's warm back and crept out of bed. She closed the bathroom door gently and tried to pee quietly, but it sounded like someone emptying a tub of water from the roof of the barn. When she went back to the other room, the three sleepers were still deep in dreamland. Dal considered crawling back into bed but knew she wasn't going to go back to sleep. If she tried to lie quietly, she would only manage to give herself a cramp in the leg. If she moved around, that would wake Maggy up. She dragged on her jeans and went through her pack to find clean socks and her sneakers, which she hadn't worn in a month. Her T-shirt was creased, but so what? And she hadn't had a chance to fight it out with her hair yet. It was post-shampoo curled tight in a wild mop, but if they didn't like it they could jump at the moon. She pulled on her jacket and put one of the room keys in her pocket, checked her hip pocket to make sure she had her wallet and eased herself out of the unit.

Half a block from the motel she saw the distinctive sign for Smithy's Pancake House. Suddenly Dal knew that Smithy and the pancakes were the only reason in the world she had come to town. She zipped her jacket and ran toward the sign. She wasn't even breathing heavily when she got there. The waitress looked at her and smiled. "Tree planter?"

"God, don't tell me I've got seedlings caught in my hair?" Dal said, grinning.

"No, but who else has a tan like that this early in the year? Coffee?"

"I'd love coffee. And I want pancakes with sausages, syrup, whipped cream and some fruit, please."

"Eggs too?"

"Sure, why not? Over easy, please."

After she finished her breakfast, Dal made a collect call home from the restaurant pay phone. Iris answered.

"Hi, Iris, this is Dal. Could I speak to Pansy?"

"Pansy! It's for you!" Iris screeched. Then she turned back to the phone. "Oh, God, Dal, you've got to come home. Daddy is real sick, and they don't think he's going to make it."

"Yeah? Are any of the kids handy?"

"Kids! It's your mother!" Iris screeched again. "They think it's his heart. And his lungs. He's got scar tissue or something, and can't breathe properly. You've got to come home."

"I'm only in town for today. We're going back to camp tomorrow."

"But you have to come home! He's probably dying."

Dal sighed, but not with sorrow. She tried to restrain herself and might have succeeded, but Iris took the silence to mean something it didn't.

"You know you've got to make peace with him. You know you have to come home."

"What good would that do? Surely to God he's got a doctor."

"Of course he's got a doctor. He's got two or three of them. When are you coming?"

"I'm not. If the doctors can't fix him up I sure can't. I need to talk to Pansy and the kids."

"What is the matter with you?" Iris was revving up, getting ready for a good explosion, when Pansy took the phone. Dal could hear Pansy telling Iris to calm down, to just get herself in hand, she knew full well all the yelling in the world wouldn't change anything.

"Hey, you," Pansy said easily. "You replaced the missing forest yet?"

"Made a teeny start on it. How's everything there? How are the kids?"

"Kids are great, but only about half of them are at home."

"They must look funny, walking around with half themselves missing. I hope it's the half with a mouth and throat, so's they can talk."

"Soccer. Everyone but Twink, Pape and Pip is at soccer. It's practice today, so I only had to drop 'em off, but tomorrow's a game and I'll get to freeze my royal Irish watching them splash in the mud. Johnny and Ricky are on teams too. Ricky's pretty good. But they didn't put him on the same team as Skipper so they're rivals, and that's not the most fun in the world."

Then Pip took the phone and talked for a while. Much of what she said was next best thing to absolute mystery, but Dal made the appropriate noises and agreed with everything. Then Pape came on and filled Dal in on the wonderful antics of the great and glorious Socks.

"He stands up on the rat catcher frame on my bike and we go for rides together. If it gets bumpy, he stands on his back legs and digs his claws into my jacket and hangs on tight. When he gets tired he starts yowling, so I stop and put him down the front of my jacket and zip it most-ways up and he sticks out his head and watches where we're going."

"Not every cat in the world can do that."

"No other cat can do that. Socks is smart."

Twink, who talked the least, actually had the most to say as far as Dal was concerned. She gave thumbnail sketches of what was going down with each of the others.

"Are *you* okay, Twink?"

"I'm fine, Momma. I miss you like crazy, though."

"I miss you too, darling. Sometimes I miss you so much it feels like toothache. But each day here is a day closer to getting home. So you give the kids big kisses for me, okay? Tell them I love them."

Twink had the good sense to hang up right away. Dal could imagine what was starting to come down on the other end. Iris would harangue Twink to give the phone back to her, she hadn't finished. Pansy would shush Iris as best she could. Twink would shrug and let it all roll off her, and if Iris pushed it too far Twink would tell her to shut up. That ought to push Iris into tears and a half-hour of recriminations, but Twink, having expressed herself fully, would just go to her room, close the door and slide the bolt. If Iris was foolish enough to follow and stand at the door yammering, Twink would lie on her bed with her earphones on and something loud and rhythmic hammering, blocking the sound of her aunt's voice. She would probably read a book at the same time. Dal wished Iris would do something different for a while. Fall on her head and knock some sense into it, maybe. She almost phoned back just to have the satisfaction of talking to, rather than listening to, her older sister. There were so many things she had wanted to say for such a long time. But she'd survived all these years without saying them. She supposed they could go unmentioned forever.

Dal stopped at the drug store and got some essentials—bubble bath, shampoo, conditioner, tampons and toothpaste. On her way out, she almost ran into the boss. He looked like someone who was just about ready to go for the throat.

"You talk to them," he growled.

"Talk to who?"

"Those assholes down at the freight office. They say the goddamn seedlings won't be in until tomorrow."

"What do you want me to say to them?"

"Tell them to get them here today, dammit!"

"Where are they?"

"Holed up in the freight warehouse in bloody Courtenay!"

"Well, isn't that the next best thing to a kick in the head. Even if I took the pickup and left now I wouldn't be back until after supper-time." The idea appealed to her. "But that's still earlier than tomor-row. You got the paycheques?"

"You want your paycheque? On top of everything else I'm supposed to issue the paycheques. Jesus Aitch!" He looked like his stomach hurt. "How about a drag instead?" he suggested.

"I'd like to." She smiled and he started to relax. "But I've got an abso-lute raft of kids who insist on eating, and…" They walked together back to the motel and went into his unit. He grumbled and snorfed to himself but opened his little gray suitcase and pawed in the accumu-lation of papers until he found his chequebook. He sucked his teeth and grumbled some more, then found a pen and started writing.

"Here. It's not the full amount, but I can't figure that out until I sit down and actually do the books."

She looked at the amount and nodded. It was only about 80 percent of what she figured she had coming to her, but—a bird in the hand.

"Would you really?" he asked. "Go get them, I mean."

"Sure, I can drive." She smiled again to take the sting out of it.

"I'll go talk to those idiots at the freight company."

"I'll go to the bank, then meet you back here."

When they met up again, the boss looked like he was about to burst a blood vessel. "They close at five. Can you make it by five?"

"What time is it now?"

"Quarter past 11."

"I think I can."

"Well, if you can't, get a hotel room and keep the receipt, then get loaded as early in the morning as you can and drive back in. Now these puckers say their truck won't even leave until one in the afternoon, minimum, because the mechanic isn't finished with it."

"The mechanic isn't finished? What, they've only got one truck, I suppose."

"Probably got nothing more than a buck-toothed kid with a little red wagon." He started laughing, the reddish purple flush fading from his face. "Would you believe," he went on, sounding more human than she'd ever heard, "I used to have nothing more to worry about than getting to work on time. I didn't even have to worry about making sure I took my lunch kit with me because there was a Ukrainian restaurant just down the street and I ate there. Lunch every day, supper most days. I didn't do payroll, I didn't keep track of the number of half-dead fuckin' baby trees each person said they put in the dirt, I didn't have to balance numbers or try to get the transport company to shape up or send people bouncing off over roads or anything. But I wanted to be an entrepreneur." He made it sound like something that was at least first cousin to the bubonic plague.

Maggy came into the unit with a black garbage bag full of something bulky. "Hey, you're an early bird," she teased. "Some of us have been busy." She looked curiously at the boss and nodded hello to him. "Did your laundry with mine. You owe me three bucks for quarters for the machines. Something up?"

That was all the invitation the boss needed to jump back into his grievances. While he gave chapter and verse, Maggy nodded and sorted the laundry. Dal went to the bathroom and did what she could to tame the mop. It didn't want to be tamed, so she gave up and grabbed toothbrush, toothpaste, shampoo, conditioner and bubble bath—just in case she got caught in Courtenay.

"I'm going with you," Maggy announced. "No need to just sit here watching the world watch me as I watch it go by."

"Don't you two get into any kind of trouble, now," the boss warned, as if they were 10 years old. "This isn't a joy ride, okay?"

But it was the next best thing to it. Dal did the driving and Maggy did the entertaining. She cracked jokes, she sang songs, and when they got stopped by bridge construction, she chatted up the flag woman. The transport company was still open, but they wouldn't release the seedlings.

"I don't know nothin' about this," the receptionist kept repeating. "Nobody told me. You don't even have an authorization paper. You got no bill of lading. And this stuff isn't destined for here, it's supposed to go up to Hemming Bay."

"Lady, please, we just came from Hemming Bay, and we came to pick up the seedlings so you don't have to go there tomorrow."

"Well, nobody told me nothin' about it and the boss isn't here. And I'm not letting anything go to someone without authorization papers unless the boss countersigns, because I don't want to lose my job. It's the best job I ever had in my life."

Dal didn't bother saying she felt sorry for anyone whose other jobs had been worse than this one. She grabbed the phone and called the motel, then had to leave a number for the boss to call her back. At 5:10 he still hadn't called and the receptionist was past impatient to downright antsy. "I don't suppose you got much else to do right now," she said, "but me, I got a life, okay? And I prob'ly won't get overtime for this."

"We can phone him from the motel," Maggy said quietly.

The boss still wasn't back in his unit when they phoned, so they left the number of the motel they were staying in. While Maggy headed out to find a takeout place, Dal phoned home again to talk to the older kids. Skipper answered, laughing.

"Pete's Morgue," he giggled. "You stab 'em, we slab 'em. What can I do you for?"

"How you doin', Skip, this is your maternal parent calling."

"I'm fine. We're all fine, but Auntie Iris is right up the damn wall. Someone died, and she's mad because you didn't come home for it and mad at us because we don't care. Who died, anyway?"

"Your grandfather, I guess."

"Did I know him?"

"Darlin', you never set eyes on him in your life."

"Then why's she mad? How can a guy cry and blubber about someone he never set eyes on?"

"You don't have to cry. Tell me about soccer."

"Ricky's not on my team. But that's okay because when we played them, we won. We have to play them again next week."

"Maybe they'll win next time."

"Maybe. He's pretty good. Auntie Iris is mad at him, though, because he told her if she moved in with her boyfriend and made Rick move with her, he'd just run away and go live with his dad. His dad's not in that treatment place, he's got a place of his own. And a new girlfriend. She doesn't have any kids. They came to see Ricky and Johnny, and took us all out to the movie, and when I asked her if she had kids she said, 'No, thank God,' and I asked did she want any, and she said she thought she'd rather catch the clap."

"Well, if she's hanging around with Duh-Whine Morgan she might."

"Yeah, and when Ricky told his dad about Auntie Iris moving in with her boyfriend and how he didn't want to go, his dad said not to worry, he could stay with us."

"Who could?"

"Ricky. And John too."

"Stay with us."

"Yeah. He even gave Auntie Pan some money. But not for Auntie Iris, he said she could pay her own way. So she's mad at him too."

By the time all the other kids had got their turns and Pansy got on the phone, Dal was feeling overloaded and tired.

"Cripes," she sighed, "those kids sure lead busy lives."

"And it isn't over yet. You have to talk to Johnny and Ricky too, they're about coming out of their skin. Iris got served papers yesterday."

"What kind of papers?"

"From the court. Dwayne's lawyer did a background check and I guess someone from welfare or somewhere went to the school and talked to the boys. It's a mess. I won't go into it on the phone but it looks like as long as she stays here, nothing changes. If she moves out and lives by herself, nothing changes. She moves in with him and, well, how do you feel about a couple of kids full-time?"

"How do you feel about Dwayne's girlfriend's idea of the clap? You know what will happen, Pan. Duh-Whine will pay support only for however long it takes to get those kids settled in and then he'll want a new truck or something, or someone will ding him for a bill he hasn't paid. And that'll be it for child support. And Iris? Hey, don't think for a minute Chummy is going to pay for kids who have told him to his face that they hate his guts."

"So what are you going to do?"

"Me? Jeez, Pan, I'm not even there to do anything!"

"It's your house."

"Right. Well, what do you think?"

"A kid or two more or less..."

"Never mind the 'or less' part of it, none of mine are going anywhere!"

"There's something else," Pansy said. "Iris is really mad at me. I mean really mad at me. I got up the other morning to get breakfast started for the kids and his car was parked outside. I think I kind of flipped. I went into Iris's bedroom and sure enough, there they are, all cuddled up together. They were asleep, but not for long. I hauled off all the covers and gave him two minutes to get his ass out of the house or I'd throw cold water on him. He started to argue with me so the mattress got soaked."

"Iris isn't sleeping in my bed!"

"I know. And I told her he could honk the horn for her and wait outside from now on, but he wasn't coming inside. And you know what she said? She said she'd already invited him to have Sunday dinner with us. So I said he wasn't getting so much as a crust of dry bread and if she wanted to eat with him she could do it at his place with either her or him doing the cooking and cleanup. She's real mad, and the old man croaking hasn't done anything to improve her mood."

"Piss on her."

"Well, you better talk to John and Rick, they're hopping from foot to foot here like a couple of fleas."

Dal didn't really want to talk to John and Rick but couldn't see any decent way to get out of it. "Hi there." She managed to sound friendly, even loving.

"So is it okay if we stay here?" John wasted no time getting to the point of the conversation. "Dad's girlfriend hates kids, and anyway, I don't want to live with him. He's bein' nice now, but you know what he's really like. And there's no way I'm living with Chummy. He's a dork."

"Darling, it's not up to me to decide who you live with. All I'm going to say is if it can be worked out with the judge and everything, and if and if and if-if-if, then yeah, you can stay where you are."

"Thanks, you better tell that to Ricky, he's as crazy as our dad is sometimes."

Dal thought she was home free when she had reassured Ricky, but before she could say goodbye and hang up, Ricky yelped and then Iris was unloading into the phone.

"You can just tell that damn Pansy she doesn't rule the world! It's not up to her to say who can visit me and who can't! It's none of her damn business!"

"Iris, listen."

"Just boss, boss, boss, as if she had been elected the life police or something."

"Iris!" Dal screamed.

"What?"

"Iris, I have never—not ever—taken one of my boyfriends home to spend the night under the same roof where my kids are sleeping. And Pansy has never brought home someone and fucked herself blind with the kids watching TV in the living room. And you, by God, aren't going to do it, either. Chummy isn't welcome in that house. He never was, not from back before the time you started sleeping with him."

"Now you're the boss, huh? Who gave you the right? What makes you think you can pick and choose for other people? Who in hell are you, anyway?"

"I'm the one owns the house, Iris. You want to fuck Chummy, do it in his car or in his apartment."

"But we like to cuddle." Iris was whining again, wouldn't you know it.

"Then cuddle at his place. But he isn't staying in my house with my kids, and he sure as hell isn't welcome. You heard what Pan said, he can wait for you outside."

"How come Pansy gets to give orders and you back her up?"

"Pansy is in charge, is why. Pansy looks after my kids, and yours too, and I know she does most of the work. The kids might help her but I'll be bloody surprised if you do. That's how it is, Iris, and if you don't like it, well, you'll have to lump it or find some other solution."

Iris started yelling and crying all at the same time, and then there were some odd noises from the phone and it was Pansy talking again.

"Hell, Dahlia, it's all kicked off again, I guess. She's back in the ozone."

"Leave the bitch in the ozone. Don't you ever get sick and tired of it?"

"I was sick and tired of it a month ago. Hear her? She's saying she's going to pack her stuff and phone him to come and get her."

"Good. One less person to clean up after, right? Listen, Pansy, I love you. If you want to kick Iris out, you go right ahead. Oh, and did I tell you I had some money transferred down to the chequing account?"

"No, you didn't say."

"Well, I did. I love you, Pan."

Dahlia hung up the phone and almost got her T-shirt off before the thing rang. "Hello?" She was half-expecting it to be Iris, full of bluff and bluster.

"Dahlia?" It was the boss.

"Hi, boss. The news isn't all that good. They wouldn't release the boxes. The receptionist said nobody gave her authorization."

"Sometimes," he said, so mildly it amazed her, "I feel as if the whole bloody world is full of absolute crazies. Well, nothing you can do about it tonight. I'll be on their backs first thing in the morning. Don't worry about it."

She still wasn't over the shock of his calm reaction when Maggy walked in with a tub of fried chicken and a box of potato salad, French fries, coleslaw and warm biscuits. "I didn't know if you liked fries or spud salad so I got both. And I didn't know if you'd prefer beer or pop, so I got some of each."

"I like 'em both." Dahlia tried to grin.

"You look like someone just threw you off the top of the building."

"Nah, nobody threw me off. I jumped."

They sat side by side on one of the beds, eating dinner and watching a movie about a bunch of people who seemed impervious to bullets, bombs and poison gas. "You believe all this, huh?" Maggy asked.

"Implicitly," Dal answered. "I myself have been through exactly this same thing in the past hour and a half."

Dahlia was bathed and in her bed when Maggy came out of the bathroom and sat on the edge of the other bed to rub her short hair with the towel.

"You okay?" she asked.

Dahlia nodded. "I'm fine." She even managed a small smile.

"Good." Maggy smiled back. She stood, then, totally naked, and walked back into the bathroom. Dahlia could hear the sounds of toothbrush, of running water, then Maggy came back. "You going to watch TV?" she asked.

"No, but if you want to it won't bother me. I don't think there's much is going to keep me awake tonight."

"Oh well, there goes the passion and orgasm I was planning." Maggy grinned, but Dahlia knew it was only half a joke.

"Huh?"

"Well, I was sort of considering putting the tap on you, but if you're worn to a nub and flat out of energy I might as well save it for another time."

"I'm not in the mood."

"Not in the mood, or only in the mood for men?"

"Spare me. I couldn't find the energy or interest if you lined up the population and told me to take my pick. I'd still pick my pillow."

"Have you ever been with a woman?"

"Yes." Dal didn't see what business it was of anybody else's, but it wasn't anything to hide.

"Seriously involved or experimentation?"

"Both. The experimentation was clumsy, but not for long and one of the best weekends of my life. The involvement was something else again."

Maggy got them each a drink from the bar fridge and settled herself down in her own bed. "So what came down with the involvement?"

"You name it, and it came down. Boy, talk about the good, the bad, the wonderful and the God-awful, it was all there, jam-packed into six of the most adrenalized and nutbar weeks of my life."

"Maybe you just picked the wrong person."

"Maybe I myself am the wrong person. I seem to get along fine with my kids, and I think I get along better with my sister Pan than most people can get along with anyone, but after that it starts to get just a tad spotty. People I get involved with seem to think that because we're sexual, they have the right to tell me what to do and how to do it"

Maggy laughed. "It sounds as if I've been involved with some of the same people you have."

"I used to think it was just that one particular person. If only he wouldn't do this, or if only she would stop doing that. But now I think it's me."

"You ever been dumped?"

Dal grinned but her voice was hard. "I do the dumping. If there's walking to be done, I seem to be the one who does it. You know how every magazine you pick up seems to have a self-help article in it? And every article seems to say we should step back and take a calm look at things? Well, not that I'm one to go overboard, or anything, but I don't step back, I start walking, and the calm look turns out to be distancing and probably even isolating. One step becomes a mile, and from that distance, it's easy to just keep hoofin'er."

"You ever been in love?"

"Probably not. I mean, those articles suggest if I was, I wouldn't take the hike, eh?"

"How are you with your kids?"

"What is this, head-shrinking time?"

"How else will I get to know you?"

"Why would you want to?"

"Well, I do. Tell me about your kids."

"They're great."

"Why, because they don't tell you what to do?"

"They run my life." Dal laughed. "Ask me if I'd even be here if it wasn't for them."

"So what would you do if you won the lottery?"

"Something stupid, probably. Stay home full-time and—oh, I don't know, take music lessons and start my own band. Maybe learn to tap dance. But probably I'd just sleep."

She snuggled into her bed, thumping her pillows, wriggling until she felt comfortable. Maggy finished her beer and put the empty can on the bedside table.

"The TV won't bother me," Dal said.

Maggy nodded and reached for the remote. Dal yawned and squirmed, then closed her eyes. The sound from the TV was low, the voices became increasingly fuzzy and she drifted into a deep and restful sleep.

In the morning they dressed, checked out of the motel, went for breakfast and were waiting outside when the freight company opened. Less than an hour later they were loaded and heading back, the pickup heavy, the steering sluggish. Maggy drove the last hour and a half of the trip and Dal was glad. The trip back, with the weight in the back, was about twice as hard to handle as the trip out had been. She wanted coffee, and settled for a can of lukewarm pop, she wanted lunch, and didn't get it until nearly two in the afternoon, but at least it was worth waiting for, and she enjoyed every bite.

The boss was in a hurry to leave. He gassed up the pickup and drove off at about the time Maggy and Dal were starting to pack away their steak and fries. The rest of the crew was checked out of the motel, their stuff already crammed into the van, and they'd all had lunch, but they still had room for pie and coffee.

"Good trip?" Cook asked.

"It was okay, but not what you'd call a holiday."

Maggy told about the woman at the freight company and managed to make it sound funny. "And so there we were," she said between bites, "waiting for the boss to phone. Sitting in this other motel with a box of takeout, feeling as if we'd been abandoned."

Dal knew that Cook and the rest of the crew were wondering how she and Maggy had spent their time. She wanted to slap her hand on the tabletop and tell them no, we didn't, not with each other or anyone else, but if she did that, she'd convince them all that they had. She wondered what they'd say if she told them about Iris and Chummy and how it used to be Pan and Chummy. Probably stop talking to her, especially if she threw in some descriptions of Duh-Whine. After all, if you're known by the company you keep...

With lunch warm in her belly and The Kid driving the van, Dal enjoyed the trip back into camp. The snow was retreating on the slopes, and the alder trees were showing the red of their first bloom. The burned-over clear-cuts were faintly tinged with a greenish fuzz, the fireweed beginning to grow, the trailing blackberry taking hold and sending out new leaves. In some places patches of what had to be grass were growing and when they finally got back to camp they could actually see the results of some of the work they had done. The baby trees showed green against the dark brown of earth, the grey of rock, the black of scorched slash. The pickup truck was parked near the cook tent and smoke was coming from the stovepipe stuck out the canvas side. In the grey of late afternoon the glowing light from the propane lamp looked inviting, promised warmth. The pickup truck with its load of heavily waxed boxes full of baby trees sat near the door.

The boss had made a pot of coffee and was sitting at a table sipping at a mug of it and smoking a cigarette. He barely looked up when they entered.

"Soon as you've had a coffee," he said, "you can start unloading the boxes."

"Excuse me?" Martin turned slowly, and Dal could almost see the string as the balloon began to go up.

"The boxes," the boss grunted, "have to be unloaded."

"You're sitting on your ass drinking coffee and telling *me* to unload the boxes?"

"What's your problem?"

"I guess my problem is I get paid by the seedling, not by the hour. I guess my problem is simply one of economics. You want me to unload and stack boxes, but you don't want to pay me for doing it."

"What in hell is this all about?"

"We finally get a couple of days off and what happens? You wind up with a unit all to yourself and we wind up crammed in together! Did you think to say, 'Hey, there's room for two or three more in my unit, why not bunk in?' No. You wind up with two big beds and a sofa, and we wind up on portable cots! You hoof'er off to the steak house and we're eating hamburgers because we haven't gotten paid yet! Now you're sitting on your ass and telling us to spend the next hour or so unloading boxes and stacking them where you want them stacked, and you don't so much as say a word about pay. You're a chintzy son of a bun is what you are."

"If you don't like it you can take a hike. Nobody's forcing you to do this job, nobody's got a gun at your head."

"And how come camp costs are so high? You don't even have a boiler set up so's there's hot water for washing! For what we're pay-ing for camp costs we ought to at least be able to wash our socks in warm water."

"You don't shut up you're gonna wind up with your termination notice in your hand."

"Sure, sure," Martin laughed. "And you'll wind up unloading all those damn boxes by yourself."

The boss looked about ready to explode. He also looked like someone who had just realized that Martin wasn't standing alone on a bare rock with the wind whipping up his soiled toga. Nobody said anything and nobody had to—it was obvious that if Martin got the boot, the whole crew would walk. The boss heaved himself to his feet and stomped out of the cook tent. The crew looked everywhere except at each other.

"Anybody want some fried egg sandwiches?" Cook asked, breaking the silence.

"Only if you promise it's the last goddamn egg I have to look at for at least three days," said Martin. "And I want you to know it isn't your wages I object to paying. You're a damn good cook. It's just that it's hard to make eggs and spaghetti taste like anything other than eggs and spaghetti. That guy is pocketing probably half what we pay for camp costs, and that pisses me off!"

They had their fried egg sandwiches and hot coffee, then brought their sleeping bags in from their tents and draped them over the tables so the warmth in the cook tent could take at least some of the clammy dampness out of them.

"I guess if we don't help that fat fart with the seedlings we'll be filling our damn bags from the bed of the pickup tomorrow morning," Dal said. "And Martin, next time you decide to have a revolution, you might let the rest of us know about it ahead of time."

They unpacked the boxes of seedlings and stacked them near the growing mountain of empty boxes, then took the groceries into the big tent and helped Cook put them away.

When the groceries were put away and the water buckets refilled, there was wood to chop and stack under the lean-to attached to the back of the cook tent. It was pitch black by then, not a star showing in the sky, the moon a sickly glow behind the thick layer of night cloud. Dal cut dried cedar into kindling for the morning and put it under a table near the stove, where it would stay dry even if the aged roof of the tent leaked, which it often did when the rain had been falling for days. Sparks from the chimney had burned tiny holes in the canvas, and no matter how many times they tried smearing tar over them, they didn't get them all. Dal washed her hands and face, brushed her teeth, then grabbed her now-warm sleeping bag and ran with it to her tent. She took off her shoes but didn't remove her clothes. After a couple of nights in a motel unit with central heating, the damp night air felt uncomfortable. "One of these days," she promised herself, "I'll sleep in a warm bed every night of my life."

Dal woke up abruptly at half past two in the morning. It took her a moment or two to realize that the things thumping and slamming against the side of the tent were the empty seedling boxes. The wind was howling, her tent billowed and strained against the pegs, and she could hear the nylon flysheet thrumming. Someone yelled and someone else hollered a reply, and off to the right something big and metal crashed, then rolled over the rocky ground, clanging and rattling. Dal groped for her work boots. First things first. Even in the dark she knew where her jacket was, and she grabbed for it, got her arms into it and fastened a couple of the snaps. Kneeling in the madly jittering tent, she scooped up her sleeping bag, tucked it under her arm, then unzipped the front and crawled out into a dark world that sounded as if it had started to come apart along the seams.

She was the first one in the cook tent. She managed to find and light a kerosene lamp, and by its dim light she spread her sleeping bag under a table, then went back out into the dark and groped her way to her tent. An empty box hammered her between the shoulders, almost knocking her to her knees. She stumbled, and then her tent was under her hands and she caught her balance. All she had to do was pull on the fibreglass rods and they came apart at the connectors. Her tent collapsed and she grabbed at it, rumpling it any which way and scooping it up, then raced back to the cook tent with it.

She dumped the bundle of tent on the floor and rushed back, but her flysheet had vanished. She was groping around, trying to find it, when she heard Shorty holler, "Someone gimme a hand here, chrissake!"

"Keep hollering so I can find you!" she called.

"I've got him," someone answered.

She slipped again and fell face down into the mud. "Oh to hell with this," she muttered, spitting the dirt and grit from her mouth.

Dal went back to the cook tent, got her foam slab and bubble pack out of the rumpled mess of tent and took them to where her sleeping bag was laid out. If she had to sleep under the table for what was left of tonight, she might as well be at least marginally comfortable. Briefly she considered going back outside to see if she could lend a hand, then she rejected the idea. All she would do was add to the confusion of bodies fumbling in the dark, trying to salvage whatever they could before the gale took everything and scattered it for miles. Her back still smarted where the heavy box had slammed into her. Maybe next time she wouldn't be as lucky. Best to stay out of everyone's way.

She finished collapsing the tent and moved the wet nylon bundle into an out-of-the-way corner. Only then did it occur to her to put some wood on the fire and light the propane cooker to boil water for coffee. When they finally gave up and sought the meagre protection of the cook tent, they might appreciate something hot.

Cook staggered into the tent, one side of her face covered with blood.

"Jesus, what happened to you?" Dal grabbed her and helped her to a chair near the stove.

"Something bashed into me." Cook dabbed ineffectually at her wet and mud-smeared clothes. "I think I got knocked out. Jesus, I feel awful."

"Here, let me have a look." Dal parted the hair where the blood seemed thickest. "You've got a cut scalp, and one hell of a goose egg here. I don't think the cut is serious, but scalp wounds always bleed like hell. I've got my pack in my tent. I'll get you something dry to wear—you're soaked to the damn skin."

"All I want to do is lie down and go to sleep."

"Well, you're not going to. Not with a bump like that on your head. Where would I find a towel or something in here?"

She found the towels, did what she could to stem the bleeding, then got Cook stripped of her wet and muddy clothes and into some of Dal's own clothes. Cook was shivering, probably as much from shock as from cold. Dal got her sleeping bag from under the table and draped it around Cook's shoulders.

"Coffee is nearly ready," she said, trying for a comforting tone and almost managing, if you overlooked the trembling in her voice.

They brought Shorty into the cook tent in even worse shape than Cook. He was white-faced with pain and his eyes were nearly popping out of his head with fear and shock.

"He fell on his planting tool," Greg panted, "He's got a hole in his ass you could shove your fist into."

"Lay him on his belly on top of the table." Nancy rummaged under the buck-she shelf that held the wash basins and brought out the industrial first aid kit.

"What in hell all's going on out there?" Dal asked, pouring water into a basin and ripping a clean tea towel in half.

"Oh, just your run-of-the-mill west coast arrival of springtime, I suppose." Nancy was busy cutting the ripped jeans away from the horrible mess that was Shorty's arse. "Some places get sylvan breezes, we get hurricanes. Nothing in this country is middle of the road. Everything winds up exaggerated to the nth degree."

The rest of the crew came into the tent, soaked to the skin and smeared with mud.

"Jesus," Maggy breathed. "That must smart something fierce."

"Christ, you're killin' me," Shorty gasped, his eyes rolling.

"G'wan with you, I haven't even touched you yet. I'll make sure you get compensation, don't worry about that."

"I don't think he's even thought about it," Maggy laughed nervously. "I think all he's worried about is whether or not he's got any butt cheek left."

Nancy gestured for Kid to shine a flashlight on the wound. "Guess the hoptycopty isn't going to get off the ground tonight. So what do you think, Kid, should we wait for daylight or are you going to drive Shorty to town tonight?"

"I'm not goin' anywhere in that van," Shorty said, and he laid his face on the tabletop and sighed like a little kid. "Jesus, all I wanted was a job, you know? Just a damn job."

Daylight arrived, but barely. The wind was still howling like fury, and the rain came sideways. Most of the tents had collapsed, or been ripped to shreds, or both. The seedling boxes were scattered from here to hell and gone and someone's bright yellow rain slicker was caught in a scorched snag, the torn edges flapping madly.

The boss redeemed himself. He didn't once moan about the boxes of seedlings, dumped and overturned in the mud. He didn't complain that the aluminum canopy for the back of the pickup had vanished from where it had been put behind the cook tent. He didn't whine about how something had gone through the windshield of the truck, or snivel about how much this was going to put him back. He just grabbed his tools, unbolted and removed the two front bench seats in the van, and then hauled his single mattress out of his trailer and wrestled it through the side door onto the floor.

"Any dry sleeping bags?" he asked. Dal went for hers. When she came back, Kid was leaning against the driver's door, wiping at the tears on his face.

"What's wrong?" the boss asked.

"Ah, hell," The Kid managed. "I'm just feelin' like a real shithead is all. I mean, there's Shorty with half his ass ripped up, and Cook with maybe a concussion, and I'm worried more about how in hell I'm going to replace that damn tent. I know I should feel lucky, and be glad more of us weren't hurt, but I borrowed that so's I could take this job, and now it's wrecked." The tears started again. "And damn it, by the time I buy a new one and pay my damn camp costs, that's it for me. I won't even have enough to buy new rain gear. Some days, so help me God, it seems as if a person can't get ahead for sliding behind, and it gripes my guts." He opened the door and thumped his butt onto the driver's seat.

"Jeez," Dal said. "Talk about Hard-Luck Harry. This is his first planting job. He's still learning—every other day he brings half his seedlings back because he didn't get them planted. Hasn't had a chance to make a dollar. And that was a damn fine tent."

"He'll be okay," the boss reassured her. "Hell, I pay enough insurance premiums to put me in the poorhouse. We'll just claim all this gear as if it was company property. Just remember, like you said, they were all of them damn fine tents. Three-four hundred a shot, right?"

"And the sleeping bags. Jesus, don't forget the top-of-the-line brand-new double thermal waterproof and gorgeous sleeping bags," Dal laughed.

He grinned at her and took the sleeping bag. "Thanks." He turned to leave, then looked over his shoulder at her. "I have to agree with him about the gripe my guts, though. Son of a bitch, eh?"

Cook came from the tent supported on one side by Nancy, who was obviously a bit frightened. Small wonder—Cook was the colour of old cottage cheese, her footsteps unsteady. Dal was sure she wasn't fully aware of where she was or what was going on.

"Don't let her go to sleep," Nancy warned, "even if you have to pinch her to keep her awake."

The guys carried Shorty from the cook tent and laid him belly down on the boss's single mattress. His face was flushed with pain and tears slid unheeded down his face.

"Hey, guy," Dal said gently. "You just hang on. You're going to be fine. They'll take good care of you."

"Lousy luck," he nodded. "Trust me, eh. Do I get a helicopter ride? No, I have to get my ass ripped off while the wind has everything grounded from here to probably California."

"You know what they say," she agreed. "For some of us, if it wasn't for bad luck we'd be shit out of luck."

"God, I hope I don't leak all over your sleeping bag."

"Don't worry about it, we're all getting new stuff. Just you take care of yourself. You know what they say. If you don't take care of your ass, nobody else will."

He tried to smile but what he managed looked more like a twisted snarl of raw agony. The towels covering his butt were already stained red and Dal could only hope he didn't wind up losing so much blood that he was in real trouble by the time he got to hospital.

They watched the van drive off, mud and water spraying from the tires. Dal didn't know how anyone else was feeling, but all she wanted to do was lie down, go to sleep and not wake up until the sun was shining and the cleanup was finished.

"We have to make a list of everything that got wrecked," said Nancy. "You heard the boss, he's got insurance."

"As far as I'm concerned," Maggy said, well on her way to sounding defiant, "we all of us lost everything, including our socks and skivvies. We sure as hell aren't going to be making any money for the next while. Those damn seedlings are scattered from hell to breakfast."

"Speaking of which," one of the guys said hopefully, "does anyone know how to cook?"

"What? You mean you don't?" Maggy shook her head in disgust. "I don't know why you guys think we're the only ones can open a can of pork and beans and heat it up. If you can't cook, you don"t deserve to eat!"

Dahlia took over as cook. She figured it wasn't all that different from turning out a big dinner at home. She had some trouble finding stuff at first, but every kitchen has its challenges. By noon she had a huge pot of soup, so full of rice, beans and macaroni that it could have passed as stew.

"Can you believe," Maggy sighed, "that just about this time yesterday we were checking out of a motel, with real beds, bathtubs and clean towels?"

"Live in the moment or you'll go crazy," Nancy warned. She tasted her soup, nodded approval, and reached for a baking powder biscuit. "I could show you how to make frybread," she offered.

"You want frybread? I'll have you some for suppertime."

"You trying to tell me you know how to make frybread? I don't believe it. You guys can't make good frybread."

"Hey, you, suck back, eh? What do you think, you invented the stuff? We'll get you on appropriation of culture if you aren't careful."

"Oh, yeah, listen to you, next you'll be telling me you brought it with you from Europe, I suppose."

"Yeah, we did, but mostly we called it bannock."

"G'wan, frybread and bannock are two different things."

"My eye they are."

"My ass if they aren't."

"Bake off," Dal challenged.

"You'll lose. You guys never learn. You'll wind up with one eye and a patch over the other. You'll see."

"You'll be the one with a patch. Where your ass was."

"Oh yeah, sure, it's always the same with you guys." She was laughing. "I know what you're up to. You just want to watch how I do it so you can swipe the recipe."

"I know the recipe."

"Nah, you only know the recipe for bannock. But you make good soup. Of course it could use a bit of meat, but under the circumstances...and aren't they just the most unreal set of them you'd want to contend with? Can you believe this? Jeez aitch, Dahlia." Nancy's eyes glistened with tears. "I swallowed the crap, you know, about how education was the key to the future and rah rah rah, and I got my grade 12. Except somehow there weren't any jobs at the bank, or the credit union, or anywhere else that paid more than minimum wage. And I didn't want to clean toilets in the local hotel or walk around with a tray of draft beer weighing down my arm. Grade god-damn 12! And here I am. I coulda done this with grade two."

"Yeah, well…here we all are, I guess."

"I used to blame you guys. Then I went down and put in my application for a job in the band office and guess what? I didn't get it." She smiled sourly. "We got our own version of political bullshit, eh?"

"Learned it from us, I suppose." Dal tried to tease Nancy out of her black mood.

"Maybe. Maybe we always had it. Who would know? Someone with a relative on the band council got the job. A guy. He had grade eight and didn't know a computer from a can of beans. They paid him good wages while he took a course on how to use one. He had to take it over again because he failed the first time. When I bitched they said, Oh but he's got a family, he needs the job. Well, I said, I need the goddamn thing too. And here I am, years later, and the only good thing about it is I've still got this lousy job and he's back on welfare. Him and his lousy relatives!"

"There, see, there's justice in the world after all."

"You believe that and you'll believe anything. Hell, you'll even believe bannock is frybread!"

By the time the boss got back with Cook, the campsite was as cleaned up as it was ever going to be and the broken glass had been swept out of the pickup and a tarp stretched over the hole. Half of Cook's hair had been shaved off, and there was a startlingly white bandage over the five stitches on her head.

"Shorty's staying in hospital," she told them before they could ask. "They're probably going to air evac him to Vancouver as soon as they can get him a ride. They say they'll probably have to do plastic surgery on that awful mess that used to be one half of his bum."

"Well, there you have it, him and half the movie stars in Hollywood. How is he?"

"At least he can make jokes about it. He's calling himself the Half-Assed Hero. I asked him what he did that was so heroic and he said he'd try to figure out a good story to tell."

The boss had new sleeping bags, and brand new tents as well. "It's too damn late to start pitching tents," he said. "Might as well just set ourselves up in the cook tent. At least it'll be warm. Got some groundsheets and some inflatable mattresses too." He grinned tiredly. "Might as well, the insurance is paying."

The weather improved, although as Dal had said, it couldn't have got much worse. For the most part the new tents were bigger and in better shape than the ruined ones had been, and the replacement sleeping bags were top-of-the-line. The crew made jokes about how, as long as he was spending the insurance company's money and not his own, the boss would settle for nothing but the best. He just grinned at them and began eating in the cook tent with them instead of carrying his meal to his trailer.

When he found out that Nancy not only knew how to run a computer but had bookkeeping and accounting courses under her belt, he sighed with relief. "Ten bucks an hour," he offered.

"Thirteen, or you can just keep on doing it yourself," she told him. He pretended to be outraged. He grabbed at his head and made as if he was pulling out the last of his hair, but he agreed.

Day by day the snowline receded and they chased it up the slopes, working longer and longer hours as the days lengthened. There wasn't much to do in camp except sit around in the cook tent and play cards or swap books and magazines. Every two weeks they called a halt to the planting and went into town for motel beds, bathtubs and some cold brews in the pub.

Everyone knew Cook and Nancy were a thing, they even made jokes about it, and more than one indirect question was asked of Dahlia and Maggy.

"Not me," Dahlia answered. "I'm too old to have the energy for that and this damn job. And if I quit, you'll know it's because I suddenly remembered what a sex life was like and made my choice."

"Oh, I'm all for it," Maggy teased, "but you heard what she said, and what can I do except slobber hopefully."

"I'll sit down beside you and do some slobbering myself." The Kid wasn't pale and skinny any more, and the harried look was gone from his face. "And if she ever makes that choice, I'll quit this job and tag on after her."

"Your problem is you've been out in the bush so long anyone looks good, even someone who's damn near old enough to be your mother," Dahlia told him. He just grinned and shook his head.

"You say you're too old," and he wasn't teasing, "but every day you plant at least twice what I do."

"Tell you what." Dal surprised herself. "You come with me. We'll plant side by side for a couple of days. You can't fight this country, you can't make it do what you want. You have to learn to use your eyes, find the places the planting tool will go in without making your arm feel as if it's gone numb. You learn which rock you can roll out of the way and which one you just leave."

"Yeah," Maggy grinned. "It's like sex, it isn't what you do it's how you do it."

"Well, that's no help." He pulled a face. "I know nothing about the other, either."

Springtime faded into summer, and the days got hotter and hotter until they all knew they were ready to wind it down and pack up the camp. They finished their last shipment of seedlings and started folding it all away. By then they were so well established it was like moving a small town. They had one last night in the motel and then Kid drove them out, through Campbell River, past Black Creek and Dove Creek, through Courtenay and down the Island Highway. They stopped once for hamburgers and fries, and three times for quick trips into the bush to drain their bladders, and then Dahlia was off-loading her stuff at the bus depot and waving frantically for one of the half-dozen waiting cabs.

"See you when the rains start again," she promised. "If you're in town, I'm in the book. And guess what, I've got a near-new sleeping bag you can use."

"Maybe I will." Nancy leaned forward and kissed Dahlia on the cheek. "But you have to promise me you won't try to get me to eat any of that stuff you call frybread. Jesus, Dahlia, you do not put raisins in frybread!"

"Of course you do," Dahlia countered. "And at least I've got you admitting that what I make is frybread."

"Bah humbug."

Dal turned to Maggy. "You remember, now, I'm in the book and there's always room, if you don't mind picking your way through God knows how many kids by now."

"I might do that. Yeah, sounds good." They hugged, but briefly, and then Dahlia was throwing her stuff in the open trunk of the cab and piling into the back seat. Every year she made the same offer and every year the rest of the crew said they'd be sure to drop by, but all they really had in common was the miserable job, and nobody had ever taken her up on her offer.

∽

The kids came pelting out of the house to help unload the cab, and Dahlia felt as if she was drowning in high-pitched voices. She wished Pinch and Duck were there too, but they'd already left on the fish boat with their dad.

"Can we?" Pape asked anxiously. "Can we, Mom?"

"What's that, darling?"

"Go camping. Auntie Pansy said maybe, if it was okay with you. Can we?"

"Camping?" Dahlia started to laugh. "Oh, sure, nothing I'd like better than the chance to sleep in a tent and burn our food over an open fire. But give me a day or two under a real roof, first, okay?"

One night was what she got before they were off on what the kids considered to be an adventure. They loaded up the car with boxes of groceries, enough to make her feel like she was really only making a supply run for the planting crew. Her tent, the bigger family tent, sleeping bags, garbage bags stuffed with clothes—the pile grew.

"Could invade Asia with this amount of gear," she grumbled. "Why does 'camping' have to mean four-star hotel to these kids? She didn't mind that Ricky and Johnny were coming with them, but she thanked all the gods and goddesses that Iris was up with Chummy and wouldn't be underfoot. Iris underfoot was always Iris complaining.

Camping also meant the place up the back of the Lakes. It wasn't a provincial campsite, it wasn't on any tourist map and the closest thing to facilities that it had was the pit Dahlia dug. "Don't forget," she lectured, "when you poop, you scoop. One of dolomite lime, one of loose dirt. Be sure the paper can't be seen."

"Last one in does dishes," Skipper yelled, and Dahlia was left standing by the hole, holding the garden trowel.

"Well," she sighed to herself, "guess who gets to go swimming and who gets to set up camp."

Nobody bothered them. The place was only accessible by overgrown brushy skidder trails, and if you didn't know how to find the entrance you wouldn't luck out and find yourself on it. They heard occasional traffic sounds but didn't even see any, screened as they were by thick alder and wild cherry.

"What do you want for supper?" Dal asked Pansy. "I do the cooking, you've been stuck with it for ages."

"Stuck? You're never going to believe I love every minute of it, are you?"

"Well, you sure can't go out and get yourself a good steady job with medical and dental and all the other benefits as long as you're —"

"Stuff it."

Dal put together a lovely thick stew, used it as a gravy over mounds of mashed spuds. The kids ate enormously, praised the scowse and wheedled until Dal agreed to make more for breakfast the next day. "But," she bargained, "you guys better get busy and catch some of the fish in that lake or you'll wind up eating spam sandwiches for lunch."

"Just about time too." Pan stifled a yawn. "And the best place to do it is off the logs over there."

The kids took their gear to the logs but they weren't ready to settle down and fish. They launched themselves into the water, and Pansy laughed. "As of right now every fish in the lake is over on the other side."

"Ah, well, the Spam sandwich was just a ruse, anyway."

"Anything for some peace and quiet?"

"Not really. I've been gone for so long just about all I want to do is watch them. If it wasn't for them needing to eat and wear clothes I'd sit at home."

"You could go on welfare."

"I'd rob banks first. Do you know most of the kids who wind up in juvenile court are kids from welfare families?"

"Doesn't have to be that way."

"Doesn't have to, but it is."

"Well, let's have a nice cup of cowboy coffee and I'll drop the brick on your foot."

"You have a brick to drop on my foot?"

"Or head, or heart. Someplace that might hurt."

"What?"

"Coffee first."

Cowboy coffee was made in the old percolator on the Coleman stove. "Don't forget the pinch of salt," Pansy warned.

"Who's making this stuff, thee or me?"

"Thee. With help from me."

"Who taught you how to make this?"

"Thee."

"There. Want some scowse with it?"

"You know it. If you look in the big box, under the package of tea bags, there's a jar of this year's raspberry jam."

"God, you spoil me."

"Yeah, but that's okay—it's mutual. You talked about how I could get a job with all these benefits. Do you ever think about how lucky I feel? No worry about a roof over my head, or food on my table, or a car to drive. I'm one of the lilies of the field, not a pansy at all. And, the best part of it is the kids."

"Think we'll get away with this, or do you figure those little vultures are going to smell the raspberry jam and come over and yard the scowse right out of our mouths?"

"Why not put a couple of batches in the coals? You know they'd eat rat-tails on toast if they came out of the ashes. I'll help."

"Friend of mine showed me a different recipe this summer. Want to try it? It's good. It's different, but it's real good."

"Let's get fat. I'll help."

While they prepared the dough, they talked of absolutely everything except the brick, but once the cast-iron pots were in the ashes and coals, and they were eating scowse and raspberry jam and drinking cowboy coffee with canned milk, Pansy patted Dahlia on the knee. "You ready?"

"Ready as I'm going to be. Is this bad news about one of the kids? Are the twins okay? The boat isn't missing, is it?" She was ready to bawl like a calf.

"None of the above," Pansy soothed. "It's about the house."

"The house?" The relief was such she almost dropped her coffee mug.

"They want to buy you out to make way for a shopping mall."

"They want to..."

"They want to buy the place, demolish the house and, as the song says, put up a parking lot. Which means it's time to move."

"Oh," said Dal. "Well..."

"It's going to be a mini-mall, Dal. And either you agree, or a parking lot will start at the property line and armies of untended kids will be swiping tomatoes and hauling apples off the trees before they're ripe."

"It makes me sick," Dal said. "Not the house, it's just boards and nails sitting on a concrete-lined hole. But something about that big mess. All the little stores squeezed out, all those families out of work."

"They don't want any bad publicity of any kind, so they've offered about twice what you'd have gotten otherwise. Never do better, Dal. And you know you were already thinking about it."

"Well." Dal took a deep breath, feeling as if she would never, in a million years of gasping, get enough air. "I suppose."

They sat quiet, as if they knew they'd come to the end of a paragraph, could see the punctuation mark floating in the air, a period, an ending. Dahlia wondered if other people communicated as much by silences as they did with words. The kids were splashing in the lake, Pape's life jacket bright red against the tea-brown water. Across the bay where they were swimming, the dark green lily pads gleamed, the yellow flowers on their long stems bobbing gently in the breeze-ruffled wavelets. A blue kingfisher hovered no more than eight feet from the kids, his wings flapping so fast they were a blur. He screeched and yelled, cursed and yammered, trying to chase them away so he could go back to his work, his crest raised in anger and defiance. Pip was asleep on a towel, shaded by the overhanging salmonberry bushes, her fingers curled, her hand still touching the plastic baby bottle with the rubber nipple. The juice inside was nearly gone and what was left was sure to be warm and unappetizing, but Dal didn't want to remove the bottle in case Pip woke up. If she was under-slept she was the crankiest thing in creation. Dal lit a cigarette and sucked deep on it. The warm smoke did what air alone hadn't been able to do. It filled her chest, let her know she was at least alive enough for that.

"So—him in the tweed jacket with the leather elbow patches. Good old wotzisname?"

Pansy waved her hand. "He's got a job starting next week. Cache Creek."

"You're kidding."

"He thinks I should go with him. I guess it's a nice enough place if you want to live somewhere that looks like a cowboy movie. Yellow grass for miles, trees so far apart the birds carry flight maps, have to make do sitting on fence posts because there's no branches. All of it so dry you can lose five pounds of body fluid just getting out of the car to take a pee. And then you don't have to, it's evaporated too." Pansy grinned. "Healthy place though. Your kidney stones turn to dust and pass from you when you fart. I need green. Lots and lots and lots of green. Shades and tones of green. And I think I'd wither up and blow away if I couldn't walk in the rain."

Pansy smiled, and it was like the safe old times, Pan sitting, legs curled under her, listening while Dal practised and practised and then practised some more, lost in the sounds she was finding, the notes she was playing. "He'd never be comfortable as part of the horde. He's used to being the maypole, not one of the ribbons."

"Maypole?" Dal laughed and nearly choked on her cigarette smoke. "Jeez, eh? How do you suppose people wind up believing that about themselves?"

"I don't know. I tried to explain to him how it was, but he kept saying he didn't understand. He said 'don't understand' so many times I finally told him he did understand, very well, but just didn't want to accept that he couldn't get his own way. He got mad."

"How mad? Noisy mad or the other kind?"

"Just noisy. He doesn't do the other kind, thank God for small mercies."

"Isn't it funny—it's as if the only emotion they can recognize or dare to show is anger."

"Or lust."

"Well, yeah, that too. Sometimes it's hard to tell the difference...or don't you find that?"

"Why, did you lose it?"

"Didn't lose it. Chucked it away."

"Yeah. So anyway, I sure as hell am not going to Cache Creek with him and leaving you and the kids down here! God, who would I talk to? I'd be all alone, and lonely, and when I told him that he yelled, 'Well, my God, Pansy, you'd have me.' So I said, 'That's not much compared to the other,' and he said, 'Oh, well, if you feel that way about it,' and I said, 'Yeah I do.'"

"You okay about it?"

"I'm fine. Really, I am. Seems to me when things start to seem like hard work, it's time to find something else to do with your time. I mean, really, when there's more frustration than contentment and more misunderstanding than agreement, and you're either angry or on edge so much of the time, well, it's time to hit the pike. I think, anyway."

"So you think we should sell?"

"If it was me, and my house and my kids, I'd do it. Hell, if you want the kids to grow up on a big hunk of pavement, we can move to the shitty."

They sat watching the sky assume the colours of sunset, watching the kids cavorting in the water, climbing onto the logs and diving off.

After a long and companionable silence, Pansy cleared her throat. "There's something else," she said.

"Oh God, is this the good-news-bad-news thing, and you've given me the good?"

"This isn't bad," Pansy smiled. "I'm pregnant."

Dal could only stare. She could see everything around her, but all she could hear was a faint roaring, thunder rolling hundreds of miles away, perhaps, or a sea crashing on a black sand beach somewhere.

"Can you say that again?"

"I'm pregnant." Pansy nodded, her smile widening.

"Did you... I mean, they said... Did you try one of those fancy medical things where they fertilize the egg in a saucer or something and then...?"

"Nope." Pansy nodded again. "Just the usual thing. I was nearly three months before I even noticed. I went to the doctor, expecting some kind of bad news. It's been years since I even dared hope." She giggled. "Even the doctor has no idea how, or why, or... He figures it must have happened just about the time you were leaving to go planting. He teases me that I'll have to call the kid Seedling, says if I want a second I'll have to ship you out again."

"Well." Dal shook her head. "Well, I'll be dipped in shit."

"I hope you're pleased. Iris is livid. Says I'm going to be as big a scandal as you are. I told her there's no scandal in any of it. She says I should get married."

"And whozit? The guy with the leather elbow patches? How's he feel about it?"

"I didn't tell him. There might be no end to him if I tell him. I am not moving to hell and gone up there!"

"He'll put two and two together. Twink's dad did. The twins' dad did."

"But they didn't expect you to move to ulcer gulch!"

"No." Dal started to speak and couldn't. Her throat slammed shut. She could only stare at Pansy and try, in vain, to identify the emotions suddenly boiling inside her.

"What? Dal?"

"Omigawd," Dahlia blurted. "Omigawd, Pansy!" And she was sobbing and talking at the same time, her words coming in bursts. "It's like a miracle! It's so...so damn wonderful. I feel... I could burst... This is going to be the most wonderful baby in the world!"

"Yes," Pansy nodded. "And I'm not going a two days' trip away from all you guys because you and the kids are why it happened. Having them full-time, on my own... I think something relaxed. I think it never happened before because I wanted it so much."

"It's great! It's unbelievable, but it's great!"

Dal woke up the next morning knowing that Pansy was right about the house. And knowing what it was they had to find as a replacement.

"Has to be near the water," she told Pansy over breakfast. "Not on, but near. And someplace where we aren't going to be mini-malled again as soon as we're unpacked."

"Not the west coast, though," Twink said clearly. "I'm always cold when we go there, and the place is full of ghosts."

"Ghosts?"

"Yeah. I don't know how come nobody else sees them. I'm not scared of them, but they're what brings that cold, it's the death chill. The thermometer might say hot but I'm always cold when I'm there."

Then the others added their requirements.

Pape: "Trees for Socks to climb."

Button: "I want a dog."

Skipper: "Maybe a pony."

John: "Ride our bikes to school."

"Not need a car ride to get to town."

They figured they knew already what the twins would want. All of the above, convenient for their dad, and a room for them to share, but only with each other.

"Need a mausoleum for this pack," Dal muttered.

"Wrong word. Mausoleum is for the dead. I think. Dark, gloomy, stale-smelling."

"Abandoned hotel, then."

They signed the agreement to sell the house the day after they got back from the camping trip. They had 60 days to find something else and get themselves moved. They searched every day through the hot month of July and said no to every possibility. The kids were like Amsterdam diamond merchants, picking up what looked like gems, finding flaws, turning thumbs down and walking away.

"Too puny," Pape said. "It looks like it'll break. Pretty little railing on the steps, cute fence, gate for a girl's dollhouse."

"Too dark," said Twink. "Windows like tall skinny eyes."

They rejected everything in the north end of town because they said there were gangs of tough kids who would go after anyone and beat them up, steal their money, their shoes, their jackets—even a belt wasn't safe. They rejected Parksville for obvious reasons, then put the nix on Qualicum for others they couldn't explain. Almost said yes to Union Bay, but Twink said the highway traffic would probably flatten the dog Button didn't yet have, and that was that. Maybe Hornby Island? Maybe Denman?

"Not!" Skipper snapped. He went into a near tirade about stupid people who don't want to face the fact that they'd be stuck in line waiting for the ferry to take the bus to and from school. "And no hockey, no swimmin', or anything." He was nearly crying, as if the mere idea made him claustrophobic.

"Okay, Skip," Dal soothed him. "We're just trying to examine every possibility. That way we can know for sure that we did our utmost and we picked the best. Nobody's gonna make you live in a paper bag, okay?"

The rest of the family was willing to look at the islands. They were like Magellan, eyes fixed far away on a place nobody had seen, or like the Salish, who considered the water part of their life, not a barrier between them and their cousins. They caught the ferry, and Skipper held his tongue. He had been comforted by reports of an ice rink, a swimming pool, soccer fields and softball diamonds, with roads connecting and buses running.

When they got there, Dal felt as if she'd been grabbed by the scruff of the neck and set back a good 25 years. The place still had fore-shore, and no condos blocked it, no sawmills or big hotels on the beach, no mess of billboards wrecking the view. Right downtown, for crying out loud, a beach with a playground for the kids, a raft float to dive off and, with any luck, no nameless dead one floating beneath, waiting to be found by strangers.

The real estate agent was young, dressed in jeans, T-shirt and sandals. She asked if they'd had lunch. They hadn't, and she took them to a fish'n'chips place near the ferry. They ate as they watched out-bounders drive into the maw of the car deck, watched the ferry return to the long blue line against the horizon. The afternoon passed quickly. There was so much to see, so much to compare, to discuss, to dismiss again. Dal worried the real estate agent would think them picky, less than serious, a bunch of gadflies with nothing better to do than waste her time.

"It's a big thing," she tried to explain, "a big move for us. The kids have to feel good about it."

"Of course," the agent smiled. "They have to live in it too. Sometimes, they live in places even more than we do. They're home more, they live in a place more intensely, more personally."

And then there it was. She waited for someone to voice doubt, find fault, even a small nit to pick. Waited and then felt obliged to raise some little hesitation of her own. She had to, they were all looking at her.

"Isn't it a bit...big?"

"That's good." Pape was intense, like the time when he'd looked at her, Socks in his hands, his heart waiting to be broken. "No mini-mall, Momma."

She saw clearly what progress had taken from her son. His entire world had been yarded out from under him and now he was looking to her to help him invent a new one.

Six

The house was built entirely above ground. Flooding basements weren't rare in this place where the massed green of second growth whispered of winter monsoons. Whoever built this place had been more interested in comfort and utility than in decoration. Wide board planks for flooring, high ceilings, big windows. The main floor had a living room, kitchen, two medium-sized bedrooms and a huge bathroom. The bathtub was mammoth. Not a coloured, moulded fibreglass luxury tub with jets in the side, but a big old claw-footed wonder with brass taps. The kids stared, grinning at each other. Dal imagined the tub cluttered with rubber ducks, plastic bowls and the Avon frog with the place in her belly to keep the soap. The kitchen would be a pain. All those cupboard doors! So much to paint, to scrub, to keep clean. Each one of them was an invitation to grubby finger marks, scuffs and stains from spills.

Upstairs there were more bedrooms and another bathroom, this one not much more than a closet with a sink, a tub and no toilet.

"Businesslike," Pansy grinned, "and nice to not have someone hammering on the door and wailing, 'But I gotta go!' Might even get to have a nice soak in peace."

"Better to soak in hot water." Dal couldn't let the opportunity pass, it was screaming to be filled with a joke, however bad.

Then they went down to see the ground floor basement space. Long low windows looked out from every wall across the fields where cows were grazing. The new furnace sat against a dividing wall, and hooked to it was an electrostatic air cleaner that smelled faintly of ozone, fresh and tingly like a late summer day after a lightning storm.

"Boys' bunkhouse," Skipper breathed. "Bunks along the wall, TV there, stereo in the other room with a couch and some chairs."

"Big oldie kind of couch," Pape agreed.

"I get the top bunk," Skipper announced.

"We could all have top bunks!" John said. "Keep our stuff under them, like in the army or something."

"We'll see," Dal said. But she knew it made sense. Maybe there were too many women in their lives. Maybe they needed to herd together to feel safe.

The agent said little, wisely letting the place do its own sales job. Dal went outside and sat on the top step, smoking a cigarette, calm as milk in a blue saucer waiting for the cat to return.

"Can we have another look tomorrow?" Pansy asked. "We need to talk about this."

The agent dug in her pocket for the key, then passed it to Pansy. "Tomorrow, my office, at two?"

She left them to wander the place on their own, and predictably, the kids charged off to the orchard to ooh and aah at trees that had been huge before Dal was born. Dal sat on the steps and tried not to hit the panic button.

"Something wrong?" Pansy asked.

"I was thinking. Remembering. Jesus, Pan, I couldn't wait to get myself to hell and gone *off* the farm! The house is great, it's the rest of this gives me the willies. Those cows are real. You know what that means—shit to shovel, hay to feed them, calves caught sideways, the vet driving up and down with a big going-to-Hawaii grin."

"This won't be the same. It already isn't the same."

"Oh, dear God," Dal moaned. "You really want this, don't you?"

They got side-by-side motel units and crammed into one with pizza and canned pop. They talked and ate and ate and talked, then talked some more until the kids forgot why they were talking and began to look like people who were asleep but too polite to close their eyes.

"Go to bed," Pansy laughed. "Go on with you, now, this is silly."

The four boys left and the two bigger girls took Pip into the second room of the unit and climbed into bed together, covers pulled up under their chins.

"You okay?" Pansy opened the last two cold pops, and handed one to Dal.

"Scary."

Pansy nodded.

"Don't know a soul. Don't know if they even have mushrooms, let alone know where they are. What's a fungus plucker to do with no fungi to pluck?"

"You could go back over for the season."

Dal shook her head. "Been gone too much already. I've hardly seen Pinch and Duck all year, and Pip obviously thinks 'Pan' means 'Momma.' Maybe there aren't any small changes in a person's life. Maybe change is like leprosy—either you have it or you don't. You never get a touch of it—you get it, and it's got you."

"Dear me," Pansy breathed. "Didn't expect that!"

"Well, my soul!" Dal felt the tears begin to flow. "I get a lot of time to think out in the clear-cuts. It was all so different when they were little. They start to grow and they get so settled! So how can they do that? Get settled, I mean. How can they do that when I don't seem to know how?"

"Maybe you bought them the time to learn to feel safe. Maybe all those nights away, all those days of hard, hard work, showed them they could dare to feel secure because they knew you'd work yourself to a nub for them and never throw it up in their faces. The things you've done to keep us all together! God, Dal, you just don't know. You really don't know what mountains you've moved. But one day you will. One day. And don't tell me it's nothing anyone else would have refused to do because the welfare rolls are plugged with the ones who have already refused and are teaching another generation to refuse, as well."

"Christ, Pan, you sound like the leader of the Reform party."

"If I was the leader of the Reform party, I'd do the country a favour and commit suicide! I'm not saying everyone can pick shrooms, and I'm not saying everyone ought to be out planting trees. I'm saying if a kid grows up not seeing even one soul who is willing to go off and do a job of work, then the kid grows up not expecting to do that herself. So she doesn't. So then her kids don't, either. And somewhere along the line, someone, somehow, has to do something or the whole bloody country is going to be sitting on its ass with its hand extended, waiting, watching the world go by."

"You and Attila?"

"The difference between me and the leader of the Reform party—or Attila for that matter—is he thinks those kids, those people, are wrong. I think the system's wrong."

"So what explains Iris?"

"There is no explanation for Iris," Pansy laughed, "unless you believe humanity is a living body and has to have an asshole."

At 10:00 the next morning they were back. The inside of the house was familiar now. The kids knew where they'd sleep and they'd even decided which bedrooms would be for Pinch and Duck when they came back from fishing. Now it was the outside called to them. They'd already seen the orchard, but out back there was a ravine, the steep sides of it choked with stuff, everything there from shards of dishes to junked chairs. The broken neck of a cheap electric guitar hung caught in the branches of a fir tree. They could hear the sound of a stream, but couldn't see it for the heavy tangle of fern and salal, wind-down alder and top-snapped cedar. The sun fought to shine through the overhang of dark and lighter green. Even the air seemed tinged with green, an Emily Carr painting that had jumped off the canvas for them. Dal imagined the place cleaned up, with access trails and maybe some steps. She imagined the water she could only hear, saw it clear and bubbling past mossy rocks, even saw the silver flash of baby fish, a salmon-spawning place, perhaps, or rainbow trout. When she looked with real eyes, she knew it was a mess. So much crap had been junked over so many years it would take four hours a day for the rest of her life and the place would still look like Golgotha. Still, it was a pleasant dream, and it wasn't exclusively hers. Nice to share something, even the impossible. And who could tell? Maybe one path down wasn't impossible. After all, someone had built the first house, someone else had built the first bridge. Some things can be done, you just start with a smaller scale, a more attainable goal. That first bridge didn't span the Fraser River, it just went over a creek somewhere.

A path down, then, and at least a section of the greenery tamed to allow sight of the stream.

The chicken house was filthy, the floor thick with old litter and shit turned to concrete.

"Be a bitch of a job to clean this," Dal muttered. "What do you know about chickens?"

"Fried, roasted, baked and stewed with dumplings."

"Right. And this. More of this than the other."

There were two barns, the smaller one showing no evidence of having been built for any other reason than to store hay. There were bales and bales of it still in the loft, some of it yellow with age, some from last year's harvest, the smell faint but pleasant. The other barn was as dirty as the hen house, cow manure stuck solid to the floor. "That's how they used to make bricks!" Dal blurted. "Mixed shit and straw and let it harden. We'll need a jackhammer to get through it."

"Or a flood," Pansy suggested.

"Why would someone leave the place so dirty?"

"Maybe they got sick?" Dal guessed. "It looks like whatever came down was...sudden. The beef is in good shape, but the place feels... unused, or empty. Maybe they got up one morning and looked at the heap of chores and thought hey, there's life to be lived, and just hoofed'er off."

"You think?"

"No. I think something happened. Maybe an accident of some kind." She was suddenly thrust back to the previous summer and the deader trapped in the space under the raft. Such a beautiful world, but anything at all could go wrong, end a life, write finis to a dream.

Heaven knew what the other buildings had been used for. One seemed to be home to half the rats in Christendom, its dirt floor pitted with holes, and the smell of rat piss strong and ugly.

"Where's Socks when you need him?" Pansy wrinkled her nose and closed the door quickly. "If Iris shows up, this is where she sleeps."

"Pray God Iris won't show up here. We won't even mail her a change of address card."

"So..." Pansy let the question hang. It jumped up and down, fingers in its ears, waggling, pulling faces, chanting nyah nyah nyah. Dal tried to ignore it, tried to concentrate on the sound of the kids' laughter.

They walked toward the field where the kids were whipping around in long grass that probably ought to be a hay crop. Dal shouted, waved them out of the field and made a mental note to explain a few basic farm facts. You can run around where the grass is short, but long grass is meant to be hay, and hay is gold. It is more than gold — it is life.

Dal stopped dead in her tracks. "Oh holy fuck," she whispered, "are we back to this again?" She shook her head. Tractors, balers, God knows what and who lifts the bales and how to get them up into that skyscraper-high loft and what did the agent mean when she said "complete" farm? A farm, Dal knew from long, sad experience, is never complete. There's always a fence needed, a gate to be replaced, bits and pieces that fall from machinery and can never be found again. Then you have to buy new ones, and old pieces of rusted mystery metal might turn up in the stomach of a dead cow.

"Oh God, please, write it across the sky, reveal the reason you have decided to jump me through these old hoops I thought I had escaped."

She almost expected to see the letters form, white clouds becoming writing, probably thick, angry, stolid Gothic: "You piss me off, bitch."

"This is going to change everything, Pan."

"Change isn't necessarily bad, Dal."

After all, it had all changed already, and not just because of the mini-mall. It was Pansy. She had paid and paid again for her chance, paid her dues and the taxes on her dues. Hours into years of loving nieces and nephews, hiding her envy and pain, and now, by all that was holy or otherwise, she would get her chance or Dal would die trying.

"So, what I need to know…" She stopped walking, took out a cigarette, turned her back to the breeze to light it and puff, inhaling greedily, snatching desperately for a bit of calm. It was a soothingly familiar ritual, something she knew how to do, had known for years how to do, something to keep her feet securely fastened to the ground. "Do you want this or is it just not-so-worse as everything else we've seen so far?"

"I want this." Pansy looked back at the house. "I already feel as if I live here. Feel as if I've been looking most of my life for exactly this place."

"That's it, then." Dal was so scared her mouth was dry, her throat hurt when she tried to swallow. She surveyed the property around her and stifled a laugh. *Jeez, the things we do for those who are so kind and gracious as to allow us to love them so totally! The things we jump up and volunteer to do, then feel good about, good all the way to the bone, in spite of all sense and reason.*

The real estate agent didn't seem the least bit surprised. Maybe any time people ask if they can look again the following day, it's a sure sign they've bitten hard and taken the entire hook.

"What does 'complete' mean?" Dal dared.

"Exactly that," the agent smiled. "The Pritchards farmed full-time right up until he had a massive stroke. She put the place on the market immediately. There's an inventory here, if you want to take a copy of it with you and study it. Or we can go out and you can check it for yourselves."

"And the critters?"

"The grandson goes over twice every day, early morning and last thing at night, and makes sure about things like feeding and watering. He's quite prepared to continue to do that right up until you take possession. He's also said he'll come for a month or so after, to make sure you're settled and not overwhelmed."

"Decent of him. I would have thought maybe the family..." Her voice trailed off. She knew full well why they hadn't, knew because she had turned her own young back on the endless do, do, do, then do more, nose pressed hard against the law of diminishing returns.

∽

July had been consumed by the search and August was going to be taken up by the move. "A lot of our stuff is not making the move," Dal warned.

"Like what?"

"Like all that ratty old shit in the living room for a start. Some of that so-called furniture came from the Sally Ann or the Goodwill years ago. I think somewhere along the line it died and we were so used to it we didn't notice."

"Going to have a funeral?"

"You betcha. And if there's anything in the basement you do want, you'd better get down there and muck through the mess because if it's there on Tuesday, it's off to the dump."

"To the dump, to the dump, to the dump, dump, dump," Button sang. "To the dump, to the du-hu-hump. Hi ho Silver!"

Bicycles, skateboards, swim fins, life jackets, roller blades and wagons, basketball, softball, track, lacrosse, soccer and hockey gear were moved to one side of the main room in the dark basement. The basketball hoops were taken down—one from the garage, the other from the woodshed. Tools, toolboxes, fishing rods and an old non-electronic hockey game were lugged to safety. "Take that to the antique store and make some money," Pansy suggested.

The kids stared, betrayed. "That's a good thing!" Skipper blurted. "Even Pape can play it!"

Dal rented a pickup truck with a trailer attached and backed it up to the basement door. "Pickup first," she told them. "When it's full, start on the trailer."

While they lugged and Pansy supervised, Dal went to the garden shed. She stood in the familiar place and felt bereft. She needed it all, even the almost empty half-gallon jug of liquid fish fertilizer. She wished she could fold up her garden and take it along. Good land shouldn't be treated so cavalierly, dammit! It isn't just dirt, it isn't something dead, something to be taken lightly. She had hand-picked the rocks, piled them near the garden shed, waited until she had the time to fashion them into a rock garden. The thought of a bulldozer flattening that rock garden caused her physical pain. She had spaded, hoed, raked, fertilized and babysat that small plot of earth and in return it had helped feed her kids. Anything she had done, anything she had given, had been returned five, even tenfold. And now the garden would be covered over with Mr. Macadam's invention. She felt like she was betraying the very earth that had fed her.

Iris and Chummy pulled up on Wednesday morning. A blind person could have seen that a move was underway. "You didn't even phone me!" she screeched.

"Phone? Where? Did you leave us a number?"

"I'm entitled to a honeymoon!" Iris wasn't going to take prisoners. She was set to dismember and disembowel. "I want my kids! Where are my kids? What have you done with them? Oh, my God, you bitch! What have you done?"

"Yeah!" Chummy didn't have sense enough to butt out of what anyone in the family would have told him was none of his business —except, of course Iris, who seemed quite willing to allow the entire town to hear it.

"You shut up," Dal roared. "And stay on the out side of the gate. This is still my place and you're not welcome here."

He ignored her and pushed through the gate, actually daring to bump into Pansy and push her aside.

Dal shoulder-checked him and sent him off the sidewalk. "You're pushing at a pregnant woman there. That'll get you five years easy."

One look at Pansy's face told him more than he wanted to know. "Christ," he managed. His lips twisted and Dal hoped it was the taste of his own bile sour in his mouth.

"Johnny!" Iris screeched. "Ricky!"

No answer. Iris moved like a schooner in full sail, up the front steps and into the house.

"Not you," Dal said, amazing herself with the amount of calm in her liar voice. "You get out of the yard, or I'll have you arrested for trespassing."

"You wouldn't dare," Chummy blustered.

"Hey, Studley, I'd love the chance." She opened the gate and waved at his car. "I'm not fooling, numb-nuts, get out of my yard."

Iris found her sons in the living room, talking a mile a minute into the phone. "Get yourselves into that car!" she yelled. "You're coming with us."

"Not me. I won't live with him," John answered.

"He's a goof," Rick agreed, "and he's weird, and I won't live with him, either."

"None of your lip! You get in that car, not just now, but right now! They can send your clothes later. Now move it!"

They did. Out the back door and almost smack into Chummy, who had thought to head, out of sight, to the back steps and sneak into the house.

"Here, you!" he said, grabbing John by the arm. He'd have been better off trying the old tiger-by-the-tail trick. The noise alone was incredible, all the kids wailing and howling, hollering and shouting, Skipper pulling at Chummy, trying to wrench his hand from John's arm.

Iris lumbered down the steps, swung her meaty arm and knocked Skipper aside.

"Easy, easy, Iris!" Pansy got there before Dal, blocking the haymaker Dal was winding up to send in defence of Skip. "No need to get violent and leave bruises on the kids."

"Don't you tell me what to do!" Iris was off and running. "I'm tired of you and your damn bossiness, telling me what to do all the time." She let the words fly at Dal, who more than ever wanted to drop Iris on her generous butt. "You dare tell me I can't drive your stupid old car, can't even sleep with my own boyfriend. Telling me about phone numbers and addresses, doing everything you can to ruin my honeymoon."

"That's a great trick, lardarse, going on a honeymoon before the divorce!"

"Lardarse? Listen to you. Well, just let me tell you something, you redheaded streetwalking slut!" Years of resentment poured like sewage from a plugged pipe suddenly unstoppered. "All my life all I hear is Dal this, Dal that. Every time I turn around all I hear is how hard Dal works, how well she's doing, how great she looks! And each and every one of those kids of yours has a different old man. Each and every one of them is a bastard! At least I was married—that's more than you ever managed. Just one bastard brat after another as if your damn uterus was an assembly line."

Dal laughed. She wanted to slap Iris hard enough to shut her up but didn't think her kids needed to see their sweet and newly returned mom hauled off to the crowbar hotel on assault charges.

"Oh, Iris!" She sounded, she knew, as if she was talking to an inconsequential idiot. "You are such a pill." She turned away and bent to pick up a fallen spade. Skipper had fallen back against a pile of stuff from the garden shed. Shovels, rakes, a four-tined digging fork, all scattered. Dal didn't want anyone tripping and falling on the fork or the sharp edge of the hoe, so she started leaning them back against the wall of the house.

Duh-Whine arrived in a squeal of brakes. Roaring with fury, he jumped from his brand new car and vaulted the fence. Chummy chose that instant to drag his belt from its loops and start swinging at the kids he was ready to claim as his own. He was holding the belt by the middle, both ends flapping, his fist clenched tight. The first whack got John across the shoulders.

Dal dropped the armload of garden tools and stepped between Chummy and the kids, shielding the enraged John. The second whack got her. Had she been standing up, it might only have strapped her across the back, but she was half-bent over John. Instead of her back or shoulders, the belt wrapped around her head and face. The pain in her eye was so bad she couldn't even speak. She jerked back, her hands flying to her face. She stepped on the upturned shovel blade. The handle whizzed up, slammed Chummy from behind across one shoulder. The tip hammered him behind his right ear. He gurgled and dropped to his knees in time to catch Dwayne's flying foot.

Dal could only hang onto her face. Something sticky was coming from her right eye.

"Doctor." Dal forced herself to speak. All the kids started sobbing.

"Kids, into the house," Dwayne said calmly. "Rick, call the cops."

"He's hurt, oh God, he's hurt!" Iris pitched herself into hysterics. "Look what you did!"

"Holy Jesus, Iris, all you are is trouble in a full sack." Dwayne picked up Pip. "C'mon Pipsqueak, you come with Uncle Dwayne. We'll go get ourselves a freezie from Mommy's freezer while Auntie Pan takes Mommy to see the nice doctor."

He glared at Chummy, bleeding from the mouth and nose. "Then we'll wait for the nice policemen to come and take this trash from Mommy's yard."

"Look what you did! Oh my God, you hurt him!"

"He ever tries to use a belt on either of my kids again and I'll bury the scum-sucking dweeb. Jesus, Iris, couldn't you have found something better'n someone Pan kicked to the curb? He's getting a pot belly, his forehead is getting bigger by the day, and there isn't a muscle to be seen. No wonder he picks on kids! He knows an adult would clean his clock. You're goin' downhill, darlin'. You did better'n him when you were a kid!"

Dal didn't get back home for four days. She didn't know much of anything for the first day and a half. The doctor took one look at what was left of her eye and the next thing she knew she was on her way to the operating room. Hours of surgery and they saved the eyeball but not the vision. Dal went home wearing a flesh-coloured patch.

"Oh my dear," Pansy sobbed.

"Hey, stop it," Dal said sternly. "I know it looks like hell, but I figure I can get me a nice little black one, you know, stylish and all. Maybe get one with sequins for fancy-up time." She let Pansy grab her in a gentle hug. "Don't make a big deal of it, Pansy, please, or I'm going to start bawling, and if I start, I don't know when I'll stop."

All Chummy needed was a whiff of ammonia and he was conscious. But they took him to the hospital to get his face fixed where the toe of Dwayne's cowboy boot had connected. Iris wound up in the pokey overnight because she had taken a swing at Dwayne. An officer told her to stop, but she tried again, and the cop took her by the arm. Iris turned on him, spewing anger, and her opinion of all cops, back several generations on both sides of their families. Out came the handcuffs.

The house was ready for the movers by the time Dal got out of the hospital. What might have taken Dal a couple of weeks to do was done quickly by those who weren't the least bit sentimental and who didn't stand mourning and dithering about what to take, what to leave.

Dwayne and his latest girlie had gone over to help Pansy.

"Come on guys," Dwayne told his boys. "If you want to get out of here, start sweating." The kids were so worried about Dal that they weren't sleeping well anyway, so they were right there, willing to do anything to get out from under the eyes of the disapproving neighbours.

"You watch," Dal muttered to Pansy. "No sooner will we be gone than they'll be talking about 'those Cassidys.'"

"We don't have to leave for them to do that, Dal. We've probably been the main topic of gossip for years. Surely to God you don't think you're the only one saw the Idiot Boy draped across the porch?"

Dwayne applied for and got a temporary order giving him custody of John and Rick. "So what do you want?" he asked them.

"Live with Auntie Pan," they said. Dal noted it was Pansy they mentioned first. She half-expected it to sting, but it didn't.

Dwayne sighed and for a moment looked as if he had a bellyache. "Anytime you want to come home," he said slowly, "the door's open. All's I want is what's best for you."

"Dal, I could hardly believe it was him!" Pansy helped Dal with her shoelaces—bending over set off terrible pains in Dal's sore eye and she still hadn't adapted to the change in her depth perception.

"Don't let it alter your opinion. You can't be a lugan for nearly 40 years and then suddenly wake up a responsible human. Wait half a day, the real one will stand up and bray."

"Maybe that detox program worked. "

"Yeah, and maybe brown cows give chocolate milk."

The moving people arrived just before the real Duh-Whine showed up drunk with yet another Suzie-the-Floozie on his arm. He gave each of the kids 10 dollars, then brought a battered old guitar case from the back seat of his car. He handed it to Dal, a wry smile on his face. "It was my uncle Blackie's. Guess it shoulda been yours a long time ago."

"I don't believe that old story," Dal said, her shoulders stiffening.

"Don't matter." He winked at her. "Everybody else does. Take 'er. My dad said so."

"Dwayne—"

"Dal, it don't matter." He sounded tired, and that was almost enough to scare the spit out of her because Duh-Whine, like all the other men in his family, never seemed to get tired. "None of it matters. Not the old story, not the ongoing gossip and bullshit, not none of it. This was Uncle Blackie's, and he could play like God-almighty-damn. Well, you can play like that too. And at this late date, do you really give a shit? What's that old crap matter? My dad said this was s'posed to be yours. Take the fucker, will you? Please?"

The concept of the Morgans asking please was such a shock that she could only nod, and take the battered case. The handle fit her hand so well she couldn't help but wonder if her hands really were, as they said, smaller versions of the rip-snorter's own.

The truck with their stuff was on the road by 11:00 in the morning on the 20th of August By 7:30 in the evening, all their belongings were in the new house, the truck and workers were heading back to the ferry and Dal felt as if she was about to collapse. Her eye was throbbing.

"Do we unpack now?" Button looked like she was ready to cry.

"Just get your sleeping bag out of the trunk of the Chev, darling, and take it to your room. Auntie Pan is going to lie down on her bed while I find the stuff to make tea. Skipper is getting the sandwiches and spud salad out of the trunk, so if you hurry, the lid will still be open."

"Does your eye hurt, Momma?"

"Hey, only a tickle, okay?" Dal lied. "Hardly enough to notice." She had a flat tin of aspirin in her pocket, and she hauled it out and took three of them.

How they got themselves unpacked and sorted out was something Dal considered to be a minor miracle. But a week later it was done, even if they did have a bit of trouble finding things in the kitchen.

"All those jeezly cupboards and everyone with their own idea of where it all ought to be put," Dal complained.

"I think we should beat them." Pansy came up behind Dal and gave her a cuddle. "You hold them and I'll whale away on them, complete with kicks and a few bites and chews for good measure."

"I feel totally discombooberated."

"Darlin', we didn't want to tell you, but you are, and have been for years."

Before they arrived at their new house the hay had been mowed, teddered, raked, baled and stored in the hay barn. The beef were in the fields now, cleaning up along the fence lines, licking up the bits missed by the baler, spreading their fertilizer directly on the field. The grandson, Nick, came only once a day now, in the evening, and didn't so much do anything as watch Dal and the kids and offer a few suggestions.

"You seem to have a pretty good idea of what to do," he said after the first day.

"My parents had a farm," Dal said. "Or, more to the point, it had them."

"Yeah," he nodded, "by the short ones, eh?" Nick stubbed the toe of his sneaker in the dirt. "So maybe you know how come the place went for sale?"

Dal nodded. "I understand it real good. What I don't understand is how, after growing up like this, my sister and I were so stupid as to buy into it all again."

"She really your sister?" His face was brick red. "I mean you look a bit alike, except for hair colour and all, but—"

"Son, I got twin daughters due home soon. And when you see them, not you or anyone else in town will need to wonder. Yeah, we're really sisters. Same mom, anyway."

"And all these kids are yours?"

"Every last one of them, plus the twins."

"But, uh, no, like, man on the place?"

Dal laughed. "No. Both my sister and I are too snarly for any man to bother even trying to live with us. Besides, who in his right mind would volunteer to put up with all these kids? And who'd want one as wasn't in his right mind?"

She didn't consider it was a lie to claim John and Rick as hers too. There hadn't been a word from Iris since the cops took her off in handcuffs, and the court gave custody to Dwayne. Dal didn't think her luck would hold forever, but until things changed, John and Rick might as well be hers.

The two main floor bedrooms were for Pansy so that when her baby came there would be private space for them and a room for the new arrival when it was older. The boys nattered about their bunk beds with storage under until Dal, who had neither the skill nor the inclination to do it herself, got the number of a handyman from the paper.

Handy Andy looked at the sketches the boys had made, then nodded. "Take a week," he told her.

"When can you start?"

"Now, if you want. Was it me, though, I'd put that stuff on the concrete that stops leaks and moisture seepage, then I'd put down an insulated false floor to keep the cold away. Concrete floors are awful cold in the winter. That'd be, oh, another 300 for materials, more if you want linoleum or carpet."

"Linoleum," said Pan.

"Good thinking. Now, do you want plywood or real boards? For the bunks and such, I mean. Plywood for the floor, it's the best. Even that new stuff, the chipboard stuff, is good."

"Real boards for the bunks."

"I got a cousin has a franchise outlet. Plain Stuff, it's called. You get good quality but it isn't finished in any way at all. The downside is you wind up painting or staining it yourself, but the upside is it's about half the cost and you get to choose your own colours."

"You tell him we'll be down." Pansy was taking over and Dal was more than willing to let her do it. "We'll need two dressers for each kid, and I wondered if you could build like a sort of assembly line desk for homework and stuff all along one wall."

The entire lot of them went to Plain Stuff to see what the cousin had as selection. Dal was overwhelmed by all the different styles and sizes on the floor. And when she saw how thick the catalogue was, she was ready to throw up her hands and head home. But Pansy knew what she had in mind and had already discussed the entire matter with the boys. Consensus had been reached easily and amicably. Two dressers each, and, because they had been quick and willing and pleasant, and because she would have indulged them almost anything at any time, a large storage box built to look like a pirate's treasure chest. "For stuff like roller blades and soccer cleats," Pansy suggested.

"And toys." Pape's eyes were shining. "And marbles and everything!"

"No treasures from outside," Pansy warned. "No frogs, no snakes, no woolly bear caterpillars."

"No. And no spiders, either," he agreed. "I keep my spiders in the stinky shed. They love it in there."

Handy Andy's estimate of two weeks was short by another, but once it was done, the noise and expense seemed worthwhile. Of course, his estimate for labour was short too, and he was openly disappointed that Dal didn't want another bathroom downstairs.

"If you change your mind, you've got my number."

"We'll be calling you," Dal promised, thinking of the kitchen and the cupboard doors she detested, thinking of the floor in her bedroom with the ugly grey paint. Hours and hours of sanding would be needed to get back to the original boards. But who said flooring had to look like hardwood? The braided rug would show up beautifully against wide white-painted boards. And maybe Handy Andy could do something with the windows, which had been painted shut so many times they might as well be cemented in place. It would be nice to be able to open the window, sleep through the summer with the fresh air filling the room. After all, what they'd been paid for the other place was incredibly more than what they'd had to put out for this place, even including the downstairs renovation.

Dal woke up at six in the morning a few days after they'd finished unpacking. The coffee maker was burping when she padded into the kitchen. She took her first cup out onto the front steps, sat drinking it and looking out over the fields. The ground was dry, the paths the cows stuck to by habit packed hard, the breeze barely lifted any dust. The hay stubble was bleached and stiff, and it crackled when the calves cavorted on it. Dal had a strong urge to do something, but nothing much to do. For those who could let themselves enjoy it, it was slack season. Dal wasn't one of those lucky souls.

She headed for the rat shed and opened the doors wide. The reek of rat piss was like a slap to the side of the head. She brought out the package of Warfarin and began dropping it down the rat holes. Wonderful stuff, she thought, and what a great way to wage war. No guns, no flame-throwers, just send in the air force and drop food, specially treated so the smell of it is more than merely inviting, it is irresistible. After the rat shed Dal turned to the green-painted slope-roofed shed, opened the doors wide and clambered up a ladder to open the loft window. Except for a musty smell, the place was fine. She examined it closely—insulated walls, electrical wiring that seemed to be in good shape, plywood beneath her feet. The floor must be insulated too, because her footsteps did not ring hollowly. She thought of paint again, and of a small pellet stove, another window in the loft, maybe a skylight cut into the roof. A guest cottage, sort of. A place to put the overflow. She'd get Handy Andy to build a queen-sized frame, buy the best mattress in town. If Pansy met someone worth bringing home she could bring him here, frolic and romp freely, no need to worry about the kids hearing. Or put bloody Iris up if she showed her petulant face. But no Chummy—not until she had full sight in both eyes and was so old and senile she forgot everything she knew about him.

Dal would have liked to believe that Iris was going to stay out of the picture, but she knew better. After all, they *were* her sons, and temporary stupidity aside, she did undeniably love them. Besides, Dal's entire life experience with her older sister had been stormy.

Iris would seethe and simmer, fuss and fester, and then explode and say the most hurtful and godawful things. When she was over her pique she'd show up and expect everyone else to be over it too. The thought that she might have hurt someone's feelings had no effect on her. Several times she had, in a fit of total fury, denounced Dal and said she would never speak to her again, and each time she had resurfaced, expecting everything would be fine, just fine. But it had never been fine between them. Even as little girls they had clashed. Iris figured she was boss because she was older. Dal figured Iris was too dumb to be boss of anything.

Dal had boxes and boxes of bulbs and corms, everything from the other place the kids had been able to dig up and bring with them. Already the azaleas, rhodies and roses were in. They would probably make it if she made sure she remembered to water them every morning and every evening. She turned on the taps, set the soaker hoses, then started opening the boxes. She had no idea which was which colour. The kids hadn't thought to label them, and they probably weren't even sure what things were called.

She dug, moved sod, dug some more. She picked out grass roots, she dug some more. She hoed, she weeded again, she raked, and, finally, she began planting, an ovoid of colour here, a long thin bed of it there. No overall plan, no carefully designed landscaping. She had seen an absolute mountain of old, old bricks in the long grass behind the rat shed that she could set around the cleared areas, leaving some space so the lawn mower wouldn't become even more of a problem than it was. Bribery would be a necessity to get this amount of yard trimmed. Dal smiled. It could look nice, maybe a bit of a fan-shaped design around the ovoid, almost like a courtyard thing, set up some chairs, maybe a bit of a table, for lemonade. Nobody drank lemonade any more, not really, but it sounds so summery, so "Sat in the courtyard, my deah, and sipped some lemonade." Sat over there on the bricks and guzzled Sprite, more likely, she thought.

The spring bulbs first—daffodil, narcissus, tulip, crocus, anemone. Lilies next, spaced at irregular intervals. Dal had no idea which was dragon lady red, which creamy white, but it didn't matter any more. Just put them in and then, finally, almost on top of the dirt, the irises. She marvelled at the size of the rhizome—she'd get four generous-sized wrist-thick ones by snapping off the excess. Plant them on the edge, 18 inches or more apart, for a clump of colour. At this rate there'd be more of them in the first year than in the other place after two or three years. Except the ovoid was full—overfull, some would say. She needed more space.

Dal started digging holes. Put them along the fence, they can take care of themselves. Get the kids busy with shovels. Three spots each should take care of these, but right now what she wanted was to wash her hands, stretch the crick out of her back, make fresh coffee, sit on the porch again, look at what she had already accomplished and dream of the flowers that would bloom.

In the last week of August, the adrenaline rush began to fade. Even the kids started to slow down, to relax into a non-routine and begin to explore and enjoy, not just whip around trying to see it all at once.

"School soon," Skipper sighed.

"Yeah, but Pinch and Duck'll be here soon," Twink consoled him. "They always make you feel happy."

Pinch and Duck's dad wasn't happy, though. He sat on the front verandah, drinking tea and scoffing down the brownies Dal had made. "Gonna seem pretty damn weird." He sounded like someone who was trying hard not to get angry. "I don't like the idea of not seein'em that much."

"You live no more'n an hour and a half from the ferry. It took you that long to drive south to pick them up, so now you just do what you always did, only you drive north. Pick them up at the terminal instead of at the other house."

He looked around at the fields, the old buildings, the grazing beef. "If I'd'a seen this place first, Dahlia, you'd never have had the chance. It's worth every cent, however much you paid."

She told him the amount and his eyes widened. "We've been look-ing for the most part of a year. Hell, you can't find this hardly any more. It's all been subdivided, bought up by developers, big compa-nies with deep pockets and grandiose ideas. Ruined."

"Tell me about it! There's a Superstore parking lot where my garden used to be."

He sighed, and she knew that if it wasn't for his wife and two kids, she'd go after him all over again, maybe tie him down this time, not just stroll away as if what came willingly wasn't worth having. The stupid damn things we do at times, she thought. Then thought maybe this mood she was feeling was one of the major stupid things in her life. How do you tell? She had never lived with him, had never lived with any man, insisted she have her space, even with this man, who she knew was one of the most easygoing and pleasant souls on earth. At the time they had been joyfully and sweatily involved, it had never even entered her head to have him move in. Yet here she was, all these years later. Obviously the whap with the belt had knocked more than eyeball jelly out of her head. She'd lost an important section of brain cells.

He had another cup of tea and then Dal drove him to his boat. The twins clung to him, eyes wet with tears.

"You know I'll be waiting at the ferry, big grin on my face. It's only for a little while."

Watching them, Dal felt jealous. Not of him but of her own twins, who had something she'd never known. She couldn't imagine herself crying because she wouldn't see her dad for a month. More likely she'd have cheered. But silently, so he wouldn't notice.

Seven

The back-to-school rush was awkward. Not just the new clothes and shoes this year. They had to register, meet a horde of new kids, redo all the post-pissing that is part and parcel of New Kid Syndrome. At least there were enough of them that they could give each other some protection.

But then there Dal was, with long days to fill and no clear idea how to fill them. Pape was at school all day now, and Pip, who really ought to still be a baby, had somehow managed to vault into girlhood and was in pre-kindergarten from noon to three. Dal drove her to school with the little bike stowed in the trunk, but Pip came home with the older kids, pedalling her little white two-wheeler with training wheels.

"Everybody's always saying how she should grow up and stop bein' such a baby," Button reasoned. "Well, how else can she do that but by doing it?"

"Is this a lawyer?" Pansy asked, "or just some mouthy kid?"

"I'm not interested in being a lawyer. I'm going to be a jet pilot."

For a moment Dal had a horrible image of Button in an air force uniform, flying off to drop napalm or air-to-ground missiles or whatever they were dropping these days, but Button had more to say. "I want to fly passenger jets. You get to see all the great places. Pyramids, the Amazon, you name it, boy, I'm going to see it."

"Wonderful." The relief Dal felt was so enormous it shook her. "What place do you especially want to see?"

"South America. All that Aztec and Mayan stuff. And China."

"They eat rat meat in China," Skipper warned.

"Now there's an idea. Probably cut the grocery bill in half if we learned how to cook it the way they do."

"Gross," Skipper said.

"Oh really? Maybe they think anybody who eats cottage cheese has rocks in their head."

"Well, they'd be right about that! It looks like—"

"Don't say it," Dal warned. "I'll boot you if you do. Right up the old wah-zoo."

There's a limit to how much time a person can spend feeling lost and bereft. Here and now leave no time nor place for might-have-been. And the farm wasn't going to put itself on hold just because Dal's heart yearned for the old garden. So Dal and Pansy found the canning jars, sterilized them in boiling water, then set to work. They canned the fruit that the crows, ravens, robins and wretched Steller's jays hadn't ruined, until the jars of jam and preserves filled all the shelves in the basement not claimed by the boys' bunkhouse. Dal bought Okanagan fruit by the case, locally grown tomatoes by the pailful, more fresh corn than even she could believe and still felt as if she was only pretending to be busy. She could smile, she could natter and tease, but something was needling, pushing, demanding her attention, and until she found out what it was, this taut-wire trembling wouldn't stop.

She played her guitar, her violins, the dobro Dwayne had given her, the tips of her fingers flattening from hours on the strings. She even looked at the list of courses from the local college and briefly toyed with the idea of maybe taking something. She just didn't know what, and couldn't imagine any part of it. Maybe she should get pregnant again. It seemed to be working for Pan—she was as content as a well-fed pig. And why not? Every minute of every day her body was busy, busy doing something real.

Dal checked out the large space that had been a garden. The fence around it was a mess. The grass, dock and plantain were trying to take over, but once she used the four-tined fork to dig out the worst of it, she could see that the dirt was dark and rich and she settled herself to the job of getting it ready to rototill. The old man might have worked the farm right up until he had his stroke, but he hadn't been able to work it all. Obviously he had cut back bit by bit, his body perhaps sensing what was coming down the pike.

She dug out the sod, stacked it in a heap and sprinkled Rot-It generously. Maybe it'd be the start of a good compost pile. Sweat ran down her face, some of it leaking under the plastic patch, stinging her eye, which hurt most of the time anyway. She tied a sweatband around her head and that helped, even if she did look like a misplaced gypsy.

When the sod was gone and the garden as good as dug, she got her old and much-loved Troy-Bilt Pony from the building she already thought of as the garden shed, and turned hours and afternoons of September into the soil. When the earth was crumbly and soft, she felt as if the patch was acquainted with her, had reason to trust her. She hauled down the old fence, pulled out the posts, trimmed off the punky ends that had been in the ground. Since they were now too short to keep the deer out, Dal went to the feed store and got new ones, smaller, green-painted with some kind of preservative. While she was there she got wire, lots of it, and more Rot-It, three bags of sweet lime and more rat poison. She came home with twice as much stuff as she had planned on buying. It helped settle her. She no longer woke up in the morning feeling as if she was in a hotel room, her bags packed, ready to catch a bus and go to some mystery place. She no longer turned suddenly, feeling as if there was something very important she had forgotten, something she absolutely had to do, right now.

Dal fastened a length of hose to the tap just by the entrance to the bigger barn. She turned it on and rusty water spouted out. The old manure was inches thick on the floor, lumped and bunched, the imprint of last year's hooves showing. Trying to do anything with a shovel was like trying to dig a concrete sidewalk. When the entire floor was soaking wet, she turned off the tap and walked away. A few hours later she turned the tap on again, left it until just before bedtime, and turned it off. In the morning the manure was a semi-soft muck.

It had been years since Dal had run a tractor. She wasn't skilled with the front bucket—in fact, she was clumsy. More than once she banged it on the floor so hard she scared herself. The first few swipes she made with it she was so tentative she barely scraped the top of the muck. But she didn't drive through the back wall of the barn, she didn't knock out a support beam, she didn't do any of the things of nightmares and jokes. The knot in her belly began to loosen.

She knew she was grinning from ear to ear when she drove the first bucket load of wet muck to the garden fence and dumped it over onto the dirt. When she got the tractor turned around to head back to the barn for another go at it, Pansy was standing in the yard, laughing, clapping and making a happy fuss. Dal made a victory salute and rode back feeling like there might yet be hope of progress. She didn't get it all off that go-round, but she knew when she parked the tractor that she had it figured out. She flooded the floor again, let it sit another night and went up to the chicken house to get started there too. The pity of that was she couldn't drive the tractor in and get right down to it—she had to go at it the old way, pre-Industrial Revolution.

It was awful. The dry litter made thick dust, and where the chicken shit had stuck to the concrete floor, she had to bang and ram with the shovel. The whole afternoon went down the tube, but four wheelbarrow loads later the place was clean. She mixed an entire bottle of Lysol in a big bucket of water and with an old string mop she smeared it on until the walls and floor were drenched. The disinfectant smell was so strong it was somehow worse than the old stale smell of droppings and feathers. She dumped the last of the water on the floor and walked out, leaving time and air to dry out the mess.

Dal slept that night as if she'd been slammed on the head with a brick, and when she woke up in the morning her muscles were tight. But it felt good. She had the barn scraped clean by lunchtime and took Pip to school feeling righteous and proud of herself, as if cleaning cowshit from a barn qualified her for a Nobel prize.

The following morning she took the tractor through the large gate into the garden and, using the bucket, shoved the accumulated cow and hen crap as evenly as she could manage over the tilled ground. The tractor tires ruined her careful tilling, of course, and left deep ruts. She parked the tractor and got the Troy Pony, then spent the rest of the day redoing what she had already done, only this time she was not only turning the soil, she was mixing aged manure into it.

"You're going to have to plant long-distance," Pansy warned. "Stand back a good four feet and toss the seeds in one at a time. Otherwise they're going to land in all that rich stuff, sprout on contact and grow up so fast they'll bash you on the chin."

"Yeah, and the real bad news is with this eye the way it is, the damn stuff will be able to blindside me."

"Oh, God, babe, I'm sorry."

"For what?"

"Reminding you."

"You didn't remind me. I don't need reminding." Even Dal heard the pain in her voice.

Pinch and Duck's father arrived with his wife and two sons for a surprise visit. They drove up in a pickup truck with a camper riding on the back.

"Fooled you," he laughed, grabbing his daughters in a big hug. His wife looked uncomfortable, a feeling Dal shared fully.

"No," Pansy said, "you are not going to sleep in that tin box. We've got scads of room in the house."

"Are you sure?"

"Don't you worry about a thing, the kids will bring in your stuff."

He seemed to know about farming. He checked over the tractor as if he had reason to believe it was being sorely neglected. He knew what "three-point hitch" meant and seemed to understand bucket and mower, baler and tedder, rake and harrow. He talked at length about the how of haying, what to do if and when. He checked out the barn, gave her unnecessary, obvious advice to use the hay in the loft of the cowbarn first, then set up the elevators and move hay from the smaller barn up into the loft. Dal knew all that, Pansy knew all that, and by now even the kids knew all that, but she nodded as if words of wisdom were coming from the guru.

"Where's your chickens?" he asked.

"I was going to wait until springtime and—"

"Now's when they're the cheapest. There has to be someone around here who does eggs in a big way. Find out who it is and ask if you can buy his culls. He'll be getting rid of probably a third to a half of his flock, replacing them with 25-week-old poults."

"Why?"

"They'll moult soon. When they moult they don't lay. You get them for next best to diddly-squat, feed them through the moult, and when they start laying again, there you are. Eggs are bigger from older birds too."

"The henhouse is so big I thought that come spring, I'd get a whack of meat birds, put them in one part, grow our own meat."

"Pigs too," he suggested. Good money to be made with pigs if you go about it the right way."

"Pigs mean killing." She could remember the horror of that, the overhead pulley, pigs hanging by their back legs, their throats slashed open, blood spouting, the pigs trying to scream protest, able only to squeak, their lungs heaving, bubbles frothing in the gore. And when they were finally dead, and it took so long, the pulley lowered them into near boiling water, then lifted them back out and everyone had to scrape, scrape, scrape, until the bristles, roots and all, were lifted from the skin.

"Sure to be someone in town does butchering." He shrugged. "Ask around. Then all you do is back the truck to the door, chase 'em in." He gave her a stern look. "You're going to need a truck, Dahlia. You can't run a farm with an old Chev, however classic it is."

Dal lay in bed that night and wished Pansy hadn't been so swift to set up the visitors in the house. She would have preferred them in the camper. She didn't feel the least bit ready for all this civilized extended-family stuff. More than ever the idea of fixing up the guest cottage seemed like a good one. These weren't the only people apt to show up. What if any of her sibs took it into their head to check things out? And then there were the half-sibs. Some of the ties that bind seem to wrap around your throat two or three times, she thought, and if they don't choke you to death they make you feel short of breath more often than not.

Nobody had ever set aside time to actually teach Dal anything at all about farming. What little she knew she had learned mainly by osmosis. She had never thought of teaching her kids the ins and outs of tractoring. But Pinch and Duck's dad obviously didn't believe in absorbing knowledge. He started teaching the kids right after breakfast, and the noise of the tractor didn't stop until it was time for supper.

After supper he packed up the camper, and the family set off for the next-to-last ferry. Dal felt a wave of sheer physical relief when the pickup was gone. She slept that night as soundly as a baby, as exhausted as if she had just finished planting an entire mountain.

The next morning she opened the back door of the barn, dropped some hay, then went to open the gates and direct the cows out of the hayfield into the upper pasture. She had anticipated a frustrating and miserable couple of hours of it, but the cows had their eye on the longer, ungrazed grass. No sooner was the gate open than they were heading where she wanted. All Dal had to do was wait until the last huge beast had lunged through, bucking, lurching, kicking and slobbering, then she closed the gate and tied it shut.

Getting them back into the barn was easy—all she needed was a flake of hay. She stood by the back door, hollered "Groceries!" and let one or two of them see her toss handfuls of fragrant bluey-green stalks. A stocky, short-legged cow bawled and began to run awkwardly, udder swaying. Grass or not, and there was good grazing in the field, it had been months since they'd had hay, and this fat-layered tub wanted some. As soon as the others saw her on the move, they were moving too. Dal dropped a trail of hay through the back door into the barn and they charged in.

She was glad now that Pinch and Duck's dad had been such a nut for large toys. He had oiled and greased every part of every bit of machinery, and anything that looked as if it might move was thick with pinkish-tinged grease. She hauled the manure spreader out from the machinery shed, then unhitched it and used the bucket of the tractor to load the rest of black butter-textured stuff she'd scraped off the barn floor. With the spreader full, she hitched it to the tractor and headed off to the hayfields. She drove around the field, the spreader clanking, clunking and throwing a fine-cut spray of manure behind her.

The next morning she drove to the Farmers' Co-op and bought several pricey sacks of lowland pasture mix seed. Then drove around and around with the cone-shaped spreader spraying grass seed behind her. Round and round. By suppertime, rain was pouring from the sky. The kids bitched about nothing to do, watched mindless TV and yawned with boredom. As she drove Pip to school on the third day of rain, Dal noticed a large sign on the side of the road: Mushroom Buyer. Something inside her began to relax. If someone was buying mushrooms, someone else had to be picking them.

Dal knew what kind of places the shrooms liked. First hint, look for fir trees. The back end of her own place was well covered with second growth, even had some big old matriarchs overlooked by the ones who had shorn the province. Feeling optimistic, she went home and changed into her drybacks and gumboots.

Pansy grinned and handed Dal a packed lunch and full thermos. "Lo, the mighty shroom-seeker girds her loins and sets off on the hunt for the wiley pines," she teased.

"Lo, the mighty shroom-seeker goes out to get wet to the ass, more like it," Dal pretended to gripe, but Pansy wasn't fooled. "I have no idea where the best places are, but to a trained eye, you know how it is."

"Yeah. You big kid."

Dal drove slowly along the unpaved road that flanked the far side of the property. There was evidence in the mud that several other vehicles had come this way recently. She was sure they had been driven by fungus pluckers on their way to their favourite picking sites. Ahead of her, parked on the side of the road, was a large old van. The grass alongside the road was trampled and she could see where several people had climbed over her fence, twisting the wire, pulling the section down, wrecking a good five feet of it. She would have to come back with replacement wire, maybe even add a few strands of barbed wire to discourage the assholes.

She parked behind the van and locked the Chev. Shouldering her pack with her gear in it, she followed the trail in the grass. Over her own fence, and through the salal and Oregon grape to places where the moss had been pulled back and left clumped. She hunkered down and smoothed the moss back into place. A deep anger began in her belly and moved up to her throat.

"Fuckers!" she muttered. She could see the marks of rake tines. "Bastards!" Everyone knew you don't rake the moss, it can ruin the area for years. You need to treat the bounty with respect, think of next year, and the year after that, think of what was best for everyone and everything. The trees needed the mycelium, and it needed the moss. She'd heard of incidents where rakers had been grabbed by shroomers, soundly trounced, their rakes taken from them, invective heaped on them, lumps left, bruises given, threats of what would happen if there was a next time. She didn't anticipate going that far, but she'd have a word or two to say when she caught up to them.

An hour later she caught up to them. "Hey, guys," she called. "This is private land."

They turned, glaring.

"I'm sorry, this place is out of bounds. And get rid of the rakes, okay, you're ruining the moss."

They stared at her as if she was speaking a foreign language.

"Fuck off, bitch," one of them said. "Haul ass or we'll kick it for you."

"You're on private land. Mine."

"Fuck off while you still can."

"Okay." She shrugged, turned and walked away as if totally intimidated.

When she was out of sight, she started to run.

When she got back to their van, she smashed a side window with a rock, reached in, grabbed the lever and popped the hood. She tore loose every wire she could see, disconnected the battery and took it to her Chev. She locked the battery in the trunk. Then, just to be sure, she let the air out of all four tires, wrote down the licence number, got in her Chev and took off as fast as she could, back to the house to phone the police, then drove back again.

She parked on the side of the road, eating thick sandwiches and drinking strong thermos coffee, alert and ready to drive off at the first sight or sound of the owners of the now disabled van. The Mounties drove up, parked their car and talked to her briefly, and together they walked in boldly, Dal directing them.

The shroom rustlers took one look at the cops, dropped their rakes and scattered, leaving their gear, leaving their baskets of carefully wrapped mushrooms, leaving everything, and peeling off in as many directions as there were bodies. The cops grinned and looked at her, then at the baskets of mushrooms. "Well," said one, "they're yours, they grew on your property. Nice of those runners to pick them for you."

She almost felt sorry for the rustlers. They'd lost more than a bonanza of shrooms—their slickers alone were worth plenty, and they'd have to be replaced. If they went down to the cop shop to claim them, they would get nothing but a bunk in the Queen's hostel. Dal expected they would hoof 'er out and find a phone, and by suppertime someone in Vancouver would report the van stolen and someone else would be on their way to pick them up and drive them home. The van wasn't worth fixing. The wiring alone would cost more than the old wreck was worth. Maybe they'd take the hint and decline to buy new rakes too.

The Mounties called for a tow truck, took Dal's statement and finished writing it before the truck arrived to hook up to the van.

"Dear, dear," the driver said, grinning. "Makes a body wonder how they even got it here, the sad shape it's in now."

"Shocking," Dal agreed. "Just shocking."

She took the baskets of shrooms to the buyer and used some of the money to buy stencils, paint and brushes at the hardware store. That night she and the kids set to work cutting shingle-sized pieces of wood from the pile of waste and scrap behind the tool shed and painting them bright orange with bold black stencilled letters: No Trespassing.

"Buggers'll probably just rip 'em down and toss 'em in the bush," she said to Pansy after the kids were in bed.

"Not if it's going to cost them their shrooms and a repair bill. By now the whole town probably knows what went on today. I don't think we'll have trouble with poachers after this," Pansy answered. Then she added, "You be careful out there, you hear?"

"Yes, ma'am."

"I mean it, Dahlia. People get funny when it comes to money."

Dal placed the signs along the fenceline as she moved through the damp gloom of early morning, picking her mushrooms. As she wrapped each one carefully in newspaper, she was buoyed and cheerful because there were so many big ones with unbroken veils, the ones that brought top price, the smileys. She picked until her back began to protest, and it took two trips to lug out all her baskets. The buyers smiled when she drove up to the station.

On Saturday morning the kids were out of bed at the crack of dawn and dressed before Dal. Pansy had a huge breakfast ready for them and had packed their lunches. Pip, thank heaven, was still asleep or she'd have wanted to go too.

Dal was impressed with the kids. No two ways about it, they knew how to work. Skipper explained things to Pape, showed him the difference between smileys and lesser grades. Pape immediately decided they should sort their own, but it all started to get too complicated.

"But I don't pick as fast as Skip does. He'll get mad if he has to share with me. He'll call me pokey and tail-of-the-cow."

"No, I won't," Skip promised. "If you get tired of picking you can help do the wrapping. That way, if I'm not wrapping, I can pick more. The more we pick, the more money we make."

They stopped for lunch and ate ravenously. Pape napped and the others rested briefly, then they were up and prowling, eyes busy, looking for the telltale white nubs poking through the thick layer of damp moss. Dal got them home in time for supper, then drove to the buyer station.

When the kids had counted their share of the money, they stared at each other, their eyes gleaming with avarice.

"Can we go again tomorrow?"

"What are you going to do with all that money?" Dal teased.

"Buy a horse," Skipper said firmly.

"Put it in the bank until I'm rich," Pape said. "I'd like to be real, real, real rich."

"Ah, darlin', you're a man after my own heart."

"What does that mean?"

"It means putting it in the bank is a good idea and I love you tons and tons."

The kids picked all Sunday until dark and would have stayed longer.

"Next time let's bring flashlights," they chimed.

"You know the ones we don't find aren't wasted, eh?" Dal said. "If we miss them, they mature, then spore. That means they pop open and their little seeds fly out to start new ones for next year. It's not as if they're wasted."

But the shroom fever was on them. They sped home from school, changed and raced down the road on their bikes, parked them in the weeds and tore into the stand of firs to pick until dark. Day after day they were on their knees, eyes searching, covering an incredible amount of ground, getting to see their place close-up.

Pansy told Dal it was a good thing. "It's a kind of bonding," she said. "This isn't just a hunk of dirt to them any more. Already they feel connected. This is *home* now."

Dal nodded, but wasn't sure she knew what Pansy was talking about. She knew about the feeling of ownership, but what was this bonding stuff, anyway?

"Never ever take all of them," she warned. "You pick four, you leave a big one to seed. If you wipe them out you'll be ess-oh-ell next year."

"Yeah?" Button sounded suspicious.

"Yeah. Don't think of this as a gold mine to be emptied. Think of it as a bank account or an investment portfolio. Here every year, money at a time when you need it most. Christmas presents, sports gear... Besides which, if anyone tries strip-mining, they'll wind up banned from shrooming."

"Maybe we could spread them," Button suggested. "Maybe we could pick some that are nearly ready to open, put them in places where there aren't many."

"You can try. If it works, great."

The rain stopped, and Indian summer settled on the land with its clear, mild days of sun. The night dews were heavy and the fungi continued to grow. Dal went out every day until noon, then collected Pip and drove her to school, took her baskets to the buying station and sold them and took the money to the bank. Sometimes she stopped at the Chev dealership to look at pickups while the salesmen and mechanics gathered around her car and talked about how they don't make 'em like that any more.

Pinch and Duck's father phoned to ask if she'd found a truck she liked, and offered to go looking for her. Dal said thanks but no thanks, saying she had her eye on a couple, just had to make her decision. She didn't have her eye on anything but didn't want him getting too involved in her life, and to Dal, picking a vehicle was as personal as picking a puppy.

"Tell him that," Pansy said. "Just say exactly that to him."

"I can't," Dal muttered. "He's their dad."

"I don't remember a time you were so shy about telling your own dad to get his somewhat over-large Irish beezer out of your business."

"Now, don't you start!" said Dal, and they both had to laugh.

~

The farm looked different with the long grass cut. There was a tidiness and a stubbornness to the place now. The fences stood guard, the gates did their jobs, the cows moved slowly or lay like big browny-red lumps, jaws moving, savouring cud. Dal wouldn't have complained if the weather stayed like that forever, would even have traded the heat of summer for a lifetime of this. But nothing is forever, and without warning, the autumn monsoons hit.

The first slam of wind against the side of the big old house jarred Dal awake. The second threw her out of bed. She went to her window and looked out, half-expecting to see the bull with his balls in an uproar, charging the house. But she didn't see much of anything except rainwater streaming down the outside of the pane. No moon. No stars. As her brain caught up to her body, she realized the wind was raging, blowing steady at gale force with gusts like massive fists, punishing and fierce. She tried to go back to sleep and managed to doze for a while, but the storm got worse. Finally she got out of bed and tiptoed downstairs. She switched on the outside lights that illuminated the barn, hoping it would prompt the cows to go inside instead of lying on wet grass with the rain lashing down on them. In the slash of brightness she could see raindrops the size of quarters. She made a pot of coffee and settled herself in the living room to watch the storm.

Pansy came out of her room, looked at Dal and shook her head. "Dear sweet lord Jesus," she said, "nobody told us about this." She went to the kitchen, then came back to the living room with her own mug of coffee.

"I wonder if it does this very often."

"All it has to do is do it once or twice a year and it's more than enough for me."

"I hope we don't lose any roofs or gates. Or anything else. Like the front of the house."

"Remember Billy Lewis's joke about the wind in Ucluelet? He said it blew from the same direction all the time, night and day, 50 to 60 miles an hour, and everything had to learn to walk leaning into it so it wouldn't blow them away. And one day it quit and all the dogs fell over."

In the morning the ground was covered with puddles, and still the monsoon dropped water on them. The puddles grew, joined together, became shallow ponds, and suddenly ducks that should probably have already migrated were paddling happily, taking off in flapping squawks when the kids gumbooted it down to get a closer look. Canada geese showed up, and one magical morning four trumpeter swans set down and, miraculously, stayed.

"Probably out there ravaging the fields," said Pansy, "munching down all the precious grass you seeded out there. You'll have a bare parking lot instead of a hayfield."

Dal didn't care. She set up her camera and got some excellent shots. Later she enlarged the best one, framed it and hung it on the living room wall, just across from the picture of Twink, face intent, practising on Dal's classical guitar. By the door there was one of Skipper, wrench in hand, busy doing something to his bike, his hands streaked with grease, and another of Pinch and Duck in yellow rain gear, hard at work gutting fish. Pape held Socks and smiled from another wall, and Button was caught forever working with crayons at the table in front of the window in her old bedroom. John and Rick stood by the Chev, arms around each other's shoulders, one grinning, one serious.

That first storm calmed, but the rain continued. Dal bought a ten-year-old pickup truck and went shrooming in it, leaving the car for Pansy to take Pip to school. Pansy went to collect the kids too. The rain was so heavy and so unrelenting that riding bikes home in it was misery. Besides, everyone else was driving to the school to pick up kids, and there was so much traffic it was hardly safe for a kid to be on a bike or even on foot on the sidewalk.

After Pansy drove them in the morning, she went home and did Pip and housework until it was time to take Pip to kindergarten, then drove back for her afternoon rest, much-deserved, ordered by the physician and the older sister. She set her alarm clock, because more and more now she was actually falling asleep, not just lying there, obedient but impatient. She was feeling the weight of the baby now, and moving with the awkward grace she had so long envied in other women. Often, in the evening when the house was quiet, or later at night before going to bed, she rubbed almond-scented massage oil on her belly and hips. Not because she dreaded stretch marks—she had wanted them for years—but because she hoped it was a way to make her baby feel loved and wanted.

Just as the shrooms were putting themselves to sleep, Dal saw a posting at the employment bureau. She phoned, talked briefly and hung up. "Paid employment!" she screeched, and Pansy jumped as if she'd been goosed.

"Jesus, Dal, I get startled for two now, you know. Another like that and I'm going to hit the ceiling with such force Bowser's going to get left behind and land on the floor."

"Brushing and thinning," Dal chanted. "Brushing and thinning but the alder is winning—hey, I could write a song." She began to sing, deliberately off-key and nasal, a third-rate c&w singer. "We're brushing and thinning, we're toiling all day, but the alder is winning, it just won't go away, we're—"

"Shut up!" Pansy pretended to ram a tea towel in Dal's mouth.

In the morning Dal got dressed in her work gear, had breakfast, and tucked her drybacks under her arm and put the lunch Pansy had fixed for her into her old backpack. Then she clumped out to her red pickup truck, her waterproofed steel-toed boots splashing in the mud. When she got to the pickup point, she had time for a cup of thermos coffee before the others began to arrive.

"Oh, good," the crew chief said. "You've got a pickup. Twenty cents a mile. We'll put our gear in the back."

He had driven up in a brand new crew-cab with a moulded plastic liner in the bed, and Dal supposed he didn't want the sharp-edged tools digging at it. She nodded, and she let him see her take a ball-point from the glove box and write her mileage in a little black note-book. No more-or-less estimates for her. Somehow they all shaved on the wrong side, and she had long ago grown tired of being on the dirty end of the stick.

They started in the pre-dawn gloom, trudging through a mess of salal, Oregon grape and alder whips. Dal estimated the place had been reforested five or six years earlier. The baby Douglas firs were still less than knee-high, and the alder was as big around as her wrist and higher than her head. Old-timers said that if you stood still and there was no wind blowing, you could hear the damn stuff growing. Alders were the biggest weeds on the coast and for years had been considered trash. Hundreds of miles' worth had been burned in slash fires before all of a sudden someone caught on to what salmonbellies had known for years—alder was hardwood, and properly kiln dried, sawed and sanded, it was excellent as flooring, ideal for window frames and sills. You just had to wait until it was well and truly dry before cutting it or it would twist something fierce.

Off to her right she heard the first snarl of a chainsaw. She checked hers and heard off to her left the ratcheting of a brushcutter. She sighed, and pulled the cord on her Stihl to start it up. After lunch the boss gave her a gizmo for ringing the alder instead of chainsawing it. All she had to do was fit it around the small tree and give one hell of a whip with her arms, turning the riggings so the sharpened chain could cut through the bark, through the cadmium layer and into the wood. It seemed easy. It probably would have been easy if there had only been a couple of dozen trees to do, but hour after hour of it and her shoulders, unused to the movements, began to holler protest.

When she got home that night, Dal's hands were swollen, her fingers too stiff to play anything but slow pieces. She wasn't used to the heavy boots. After months in sneakers, the muscles in her calves were tight and hard. She could feel the strain when she sat down—her butt felt stretched. But she shed her drybacks and hung them on the hook in the hallway, unlaced her boots and stood them on the hot-air register to dry, then padded to the bathroom to start the tub.

After her bath she pulled on clean clothes, rinsed the tub, then went down to the kitchen, drawn by the smell of one of Pansy's bang-up suppers.

"Ah, you're a darlin'." She kissed Pansy on the cheek and sighed appreciatively. "I won't perish after all." She checked the stove, peeked in the oven, and sighed again. "Grilled liver."

"Onions separate *and* in the gravy," Pansy said, "with oven-done bannock. And the first jar of pickled beets. They're a bit mild, but Pape likes them that way."

"You spoil me, Pansy. You spoil all of us."

"I know," Pansy agreed, beaming, her face flushed with pleasure and cooking heat. "But you're all worth it. Raisin pie for dessert and a chocolate cake with peppermint frosting. The boiled kind, everybody's favourite."

After supper, while the kids did the dishes and cleaned the kitchen, Dal went out to the barn and tossed down hay to the cows. They pushed and shoved, then settled themselves, and the sound of their munching was soothing. She could easily have pulled up a couple of bales, lain down and gone to sleep. Instead she went back to the house and started the tub for Pip. Dal lasted through that bath, and through Pape's homework. He was to read five pages of his book to her and she was amazed at how well he did.

"Oh, you are my darling." She cuddled him, nuzzling the little hollow in the back of his neck. "You're just so good at what you're learning."

"I want to learn lots, so's I can get rich."

"Yeah? What kind of job do you want?"

"Garbage truck," he said promptly. "They got lots of work and nobody'll be tryin' to take *that* job away from me."

By the time Saturday morning dawned and she could sleep in, she was so accustomed to the routine that she woke up at her usual time. She went out to the barn and found that the cows were waiting—they had adjusted to her schedule as well.

"Dear God, Dahlia," Pinch and Duck's father marvelled, "there's no need for you to do dog work like that! Hell, you can play just about any instrument made, and you ought to be able to make a living doing that."

"Can't put 'ought' in the bank and get credit for it." She did wish the man would try to learn to mind his own business. Was that why she hadn't been quick to grab him when he was available?

"Well, you're a smart woman! Go to school, get a trade, stop beating yourself up this way."

"I think maybe," she said slowly, "you need to look at something. If I went to school, did my upgrading, went to college or trade school, got myself all taught and trained and tickety-boo, I'd still be a woman, and I'd still be in a work force where women make something like 60 cents for every dollar a man makes. That means we lose 40 cents, okay? Not a lot, until you multiply it by all the hours and days in a workweek.

On top of which there's the clothes. You don't go work some 'woman's job' in work duds, you know. You go in drag. All that to wind up doing something that bores me numb or gives me the pip?"

"Well, hell…"

"Why you still fishing? You know damn well the west coast is going to follow the east coast into bureaucracy-induced bankruptcy. You know damn well the best of it's been caught and canned and sold. You know all this stuff about stream rehab and rah rah rah is just so much bullshit to keep you baffled until they shut you down. So what kind of retraining have you signed on for? When are we going to see you selling real estate?"

The silence on the other end of the phone stretched out until she thought the dime had dropped and he was going to butt the hell out.

"It don't have to be real estate, Dahlia. It don't have to be used cars. What about lab technician or X-ray or something? There's always going to be sick people."

"Tell you what, I'll call myself a psychiatrist. There's more crazies than sickies." She handed the phone to Pinch to say goodbye.

✍

Dal had known before she signed on the dotted line that the farm was going to mean the end of tree planting. There were just too many chores for one pregnant woman and a bunch of kids, however willing they might be. She had thought it would be easy to just stay home, but increasingly through the wet autumn she felt a tug of what she finally decided was nostalgia. Year after year she had headed out, right after shroom season, to plant from daybreak to dark, and now, once again, she felt that sense of discombooberation. It was the feeling that something had been left undone, that there was something she absolutely had to do or something dreadful would happen.

And then one night she stepped out of a deep tub of sudsy hot water, dried herself on a thick, fluffy pink towel, pulled on dryer-fresh pyjamas and walked barefoot through a warm house to her bedroom. She sat on the edge of her bed and started to laugh. "Awkitchabitchin', Dahlia," she said aloud. "Here you are, warmer and more comfortable than you've been since before the twins were born, and they're trying to bed down in sleeping bags." The thought of Cook, Nancy and Maggy living in tents thrumming with gale force winds made her present position seem downright luxurious. Well, she told herself, wasn't it Simone Signoret who said nostalgia ain't what it used to be?

Just before Christmas the monsoon stopped and the Arctic front moved in with a vengeance. The ground froze as hard as rock and the cows had hell's own time getting around when the ruts and holes they had made in the mud turned treacherous and hurt them. Instead of rain, the sky dropped snow, probably six inches of it, and the kids were busy making snowmen and snow women and even little snow children. Twink built an abstract construct and sprayed it with water, and the next morning Pape helped her sprinkle some food colouring on it. That night, with the temperature still plunging, they sprayed more water, then left the hose dribbling on one section. In the morning, nothing would do but out with the camera and shoot a whole roll of film. Dal knew she would get at least a couple of shots worth enlarging.

Two weeks later the dog found them. Dal went out to the barn in the near dark and a black form lurched up out of a little pile of waste hay. "Whoa," she yelled, suddenly afraid. What if it bit? What if it was a wolf? She'd heard them howling. The animal stared at her, eyes dull, then slowly lay back down again, cringing. Dal went up to the loft to throw down hay for the cows. The dog just lay there, and when she went back down it barely raised its head.

"So who in hell are you?" She hunkered down beside it. There was still some shine to its brown and black fur, but beneath it she could feel ribs and hip bones. Its eyes were dull and it shivered steadily, and when she tried to get it to stand up, it wavered and wobbled so much she finally picked it up and carried it back to the house. "You bite, you bugger, and it'll be the last thing you do before you hear the angels sing."

She got some warm milk into it, spooning at first. Then the dog lifted its head to lap weakly. In the light she could see cuts on its face, a raw and oozing strip around its neck where the hair had been worn off, the skin rubbed and torn. There were unhealed cuts on the front legs and the pads of all four feet were swollen, the skin between the toes bleeding.

"What a fuckin' mess you are," she crooned. "Looks like someone got fed up with you and tied you to a tree in the bush, left you there to die. Probably would have too, if that rope had been any tighter. Looks like you lost enough weight off your neck you were able to fight your way out of the noose. You're some lucky pup."

Dal had to hurry to get ready for work, and she barely had time to tell Pansy about the refugee in the kitchen before she had to race off, breaking the speed limit to be at the pick-up point in time. When she came home, the dog, mostly border collie with a touch of shepherd, was lying on an old blanket in the hallway with a bowl of water and a bowl of food within easy reach.

"Just goes to show you," Dal said to the dog. "I'd'a taken you for an outside dog, myself. What you doin' in the house, anyway? You paid your rent yet?"

"Queens don't have to pay rent," Pansy said, coming to help with the backpack and thermoses. "The vet says she'll probably be fine, no heart trouble or hip problems, just exposure, hunger and the aftermath of one hell of a bad beating. Gave us some special food for her and some vitamin drops."

"I'd bet the farm the vet didn't *give* a goddamn thing. I bet you paid through the nose for it all."

"Oh, listen to you! You aren't happy unless you can make people believe you're complaining. Give it a rest. You know you'd have done the same thing! Who brought her in the house, anyway?"

"Right. Her. I'll bet you dollars to donuts she isn't spayed, either."

"Psychic. The woman is psychic. Or physic more like it."

"Or psychiatric. I told you I was going to be a shrink."

"You didn't tell me, you told him."

"Ah, him. Yes indeed. Okay, Queenie, stop shaking, nothing's coming down on your head. I guess the kids are madly in love with her."

"I told you—psychic."

It wasn't hard to fall in love with Queenie. Once the food and the vitamins began to work and she could stand without trembling and walk without staggering, she appointed herself Faithful Companion. When Dal went out to the barn in the morning, Queenie went with her, and everyone was convinced that had the dog been able, she would have helped with the chores. She walked back to the house when Dal did, she whined hopefully when Dal left for work. Once Dal was gone, Queenie latched on to the kids, and when they left for school, she glommed on to Pansy and Pip. Pansy attributed it to the natural herding instinct of the border collie combined with the protective nature of the German shepherd. Pape had a less specific but equally believable explanation: "She's a real good dog."

Dal had half-expected Socks to pull a cartoon cat and go into orbit the first time he saw a dog in what he had every right to consider his house. The third morning after Queenie arrived, Dal came down the stairs in the morning and found the two animals curled up together on the blanket, Socks snugged right up against the dog, comfortable and unperturbed. Dal tried to get a picture, but Socks knew all about that little black box and the sudden bright flash, and before Dal had the camera focussed, the cat was walking away, tail upright.

Dal wasn't surprised when Iris phoned. This close to turkey day you're apt to hear from just about anybody. People you don't care to hear from seem determined to use bah humbug time as an excuse to pretend the spirit of goodwill has overtaken them and not only do they want you to think they've forgiven you, they try to convince you that they know you've forgiven them.

"Hi, little sister," Iris trilled into the phone.

"Hi, Iris. What can I do for you?"

"How are you?"

"Just great."

"And the kids?"

"They're fine."

"Johnny and Rick?"

"They're fine."

"How's Pan?"

"She's fine."

"Are you all ready for Christmas?"

"As ready as I'll ever be, I suppose."

"Have you put up your tree?"

"Not yet."

"Are you buying a real one or one of those nice permanent ones?"

"Going to cut one on the property."

"Is you-know-who going to be there for the big day?"

"Who?"

"Dwayne."

"No, last I heard he and his latest kissy-face were going to Whistler, supposedly to go skiing."

"He can't ski!"

"I guess Whistler doesn't care if you can or can't. They'll take your money either way."

"So can I come spend Xmas with the kids? They *are* my kids."

Dal considered a number of possible responses. She could just say no and hang up the phone. She could ask if Iris had permission from the court. She could screech, "Leave me out of it!" and tell Iris to ask Dwayne—he was the one with custody. She could offer to put the boys on the ferry and Iris could meet them on the other side. But in the end, all she said was "Don't bring old wotzisname with you."

"God, you're mean!"

"Iris, I'm not mean at all," Dal said, feeling bone-weary. "There are some things people don't do, that's all. There's boundaries, limits in life, and you just don't shag your sister's boyfriend, whether he's current or ex."

"You've got no right at all to tell me who I can—"

"I'm not telling you anything. Well, nothing that isn't my own business, anyway. You want to hang out with Chummy, that's up to you. Just don't bring him here. I didn't like that sucker when he was lying across my doorway moaning his heart was broken and he'd die if he didn't get back together with Pansy and I don't like him any better since he started beating on the kids and wrecked my eye."

"How *is* your eye?"

"It's blind, you asshole. And it hurts. And I have to wear a patch over it all the time because the light makes it hurt worse. But my eye isn't why that jerk isn't welcome. He wasn't welcome before that."

"You're asking me to choose between my flesh and blood and my very heart!"

"Oh put a sock in it, Iris. This isn't daytime TV. You don't have to choose between anything, not even between being fried and being boiled. Even I can figure out the logistics. You can stay in a motel and bring him on the trip if you have to—just leave him in the god-damn motel when you come out to see the kids."

"So what does he do for Christmas dinner? Or aren't I invited, either?"

"God didn't put me in charge of planning your life. You could have talked to Dwayne, you know, and made arrangements to have the boys go there or something. But no, phone Dal and dump it on her lap. Well, you do whatever in hell you want to do, just don't bring that tub of shit onto this piece of property. And I mean that, Iris. I'll have the cops run the both of you off if shit-for-brains shows up here. You, I'll put up with, you're Johnny and Rick's mother. Him? I'd as soon shoot him."

"How did you ever grow up to be so cold-hearted?"

"I practised, Iris. Just a little bit every day at first, but more and more as time went on, and now I do it pretty much full-time."

"Well, let me talk to my sons. They are my sons, if you remember."

"Iris, for crying in the night, it's all just too fuckin' ridiculous. There's no need for all these hysterics."

Dal passed the phone to Johnny who took it as if he thought it might blow up in his face. She didn't stay to hear the conversation. She went into the kitchen and got a drink of water. Even so she heard Rick holler that he wasn't going to talk. She supposed Iris had heard too.

"I could probably ignore Chummy if he showed up," Pansy suggested. "I mean, it's not as if the guy was important."

"I am damned to hell for all eternity, Pansy, if I'm going to have that gomer showing up in my life at any time of the year, let alone this time. I'm not going to sit one-eyed watching him be an asshole when he can sit there two-eyed and be one."

Pansy nodded and turned away sadly, and Dal wished she hadn't mentioned her eye.

John hung up the phone and came into the kitchen. He put his arms around Dal and held her gently, and she was amazed to realize he was as tall as she was. When had he gone ahead and done that?

"I could phone Dad."

"No need. All that would do is stir the stew with a great big stick."

"She's coming. Ricky'll have a shit fit about it."

"Ricky will do no such thing. Ricky'll behave himself, be polite and knock her socks off with his gentlemanly behaviour. Is she staying at a motel?"

"No luck," he sighed. "The asshole is going to his parents' place anyway. All that go-round and hoo-rah and she knew it before she even phoned."

Iris phoned again, but it was Pansy talked to her. Dal was at work. Pansy didn't drop the brick on her until supper was finished and the chores all done, Pip in bed asleep and Pape in the tub with his flotilla. "Iris is coming Saturday."

"What time?" Dal sighed. "Early, I suppose, so she can wreck the whole damn day."

"Yeah. She says don't go cut the tree until she's here."

"I don't think so." Dal smiled. "We've already planned to hoof off right after morning chores, and I don't feel the least bit ready to change the plan just to satisfy her."

"I'm to pick her up at the ferry. I think I'll drive her crazy as well as drive her home. I think I'll take the Chev—it'll piss her off just looking at it."

Eight

The next morning the boss handed them all their Christmas presents—lay-off notices. Dal wasn't surprised. The snow might only be ankle-deep at home, but up here it was almost to their knees and things were getting more than a tad dangerous, especially with chainsaws in the equation. She didn't bother to tell Pansy about it when she got home. It was Christmas concert night at the school and there was no need to put a damper on things by bringing up the tacky subject of unemployment.

Dal hurried through the chores, the kids helping, then rushed through supper and was the first one in the bathroom to get ready. Pape had bragged to his class about how his mom could play violin and guitar, and somehow, Dal wasn't sure how, she had wound up being volunteered to play at the concert. She looked at herself in the mirror and considered not wearing a patch. The injured eye was smaller than the other, and the coloured part of it was no longer a perfect circle, but other than that it looked pretty normal. But no, the light jabbed at her after even a few seconds without the patch. Well, so what if she looked like Long Jane Silver? If you can't hide it, flaunt it. She chose a patch that Pansy had covered with black velvet. "Looks okay," she told her reflection. "Who knows? I might start a fashion trend."

They arrived at the school 15 minutes early, and Dal found that she had not only been enlisted to play while Pape's class sang "Hark! the Herald Angels Sing," she had a full 10 minutes on the program all to herself. She figured the kids were probably going to do all the carols and she hadn't practised any of them, so she played what she knew best—three fast fiddle tunes, then Hungarian Dance Number 5, a sure hit.

After the concert was over, Dal was invited to play at the extended care unit and the old folks' home as well as with a band. "We're booked for New Year's Eve," the guy told her, "and we're getting paid a bit too." She almost said no, but then asked herself what else she was going to do that night.

Saturday morning Dal loaded kids and dog into the pickup. Pip was furious at first, because she had to ride in the cab and all the other kids got to sit in the back with the dog. But Button tapped on the window and when Pip turned her head all the kids were grinning and waving at her. They parked the pickup near the place Dal had parked when she was in pursuit of pine mushrooms, then helped each other over the repaired fence and trudged through ankle-deep snow. Dal carried the small chainsaw for a while, then Ricky took it. God, she thought, here's another one doing it—his head is past my shoulders! He'll be looking me in the eye next week.

The snow was marked with little holes where the kids had trudged on their scouting trips, and it was easy to see which five-foot wonder they'd chosen. It had surveyor tape tied to a branch.

"What do you think?" Skipper led Dal twice around the tree. "Pretty even, huh? Not too big, not too small. Think it'll do?"

"It's great," she said, with an enthusiasm she didn't feel.

Maybe she was worried she'd take one look at Iris and drift her a good one. But mostly Dal had no idea why she was less than overcome with joy. People talked so much about how they felt, and when she mulled it over, Dal was aware of some of her own emotions. She knew, for example, when she was angry. She knew happy, she knew contented, she knew lustful, but what were these other things? Uncertainty, anxiety and what seemed like scads of others. How did people know what they were feeling? Here she was in one of the nicest places on the planet, with a pack of kids she would die for, and she wasn't enjoying it as wholeheartedly as she had enjoyed in many previous years, and she didn't know why. Maybe she was incomplete. Maybe there was more than the sight of one eye missing. What was the difference between feeling alone and feeling lonely? How come you could watch daytime talk shows on TV and people no more verbally skilled than yourself talked away so easily about things like "feeling vulnerable"? One woman had said she felt "abandoned." How was that different from "lonely"? How did they even learn to recognize all this stuff? Did someone take them aside in high school and give them little talks about it?

They had the tree set up by the time Pansy came back with Iris, and already Pansy looked as if what she felt was a strong impulse to kick, shinward. As usual, Iris was pretending everything was absolutely hunky-dory. You'd have been forgiven for thinking she saw herself as the flowers in May. She had at least remembered to bring a few presents for the kids. She made a big fuss—everyone had to get hugged, even Dal, and then Iris dug in her shopping bag and came out with a tin of store-bought shortbread, which she handed over as if it was the Crown jewels.

The kids concentrated on decorating the tree. Dal had already had several long conversations with John and Rick, who had vented enough anger and grief that now they could be polite, even when Iris started trying to organize the decorating. "The short kids should do the bottom of the tree, the tall kids the top and the in-betweens can do the middle."

"The tree is only five feet tall," Pinch said. "It hardly has a middle. Besides, the little ones really get off on this." She turned from her aunt to an eager Pape, who was holding up a glass bird. "Where do you want to put that one, Papers?" She lifted him so he could reach his chosen branch.

"Is it okay?" he asked anxiously.

"Looks real good." Pinch winked at him, then called to Skipper, "You got those damn lights fixed?"

"Just about. It looks like someone stepped on the plug. The prongs are bent. Okay, stand back, let's see how it goes."

The lights went on and Pip cheered, clapping her hands and jumping up and down.

"Someone do something about that kid," Iris snapped. "She's going to drive me nuts. Doesn't anybody ever do anything about the way she behaves?"

"You know where the door is," Pansy said.

"Well, a fine thing!" And Iris sat glaring, sulking.

John stared at her and for a moment Dahlia was afraid he was going to pull a Duh-Whine and cut loose. Instead he pulled a Pansy, and even made it convincing. "She's just a small sib, Mom. You know how it is, they get kind of bent out of shape about turkey day."

The incipient explosions moved to the back burner and might have stayed there except that after supper, and after the kids had helped with the chores, they clamoured for Dal to play for them.

Iris took one look and nearly shed her skin. "Dahlia!" she gasped. "Dahlia Jane Cassidy! A person would think you'd have more pride! That's *Blackie's* tin-top!"

"Dad gave it to her," John said.

"Grandpa told him to," Rick added.

"I don't care what the damn Morgans decided." Iris was working herself into a good one. "People see you with that and all those awful old stories are going to surface all over again."

"Oh, for heaven's sake," Pansy said wearily. "Number one, nobody but you is the least bit worried about ancient bullshit like that. Number two, if they are, nobody in this town has even heard those stories! Nobody for miles would know bugger nothing about them. Give it over, Iris. Just stop it."

"Well, I'd know." Iris seemed suddenly very satisfied. Why not? She'd finally got a good rise out of Pansy.

Sunday was worse. It started off all right. The tree was up and the presents wrapped and waiting, hidden under beds and in closets because Pip still believed in Santa and Pape wanted to believe. Pansy was baking up a storm and the kids were working overtime as quality control engineers and product samplers. But Dahlia couldn't find enough outside work to keep her away from Iris, who kept coming back to the same old refrain. "It's not fair, Dahlia. They're my kids and you won't even let me see them."

"Iris, if you want to move here, you move here, but not to this house. Get yourself a place of your own."

"And live by myself? You know Dwayne isn't going to sign over custody. The only way I'm going to get to see my own kids is if I live here."

"Well, you're not going to. With or without your gomer, you aren't living under the same roof as me ever again. The last time I saw you, you were screaming at me and calling me a street-walking slut. It doesn't work. You can't stand me and I can't stand you."

"What an awful thing to say."

"It's true, though, awful or not. Everything about me picks your ass. And everything about you makes me want to punch you right in the mouth."

"But Pansy can live here."

"Pansy pulls her weight, you don't."

"Pansy doesn't pull her weight, you pay her way."

"Oh bullshit. Do you have any idea how much it would cost me to hire someone to do what Pan does? And what does she get out of it?"

"She gets a place to live. A place she could never afford on her own! She gets all her food! She's always got money in her pocket!"

"If I didn't have Pan to help me we could never afford this place! And what business of yours is it anyway? When you stayed with us, what did you do? You didn't even look after your own kids!"

"I'm not your damn maid! Pansy might be willing to save you the cost of bringing a nanny in from the Philippines, but I'm not!"

"Right. And you're not staying here any longer than the 27th, either."

"You're a bitch, Dahlia Jane."

"You got 'er, Iris Jane."

Iris stomped off, her pudgy body jiggling with indignation.

Dahlia went into the kitchen. "I need five minutes with Auntie Pansy," she said quietly.

"Uh oh." Pinch picked up Pip and headed out of the room. The others followed quickly.

Dahlia told Pansy about her argument with Iris. Pansy just kept on cutting cookies and putting them on the sheet. Little tree shapes, snowman shapes, stars, Santas and elves.

"And?" she said when Dahlia had finished.

"And so I need to know—do I treat you like a Filipino nanny?"

"Hell no!"

Pansy laughed freely. "Iris is right, partly, anyway. I've got it made. Look where I live. Look how I live. I can even write cheques on your account. On top of which, somehow, no matter what I spend, there's money in *my* account. Woman, I could take you to the cleaners if I wanted to."

"But you wouldn't do that, Pansy. Not in a million years. And if you did, you'd have a good reason." Dahlia was suddenly fighting tears. "Damn!" She lifted her eye patch to wipe under it with the sleeve of her shirt. "Now look at me!"

"Don't bother wasting your tears," Pansy lectured her. "It's jolly ho-ho, remember? Listen, goof, I know, the way I know what you got the kids for Christmas, that I don't have a worry in the world. Now you just go have a bath. Anytime you start shedding tears it's a sure sign you're overtired."

Dahlia had a bath, washed her hair, then went to her room and had a two-hour nap. When she woke up she felt ready for anything, even her older sister.

"Here," Pansy said, handing her a scrap of paper. "Some guy phoned about a New Year's Eve dance."

His name was Jim and before the first cup of coffee was finished, Dahlia and Pansy both knew he was divorced with two kids, his ex-wife had remarried and he was working up the courage to put the tap on Dahlia. She studied the list of songs the band had chosen and nodded confidently. "I know them all."

"Well, we're having a rehearsal the night of the 27th, and another the night of the 28th. Can you make them?"

"No problem."

He reached for another butter tart. "So do your husbands work out of town?"

Dahlia supposed he thought he was slick. "No husbands in sight and no boyfriends, either. That's how we like it."

He nodded, but she was sure he didn't believe her. He was probably a very nice guy and dozens of women would probably be more than willing to step out with him. But Dal couldn't work up the slightest interest. She hoped that wasn't going to be a problem. Her life was not only full, but a tad overfull.

No sooner had Jim left than Pinch and Duck's father phoned.

"Hey, Dal," he said cheerfully, "how's things?"

Dahlia started to laugh. "Oh hell," she managed, "how else would they be?"

"Well, what I'm phonin' about is, can we have all the kids? From the 28th until the 5th? They go back to school on the 6th, right?"

"Let me talk to Linda."

When Linda got on the phone she sounded fine. "Is this okay with you?" Dahlia asked bluntly. "I mean, only two of them are his, and I'd understand if—"

"Dahlia, you know as well as I do what he's like. And I would far sooner have the kids come here, where I feel at home, than have us show up at your place, where I can't help but feel just a bit off-balance. I know there's no reason why I should, but I do, and that's how it is."

"Linda?"

"Yeah?"

"Do you ever stop everything you're doing and look around and wonder how, in the name of all that's holy, you wound up in what must seem to everyone else in the world like a rock'n'roll road show?"

"Doctor Fidget's Travelling Medicine Wagon? A dollar a bottle, good for what ails you, man or beast?"

"So does it ever end?"

"I think it just gets busier. Have you thought what it's going to be like when all the kids start having kids?"

"We got the dog spayed."

"It's an idea." Linda was howling with laughter. "You should have had yourself done years ago—you wouldn't be in the pickle you're in now."

Sometimes Dal would watch her children heading off to school and an image of herself at the same age would come unbidden. Her kids were well dressed, and she hadn't been. They had good shoes, hers had usually been worn and shabby. Her kids looked like any other kids in town, better looking, in fact. Of course they were better looking! They had the Cassidy hair and eyes—that alone put them ahead of the pack. She'd had them too but had been scorned for being who she was. She wanted to reach out to the lonely, sullen ragamuffin she'd been, wanted to say "Hang in, you can make it better, and you will," but the phantom child couldn't hear her over the sound of her own fears.

Those fears still lurked in adult Dal, and she knew it. She wanted to believe her own kids had no fears, but she knew they did, in spite of all she'd tried to spare them. Twink, well, she had something deep inside her about ghosts, about lives cut too short, spirits who mourned their lost chances. Dal wondered if Twink's obsession had started at birth, when her own twin sister had died. Did the legendary bond between twins really exist? All those studies and stories, twins raised apart and both marry men named Jeff on the same date in August, have children 15 months later, one named Colin and the other Colleen. Could they be true? Was there a bond, or was it co-inky-dinky, or yet another manifestation of the glorious chaos that was the infinite universe? Dal herself hadn't mourned much. She already had Pinch and Duck, up on their sturdy legs, truckin' energetically, her going concerns. Besides, she hadn't met the infant who was born dying. She did feel sadness, but she shocked the nurses, who expected her to go into hysterics. She cradled the child until even she knew the short life was finished. Then she handed her to a nurse and stared at the wall for a few minutes. Then she asked to see the other, the survivor, Twink. And she was too grateful to have at least one alive, healthy, raising hell, to be able to wrench her soul with mourning.

Between Pansy and the babysitter the twins were okay, and Dal had headed in to plant trees with Twink in a Snugli. At the time she had thought that Twink was just a very quiet, very gentle little soul. Now she wondered if all those hours of cuddling close to her had been the way Twink grieved for her other half. Maybe it hadn't been placidity but sorrow, deep to the bone, cold in the gut, and the baby unable to explain until the silence had grown so strong that even now it was a preponderant part of the girl's personality. Would it do any good to go into the orchard with Twink, put an arm around her shoulders and talk about the dead half? Would it help, or would it stir the pot, revive the mourning, add to the burden? Twink knew she'd had a twin who had died shortly after birth, but perhaps she needed to talk about it. And yet she had never asked. Dal hoped she was right in taking her lead from Twink. But sometimes she wondered. She had made so many other mistakes in her life, and maybe this was just another huge one.

Pan's son arrived just in time for Valentine's Day, seven pounds six ounces of what looked like a hundred percent Cassidy.

"Duncan?" Dal teased. "What in hell kind of name is Duncan? Sounds like some kind of heather-hopper."

"It's the name of the town where he got started, you fool."

"Good job you didn't get pregnant in Bowser! Or, God forbid, Spuzzum, or Horsefly."

"Does he have hair?" Twink asked Dal.

"Lots of it, and it's as black as tar."

"If it stays that way," Pinch suggested, "we can call him Blackie Cassidy, and send Auntie Iris into permanent hysterics."

Pansy sat in a rocking chair near the wicker bassinet that had held all of Dal's kids and watched the miracle breathe. Dal figured Pansy deserved every minute of her joy. She could remember only too well how quickly she'd had to call for a sitter while she headed out to make some money. Thank God for Pansy, still in high school at the time and not only willing but actually eager to come lend a hand.

"Okay, kids," Dal said quietly, "we all have to stretch ourselves and do more of the drudge-work around here. Auntie Pan has done so much for us for so long, and now's our chance to pay it back. I know you all do a good share, and I know a lot of what seems like argument over chores really isn't, it's just another way of teasing each other, but for the next couple of months it has to stop, okay? Auntie Pan is going to be nothing but nerves and emotion. If she hears a nitter-natter over whose turn it is to wash dishes, she's apt to jump up and start doing them herself, or else lie on her bed and weep because she thinks she's letting us down."

"I'll do the dishes," Skipper said. "I'll wash them every night, and wipe the counters and table."

"I can clear the table." Pape smiled up at her and Dal could have scooped him up and smothered him with kisses. You aren't supposed to have a favourite, and God knows you love them all and would die for any one of them, but Pape's smile and those incredible eyes could turn her love inside her until it threatened to burst out of her skin.

"I'll dry." Button said.

The other chores were picked up just as matter-of-factly. John and Rick took the bathrooms, promising to keep them clean and tidy. Pinch and Duck took the laundry. Pip insisted she could run the vacuum cleaner and everyone agreed with her, even though they knew someone else would wind up actually doing it.

Dal went back to work brushing and thinning again, going to work in the dark, coming home in the dark. She checked the cows as soon as she got home, although the kids were dropping the hay now, and could be depended on to do it, especially after they made the rule that those who did the hay were excused from doing the living room and hallway. Several times the cows got fed more than once, and Dahlia was stuck with the hallway, picking up gumboots and the mud-stained sheets of newspaper they'd put down to soak up some of the muck.

And in the morning Dahlia was the one went out to the barn and chored. She turned on the lights to the loft, hauled bales from the stack and laid them along the waiting hole in the floor, a two-and-a-half-foot slit that ran the length of the loft from front to back. She broke the bale into flakes and dropped them through the hole, spreading the flakes as evenly as she could, and even so the cows pushed and shoved each other, swinging their heads, ramming each other's bellies, firing kicks. But each bale broken open released the smell of summertime, and high up in the darkness of the barn roof, snugged against the massive beams were nests of barn owls, which ran control on the mice and rats. Sometimes Dal saw bats up there, folded up like magical umbrellas. The smell of cows was comforting. They were fat and slow now, and starting to look sleepy.

The third weekend in February, Dal and the kids got the bull separated from the herd and in his own field.

"He's going to be lonely," Skipper protested. "He doesn't understand!"

"Skip, he won't be there that long," Dal tried to explain. "Once all the calves are born, and the mother cows have had a month or two to rest up, he'll be put back in with them."

"But he doesn't understand!"

"No, and I'm sorry I can't explain it to him. But it's the only way I know of to make sure all the calves come at just about the same time. Otherwise, the cows would get rundown and we'd be having calves spread out over a three or four-month period."

"What difference does it make?"

"A big one. This way we can make sure our calves come just as the grass is starting to get green and rich. You don't want to come out some winter morning and find a dying calf lying in the cold mud, do you? What if it was pissin' down rain and the cow had the calf and it drowned in a big puddle? How would you feel then?"

"Poor old guy."

"Yeah." She put her arm around her son's shoulder and squeezed him gently against her body. "It's rough. For everybody."

"Makes a guy wonder about eating meat," he whispered.

"I know. Make you a promise?"

"What?"

"You don't ever have to eat someone you know. We'll sell our calves and if we need meat, we'll buy it from a different farm."

"And eat someone they know."

"That's how it is. Even little dickie birds eat worms."

"Yeah."

"I guess, if you think of how we used to be cave men and women, and you think about everything you've seen on TV about adaptation and Darwin and the Galapagos Islands and all, I guess our appetites developed before our empathy did."

Of course, Iris absolutely had to come up to see the baby. And of course, when she heard one of the kids call him "Blackie," she went into orbit. The older kids watched her, faint smiles on their faces, as if they were watching TV and Tim Conway was doing his old man routine. That got Iris even more bent out of shape.

"Your kids are the most impudent little bastards I've ever seen!" she raged.

"If you put on your coat now, you'll make the ferry with probably five minutes to spare," Dal said calmly.

"What?" Iris got all set to pitch yet another fit.

"You can either shape up, girl, or you can ship out." Dal waited to feel her own anger mount, waited for the all-too-familiar frustration to burst loose in hot words. Nothing happened. All she felt was calm and determined.

"Now, you listen here, Dahlia Cassidy—" Iris began.

"Iris, this is my house. Either behave in it or fuck off. You don't call my kids names, you don't swear at them, you don't throw your all too ample weight around and you do try to behave as if you have, just once or twice in your life, seen how real people live. Or I'll drive you back to the ferry."

"Well, I never."

"That's right, you never did, but now's the time to start." Dal walked off feeling as if she'd won something, and not just another fight with her older sister. Something more, but she'd be damned if she knew what it was.

She went to the barn, leaned on the half-wall and watched the cows gazing off into something only cows see and understand, their jaws moving slowly as they packed incredible amounts of hay down their throats, to be chewed as cud, later. One by one her kids came into the barn and lined themselves up side by each, some to her left, some to her right. "Momma," Pinch said, "why does Auntie Iris get so crazy when anyone says anything at all about Blackie?"

"It's a long story," Dal sighed.

"Tell us, please." John sounded so much like a grown man that Dal was surprised.

"Oh, hell." She lit a cigarette and inhaled deeply.

"Blackie Morgan was your grandfather's brother." She looked at John and smiled. "He looked a lot like you do. Or you look a lot like him, whichever. Handsome? Hey, if you took Richard Gere and gave him the most incredible set of muscles and a body that just never stopped, you'd have about half of what your great-uncle was. And as if that wasn't enough, God shortchanged about six other people to give Blackie his singing voice and his music. I never heard another living soul could play like he did. Of course, he drank more than was good for him, and he left kids scattered up and down the Island, there wasn't a woman safe, especially other men's wives. And there were people, lots of people—most people, in fact—who said Blackie Morgan was my dad."

"Was he?"

"How would I know? I used to hope so. I used to dream he'd drive up in that pickup truck of his and say, 'Hey, Dahlia, darlin', I'm your daddy, jump in the truck and come live with me.' But he never did, and the closest I ever was to him was one night at a dance when I was about oh, 15 or 16, and he was playing in the band. That man took a comb and some tissue paper and played the 'Tennessee Waltz' on it. Every time I hear that song I think of him and his damn comb. He'd lost the black in his hair by then and he had lines in his face and I guess he was starting to look like a bit of a wreck, but you could see who and what he'd been, all the same."

"And that's why—"

"Iris is older than me, so she was in school when I was born, old enough to hear the jokes and the rumours, and maybe she had a rough time of it, I don't know. I once heard a story about how Lolly Rhys teased Iris and said Momma had been stepping out the back door and got me, and from what I heard Iris punched the shit out of her. Of course that only helped build the Cassidy reputation."

"Yeah." Twink spoke up, unexpectedly, as always. "We got some reputation, for sure. White trash is what they told me."

"That's what we are, darlin', white trash," Dahlia agreed. "Of course, the ones who say so are the spoon-clattering tobacco-chewing cousin-fucking fugitives from Deliverance who give good white trash like us a real bad name."

"Cousin fucking?" Duck gurgled with laughter. "Momma! Shame on you! I didn't even know you had cousins. Is that what explains all of us?" And the kids were laughing off something that had ground at Dahlia for years, something still grinding in Iris's guts.

"So do you think Uncle Blackie *was* your dad?" John persisted.

"I doubt it very much, darling. I don't think for one minute your grandma would have stepped out the back door with someone she knew for a fact wasn't going to be around full-time. On the other hand, we all do wing-nut things and if there's one thing everyone agrees on, it's that Blackie Morgan was one hell of a lot of fun. And God knows the man she was married to was no fun at all. So maybe she wasn't looking for long-term and better, maybe she was just desperate to have something bright and happy and shiny to hang onto and remember. I don't know. I do know that when she found someone who seemed to be settled and calmed-down and at least reasonable, she was packed and gone. Took the youngest ones with her, although the old man went nuts and headed off with a shotgun and brought 'em back. Then the cops came with a court order. But by then I was on my own and not paying very much attention. And then the old man moved someone in with him, and she left so he moved in someone else. Then your grandma had another baby, so of course the old man had to match her — prove he was still as skookum as she was and more skookum than the new guy — and it just went on and on and on until it got too hard and too boring to keep track of things."

"Is that why they call us 'those Cassidys' and 'that Cassidy bunch'?" Button asked quietly.

"Oh, hell, no, sweetheart. They've got lots of other reasons for saying that! Uncle Boo can get in a fight with his own shadow, and he's not the only one. Uncle Cliff, well, we all know *that* story. And then Iris. She and Dwayne were like a forest fire blazing against the night sky. But I, of course, have been an absolute model of decorum and decency and…why? Do the kids tease you?"

"Not here," Button smiled. "Nobody knows any of those stupid old stories."

"There you have it, then. That's all they are. Stupid old stories that have nothing to do with you at all. Hell, we haven't even started discussing your Grandpa Blue's brothers and sisters, but you can imagine what they were like when I tell you the old man was one of the tame ones."

"Is it true Blackie Morgan saved a kid's life?" asked Rick

"You know how high the Nanaimo River Bridge is? The old one, not the new one. Well, Blackie was riding in the crummy, coming home from work, and he started yelling to stop the thing, quick. The driver did, but said later he thought Blackie was going to barf or something because he hadn't seen anything. Blackie whipped open the door, ran three or four feet and went over the railing and into the river, with his work clothes on. He'd changed from caulks to romeos or he might have sunk like a stone, but that probably wouldn't have slowed him down anyway. And everyone else piled out, grabbed ropes and all, thinking it was Blackie they'd have to save, and that is when they saw little Georgie Clancy, hanging onto some branches, already half-drowned. Blackie grabbed him around the waist with one hand and grabbed the branches with the other, and one-armed, he hauled both of them out of the drink. When the others got there, Blackie was cuddling that kid and talking to him and telling him everything was fine, he'd be all right. Yeah, it's true, Blackie saved that kid's life."

"So he wasn't all bad, then."

"Few are. Blackie was just someone who lived his whole life right out in the open where everybody could see it and either like it or lump it, mind their own business or kiss his ass."

"So why does Iris go up like skyrockets?"

"Gives her a good excuse, I guess. I don't know. I love Iris—she's my big sister. But she gives me the pip and there's no denying it. She's too bossy."

"Oh, she is, is she? And you aren't?" Twink was looking eye to eye with Dahlia, laughing so hard that the other kids started too. If Dahlia had laughed like that, her old man would have lifted her such a good one she'd have slept for an hour. But however many mistakes she had made and still would make, she had never lifted any of her kids like that. And wouldn't.

At the start of March, Iris went back home. She'd dropped any number of hints about moving in with them, but each hint had been shot down, firmly and promptly. She was still living with Chummy, and Dahlia knew Iris wasn't going to move on until she had some other situation set up where she could do as little as possible and still have a roof over her head. She complained constantly about Dwayne, said over and over again what a loser he was, but whatever else could be said about Dwayne, he was sending support money for his sons. Dahlia had never understood how in the name of hell, feeling as she did about Blackie and all other Morgans, Iris had hooked herself up with Dwayne who was, at best, a faded copy of his uncle. Talk about giving the sib-fuckers something to gossip about! A shrink would have a field day.

No sooner had Iris left than the patched-elbow social worker showed up, carrying a big bouquet of roses and a lovely crib-sized quilt for the baby. Blue, of course. Pansy was so polite a person would have thought she didn't even know him. He gazed down at his son and his pale eyes filled with tears. "Oh, Pansy," he breathed, "he's gorgeous."

"I know," Pansy smiled. "He looks like all of Dahlia's babies did when they were small. And he's a good baby."

"Pansy, for God's sake, he's my son!" The poor bugger looked desperate. "Marry me, Pansy, come and live with me. Let's be a real family."

"But we *are* a family. Look at us. He's got all these cousins falling over their own feet just for the chance to hold him, play with him, teach him kid things, love him to death..."

"Oh, God." He started to cry. Dal looked at the kids and they all left the room together.

The poor guy stayed a week. By the time he had got himself ready to drive off in his new hatchback, Dal had softened enough to feel sorry for him. She tried to tell him all he had to do was get a job in town, and chances were he'd wind up living in the main floor bedrooms with Pansy and Blackie, and he just looked at her as if she was talking Urdu.

"Jesus," he snarled, "everything they say about you lot is true. You're all nuts! Me? Live here? Like this?"

"Now, is that a nice thing to say?" Dahlia was shocked.

"Dahlia, there's people back home saying you and Pansy are queer for each other and that what's going on here is some kind of real twisted incest. Up until now, I've told them they're wrong, but after this visit, I have to tell you, I have my own doubts."

"You should go see somebody," she said coldly. "Maybe they've got pills for that sick mind of yours. Jesus, I hope Blackie didn't inherit any part of it, because if he did we're going to have to put him in the circus geek show with the rest of your fuckin' family."

The snowdrops bloomed and were replaced by crocuses, daffodils and tulips. The entire front yard sprouted flowers and columbine grew and blossomed beside the house. The lilac trees bloomed, lavender, dark purple and white, the fragrance enough to baffle the senses. What had looked like a tangle of messy sticks sprouted clematis blossoms, and another tangle produced blossoms bunched like grapes in clusters a foot long, dark blue and purple with a heavy fruity scent. The days lengthened, the fields turned green, the cows and their calves gorged themselves on fresh grass, then shat streams of liquid and the kids yelled to each other, "Don't stand behind them!" giggling wildly.

Dahlia ordered tons of 18-18-18 from the Farmers' Co-op and got to spend one entire weekend driving round and round the hayfields, the sprayer whizzing, firing out the tricolour pellets. Two hours before she finished the job, the rain came with a vengeance. She was soaked to the skin and happy as a clam by the time she was done and the kids were rinsing out the hopper.

"Look at that," she cheered, "good old Mother Nature is on our side, washing it in so the grass can soak it up. And we won't lose the nitrogen to the sunshine, either." Two weeks later she planted grass seed, mostly tall fescue with maybe a quarter Kentucky blue.

"We should grow grass seed," Pansy teased. "The cost of it is about equal to the cost of gold! Make better money than you make selling hay and beef."

"What I should do is win the 6/49. One of the big ones. Twelve-point-six million ought to just about see us through the next four or five years."

It would have been easy to get carried away with spring fever, but Dal was brushing and thinning full-time, and she only had her evenings and weekends to get drunk on the season. She took the advice of Pinch and Duck's dad and bought a dozen cull hens but ordered day-olds from the Co-op as well. When they arrived, the kids stared. "I never saw no chicken without feathers on its neck," Pape said slowly. "Are they sick?"

"That's the kind they are," Dal said. "Someone told me they came from Transylvania, and their necks are like that so the vampires can have snacks."

Pape stared, then shook his head. "Oh, Mom," he told her, "you'll believe anything."

Dahlia didn't, though. She believed very little. When Jim asked her if she'd like to go for a drink after band practice, Dahlia smiled and said no thank you.

"Oh, come on. What's the harm in one drink?"

"Well, I'll tell you, it's like building a skyscraper. They never start with the top floor. I go for one drink and next it'll be a couple. If I say no to that, you'll say hey, you went for one, and I behaved, and nothing happened and you were safe, so why not? If I go for a couple, the next thing it'll be supper and a few—"

"You're making a big deal out of one drink."

"Who else did you ask out for a drink? Have you asked Bob out? Have you ever taken Louie out? No. Me. Because we aren't really talking one cool beer, and we both know it. This is the start of a hustle. And I don't want that kind of complication in my life."

"Dahlia…"

"Jim, I'm not flirting with you. I don't want a beer, I don't want a couple, I don't want supper, I don't want a date, I don't want a night in a motel, I don't want to sleep over at your apartment. I don't want any part of this. Not with anybody."

"You're serious."

"I'm serious. It's not you—you're a nice guy. I'm just too busy for this stuff."

"If you're too busy," he said, his tone cooler now, "then there's something seriously wrong with your life. Maybe you should look at it, pare things back, free up some time for what's really important."

"You're right." She smiled, and continued putting her instruments in the back seat of the Chev. "I think I'll do that. It's a good idea, freeing up some time. I mean, here I've been coming home from work, rushing through supper, racing through chores, going around like a flea in a fit just to get to band practice on time. Free up time? Sounds great."

She got in the Chev, rolled down her window and looked him in the eye. "Find someone else for the band. I quit." She drove away slowly, careful not to spurt any gravel or leave tracks in the dirt. She didn't feel the least bit angry, but she did wish people would believe her when she told them the truth. Make time for the important things in life? What was more important than kids, baby, making enough money to hold it together, living her life to the fullest and on her own terms? What in hell was so important about drinking a few beer when she could just as easy be learning how to be an auntie as well as a mom?

The days slipped by easily, the hours of her life marked by the kids, the place, her life, work. Every morning she did her chores, then left for a ten-hour day of brushing and thinning. Every evening after chores and supper it was time for music lessons. Dal had most of them playing, and the only holdup was the wait for instruments. She enjoyed this time with them and knew they enjoyed it too. It was like old times, when cousins, aunts and uncles had gathered with everything from kitchen spoons to banjos, and those who didn't play at least sang or danced.

Dal would gladly have stayed with the music all night, but Pansy deserved a break, so Dal took charge of getting Blackie and Pip and Pape bathed and ready for bed. By then she was so tired her ears were buzzing. Once Pape was in bed with his zoo of stuffed animals, Dal hit the couch and flopped. At this point one of the older kids was guaranteed to bring her a cup of tea and a piece of cake or some cookies. She visited with them and looked at homework, most of which she didn't understand. Shortly after, Dal headed for bed and slept like someone drugged until it was time to get up and start it all over again.

Dal took a week off work at the end of May. Haying time, not holiday. It was awful. It was terrible. It was ghastly. Around and around the field she went, the tractor moving steadily, the mower coming behind, rotary blades whirling. It was more boring than tree planting could ever be. She couldn't hear the song of the birds, couldn't hear anything but machinery. No scent of ground blackberry, no perfume of salmonberry, just hot oil, diesel fuel and exhaust. The heat from the engine flew back at her and she felt as if she was driving into hell's outer rim—one false move and she'd tip over and spend eternity there, with too many of her family. Around and around and then she looked up and the twins' dad was there, grinning, waving at her. She stopped the tractor and he motioned for her to get down. Laughing softly, he climbed on the tractor and took over.

Dal walked to the house, certain she was going to phone the real estate agent and sell the damn place here and now, crop and all. Better to live in the Superstore itself and go fungus plucking to pay for the groceries the kids devoured. Maybe they could put on roller blades and get jobs restocking the shelves. They could sleep on the floor, watch the stacks of TVs, demonstrate how comfortable the beanbag chairs were. Why try to stay here, continue this torture? Even a mother's love could be allowed some limits.

"Into the tub." Pansy was so brisk and smiling, so damn at home, farm woman personified—something baking in the oven, cold juice in the fridge.

"When did he get here?"

"Just now. The kids were talking to him on the phone the other night, and Duck said you were getting ready to hay. Here, drink this."

Dal drank, her mouth so insulted by diesel she had no idea what flavour the drink was supposed to be. She lay in the tub feeling like a sponge. She would soak up this lukewarm water, heave out of here four times her real size, slosh and drip all over the house. Her tits would be as big as 40-gallon oil drums and her arms would rival tugboats. Let someone try to even get near her clit! It would be bigger than a banana, and her orgasms would cause mountains to crumble. She'd be known as the mother of the new world. The Rockies would no longer stand tall and the country would enlarge by several new provinces.

Pansy came in again with a sandwich and suddenly Dal was starving. "Thanks, Pansy. I didn't know I was hungry."

"Don't know how you could forget a thing like that. Jeez, Dal, you were out there for four and a half hours."

She ate the sandwich, drank more juice, got out of the tub, dried, dressed and went to sit on the front steps watching the man she had never wanted to marry drive her tractor around her field, laughing happily and probably singing in his awful off-key voice. Then she must have napped, because suddenly Pansy was sitting beside her and Blackie was reaching for her hair, yelping and laughing.

"Oh, my," Dal said quietly. "Life on the farm is so mellow that one day just slips quietly into another." She left the steps, the soft sound of Pansy's chuckle following her.

Dal stood where the dropped grass met the still-standing and waited until the tractor finished the circuit. The man she had never wanted to marry climbed down, rubbing the small of his back.

"Fuck, Dahlia, couldn't you have put your money in a fish boat? The work isn't as hard, and it doesn't smell any worse."

He walked back toward the house and Dal got up on the tractor, adjusted the seat and put the machine in gear. Around and around some more, machinery rattling, banging, grinding. God, is it supposed to make that noise? Turkey vultures were circling the field. "I'm still breathing," she shouted. "I only feel like I'm dyin', gang. I'm not dead yet." The turkey vultures dropped into the mowed grass at the far end of the field, hopping with awkward grace. They seemed much smaller on the ground, their long wings folded and their bodies revealed as slight and fine-boned. When the tractor didn't attack, the ravens came down too, quarrelling, bossing the world, telling all of creation what to do and how to do it. Well, why not? Raven was herself responsible for creation. She was the one who had flown off, found the mountain peaks poking up out of the flood, hurried back to Banba and her grandchildren and directed them to safety. Banba had navigated by the call of Raven's voice cutting the fog, had deliberately beached her boat at the very tip of the highest mountain peak.

A cat, not Socks, streaked from the long grass just ahead of the tractor. Dal almost kept going but something—she wasn't sure what, but it made the hair stiffen on her neck—stopped her. She heard them before she saw them. Four kittens, huddled together, wide-eyed, terrified. She took off her shirt, put in the kittens, pulled the shirt into a sort-of bag and started walking back from the field. Pansy was running toward her and the man she had never wanted to marry followed. Dal waved, trying to signal that nothing was wrong, she hadn't hurt herself, the tractor wasn't toast.

"Here," she said, handing the shirt to Pansy. "I don't know where their mother went to. More vet bills, I guess."

"Oh, the poor things, they're terrified."

"Everything in that field except elephants and who knows? They might be there too. I'll know better when I'm finished."

She went back to the tractor and started it again. Around and around, the field behind her full of birds. Even the eagles decided to come and join in the open-air picnic, the snake sushi, the chopped-mouse pâté.

The hay was down by suppertime, but only because Pansy had delayed the meal. The western sky was streaked with sunset, fading now, and darkness was creeping up from the long dark shape against the horizon, the Island, where the rest of Dal's family—the ones she called the crazy clanjamfrie—still lived, only a few of them leaving behind the tacky low-rent stupidity of generations.

Dal sat down at the table so tired she couldn't even pay attention to the chatter and jokes. Pinch and Duck sat on either side of their dad and it was Dad this, Dad that, what do you think, Dad? And the man might well go through life with no name of his own. The man Dal had never wanted to marry, Pinch and Duck's dad, Linda's husband, Pansy's never-brother-in-law. He didn't seem to mind being called Dad by all the kids at the table and Dal wondered what he would do if she called him Dad.

The next day the sun shone and the wind blew and the grass dried, a blue-green cover on the field. The twins' father talked of protein content, of curing, of learning to tell its quality by the taste or feel of it, and between lectures he buggered about with the machinery, greasing and oiling, tightening and loosening. Dal could easily have got sick and tired of the sound of his voice, but she was too focussed on what was happening in the field. The third day, Dal was back on the tractor at noon, turning the hay. More round and round, but at least the clatter of the tedder was less than the noise of the mower. The ravens and turkey vultures, no longer afraid of the equipment, waited for the next banquet of dead snakes, mice, bush rats and dead-in-their-nest fledgling ground birds. Eagles circled or sat in trees, too chickenshit to land with people in the field, jealous of the bold ones. The turkey vultures ignored even Queenie, who had followed Dal to the field. But they had a bargain with creation itself, had vowed never to kill anything, not even for food, and in return creation had promised that there would always be more than enough for them to eat.

Was Dal going to have to take chunks of her life and feed them to the vultures too? Every year, twice a year, gambling on sunshine, riding some kind of stupid roulette wheel, piling up hours, piling up drying grass, her head baking even under the new straw hat the kids had given her. Dust, grass seed, maybe even flakes of dead critter thick on her skin, and itching, itching—oh jeez, I'll go mad with the itching.

Then it was time to rake, and finally, God she had feared the day would never come, time to hitch the baler. The twins' dad was just about popping the buttons on his shirt, his grin practically wrapped twice around his face. "You start," she suggested, and he was on the tractor and heading for the field. The kids stayed home from school even though they were all still too young to help. The excitement was so contagious that she half-expected to see Blackie in his diaper, determinedly crawling out to be part of the crew.

The crew, most of the soccer team from the reserve, arrived in good spirits. They hitched the wagon to the riggins on the back of the pickup truck and headed into the field, following behind the tractor. They grabbed bales by the binder twine and swung them to the wagon, other gloved hands grabbed, stacked and piled, and when the engine of the pickup started to protest, they headed for the barn to send bales up the conveyor, and start stacking in the shaded cool of the loft.

The kids came in handy then. They laced the bales with salt, they kept the chaff swept off the floor so nobody risked slipping, and they were back and forth with cold juice.

Pansy had chickens that had been slow-roasted in the oven, spud salad, green salad, a big pot of chili, another of spaghetti. Dal didn't know how she did it all with Blackie underfoot or on her hip. How did any of them? Jesus, all these kids in the field, climbing on the hay wagon, clambering on the bales. Who could drive, keep an eye on the equipment, steer alongside the bales on the ground and still know where those kids were? What if one of them fell, was crushed under a wheel? Why was she the only one concerned, why was everyone else laughing, a guy who was all muscles and smile grabbing Button mere seconds before she fell back off the wagon? She could land the wrong way on the hard ground, snap her neck. Instead she was set back on her feet, safe, and the guy was reminding her that it was a long way down with a thump at the bottom. She nodded, he nodded and they both laughed, while Dal tried to swallow the lump in her throat. Where in hell was Papers in all of this? And then the conveyors, the hay elevators. If a kid fell on them, they'd be stabbed, ripped, torn, all this equipment nothing but disfigurement, even death, waiting to grab soft and tender flesh.

Trip after trip, the excitement mounting, the end in sight, now, just two more loads, guys, let's get 'er done here! One of the guys yelled to her, "Boy, you guys got strange ideas of what's fun. Is this what you call your Protestant work ethic, eh?" She laughed and told him it was insanity, nothing more nor less. They all laughed, made jokes about land claims—wait'll this belongs to us again, it'll look different, we'll put all this equipment on display, a museum, a monument to foolishness. How could they do such brutal work, do it for hours, and still laugh?

The loft was full, the wagon moving cumbersomely to the hay barn, the elevators reset, the same stacking pattern in effect—one row lengthwise, one widthwise, like Lego. If it is done properly, it will stand solid and secure. If done wrong, it's going to come down on your head, a hundred pounds plummeting, accordion your spine, shorten you by six inches, helluva headache.

She made them stop. Time to refuel the tractor, to add oil, to check all the connections, to squirt some grease here, some more there. Come on, don't be shy, those are good salmon sandwiches, the tractor isn't the only one needs fuel. Get some of them into you and have some egg salad too, and a cup of tea, I know it's a hot day and you yearn for something cold, but tea will keep you sweating and the breeze cools you better. Here, another one. I don't want your mom thinking we worked you to death. And pie, your choice—raisin, rhubarb or lemon. You need the sugar for energy.

"Can't eat too much," one of them blurted, "or we'll get lazy, and next thing you know we'll all be lying down in the shade snoring up a storm."

They soaked themselves with the hose while Dal made the twins' dad get down off the tractor. He protested, but did it while climbing down—there's a limit to how much the human body can endure. Dal took over on the tractor and the kids fussed over the communal dad, but only briefly. The bales were calling and the kids had found things they could do to help. They could flip the bales so the strings were up, they could ride the wagon, slide bales closer to the pile and save the stackers one or two steps—not much if it's only one or two bales, but with 300 bales to a load, one load after another, whole miles are saved. When those kids wore out, there were others more than willing to replace them.

Pape sat against a fence, his face beet red, his cottonfluff hair wet and sticking to him. He waved at Dal when the tractor went past, but either could not or preferred not to get to his feet, not even to beg to ride on her knee. She waved at him, kept driving, around and around, around and around. But she didn't go fast. The loaders could only do what they could do, and there was no benefit at all to racing like morons.

The small field was done and she was into the fallow pasture, the grass not as high, the ground bumpier, all those feet walking around in the winter mud. Only now it had dried and the deep footprints were rattling her teeth out of her gums. The loaders stumbled now and the work seemed more brutal. The smiling was gone, the joking finished. They had the set faces of people stubbornly determined to finish what they had started, just get 'er done for the love of whatever it is you hold dear.

And then it was done. Quite suddenly, surprisingly, it was done. Every bale was in the loft, the left side full, the right side waiting empty for the second cut, almost two months away. The tractor was parked, the conveyor taken down and stored, the hay wagon back where it sat, and they all stood looking at each other, suddenly worn to nubs.

"Fuck, lady," one of the soccer team sighed, "you guys sure do work hard just for the chance to live in the country."

Dahlia started to laugh. "Those condo-moan-iums in town are starting to look pretty damn good to me," she admitted.

They washed up in the yard and followed the kids into the house for the meal Pansy had prepared. There they suddenly became shy, the laughter and teasing left behind, and Dahlia worried they wouldn't feel at home, wouldn't be able to enjoy the meal set out for them. Pansy set Blackie in his high chair, then lit the smudge and smiled. "We do this only for special occasions," she told them. "This seems like a real special time." They looked at each other, then at Pansy, at Dahlia, at the kids. Something eased, wafted away with the smudge smoke, and the meal was underway. They crowded together at the table, ate hugely.

Pinch and Duck's father left the next day. "Thank you," Dahlia said. "It was real nice of you to come."

"Any time, Dahlia." He grabbed her and gave her a hug, surprising her. It was heartfelt, though with none of the undercurrent that had run between them at one time.

Nine

The kittens meowed and wailed, climbed out of their box and ran madly through the house looking for an escape. Finally Dal got fed up. She opened the front door and let them out. "Starve," she invited them. "Get eaten by a hawk or something." The kids stared at her, betrayed. She put dishes of food outside, more for the kids than the kittens, anything to stop the looks. When she headed out to check the critters and gather the eggs, the mother cat and all four kittens were grouped around the dishes, eating ravenously while Socks sat cleaning his feet, looking as if he was convinced the mother cat was his beloved, the kittens his.

"Well, look at this cozy little scene," Dal said. The mother cat looked up at her. Dal waited for her to streak off, but instead she left the dish, came over, did figure eights around Dal's legs and between her feet, purring. The kids knew more of what was going on in town than Dal did. "There's a farmer's market every weekend," Button announced at supper. "You take your stuff there and people come and buy it. We should sell our eggs there."

"Darling, there's so many of us that even if those chickens all worked overtime, we'd use up the eggs."

"We could get more chickens."

"We could." She had no intention of getting more—she was learning all over again just what a bother the buggers were.

"Some people sell garden stuff. Of course, they have to wait for it to grow," Button said reasonably. "But there's bread there and pies and stuff. Maybe we could go and you could see?"

Saturday morning they went to the market. The gardens were barely begun, so there wasn't much fresh produce, but there were eggs, more than Dal had expected. Ten minutes after the market opened, you couldn't have found an egg for sale no matter how much you were willing to spend. The townies were pushing and shoving in their eagerness for last year's honey and other people's home baking. Pansy was enthralled. She bought some doilies and a little doll in a crocheted hoop skirt to put on top of a roll of toilet paper.

Dal wasn't all that impressed, but the kids were content, buying cinnamon buns as if they didn't get any at home. Then the music started. She turned slowly. She hadn't seen the little bandstand even though she had walked right past it on her way from the parking lot. Seven people were sitting on folding chairs, playing energetically. A guitar, a mandolin, a woman with an accordion, a violin, a guy on a banjo, a woman with spoons and a fellow with a bodhran, the Celtic drum.

"You should go play with them," Pape told her. "Look, they've got an extra violin."

"Oh, I don't think they—"

"Sure, look, that guy with the guitar. He just walked up and now he's getting ready to play with them. You should, Momma."

Dal smiled and pretended to be very interested in the handicrafts. She didn't notice Pape walk over and talk to someone on the bandstand. Then he was back again, tugging at her arm. "I asked, Momma. They said, 'Tell her to come and sit right in.' Please?"

"Pape, honey, I—"

"Dahlia." Pansy was stern. "Why do you think we came here? This is a set-up. You aren't playing except at music lesson time, or didn't you know that? So are we going to waste the trip?"

Dal gave in. She went to the bandstand, such as it was, and she accepted the violin, feeling shy and awkward, plunking the strings gently. It was in tune, but it wasn't much by way of being a violin. It sounded as if it had a pinewood top. She did wish they'd stop using pinewood and stick to maple.

Two hours later the townies were leaving, the vendors were packing up and the band was starting to flag.

"Tomorrow?" one of the guitar players asked.

"One o'clock," someone agreed.

"I hope you'll join us," the accordion woman said to Dal. "We'd like more people to come and play with us."

"Thank you." She felt excited, as if she hadn't had the chance for years, as if she couldn't have played with Jim and his band any time she wanted, as if she and the kids didn't play every night.

She was there the next afternoon, with her own violin and Blackie Morgan's dobro. The kids had their instruments too. "If you can weasel me into it," she teased, "I'll weasel you too."

The kids played, but not for long. There was too much to see, and anyway, they didn't know most of the songs the group played. Once they'd played "Wabash Cannonball" and "Big Rock Candy Mountain," "Shenandoah" and "Red River Valley," the kids were on unfamiliar ground. They'd never heard of "Crooked Stovepipe" or "Whisper Waltz," and Dal blamed herself for the gap in their repertoire. She vowed to fill it, and quickly. How could she have been so slackass? The ghost of Blackie Morgan must be ranting and raving through the hallways of hell at the thought that his own brother's grandsons couldn't play "Old Zip" or "Bill Clancy's Reel." If she didn't do something about it and do it damn fast, she'd waken one night to the sound of rattling chains. For that matter, why hadn't she taught them "Blackie Morgan's Madness"? Even more to the point, why hadn't she played it herself? It had been years, God knew how many years, since she'd made her fingers fly on that one.

"Does anyone know 'Achy Breaky Heart'?" Pinch asked hopefully.

"Know *what?*" the banjo player asked.

⌔

Dahlia was busy in the garden, down on her knees doing the gardener's inverted prayer, hands busy in the soil, inhaling the rich smells of the earth, the morning sun not yet hot, the dew still thick on the grass. Beside her, a cup of coffee steamed, and up in the hen yard one of the naked-necked roosters was learning to crow. He didn't have it all together yet, but give the little guy time.

She heard the sound of a car engine, but she wasn't expecting anybody so she didn't get up and go to the house. It was probably just another townie who had taken the wrong turn, then ignored all three Private Drive signs and both No Trespassing signs and who was now peering with puzzlement at the house, wondering where in hell the road had gone to. Now a car door opened and closed, then another, and Dal supposed the dumb buggers were going to go to the house and knock knock knock on the door until someone left what they were doing and went to answer. They would want directions. Some of them even asked, "Well, why don't you have a gate or something, how is a person to know?"

"Dal?" Pansy called from the back door. "Someone here to see you."

She couldn't imagine who it could be. Anybody she knew would have come to the garden to visit over the fence. Oh, well, the soil would wait, it always did.

They sat side by side on the sofa, a man and a woman, both of them very nervous. The man's shirt was buttoned right up to the top and his hair was recently combed, still damp, the little rows left by the teeth still showing.

"I'm Dahlia Cassidy, could I help you?" Surely they didn't want to buy a calf, thinking they could raise it to slaughter-size on grass clippings from the lawn?

"The police gave us your name," the man said, and she could see he was feeling embarrassed, didn't want to impose. "We went to your other place first but of course you weren't there. The people at the store knew what town you'd moved to and we found you in the phone book. We were going to phone, but...it's hard enough talking face to face." Helpless, he looked at the woman.

"We're Kyle's parents," she said, as if that explained everything.

Dahlia waited to hear something she might understand.

"You found Kyle, last summer. He was..."

"Oh, my God." Dahlia sat down quickly. "I'm sorry. The police never did tell me his name. I didn't know they'd identified... I mean..."

"I think some coffee would be nice," said Pansy, sweeping in with a tray and saving them all from terminal embarrassment. "And some fresh cinnamon buns." She poured coffee and passed plates. "Tell us about Kyle," she suggested gently. "How old was he? What was he like?"

"How old? Uh, 28. Kyle was...unsettled, some said adventurous, others said footloose. He liked to travel—he'd been to Mexico and all over Europe..." The father's voice trailed off, and he bit into his cinnamon bun as if it was the only hope he had of not running off at the mouth for the rest of his life.

"He'd come out here to hike the West Coast Trail." Something in the mother had relaxed and she was suddenly more at ease than her husband. "We'd had a postcard from Calgary and two from Vancouver, and then we didn't hear anything. But he'd written about the trail, you see, and we thought he was just hiking, so at first didn't think much about it. And then we started to worry but we didn't think to contact the police until much later." She paused for a moment. "It's quite awkward," she blurted, "but I had to meet you, face to face, and say thank you. I mean, I know you didn't go looking for him, but you did find him and if you hadn't—well, I might never have known, never been able to put it to rest. Put him to rest. Put myself to rest."

"It must be a terrible thing to lose a child. I'm very sorry." Dahlia looked into her coffee mug, saw the sunlight glistening on the water, saw the raft, her own children clambering on it, tried to imagine if it had been one of them under that raft, couldn't even begin to think about what it would have done to her. "They cremated him," Kyle's mother said. "And they still had the urn at the funeral parlour. We're taking him home."

"The autopsy," the father blurted. "He had a bad bump on his head. They think he was unconscious when he fell in the water. They think probably someone knocked him out. They've never found any of his stuff—not his wallet, not his backpack..."

"Jesus," Pansy breathed. "That must be awful for you."

"Yes," Kyle's father nodded. "It makes me very angry."

"To kill someone," Kyle's mother's voice shook, "for a few dollars. He never carried much money with him and there wouldn't be anything in his pack but some clothes and his journal."

Dahlia wasn't convinced that Kyle had been murdered. The body she had found was wearing a bathing suit. No need to murder someone for their backpack and clothes if that person is lying asleep on a raft with the desired items left unguarded on the shore. She almost said as much, then held her tongue. It wouldn't make them feel any better. They'd made their peace with the images brought to mind by the police report. There was no need to disrupt the calm acceptance beginning to grow in them.

She was glad when they left, and knew they were glad to go. They'd come to finish the first part of laying their kid to rest, and now they could go home and end it by putting the urn in the family burial plot. She went back to the garden but the glow was off the day. She knelt in the warmth of the sun and her tears made dark spots on the earth. Why would they prefer to think their child had been murdered? Was it easier to bear when you blamed someone else? Death cannot be blamed. It just is. All of us are born to die, start dying at the moment of conception, move toward it steadily, no matter what we do. And all of us so frail, so delicate, so easily made dead. Who to blame? What to blame? All of us. Even the middle son smoking dope on a raft, falling asleep, getting sunstroke, banging his damn head, falling into the water and under the raft, to drown for Jesus sake when all he had to do was collect his wits.

But she had to stop weeping or the salt from the tears would ruin the soil, and the garden, that place of life, deserved better.

↜

Dahlia was on Unemployment Enjoyment when the second crop of hay was ripe. No help from Pinch and Duck's dad this time—he was on the fishing grounds with the twins, his oldest boy and Skipper.

Twink didn't want to go fishing, but she did want, very much, to help with the haying. Dahlia would have said no, but Pansy got there first.

"It's rotten work!" Dal protested. "It'll rattle her insides and pound her back."

"She wants to do it. She's old enough, and she knows it."

"She doesn't know how hard it is."

"You didn't say no to Rick or John. Give someone else a half a chance to be superwoman too, will you!"

Second haying was much more miserable than first. For a start, they had the heat to contend with, and broad-brimmed hat or not, they came off the tractor feeling like their brains had been cooked for supper. Dahlia insisted they wear long-sleeved shirts and slathers of sunblock, and even so they tanned and baked. Each stint on the machinery was shorter than the one before.

Fatigue etched their faces, and even Rick winced and pressed his hand to the small of his back, arching, trying to ease out the crick.

"Take a break," Dahlia said gently. "Ask Auntie Pan to drive you to the lake."

"After supper," Twink said, "when it's all done and you can come too." Dahlia would have sold the place for a buck and a quarter right then and there.

The sky was the colour of faded jeans and not a sign of a cloud to be seen. The only breeze came from the movement of the tractor, and the hot air sucked moisture from them faster than they could drink enough fluid to replace it. Dal felt none of the pressure of first haying. No chance of rain meant no worry about it, either, and though she could have put in a couple more hours, she quit mowing in time for them all to head to the lake. They didn't so much swim as lie in the water, soaking up moisture, finally relaxing, and Dal could have fallen asleep floating on her back. But, instead she took Blackie so that Pansy could have a good swim, and he had so much fun splashing and flailing that her exhaustion faded. She wondered if she was absorbing some of his energy. God knows he had enough for an entire kindergarten.

After the heat eased, when the darkness was rising from the lake and the colour fading from the sky, they headed home for a belated supper. A good night's sleep, naked under a cotton sheet, not for warmth as much as to soak up the sweat, and then it was morning and she was up, ready to get a good swatch done before the kids woke up. With any luck they'd sleep the sleep of the exhausted and she'd get to do the rest herself. But that didn't happen, and before much longer they were there, insisting she get down off the tractor, let them take their turns, as if it was all fun. The last of the hay was down by 11:00 and Pansy had lunch ready. Dal sipped a glass of chilled pineapple juice and stretched. "Why don't the whole lot of you stuff the coolers and head off to the lake for the rest of the day?"

"What about you?"

"Me?" She grinned wickedly. "There's a bed upstairs with my name written on it and I intend to make full use of it. I'm too old to mow hay all morning and then join the Olympic swim team for the rest of the day and evening. Have pity." She moaned and flopped her head to the top of the table, as if totally stricken.

They were gone inside of 15 minutes. Dal waited until they were out of sight, then went to the fridge and got the plate of sliced ham and potato salad, the meal she had vowed she was too tired to eat, and she packed it all away. With a thermos of cold juice and a plastic bottle of ice, she headed for the barn to replace the mower with the tedder and start turning the hay in the first field.

Tedding was quicker work than cutting. She had two of the fields finished by the time the thermos was empty and the ice had melted to water and been guzzled. She considered heading into the field she had finished cutting that morning, then gave herself the lecture she usually delivered to the kids when enthusiasm was overpowering good sense. She'd been bouncing her kidneys on this machine for over 12 hours. Enough is enough, and anything more than that is too much.

When the swimmers came home, water-bleached clean and looking both refreshed and tired, Dal was sitting on the porch in clean cut-offs, sandals and sleeveless T-shirt, her fresh-washed hair still damp. She was busy packing away a fresh garden salad and looked like two million dollars tax-free.

"There's lots in the fridge," she offered, and the kids headed for the kitchen, not even noticing the neat rows of turned hay. Pansy noticed, though, and shook her head, smiling. "What a bum you are."

"Bum yourself. All afternoon on a hot rock with a pack of kids, pretending it's all more fun than you could ever say."

"Not the lake today, the beach. The kids insisted we had to go somewhere we could find shade for the baby. I've been sitting on sand, leaning against an old log in the shade watching while they all played with Blackie in the water. He fell asleep on them so they brought him over and he and I napped. Where's the work in any of that?"

Dahlia fell asleep as if she had been hit on the head with a brick. She was wide awake at 4:30 and out checking the fields for dew, but the grass was dry. Even at night there wasn't enough moisture in the air to make any difference. The coffee was ready when she went back into the house, and she filled her thermos and went back out with the tedder. Before the kids were up and eating pancakes, she had the last field turned.

"You cheated," Twink said.

"I didn't cheat. I slept so much yesterday afternoon I woke up early."

"You lie. My mother says if you lie, the devil will take you to hell when you die."

"Yeah, but what your mother didn't tell you was that I don't intend to die, so it's no worry for me."

She refilled the tractor with diesel and checked all its bits and parts, and after breakfast Twink was up on the seat, learning about raking. At noon Dahlia insisted that she needed to nap, and Pansy had the coolers packed and waiting. Once again, no sooner were they out of sight than Dahlia was up on the tractor, back and forth, up and down, raking the hay into windrows for the baler. She checked the hay often, testing it, bending it, biting it, and as near as she could tell it was all crisp, dry and cured, more than ready for the baler.

One whole day eaten by baling, and no way she could convince the kids to take a break. They spelled each other, the tractor stopping only for a refill of fuel, then back out again, baling, baling, clatter bang thump. Even Pip and Paper were tired of taking turns riding with the driver and Button had a cramp in her foot from stretching to the gas pedal. Dahlia didn't like the idea of a kid as young as Button trying to do a full share of hay work, but she knew Pansy would go up her face if she tried to get tired little Butts off the uncomfortable seat. She wasn't at all sorry when darkness rose up and she discovered the headlights on the tractor were actually too dim for her to continue. She slept heavily and didn't waken until six. By 6:30 she was on the tractor, the kids still asleep, not a bit disturbed even by the clunkety-clatter.

At noon the soccer team arrived. They worked until 11:30 that night and still had a field to do the next day. The first flat deck arrived at 10:30 in the morning and the soccer team loaded it to capacity while Twink counted the number of bales. The truck left, and another took its place. When it was loaded and gone, the crew went back to loading the hay wagon. The flat decks returned and the last of the bales were loaded. They stood in a loose grouping, shoulders sagging, watching wearily as the trucks drove away. They had 'er done!

Now the cleanup, then the feast. After they had been paid and had driven off with huge grins on their faces, Dal took a cup of coffee to the front porch and stared at the fields, stared at what had been accomplished. The barn was absolutely stuffed.

The flat decks had taken more than a thousand bales. At $4 a bale, the hay had paid for its own harvesting. More than enough to cover the cost of fertilizer, seed, fuel and the crew's wages. The calf money would be total profit. Except, of course, you'd have to convince yourself you'd got the cows for free. Dal figured she would have made better money if she'd spent the last year slinging beer at so much an hour plus tips. Ah, she thought, but then, you silly fool, you'd have had to pay rent. Pansy and the kids thought Dal was laughing in celebration. She didn't tell them differently.

She gave herself a lecture as she got ready for bed and told her inner alarm clock that the push was over, she could sleep in as late as she wanted. She was up and drinking coffee by seven, busy in her garden by eight. At ten, the saga of the jars and lids started and the quarts of green beans began to accumulate. They went on the shelves in the basement and were soon joined by quarts of cherries and the first of the plum jam. But the afternoons were for swimming, the law inflexible and willingly obeyed—if it isn't done by 1:00 in the afternoon, forget it.

The 18-18-18 waited, the dolomite lime waited and the shorn fields waited for rain that didn't arrive. The calves chased their mothers, chased each other, chased Queenie if she went into the field, and they grew so quickly it was hard to believe they had so recently been spindle-legged and wobbly. Dahlia knew she should have steered the bull calves before now, but she couldn't bring herself to envision what it would entail. Let someone else deal with it. She was going to sell them in the fall, not keep them over the winter and do the slaughtering herself. But then she saw how sexually precocious they were, and rather than wind up with a six-month-old heifer pregnant by her own half-brother, they corralled the calves, separated the males and watched as the vet did what needed done. When the sedated steers were let out of the corral and all the people were having a cold drink together, Dal and Pansy talked to the vet about castration, and Dal decided that whatever it cost, she was going to have the vet out the following year too. Yes, she could learn how. She just didn't know when she was going to find the damn time! Or, for that matter, the stomach.

On their way home from an afternoon at the lake, Dal and Pansy and the kids saw some softball teams warming up, and nothing would do but that they pull over to watch. They sat down at the edge of the field, the kids looking in the backpacks for sandwiches, oranges, any kind of food that might have been overlooked.

"We're short," a woman called.

"We can't wait forever," another said.

"Guess we forfeit. Damn! And just when I was all set to play the best game of my life. Wouldn't you know it, eh."

"We could play pickup or scrub. That way you could show us how much you've improved since the other night when you fanned out each time you were at the plate."

"Practising, that's all, just practising my swing." She looked over at the group on the grass. "Anybody over there know how to play ball?"

"I do." Twink stood up eagerly.

Pansy looked at Dal, who looked at Pansy, then both of them looked at Twink, who never spoke up, never put herself to the front of any-thing. "But I don't have my glove with me."

"Someone at bats can loan you hers. Anyone else?"

"My mom plays," Twink grinned.

"Yeah, come on Mom, show them how."

"I haven't played in years!" Dal protested.

"Then it's damn well time you did! Come on."

Laughing, Dal got up, brushed the grass from her butt and walked onto the field.

"I can play," John called.

"Sorry, guy. Shemales only. Why don't you pretend to be ump?"

Dahlia couldn't believe how much she had lost. She missed an overhead fly she would have sniped easily only a few years ago. When it was her turn to bat, she got a hit that should have put her on second and she barely made first. Where was the easy unthinking co-ordination? Where were the reflexes that took her hand to the right place at the right time to snag the ball? And where, pray tell, was the depth and height perception she'd had before she became the one-eyed woman?

It looked as if all of that had left home, packed its karazinka and moved over to Twink. The kid was amazing. Dal didn't know she was looking at herself at the same age, but she did know that was her kid out there and she was a ball player.

"Hey, kid, what's your name?"

"Twink. What's yours?"

"Peggy. So, you want to play on our team?"

"I don't mind. Am I old enough?"

"You can walk, can't you? You're old enough. It's just beer league anyway. It's not like we were bent out of shape or something. So what's your best position?"

"Wherever you need me."

"Jesus, you're confident if nothing else. Ever try catcher?"

"Yeah."

"Gear up, let's see."

Dahlia filled a hole in left field and watched as Twink, hidden in safety gear, crouched behind the plate, looking as if she had some idea what a catcher was supposed to do.

"Way to go, babe," she called. "Show what you know, that's the way."

They played for two and a half hours and quit when the light started to fade and the mosquitoes began to drive them nuts. Dahlia thought she might make it home. Twink walked easily, her shirt dry, her face slightly pink, her breathing smooth.

"To you," Dal intoned, "from failing hands we throw the torch."

"Carry your own damn flashlight," Twink growled, then winked.

Dal woke up in the middle of the night and, unable to go back to sleep, got out of bed and went to sit on the back porch. The moon was almost full and she could see her garden—not the individual plants but the rows, straight and tidy as nothing in nature. Socks jumped up on her lap and lay purring against her belly. Queenie lay pressed against Dal's back. Kit and her kittens positioned themselves on the steps, staring at her, waiting for a hint, a clue, a reason for her to be here.

The screen door opened and Pansy sat beside her, yawning.

"So what do you think of that kid?" Pansy asked. "Just as bold as brass. Anybody play ball? I do."

"It was no lie. When did it happen? And how? One minute she's quiet Twink, the one who never talks, the next minute she's insisting on driving the tractor, and then she's hunched behind the plate, being downright good."

"Did you hear her? Way to go chucker-baby, way to be, show 'em what you got — it was as if it was someone else there, not cat-got-your-tongue Twink."

"Life sure can get busy. Now I guess we've got what? A practice and a game a week?"

"Seems to me when you were first playing, you headed off on your bike. Nobody drove you."

"Seems to me there wasn't as much traffic, and what there was, wasn't crazy."

"Seems to me," Pansy teased, "if you're going to drive her to practice and the games, you'd better get some WD-40 and spray it on your joints because you're a bit stiff, old girl. Your fine-honed edge has dulled and you ain't the woman you used to think you were. They'll get you playing too, and if you aren't in better shape, you'll get hurt."

Dal nodded and sat staring out at nothing. She didn't even hear Pansy go back into the house. Her life was getting very full. Market band every weekend, lake or beach every day, chickens to feed, eggs to gather — even with the kids helping, the chores had a way of dominating life. Work done at home wasn't the same as work done elsewhere. You never got to drive away from it and there was no out of sight, out of mind. But at least you could find diversion. And she already had more of a social life happening than she'd had for a long time. She wasn't on a shaved slope, miles from other people. She had her weekend music, and conversations between songs, and after the market closed. It was surprising how many friends a person got by just being seen! People she didn't really know spoke to her in the supermarket, stopped her on the street, smiled when they passed, honked horns and waved.

She felt as if her year was being divided into a new kind of calendar. First calves in February, close the gates to the hayfield before the start of March, first haying end of May, second haying end of July—more-or-less so-to-speak, open the hayfield gates, let the cows in to clean up and fertilize. Soon, all too soon, it would be take calves to market, but not yet, please, let us have some slack time, just a week or two of it. We promise we'll be good, eat our veggies, brush our teeth.

It was the middle of August, the grass yellowed by the extended dry spell, and they were at the field, getting ready for a game. Twink said something Dal didn't hear, Dal turned around to ask her to repeat it, and she knew she was in trouble—deep deep trouble. Dal recognized this type of trouble. She'd had kids because of this kind of trouble. This kind of trouble had smiled at her from the dance floor, this kind of trouble had strolled over, to speak to her, this kind of trouble had ridden up on a motorcycle. This kind of trouble had kicked off this kind of flutter before, and the flutter, though always short-lived, had been enough to affect what Dahlia often thought of as a weak mind. This kind of trouble did something in her chest, where her wishbone would have been if she'd been a real turkey instead of this kind of turkey. This kind of trouble made something just above her pelvic bones tighten, clench, then loosen. It was the feeling you got when you went all the way up the ladder to the top step, then looked down and realized just how high up you were. It was what happened when you went over the train tracks too fast in the car, or sent the toboggan down a slick steep hill with a bump partway down the slope. Lurch. She had turned to hear Twink, but it wasn't Twink who had put her in this state of trouble. It was the woman standing just behind her, the one who half-turned when Dal turned, the one who looked at Dal with exactly the same sort of surprise Dal felt on her own face.

She did nothing about it and she had no idea why. She had never believed in all that chastity stuff—just count the kids and remember what a person needs to do to get one. Dahlia hadn't been "caught" with any of them. She had checked out quite a few men before settling on the ones who got invited to donate to the gene pools. Sometimes she looked at the kids, gathered at the table or in the music room, laughing and playing, each of them stamped with the Cassidy look, each of them also displaying resemblances to others, and she almost laughed aloud thinking of the old Vancouver Island description: if she had as many showing out as she'd had in, she'd look like a porcupine. It didn't hurt her feelings. She had grown up knowing about double standards, and had rejected them and a good number of other kinds as well.

So it wasn't anything to do with that. It wasn't because of the shared gender stuff. Dahlia had checked out more than potential sperm donors. Her experiences with women had been fun-filled and enjoyable, brief affairs easily begun and as easily ended. Or so it seemed now, safely distanced from the hurt feelings and accusations when she ended the affairs. And there was the rub, the reason she did nothing to kick off anything with Dianne. The lurch she felt in her gut was too strong—it told her she wasn't playing with a weekend or two at a motel. This was deep water, not something you paddled in but something you avoided. No going in only ankle-deep and cavorting. One step and you were in over your head, and you'd better know how to swim. It scared her. Scared her because she didn't trust herself.

Dammit, she'd seen what happened when a person took that step and walked off the ledge. Her mother was the first fine example. No matter what the old fart did, no matter how many times he stepped out and pole-vaulted into someone else's bed, there it was, the old forgive-and-forget cow cack, putting up with the unspeakable because of what was called love. Put up with it until putting up was impossible, and so what did she do? What else but walk out of one mess and into something not one helluva lot better? Well, at least wotzit didn't beat on her. As if that was a recommendation for sainthood, instead of being what it ought to be—just normal, accepted behaviour.

Her older sister Rose, suddenly not herself at all, trading in her jeans and ball bat for the white dress and pinch-foot satin pumps, looking like a total stranger, her allegiance shifted from siblings to the mechanic who grinned shyly and said little. "I love him," Rose had said. "Wait until it's your turn, Bubba, and you'll understand." And Iris, for crying out loud. How many times had she said "I love him," and then soaked her pillow with hot tears because of it?

Dahlia might have let herself fall in love with Twink's dad, if she'd met him further on down the line. But she was young, and it was too soon after her stubborn escape from the patch-ass life as one of those Cassidys. She could too well remember the quarrels, the arguments, the fights, the times the old bugger blew his cool and laid beatings on whichever of the ones smaller than himself came too close to him. None of that for her. And when she found herself waiting for the phone to ring, wanting it to ring, wanting to hear the "Hey, babe, guess who?" she panicked and put it behind her.

Pinch and Duck's dad might have been a good reason to step off the ledge into deep water, but he had this kindly way of never quite managing to mind his own damn business. "Dahlia, why don't you..." or, "Did you ever think of..."

There had been a woman who had made her feel the first stirrings of exactly this kind of trouble, a woman who was everything Dahlia's mother had wanted her to be—educated, poised, with a well-paying steady job—but the poise was only outward, and only when in public. One screeching fit too many, one jealous fury too many and Dahlia had known this one was going to be too much like what her mother had put up with, what Dal had vowed she would never allow for herself. The emotional battering seemed even worse than the other kind. When you're used to unwarranted whaps and sudden shoves, pushes and slaps, you deal with them by denying their importance, until you reach the point where a wallop is important for only as long it smarts. That other, the accusations, the nagging, the blame blame blame—that doesn't go away. It festers, it burns, it gets to you until you are no longer exactly sure who it was you thought you were. So she hit the pike. Hit the pike and vowed that she would never again run the same risk.

It's too risky. Dahlia knew of no way to be halfway to this kind of intimacy, this kind of trust, this kind of dependency. That's what the word "involved" means. It's messy—everything gets tangled up with everything else. There's a reason they call it head over heels. The ties that bind really do, and all too often they fasten around your throat, and then there you are, and it hurts, and it's scary, and who in hell wants to be on the verge of out of control all the damn time, especially when having some control has been the only thing that kept you from giving in to the fury, the anger, the fear? Giving in to it year after year until fear becomes so ordinary you don't even know you're afraid, except for the scream that seems to be perpetually lodged in the back of your throat, just waiting for you to let down some of your hard-won control so it can come out, breaking the days and nights of your life into sharp, slashing pieces. And if you start screaming, what if you never stop and they take you off in a straitjacket, put you in the rubber room and you never see your kids again? Or worse, what if you start screaming and your mind snaps and you kill every living thing, including those kids, before you slash your own wrists? And why do they never do the job on the wrists first and leave the kids alone, never mind the multiple murders followed by suicide? Just do that part first and get on with the trip to that other hell, which cannot be worse than the one into which you were born. No, you don't dare lose control. Control is all that is keeping you from being as wretchedly horrible as the ones who made you that way.

Dahlia had never been able to figure out the how and why of things. Rosie, now, the firstborn daughter, the one who had to forge the way, hammer at the boundaries and borders, the one on whom most of the expec-fuckin-tations were piled, the one saddled with the babysitting, the one who had to help with the meals when she was less than six, the one who had to bring in the washing and do the bulk of the ironing, the one who hardly had any childhood at all. You'd think she'd never been given a slam on the side of the head, had never worn belt lashings on her legs. Rosie was the one would step in front of the frightened smaller one and collect the wallop, Rosie was the one cuddled the sobbing one and said now, now, hush bubba hush, it's all right, Rosie's here. Did Rosie bear any grudges? Not so's you'd notice. Rosie lived in her four-bedroom split-level on a double-sized lot in Victoria and her life looked like something to envy—kids in university, mechanic husband in charge of the shop, and every year they took their holidays and went to the Calgary Stampede, driving a GMC pickup with a fully equipped camper. Did Rosie wake up sometimes, caught in a nightmare that sent her out of the bedroom to pace back and forth in the cold of night, looking up at the stars through tear-filled eyes, wanting to howl why? Not so's you'd notice.

Iris, of course, was a horse of another garage. Iris should have helped Rosie, but from the get-go Iris fucked the dog. Iris was an expert at finding places to hide, finding do-nothing pretend jobs. When the washing needed brought in and the table needed setting, when there was a sick kid puking and the old man in a foul mood, there would be Rosie, looking anxious, moving at top speed, and their mother calling "Iris, you help your sister," and no sign of Iris. But just ask Iris and you'd get this glowing Walton-family bullshit about life on the farm-ee-oh, unless she was feeling hard done by and went into her litany of how hard she had to work while everyone else just played music and snarled at her. But be angry? Maybe it took more energy than Iris had. Maybe she was such a damn martyr it all got translated into blubbering.

Lose control? Dal would go to hell before she turned into such a whimpering go-nowhere do-nothing. When Dahlia Cassidy cried, she cried alone in her room—except for a few times when she couldn't get up the stairs fast enough, and then it was only Pansy who knew.

Pansy—God, how did people like Pansy happen? Pansy, who was born bending over backwards to be good. Pansy, who could barely toddle and yet was there on a chair, trying to help Dahlia wash dishes, trying to help Rosie with her chores, as if it was all such fun, as if the shouting and yelling and hollering and hitting were just the sounds people made as they went about their lives. Pansy, not yet five years old, up on the chair again, carefully cracking eggs into a big bowl, chattering away to Rosie about how you have to be careful not to get any shell in or the scrambled eggs will be crunchy, as if Rosie hadn't taught Pansy exactly that the day before, and Rosie nodding, as if it was the *Encyclopedia Britannica* up there on the chair. The old man came in the house, took one look and hollered "Jesus Christ, Rosie, what if that kid spills the whole damn thing or falls off the chair and cracks her head open, where's your goddamn brains, anyway!" And before Rosie could say a word, Pansy was telling the old bugger all about cracking eggs. "I'm helpin'," she said, and turned to him with that Pansy-smile. His anger vanished as if it had never been, and he, who was kind only to his dogs, who showed gentleness only to a cow having trouble calving, whose voice was as harsh as a ravens, had put his arms around the little girl. "Well, then," he said, "and good for Rosie for showing you how." That was as close to an apology as he had ever come in his life.

Lose control? There was too much at risk. She'd done okay so far, she was making her own way just fine. All she had to do was make sure she controlled herself, make sure she in no way even so much as hinted of what she was feeling when she was around Dianne. Nothing to it, really, all she had to do was turn her back on what she was feeling. She'd done that before in her life. She'd spent years of her life making sure she put things in bottles and hammered stoppers on top.

They came home from the lake one evening and there was Iris, making herself at home. That's what you get for not locking your doors. Iris was on the porch with a pot of tea and a sandwich, smiling from ear to ear, as if they were coming to visit her instead of the other way around.

"I'll do the chores," Dahlia said. She needed some time. Talk about get control! She'd have to grab onto some, and fast, if she wanted to deal with Iris in any way other than a bop on the beak.

There weren't many chores. Some doors to close, some eggs to gather, a trip to the back pasture to check on the cows, which had the pasture pretty much chewed down. Dal decided she'd open up the hayfield in the morning and put them back in there. If it didn't rain soon, the grass would be dust. It was already hard, dry, yellow stalks, the clover was wilting, the flower heads turned to brown seeds. She turned on the taps and the hoses spurted water into the bathtubs set along the fences. The dog walked beside her, nudging her hand with a damp nose, and the cats came behind, tails up like banners. She stopped in the driveway to pick blackberies, not so much chewing them as pressing them against the roof of her mouth, squishing out the juice, swallowing the pulp. Dog nudged, hinting, and Dal picked a few for her. She'd already cleaned off the ones at the bottom of the stabbing vines and now she depended on others for her treats.

The bathtubs were full, the water dribbling over the side, soaking into the dry earth, but the grass near the tubs didn't benefit. All those hard hooves pushing, shoving, digging into and turning over the sod as the huge beasts vied for position had killed the grass, leaving a big, rough bare patch of dirt. Dahlia had given up seeding those areas, given up trying to find something tough enough to survive. The western sky was a glory of colour, the evening sunset a replay of what waited for her in the morning, when the eastern sky would come light and the new day move in quickly from the other side of the world. Pape talked often of how their sunset was dawn in China, and he wondered aloud if someone there was looking at the colours and thinking how it was sunset somewhere else. Dal couldn't imagine how she'd given birth to a kid who thought about things like that.

And now she couldn't put it off any longer. She had to go back to the house and deal with Iris and her damn ongoing soap opera of a life. Was it never to end? Couldn't Iris just stop waiting for the knight on the white horse, get herself a job, go to it, do it, collect her pay, take it home and support herself, if not herself and her kids? If Dal had to hear one more time the "Oh, you're so lucky" story or the "It's easy for you, you're a strong woman and I'm not" whine, she wasn't sure what she was going to do.

Iris seemed very subdued, almost shy. John and Rick obviously weren't sure how to relax with her, although they were going through all the polite motions—making another pot of tea, asking if there was anything she would like, another sandwich, perhaps? Iris accepted the tea but said no thank you to the sandwich, and sat watching Pansy with Blackie, who had decided that if there was someone new in the house he, by damn, wasn't going to go to sleep and miss something.

"He's a nice little boy," Iris said. "He reminds me of Johnny when he was the same age. Johnny was nice too."

"John still is nice," Pansy said gently. "All these kids are nice."

"It looks good on you." Iris actually blushed. "I'm happy for you, Pansy, you waited a long time."

Dahlia sat in the big chair, the one she seldom used. Iris was in the chair Dal preferred. How did Iris always manage to do things like that? Rick brought her a cup of tea and Dahlia smiled her thanks at him, reached out and patted his bum. "You're a love," she said.

He winked. "I'm just practising. One day I'll make some woman fall in love with me just because I know how to get her a cup of tea when she's tired."

Dal quoted something she had heard Blackie Morgan yell drunkenly at a dance one night. "Love is but a gust of wind, proceeding from the heart; if it should take a downward course, it's commonly called—"

"Dahlia Cassidy, what an awful thing to say!" Iris scolded, but she seemed good-natured. "You're supposed to set a good example for these kids, not teach them stuff like that."

Dahlia would gladly have forgone music practice, but Iris wanted to hear the kids and the kids were more than willing to throw a concert for the out-of-town contingent. Dahlia sat in the chair she didn't particularly like while they hurried to get their instruments. Iris went to the bathroom and Dahlia switched chairs. Iris came back, opened her mouth to say something, then closed it again and sat down.

The kids played well. Of course it sounded better when Pinch, Duck and Skipper were there too, but they'd be back soon. Not soon enough as far as Dal was concerned, but you don't get everything in life. Sometimes, you hardly get anything at all.

"They're good." Iris sounded amazed.

"They're damn good. Gonna rent 'em out and live off the royalties from all their gold records, let them keep me in the style to which I would most dearly love to become accustomed."

"They won't make gold records." Iris didn't sound as if she was arguing, she was just stating a fact. "There hasn't been a Cassidy, or a Morgan for that matter, who got rich on music. Hasn't even been one managed to pay their bills from it."

"Why do you suppose that is?" Pansy laughed. "It's true, but it's astounding too, because other people who aren't anywhere near as good wind up making decent money at it."

"Nobody gets paid for breathing," Dahlia yawned. "Everybody in the world breathes, nobody gets money for doing it. And that's what it's like for these kids. Breathing. It's just so damn much fun they'd do it for nothing."

Dahlia would have fallen asleep in her chair if the music had lasted very much longer, but the kids were tired too. The combination of hot August sun and cool lake water had taken their energy and they were ready for an early bed. But when Dahlia went to bed, tired as she was, she couldn't get to sleep. Was this what they called an anxiety attack? Her brain felt like it was spinning on the tip of her spinal cord. Her skin felt itchy and the muscles in her legs jerked. She couldn't decide what was worse—having a sheet over her or kicking it off and feeling the night air on her body.

She thought about finances, about pogey in and money out, she worried about the lack of rain, she fussed herself about how long it would be before her kids came back off the fish boat, she bothered herself with the thought of Iris and how long she might stay, and she wondered if Pansy really was as happy as she seemed, or if she too had times of exhausting tension. Finally, so weary she wanted to weep, Dahlia got out of bed and went to the front steps with her tobacco, papers and lighter. She rolled a smoke, lit it and stared out at the shadows. When she heard the door open behind, she did not turn, supposing that Pansy was awake too. They sat out here often, drifting in the nighttime calm and quiet.

But it was Iris, her eyes swollen, her face flushed. Oh shit, she's crying. Again.

"Dahlia, I have to do something with my life and I don't know what."

"Huh?"

"I don't like the way things are. Everybody's always mad at me. Even my own kids, hard as they try, can barely be polite. I saw Ricky wink at you. I saw how easy he is with you. He's not like that with me."

"Try calling him Rick instead of Ricky."

"But I think of him as my little Ricky."

"Iris, none of us get it our own way all the time, okay? You want things to change between you and your kids, then you have to be the one to start making the first changes. God isn't going to wave her magic wand. Pansy can't say the magic words for you and I can't do the magic thing for you. He hates being called Ricky. He's not a baby—he's three-quarters of the way to being a man. And he doesn't want to be a man named Ricky."

"And John?"

"What about him?"

"How is it you manage to get along with him so well and I can't?"

"I don't know."

"You do it so easily. You get along with all those kids."

"Not Pip." Dahlia sighed. "Pip and I are going to wind up at each other's throats the way things are going. She whines. She sulks. She makes me want to take her to the market and see if I can give her away, maybe trade her in on one of those little dolls that fit over top the toilet roll."

"Well, she was everybody's doll baby until Duncan arrived."

"Who? Oh, right, Blackie."

"I hate that name."

Dahlia wished she was alone, wished Iris would go back in the house and take all her mini-problems with her.

"We're split up," Iris blurted.

"I figured," Dahlia yawned. She couldn't help it.

"Do I bore you that much?" Iris snapped.

"Oh, fuck, Iris, it's what, midnight? One in the morning? I've been up since six. I'm tired and I can't sleep. My mind is whirling in circles and my body wants to crawl under a rock and hibernate, but it can't. I yawned, and you're going to make a federal case out of it? Gimme a fuckin' break. I'm tired."

"Aren't you going to ask why we split up?"

"No. It doesn't matter why."

"Doesn't matter!"

"Iris, listen, please. You knew Pansy had put him on the reject pile. You knew I thought he was a horse's goddamn badoinky, you knew your kids hated everything about him, and what did you do? You didn't just walk into it, you didn't just run into it, you put your head down like a stubborn cow and with both eyes wide open you charged into it. And fuck everybody else, Iris was in love. Same goddamn thing as with Duh-Whine. You knew he was a Morgan, Iris! But Iris was in love, and the whole world had to come to a halt because of it. So it doesn't matter what it was finally ended it. If it's even ended."

"Of course it's ended. I said so, didn't I?" Iris was angry. What else was new?

"Things have been ended for you before, and we've dried your tears and cheered you up and listened while you said Never Again, That's It, and the next tune to be played is Things Will Be Better Now. And always, I Love Him."

"Not this time." Iris sounded so weary that Dahlia believed her.

"What did he do?" Maybe if Iris spilled it out she'd be satisfied and leave Dahlia alone.

"Nothing. Nothing new, anyway. I just... I miss my kids, I miss Pansy, I miss you."

"Me?" Dahlia laughed. She couldn't help it. "Iris, you can't stand me! Ever since we were little kids, you and I have been gas and matches. I piss you off, and that's fine because you piss me off. Even now, when you're trying so hard to be nice and have some kind of sisterly conversation, you can't help it. I'm pissed off because I don't want to know all this shit. I don't want to get all tangled up in your life. I don't want to hear the sad story of yet another broken heart. I don't want to have to carry that around with me. I don't want to feel sorry for you. None of this is my business."

"And that," Iris said gently, "is the very thing about you that has always pissed me off, Dahlia. You think I'm an idiot because I dare to take a risk and fall in love. You're the idiot. You don't have the guts or the gumption to fall in love. Sometimes it's as if you don't even love yourself."

"Oh, Iris, go back to bed, will you."

"Dahlia, give your head a fuckin' shake, will you?" Iris leaned forward and kissed Dahlia on the cheek. "You piss me off to no end, but I love you all the same." She got up and went into the house, leaving Dahlia with more to think about than she could handle.

At 8:00 in the morning Handy Andy arrived, not the least bit ticked off at being wakened by the phone at 6:30. When the building supply store opened at 9:00, Dahlia was sitting in the pickup truck, on the parking lot, list in hand, waiting. She took the load of two-by-fours and plywood, the box of nails, the tubes of caulking and the brown bags of things she didn't recognize and couldn't guess the use of, and Andy already had the shed stripped back to joists and supports. John and Rick were working on the floor, hammering nails flat, countersinking them, putting in long screws every eight or nine inches, the whine of the electric screwdrivers sounding almost exactly like the whine of a dentist's drill. Andy came down off the roof and Dahlia waited to hear that it was going to cost her a thousand dollars to fix it. Instead, Andy carefully stuffed his bottom lip with snoose, then turned aside to spit politely. "Roof's good for another 20 years," he told her. "You get that insulation?"

"Cleaned them out," she nodded. "Wasn't room in the pickup for it so they're delivering it with their first run. The guy said probably just a bit past noon."

"Well, that's good timing. I can run a stair ladder up to the loft from inside. You might want to look at the kind that can be pulled down when needed, then lift it up out of the way when not needed. Save a lot of space. There's room up there for a bedroom. Nothing else, but it could be a good-size room, maybe a queen-size bed and a coupla dressers. Wiring's fine. Can't be more than five or six years old. I think old man Pritchard put it in so's the missus could have her broody house here, but she never did move it from up in the big shed, don't know why."

Dahlia climbed up into the loft to sweep and sweep again, then came down and went to the house for two pails of blistering hot water, scrub brushes and heavy-duty commercial cleanser. She had the place swabbed and scrubbed when Andy came up with his pry bar. As carefully as if he was preparing to do brain surgery, he loosened the old boards on the wall, the very ones Dahlia had just scrubbed.

"Yeah, see, it's that old shit. We can leave it in and just put the fibreglass stuff over top."

"I just washed all that and you're going to take it down?"

"No, you're going to take it down. If I was you I'd put rat poison in here too. Looks like someone did when the wiring was put in. See?" He picked up a little bit of something and held it out in his gloved hand. Dahlia looked, then looked again.

"I have to look twice," she joked, "what with only having one eye and all. Is that what it looks like?"

"Is so," he said, actually smiling. "You have any trouble with the eye?"

"The damn thing leaks all the time," she told him, as casually as if they were discussing her pickup. "I keep hoping something will happen to make it stop, but...the doctor tells me it will, one day. He can be breezy about it, you see, because he's not the one with the problem. Hurts sometimes, aches and throbs, but less now than when it first happened."

"Change your depth perception?"

"Change my what?" she grinned, and Handy Andy laughed freely.

"Way to be, woman," he said, handing her the pry bar. "Here you go. Careful of those old nails—you don't want lockjaw. Watch the splinters too. When wood gets old, it gets so hard it's like getting a chunka metal drove in you."

She was well started on the job when John and Rick came up to help. Rick had the thermos in his hand and grinned as he passed it to Dahlia. "My mother said to tell you to sit on your patoo and have a transfusion."

"She didn't say *have* a transfusion," John corrected him. "She said *swill* a transfusion."

"Pigs swill."

"You'd know, nimrod."

"I'm gonna tattle on you for calling me a nimrod."

"Right, you're right, nimrod isn't what you are. Dumbass dork-head is more like it."

But they were easy with each other, pretending to natter and nag, not really getting into it. Dahlia sat on the floor, her knees up, sipping coffee, smoking a cigarette, wondering if she was out of her damn mind or if it had just taken a holiday. There's a novel concept! A holiday.

Five days later the shed was no longer a shed, it was a guest bungalow. "You can move in there if you want," she told Iris gruffly. "Think on it and let me know. We can head in to the furniture store and get, like, a bed, some dressers. You could pick your own colour of paint."

"Dahlia..." For once in her life, Iris seemed devoid of words.

"Might make your visit more comfortable, give you a place to visit with your kids without having the whole clanjamfrie crowding around."

"She's not going to *stay*, is she?" Button asked later, when she was alone with Dahlia. "She's on my case all the time. Button, dear, would you...Button, a little lady doesn't...Button here and Button there and if she's *really* on her broom it's Charlene, my precious... Why did you call me Charlene, anyway? I *hate* that name."

"Your dad's name was Charlie. What was I supposed to call you? Moira?"

"You could have called me Charlie. It's better than Charlene!"

"I *asked* you if you had any particular preference, and all you did was poop all down your leg. I didn't think you wanted me to call you Poop, so..."

"So you picked the shittiest name you could think of, right?"

"You got 'er, babe."

But it was Button who went to the hospital auxiliary thrift store and got three oversized men's shirts, took them to the guest cottage, handed one to Iris, donned another herself and helped paint the dresser, and it was Button who plugged in the kettle and made a pot of tea.

"Mom says maybe she'll be able to find one of those little half-size fridges," she said. "You could keep milk or cream or something in it, for your tea."

"I think I'll just learn to like it without. Your momma has already bent over backward for me. Guess you know we have trouble communicating, eh."

"I know you behave as if you were still kids. If any of *us* acted like that we'd get our backsides warmed and be grounded for a week. A person would think you'd know better."

"Oh, we do. We know better, we just don't do anything about what we know."

"You don't want to go painting the sides of the drawers, Auntie Iris. They won't close properly if you do."

"Charlene, one of the reasons you and I have problems communicating is that you are so *much* like your mother. Now how do you know that?"

"Just look at it, Auntie Iris. It all fits, just so. It only makes sense that if you put a layer of paint on either side of the drawer, you'll make the drawer just that much bigger and it won't fit."

"See, just as I thought, exactly the way your mother's brain works. Even the tone of your voice. You aren't explaining anything to me, you're giving me a lecture. As if not knowing something I had no reason to know was a great big sin."

"Maybe you've never done it before but did you ever pull open a drawer and see it painted on the sides?"

When the others came back from fishing, Iris was still there, still pretending that this was nothing more than a visit with her kids. More than once Dahlia had wanted to say, "Iris, pack your stuff and go home, please. All good things come to an end." But she couldn't say it. Iris didn't have a home to go to, had never learned how to make one for herself. Dal half-expected Chummy to show up and drape himself over a fence or something, but he didn't even phone. He must not believe that Iris had gone. She had taken a hike and come home again once too often, and even Chummy expected her to cave in.

The kids were tanned, and in one summer Skipper had taken the leap from kid to on-the-verge—right up there with John and Rick, and Pape and Blackie were the only little boys left to Dal. She almost felt like going into mourning. It hadn't been like this when Pinch and Duck, then Twink, had gone from little girls to almost women. Why feel such sadness when the boys became almost men? Even testosterone poisoning couldn't change them that much, could it? But they seemed so damn secretive so much of the time. Maybe it was all that male bonding stuff—the knowing looks, the way they talked without looking at one another, their bodies turned away, no eye contact, no communicative body language. The girls weren't like that. They looked at each other, made strong eye contact, their bodies leaning in, hands touching, intent on what they were saying. Dahlia understood that language. It was the other, the male thing, that confused her. They weren't hers any more. They had become their own people, with their own ideas, their own little streaks of stubbornness, their own way of doing things, seeing things and taking stands.

They took a stand on the issue of school, school clothes and the money they had made fishing. "You don't have to do that. I do that!" Dal protested.

Pinch looked at her with such love that Dal felt suddenly shy. "Momma, you've been doing it all my life. Now it's my turn, okay?"

"But—"

"We've talked about it, more than once. And this is how we want it."

There wasn't much Dal could say about that. It was their money. If they wanted to use some of it for school clothes, for winter jackets and warm winter boots, she supposed she didn't have a right to tell them they had to put it in the bank instead.

God, but it was all getting so complicated!

Skipper stood in front of her, looking as if he expected to have to argue and raise at least one corner of hell.

"And have you actually tried this critter?" Dal asked gently.

"I've been on three trail rides. He's trained—real good too. And he's real calm. He's not one of the ones who spend half their time standing on their back legs pawing at the sky."

"How old is he?"

"He's nine years old. That's not old for a horse," he added hurriedly.

"So what is he, a thoroughbred, an Arab, a…" She felt at a total loss. What did she know about horses, anyway, the differences between this kind and that kind?

"He's not any particular kind, he's what they call a 'grade.' He's got some of this and some of that, I guess. But he's not a mutt!"

The animal was reddish brown, his mane and tail a lighter shade than the rest of his body. On his withers were several small white patches. It seemed an odd place for a solid-coloured animal to have any markings, so Dahlia asked about it.

"Bad-fitting saddle," the riding stable owner admitted. "He was a cow horse, up-country, and it looks as if he was kind of loose-treated. Those white spots are where he had gall sores, from the saddle rubbing him raw. He's sound—I've had him vetted—but if you'd feel better about it, well, it's fine by me if you have your own vet come."

Dahlia didn't need the vet. All she needed was to see Skip, his cheek pressed against the muscular neck of the big gelding.

The stable owner made a soft clucking noise deep in her throat, and smiled gently. "Isn't it something?" she said softly. "It doesn't happen all the time. Lots of people, maybe most people, get a horse and they're good to it, really good, and the animal trusts them, does well by them, is biddable and willing, and everything goes just fine. But every now and again, and I have no idea why, a person shows up and a horse—well, to some it sounds overly dramatic, but it's as though the horse falls in love." She kicked at the dry dirt with the toe of her worn paddock boot and took a deep breath. "Guess I might as well 'fess up. That horse wasn't really for sale. The two I had for sale are over there, in the side paddock. Then Grant arrived and was looking around, looking at the animals, asking questions, you know, the way a kid does." For a moment Dahlia wasn't sure she was listening to the same conversation, but then her brain caught up and she realized the woman was calling Skipper by his official registered name. "He asked about riding lessons, and that's a good idea if it's your first horse, so I put him on Rainbow. That's the grey in the paddock. Called Rainbow because there was one in the sky the day she was born. That went okay, and the second time he came I gave him Blazer, the sorrel who's in with the grey. That was fine too. Then he's unsaddling Blazer, getting ready to brush him down, and doesn't Chunky move over and stand next to him. Even tried nudging the Blazer out of the way. So Grant finishes grooming Blazer, and Chunk just steps in place and he gets groomed too. Next thing I know the two of them are walking off together, no lead rope, no need for a hand on the halter, just like a kid with his dog. Four days later and Grant is back. His auntie brought him, the lady with the baby? Chunk was way over in that back field. Grant had a couple of carrots. He calls out hey Chunk, and doesn't that gelding start running. So I sent Grant out on him for the trail ride and lesson. By the time they got back two hours or so later, that boy couldn't even see either of the two that were for sale. All he could see was Chunky."

"And so you're willing to sell him, even though originally...?"

"Yeah. I know. It's dumb moves like this keep this place a shoestring enterprise. My partner tells me time and time again, a person is supposed to use their head in business, not their heart, but..."

The farrier put Chunky in her horse trailer and brought him out the next afternoon. Skipper was as good as walking two feet above the surface of the earth. With Chunky came a well-used but excellently cared-for saddle, and a bridle he was used to.

"It needs a new bit, though." Skip sounded as knowledgeable as someone raised on a horse ranch. "I want to get him a copper one, you can get them with, like, sections? And they can play with the sections, with their tongues, and then they don't mind wearing the bit so much. And he needs a saddle pad." He looked worried. "And some hoof stuff, and a curry comb and..."

"I imagine it will cost a lot to get set up," Dal agreed, "but maybe after you've got what you need, it won't seem so bad." She turned to the farrier. "What about shoes? He doesn't have any."

"Depends where you're going to be riding him. He's got feet like flint, good feet, and he hasn't needed shoes because the trails they use at the riding stable are pretty much groomed, free of rocks and all. He's due for a trim in about two weeks. I'll know by then if he's chipping or not."

The other kids watched, green with envy. Dal waited, offering nothing, especially not encouragement.

"How much would you charge a guy to take a ride?" John asked.

"First one is free," Skipper grinned. "After that, well...how does two bucks sound?"

"Two bucks? For how long?"

"Half an hour."

"So that's four bucks an hour?"

"Yeah. Two hours and he's bought himself a bag of feed."

"I can see it now," Pansy whispered. "They'll be lined up, allowances in hand."

"Maybe not," Iris offered. "I can see Pinch and Twink talking up a storm. Button, well, she's thinking about something, you can tell, you can nearly see the smoke coming from her ears."

Rainbow and Blazer arrived in the farrier's trailer three days later. "That's *it*," Dal warned. "Eight kids, three horses. If you can't figure it out and agree, well, you can fight it out, down and dirty, behind the barn."

"Two horses," Skipper corrected her. "Nine kids, counting Blackie. Chunky is mine."

"You're right," Dahlia agreed. "I'm sorry. And I didn't really count Blackie and Pip—they're kind of small."

"I can ride!" Pip insisted. "I can *so!*"

Neither of the two communal horses had gear. Dal couldn't believe how much money flew out of her hand when she went to the tack store. Even second-hand gear was spendy. While she was at it, she got Skipper a saddle pad too. She also got worm medicine, vitamin and mineral feed additive, some special conditioner for manes and tails, supposed to make them easier to brush and comb. Then nothing would do but she get a big plastic jug with a sprayer top, a mix in it for the body coat. "Makes them shine, and it's good for their skin," the store owner explained. "You don't need it, but if it ever rains, it helps the water run off them, helps against rain scald."

"What in hell is rain scald? Sounds expensive."

"Everything that has to do with horses is expensive."

In the middle of the night, the August full moon seemed so big it was close enough to touch — well, you'd have to climb the grandmother cedar to do it, but she'd be easy enough to climb. Her branches were large and evenly spaced, and she'd be a living ladder. The dog was lying beside her and Kit was on her lap, her belly still naked although the stitches had healed well. Of course they'd been late getting to the vet, so even though they'd found homes for the litter from the hayfield, there was another litter to contend with, and finding homes for these ones would be easy except for the resistance from the kids. Kit herself showed no signs of Siamese or Burmese or any other exotic sort of cat — she was a hundred percent back alley and vacant lot. But the kittens were undeniably part something. They were beautifully box-shaped, sturdy, square and big, but their colouring guaranteed they'd get homes. Most of them had grey or honey-coloured bodies, with tips and points either black, tabby or, on two of them, a strange lilac colour. Pape insisted that those two were twins. Dahlia had tried to explain to him the concept of twins, pointing out to him that the entire litter was like twins, but more, all born within the same hour. "No." He sat on her lap and snuggled close, looking up at her with that special expression that kids wear when they think their mom is very lovable but dumb as a post. "That's not what I mean. These ones are exactly twins. Pinch and Duck said they looked mirror-image, from the way the egg split. Like them, and Pinch is right-handed, Duck is left-handed. These two are like that. And they're both boys, we checked."

Every mother and father knows that when kittens grow up to be tom cats, the kid is getting prepared to lay claim. Even Dal didn't believe she was going to be able to hold firm and say no.

"So whatever possessed you to buy two horses?" Iris said, sitting on the porch and pulling her sweater close around her.

"Some of the kids have money from fishing, and other kids don't. John and Rick worked like hell around here, and so did Twink. I could have let the twins buy horses, but I was afraid we'd wind up with our own herd. Already they're making noises about how Rainbow is a

girl so maybe we should find a boy and she can have a baby, and..."
She sighed.

"You don't have to buy expensive stuff for John and Rick." Iris didn't
sound as if she wanted to get into a fight, so Dal decided to forgo the
endeavour.

"I know I don't have to," she said gently, "but hell, a kid is a kid is a
kid is a kid, eh."

"Sometimes. And I have to admit this is one of them." Iris rose and
pretended to yawn. "I really do like you, Dahlia." And off she walked
toward the guest cottage. Dahlia watched her go and realized that
Iris wasn't as fat as she had been. She would never be thin, or even
merely soft. She would always be a large woman. But the weight she
was carrying now was almost solid—it didn't jiggle and sway as it
had, and that awful apron thing was gone. What *is* that thing, anyway, that slab that hangs down at the front? And why do so many
Moby Dicks wear spandex slacks, which make it more visible?

For the brief time left before school opened, it was horse horse
horse, and if there were arguments, Dal didn't hear them or hear
about them. Skipper and Chunk went riding the 60 acres with Pinch
and Duck, and when it was Rick and John's turn on the communal
horses, Skipper and Chunk went with them too. Often Skipper let Pip
ride in front of him, but she never got to hold the reins, and he had
some firm rules. "You don't talk in that high, squeaky, whiney voice,"
he said sternly. "You talk low, in a normal voice, or you'll scare him.
And you do *not* bounce and kick your legs and holler, or you'll be
down on the ground, walking. You are going for a ride, you are not
in charge of the horse. He is *my* horse, and I don't have to take you
anywhere."

"I want to steer him! I want to make him gallop!"

"Then stay home and wait until you have your own horse."

Skipper would have left without her, but Pip did a turnabout unlike
any Dahlia had seen her do. When they came back, Pip was very
quiet and went to her room by herself.

"What's up?"

"She got put on the ground and told to walk home," Skipper said, all
set to stand his ground and to argue if necessary.

"How far did she walk?"

"Oh, fifteen minutes, maybe. She'd be a good rider if she wasn't such a..." He paused and shook his head.

"Yeah," Dal agreed. "Well, we're all trying, Skip. What more can I tell you? If I was you—and I'm not saying this is how it *has* to be—next time she pesters you to go for a ride, I'd tell her no. She'll whine and grizzle and do the why-not stuff, but I'd just tell her that her bad behaviour is boring. Tell her it's no fun going anywhere with her because she can't behave."

"I already told her that. She's a lot like Auntie Iris."

"Die!" Dahlia lunged at him, got him in a headlock, pretended to bash his head into the door jamb. "Die, oh dreadful little horror." And then the foolishness was gone and they were having a quick hug. She kissed him on the cheek. "Skip, you smell like a horse. Not all of us appreciate the scent."

All too soon they headed off to school. Dahlia could have howled in the sudden silence. The house seemed cavernous. The only thing she could think of to do was pour a bath and soak in it. Now what? She heard Blackie wailing and heard Pansy talking to him, soothing him. All too soon he'd be off to preschool, then kindergarten, then grade one. Is that all we get of them, four lousy years?

Ten

Two weeks after school started up, the rain finally arrived. Three days of downpour and by the middle of the second day the grass began to green up again. The rain stopped and the sun came out, but everything felt different—they had moved from one season to another. They could expect more rain, a day here, two days there until the monsoons were on them and puddles straining to become ponds, the earth sodden and swollen with too much water. But not yet, not the near-floods yet, just gentle rain, coaxing the fungi awake. The white treasures wouldn't begin to grow until the earth was wet, and Dal imagined them sending out tendrils, encountering dry earth, yelping to each other about being scratched.

The kids invented their own routines. They rushed home from school, changed into grubbies and headed for the barn. "Groceries!" Skip called. Chunky was already on the move. He sped up his pace, his tail up and drifting behind him. His head was proportionally much bigger than those of the other two, and his legs thicker, especially down toward the hoof—near the ankle, or whatever you called it in a horse. There was an entire vocabulary here, one that Skip spoke easily and understood completely, one that Dahlia could not seem to get fixed in her head. When she commented on the differences in conformation, Skipper nodded, and said he was pretty sure Chunk had a grandparent or maybe great-grandparent who had been a work horse, "probably part Clydesdale," but he couldn't explain why he thought so. "It's what helps give him that laid-back disposition." Dahlia, feeling horsed out, didn't ask any more questions.

Skip gave Chunk a small measure of grain, brushed him, saddled him and fussed until the animal had finished his treat. Then it was on with the bozell, mount up and head off. Even with the new bit—copper, with riggins for Chunk to play with—the animal grumbled each time, and while he never refused it, he obviously hated it. Dahlia asked the woman at the tack store what could be done. "Is there a paste or something, like toothpaste, flavoured with whatever horses like? Carrots, apples, whatever, and you can smear it on the bit so the argument won't happen?"

"Nothing like that, not that I know of. Did you get the horse locally?"

"Yeah, from the riding stable. He's the cow horse from up-country, Chunky."

"Oh, him." She nodded. "Well, he's always been a bugger about a bit. I figure it's because he was raised and trained by a guy on the Alkali Lake reserve and a lot of those guys use a permanent hackamore. Lots of them make their own, like a halter, only different enough to give a bit of control. Here, see this?" She reached for a device hanging from a peg by the door. "This is a bozell. See this bit that goes over the nose? See how stiff and hard it is? It does pretty much what a bit does, only it works with pressure on the nose. Their noses are really sensitive, eh."

Dal listened, feeling that she needed a translator or interpretor, but she bought the bozell and took it home. There she conveyed the information she didn't fully understand to her son, who seemed to know exactly what she was talking about.

"Try it," she suggested. "If it works, it might solve the problem, take that little bit of unwillingness away, and then each ride will be wonderful right from the get-go."

"How much do I owe you?" Skip asked.

"A kiss. On the cheek." She tapped and Skip leaned forward, grinning, gave her the thank-you peck, then hugged her. She could barely see over the top of his head.

"Oh, Skippy, I do love you," she sighed.

"How much?" he teased.

"Way much."

"Do anything I ask kind of love?"

"I am enslaved." She rolled her eyes. "I am trapped in the cage of my love for you."

"Could we try to stop calling me Skippy? It's kind of like a dog's name, eh."

Dahlia felt her eyes filling with tears. "Sorry. I'll try to remember to call you Grant, I really will. If I slip and call you Skipper, you could maybe say excuse me, Mom, our dog is called Queenie. I'm Grant."

"No you aren't." He rested his head on her shoulder. "*I'm* Grant. You're Mom."

Chunk obviously knew the bozell. He even lowered his head to make it easier for Grant to get it on him. Dahlia watched them head off, the horse responding easily. Skipper—Grant!—had his pack and was determined to find at least enough mushrooms for supper. When he was late coming home, Dahlia began to worry. My God, what if, what if, what if Chunk had rebelled, what if there wasn't enough control without the bit, what if Skipper was hurt, what if he'd fallen off, hit his head, my God, the things that could go wrong! And if nothing had gone wrong, if he was just ignoring the rules, she'd fix him. She'd whale him until he howled.

They were having dessert when Skip walked in, his clothes wet, a grin across his face, his pack heavy in his hand.

"I get the prize," he told her. "I found the first ones."

"You're kidding!" She forgot all about beating him to a pulp. "Are they good ones?"

"Smileys, Momma."

"Way to go, Skipper," Button laughed.

"Grant," Dahlia said quietly. "He wants to be called Grant."

They raced home from school every day, and while they changed their clothes, Pansy filled the thermoses with hot, sweet tea. They picked up their sandwiches, got their shrooming bags and their newspaper for wrapping each one separately, and then they headed off, riding double on the horses, the surplus kids pedalling furiously. Within a couple of days they had the logistics figured out to their satisfaction. Pip stayed home—nobody wanted to be bothered with her—but Pape was more than welcome. He was their good-luck charm, guaranteed a ride with Grant.

"Nah," John laughed softly. "I'll take my bike, I'm not all that much of a horse person." They all knew he meant it, that he wasn't just stepping aside because he felt like a charity case or a not-really in the family. "Anyway," he teased, "the rest of them will wind up with big butts and bowed legs and I'll be the most in-shape soccer player in town."

They came home when darkness began to claim the world, and Dahlia drove them to the mushroom buyer. On the subject of money and horse expenses, Grant relaxed, knowing he had enough put away to see Chunky through the winter, right up until it was time to go fishing again.

Dahlia went picking as soon as the kids left for school and stayed out until just before they all got home in the afternoon. That gave her plenty of time to pick enough to make it more than just worth her while, and it meant she had plenty of time to do the farm chores before the light began to fade. It also meant she had time with Pip, time to wrangle with the pain-in-the-face behaviour and the I-wanna personality.

"Maybe," she said to Pansy, "maybe I should stop calling her Pipsqueak. Maybe if I didn't call her that, she wouldn't be one."

"Yeah?" Pansy winked, warning of a joke. "What *is* that kid's name, anyway?"

"Uh, I'm not sure. Belinda, Melinda, Lucinda...something like that."

"Lucy sounds like a nice person. Calm, sort of. But fun, lots of fun."

"Pray hard, Pansy. You never know, it might work."

The calves were sold at the start of October. Dahlia deposited the cheque in the farm account and drove home feeling glum. It didn't help to know the calves had another year ahead of them, a year of almost unlimited food. When she got home, the kids were notice-able by their absence. Dahlia was glad of that, she wasn't ready for the accusing looks. They'd promised each other over and over that they weren't going to get attached to the calves, weren't going to give them names, or make pets of them. But it wasn't a load of nothing at all had driven off, it was Mudface and Beano, it was Cutie and Curly, it was Champ and Fred and Toby and Lily, and she knew the same thing would happen again with the next crop of calves, and the next, and the ones after that as well. Maybe if a person had 500 of them they'd begin to be anonymous.

The brushing and thinning crew had gone without her, off to the back of beyond. They would live in the unpainted jerry-built remnants of what had once been a logging camp, then a shake-bolt camp, then a reforestation camp where other people tried, with pitiful results, to replace what had been treated so mindlessly, so that at some point long in the future, others could come and wreak havoc all over again. She wondered if the mice and snakes in the hayfield felt the same way about her and all that goddamn clattering equipment. At some other time she might have gone with them, but not now. Now she was too aware of time, and how it whipped past faster then the speed of sound or light or anything you could turn your mind to. Dammit, they were buying their own school clothes, using their own money to buy shoes and jackets. She wanted to grab them, cram them into their Christmas stockings and hang them up, keep them with her, but she couldn't.

Dal knew there was a near horde of people would tell her that her success as a mom was measured by the self-reliance of her kids, tell her that whatever mistakes she had made in the name of love had been small ones, possibly even good ones, that she had set an example that they were following, earning their own way in the world, actually trying to make plans for the future. They had seen what manual labour got you, and what you got for working for other people, and they had their sights set elsewhere. Skipper said he was going to skipper school, to learn navigation and who knows what all, so that he could not only work the tugs taking bargeloads of God knows what to Japan and China, he could be in charge. Twink had her eye on law, and Pinch and Duck were calmly certain they would find a way to get their own fish boat. She still had Button, but not for long—she was straining to leap the invisible barrier and join Skip and the others. Pape, darling Pape, was still hers. She had a feeling he would be hers when he was six feet tall and living his dream of driving a garbage truck. Pip already wasn't hers and never had been, really. She was too much like Iris and too attached to Pansy. Well, that was good. Pip didn't annoy Pansy, didn't make Pansy feel like giving her a boot on the arse just on general principles. Pansy thought Pip was a great kid. Dahlia wished she did. But things were the way they were and hard as you tried to change them, trying didn't make it so. Maybe she had run thin on patience by the time Pip came along. Or maybe you give birth to individuals, and nobody gets along with everybody.

Only a little while ago they had been in diapers, and now they were almost ready to jump into their own cars and pickup trucks and drive off, to lives that Dal wouldn't share. If she was lucky, she'd see them high days and holidays. If she was unbelievably lucky, one or two of them might decide to live near her. But law school isn't just down the road, and skipper school isn't half a mile away, and your own fish boat means half the year tangled in nets and lines. They were not going to be entangled in her life. That, bad luck and all, was that. Dal wasn't losing a moment of it by living in a jackknife-whittled ex-bunkhouse, coming home one weekend out of every three or four. She'd had to spend too much time away from them already. No way. Not a chance.

Dal had almost been ready to get a tin cup and some pencils and set herself up at the busiest corner in town, and then there she was with a job at the oyster plant. It took a lot of getting used to. Dal wasn't accustomed to working inside, she wasn't accustomed to being in more or less the same spot for hours on end and she wasn't used to having people working so close by that she could carry on conversations, tell jokes, find out more about their lives than she was interested in knowing. But she had what was needed for the job—strong hands and forearms. It wasn't anything you'd learn in school, and they didn't give courses on how to shuck shellfish, yet it wasn't something any old body could walk in off the highway and set about doing. It took skill to open the oysters without impaling the thick of your thumb or the palm of your hand on the shucking knife. It didn't pay huge amounts, either, but Dahlia was used to that kind of money, and at least it was the kind of job where the more you did, the more you got. She'd never be known as Dahlia Cassidy, the fastest shucker on the coast, but she could make enough to cover the necessities. As for the rest, well, there was always fungus plucking, and salal picking, and the off chance she would win Lotto 6/49.

She had to admit that Iris was less of a pain in the arse now than at any other time in her life. Was that because Iris was making an effort? Or was it because Dal had other things on her mind? Gone were the rantings and ravings about how Pansy was the favourite, the favoured, the lucky. Maybe Iris considered herself lucky, for once. After all, she had her own room and could see her kids any time she wanted. She had even started doing things—little things at first, the dishes or a load of laundry. That was nice. It gave Pansy a break and took a large measure of the load off Dal. And Dal could use the reduction. She was so busy that she was trying to figure out a way to borrow against the future. Dal wondered if it would help if she got roller skates glued to her feet, so she could zip around like those poor kids in the Superstore. Helluva note when walking or running isn't fast enough to keep the boss happy. But there sure did seem to be a lot of work in the world, and most of it was dirty, uncomfortable and poorly paid, if it was paid at all.

Then Iris pulled something that set Dal back on her butt, wondering if the earth was still in its appointed orbit. Iris got a job. Even more amazing, she didn't quit or get fired in the first week. Every evening after supper, Iris headed for the shower, then pulled on a pair of slacks and an amusingly serious starched white shirt with a little bow tie on an elastic. She did her Cassidy hair in a loose bun that had no chance of holding all that incredibly independent curl and would soon be coming loose, tendril by tendril, until it framed her face and made her look years younger than her actual age. She wore runners—black leather—which Rick kept shined to a fare-thee-well, and off she hied to sling beer and joke with the customers. The wages weren't high but the tips were great, and basically tax-free. When she got her first paycheque she handed it to Dahlia.

"Huh?" was the best Dahlia could manage.

"Take it." Iris was dead serious. "I've got my tips for walking-around money. And there's three of us here."

"Duh-Whine pays—"

"Don't argue with me, Dahlia, for God's sake. Stop bending over backward all the time, turning yourself inside out so you can be wonderful! Take the goddamn money."

Two weeks later Iris told Dahlia to go down to the pub and talk to the owner. "He's looking for music, and it might as well be you as some other yee-haw."

"Better a yee-haw you know than one you don't?"

"Better good music than the other kind." Iris looked at Dahlia, then nodded. "You climb into the shower and wash your hair, then come sit while I trim the ends for you. You've been on that damn tractor for so long and sitting in the sun at the lake for so many hours that your hair is six colours and dry at the ends. And I won't have my sister getting up in front of a crowd of people with frizz."

It was like being 10 all over again. Sitting on the high stool with newspaper on the floor to catch the snippets and more newspaper safety-pinned around her like an oversized bib, and Iris snip snip snipping, doing the best she could to bring order to the defiant mop.

"God knows, if you have absolutely got to have the most Cassidy hair of any of us, the least you can do is make the most of it."

The kids sat around watching, impressed by Iris's skill. "You should work in a salon," Button said.

"No thank you," Iris laughed. "I tried that. Enough to give a person the grizzlies. And the pay isn't anywhere near what I'm making now. If you have to work, sweetheart, you might as well get properly paid for it."

Dal got the job playing at the pub, four hours a night, Tuesday to Saturday. It wasn't Toby's, the crowd wasn't as large, it wasn't as free and companionable, but the tips were good, the pay was every bit as good and the regulars were friendly. It was like coming home. Maybe the house had been repainted, a few rooms added or altered, but it was home and it felt great to feed on the energy from the crowd and turn that energy into music. When she cut loose and sang "I Fall to Pieces," the owner hollered approval and the guys in the wide orange suspenders and work-stained jeans stood up and cheered.

On her first Saturday night, the place was packed. She had Blackie's silvertop and was playing it as if there wasn't going to be a tomorrow, playing as much for herself as for the crowd, and she could almost see the old reprobate himself seated at a table, nodding approval. Was that why she so enjoyed making music for the weekend crowd? Did it prove to her that she was alive?

The women from the softball team had a table to themselves, and when she took her break they waved her over, but she shook her head, smiled, pointed at the loo and headed there, only to find it full to bursting. She was in no mood to wait, so she ducked back out again and went to the back, to the Employees Only biffy. It was quieter there, blessedly. The sound of the jukebox drifted in only faintly.

She peed, ran cold water into the basin and cooled her face and neck. She stared at her reflection in the mirror. No wonder Twink's teacher had seemed surprised when she saw Dahlia. But then there was no way the teacher could know that Dal hadn't been much older than Twink was now when the twins were conceived. But still, Dal didn't look her age. Or maybe she did, and it was others, weighted down with convention and respectability, who looked older than they really were.

Iris looked so much younger, so much more vibrant these past couple of months. There was something in her eyes that made her look more youthful than she had at eighteen, when she already seemed older and tireder than Rosie, who was married and a mother and said she had never been so happy in her life.

Dahlia liked the way her hair behaved since Iris had snipped her mop. Dal had suggested that Iris whack off a ton of it, and Iris had told her to shut the hell up. "When do you ever actually see your own hair, anyway? The best you get is a reflection in a mirror, and then you only see one part at a time. It's the rest of us get to see it. We know, don't we, kids?"

The kids had noisily agreed, and now the mop wasn't any shorter but it had shape, and the bleached-by-the-sun tips were gone. Wasn't that a trick, removing them without making the hair seem any shorter?

Dahlia went back out onstage and the women from the softball team cheered. She grabbed her banjo and played "Pluck Pluck Said the Duck," and Dianne smiled as if she knew something the rest of the crowd hadn't yet learned. Dal felt her face flushing. It was like that stupid kids' game of I know, I know you know, I know you know I know you know. Dianne knew what Dal was feeling in the pit of her pelvis, and Dal knew Dianne knew. What's more, Dianne knew that Dal knew that Dianne knew, because they both knew that Dianne felt the same lurch. And with all that static energy surging, how could the entire ball team not be aware as well? Or were they? Who knew?

It was like a dare, best answered with the fiddle, and Dal played maritime tunes one after the other until the transplanted Newfies and herring chokers were roaring out the words, swaying together with their arms around each other's shoulders, closer to hysterical than harmonious. Iris wove her way between the tables, her tray of beer easily balanced, a wide smile on her face, as if she was at a party instead of at work.

∽

The rains settled in for real, day after day of heavy grey skies and dripping leaves and branches, the driveway puddled, the area in front of the house always with an inch of water on it, and around the barn the mud was starting to spread, to thicken and deepen. The farrier came out and removed Rainbow's shoes. "The mud gets so thick here it starts to form a suction when they step, and that puts pressure on the shoes. The nails start to wobble, and that breaks down the wall of the hoof. The next thing you know, the shoe is yanked off and you're lucky if the wall of the hoof isn't damaged."

The rain persisted. Dal had time after her shucking job to head out for an hour or two of shrooming, but it was getting dark earlier each night, and with so many people out looking and finding the fungi, the prices were going down down down to the point where the kids called a family conference.

"What we've been wondering," said Rick, as speaker for the group, "is would we be better off to let the rest of them just do their thing, and spore?"

"It would make for more mushrooms next year," Dal agreed.

"That's what we were thinking. We aren't making anywhere near the kind of money we were making at the beginning, and by the time we get there and get ourselves set up, it's almost time to pack it away and head home again. Last night we were soaked to the skin. Pape was so cold he couldn't even talk for shivering, and what did we make? Twenty-three bucks between the bunch of us."

"It's not that long ago 23 bucks would have seemed like a fortune," Pansy interjected.

"Yeah. We thought of that too. And it's almost three bags of feed, but..."

"I think letting them spore is a damn good idea," Dal said firmly. They were kids, and maybe most kids on the globe wind up scouring garbage dumps, looking for their supper in the throwaways of other peoples' lives. But not her kids. Not these kids. There would be years and years and years of work staring them in the face soon enough. Let them have some enjoyment while they had some choice. "We'll make it up at the beginning of the season next year. Maybe we ought to get ourselves all set up, and work it so we go full bore when the price is high, have a collecting shed or something. You could make up teams, and one of you takes full boxes to the shed and the other two are picking and packing. You could switch every hour or so. That way nobody's legs would get worn out. Then I'd go down, or Pan could, or maybe even Iris, load up the pickup, and by the time you were ready to call it a day and leave, we'd be organized. You guys could bring your bikes and horses home, and whoever was driving could go straight to the buyer—get there first, before the volume began to drive the prices down."

"Good." Pape sighed with relief. "It wasn't even fun any more."

"That's why they call it work," Iris said gently. "The other stuff is called fun, and you don't often get paid for it. So you have to find fun where you can, sweetheart, and usually make your own. Which is why your momma has been teaching you to play music."

"Do you play music?"

"A little bit. So does Auntie Pansy."

"Auntie Pansy's the best singer of everyone," Twink said. "She's the one taught me how to sing. If you're good, she might teach you."

"What music do you play, Auntie Iris?"

"Oh, I haven't played for years. But when I did, I played the mouth organ. And the accordion. But mostly the spoons and bones."

"I can do spoons. But not bones. What bones?"

"Rib bones. Tell you what, we'll look for some of the right kind at the butcher store, then see if we can whine and snivel until Auntie Pansy cooks up her world-famous ribs. Then, instead of giving the bones to the dog, we'll put them on a cookie sheet and we'll bake them in the oven until they're hard hard hard. And then—you'll see, we'll have fun."

Before they had that fun, it was time to get out the manure spreader, fill it with the aged black gold in the cement-lined storage area, then hook up the tractor and head out to the hayfields to drive around and around and around and around while the clods, lumps and bits flew. Then back to the huge pile, to unhook the tractor and use the bucket on it to reload the manure spreader. Then hook up the tractor and back out again, around and around and around and around, spreading the manure so the rain could do its work and the roots of the grass could suck up the nutrients. Another Saturday given a poke in the eye—some of the kids off at soccer practice, other kids doing horse chores or helping vacuum the living room, Dahlia on the tractor, around and around, the thermos coffee barely fighting off the chill.

And Iris togged herself in work clothes, pulled on John's gumboots and trudged out to the field determinedly. "Someone at the house to see you," she said, and she actually smiled. "I'll take over with this."

"You?" Dal blurted.

"Of course me," Iris laughed. "I was running a tractor when you were still learning how to pee in the toilet instead of your own pants. Get off and give an expert a go at it."

Dal did, unwillingly. Then stood there feeling like a fool as Iris settled herself on the hard tractor seat as if she had never sat anywhere else in her life. Dal had sudden flashes of times forgotten, of Iris coming into the kitchen red-faced and exhausted, sinking onto a chair and reaching with trembling hands for the glass of lemonade their mother offered. Iris sitting on the damn old always-in-need-of-repair tractor as Dal headed off, violin case in hand, for her music lesson. Maybe that was when Iris had started to feel hard done by. Maybe it took a while to be able to get all of you, soul especially, down off the damn noisy stinking thing, especially when there went the other one, tippy-toe down the road to a place where someone fussed over her and made her feel special. Rosie in the house, busy doing things that would get her praise and grunted compliments—good spuds, Rosie, you got the skin on the chook just right too. Maybe so. Dal would have to ask.

And she knew she wouldn't. Some things just are, and no amount of talking over or explaining can change anything. All Dal had to do was remember the second haying, how many hours of tedding she had done without any of the kids realizing she hadn't been napping.

And other things too. The middle of the night and Iris getting out of bed, so tired she was on the verge of weeping, heading off because the old man was ordering it, going to the field to help bring in a too-weak night-born calf, for no reason other than she was older than Boo, and nobody could wake him up anyway. And Rosie, well, she needed her sleep because she had to get up early to give a hand with breakfast. Dahlia was too young, Pansy still a toddler, and the older boys were still out drinking homemade goof and busy maintaining that time-honoured male tradition of sowing wild oats. Iris put the tractor in gear and headed off, every bit as easily as Dahlia. In fact she was easier. Iris was relaxed as she drove. Dahlia sat up there as if she had a pin on the seat, ready to jab her ass if she bounced loose. Well, damn, the things you don't notice, and then can't remember.

She didn't recognize the car parked in the driveway and she hoped it wasn't Jim come to ask, yet again, if she'd rejoin the band. She hoped he'd decided to lay off the hustle, or better yet, that he'd found someone else, someone who welcomed the smiling invitation to go for a coffee. Jim was a nice guy, and he probably wouldn't get drunk and almost amputate that most precious part of her anatomy. He'd probably treat it with respect, even if it did baffle him. So much baffled them—sometimes the mysteries seemed unfathomable. Why did God make things that way? Was it God who had done it, made men and women such separate and prickly things? Supposed to be the two halves of a whole, but trying to fit them together was more difficult than imagining how porcupines managed to get pregnant.

"Hi, am I keeping you from something important?" It was Dianne, grinning at her from the sofa, with Pip sitting beside her as if she was civilized, sharing a Dr. Seuss story.

"Important? Uh, no, uh, not really. Manure spreading time is all."

"Manure spreading." Dianne said it as if it was on a level with brain surgery. Dal had the nervous impulse to go into a long-winded explanation, but was saved from making a fool of herself by Pip, who chose that moment to put Dr. Seuss on the coffee table and almost tipped herself on to the floor.

"Easy, sweetheart." Dianne caught her. "You have to be very careful with yourself, you know. Precious things are always breaking, it's one of the sad truths of life, and we wouldn't want you to put bruises on your precious self."

"Do you break?" Pip asked.

"My heart, mostly." Dianne laughed softly. "But that's okay. It's worth it."

Dal finished unlacing her boots and padded into her own living room, feeling as if she was walking toward the edge of a precipice. It was up to her, and she knew it. She'd always wondered how people could do it, and here she was without the sense to turn and head for higher, safer ground. People splitting their loyalties—you dare to love someone, and then you have kids and look what that does. The kids demand attention and distract you from the loved one, who all too often, without even knowing it's happening, also distracts you, or rebels, or resents the attention that's going to the kids. Look at Iris and Duh-Whine, everything fine for a while and then… And why not? Who would not have become totally involved with Johnny? And Duh-Whine had been jealous. Hell, the Morgans were born with a streak of possessiveness a mile wide. Never mind the Morgans, look at her own precious mother, who had kept her bargain—through, as they say, thick and thin. She had promised to love, honour and cherish, and she did, long past the time when it made any sense to continue. Her allegiance had been promised and it never shifted, even when her children had bruises, even when they had the marks of a belt, even when she should have headed for the horizon with them and left him to fester in his own septic rage. Dahlia had grown up knowing she would never, no matter what, hand over her life and the lives of her kids to such danger. And by God, she hadn't.

She should turn and run. She should race away, but she wanted to see and not just imagine the length of leg, the curve of buttock, the soft slope of back. If she was going to lose sleep, dammit, it might as well be *for* something, not because of the lack of it.

"Hey, Pip," Pansy called. "We're all headin' out, you coming?"

"Where you going?"

"Going out to watch Auntie Iris with the tractor." As if watching the tractor was a big deal. But Pip must have thought so—she was already off the sofa and running out of the room.

"Haven't seen you since ball season ended. Well, except at the bar the other night. And that's not the same—didn't get to talk or anything."

"Uh, no, I, uh, guess not." Jesus, where was the Cassidy gift of gab when you needed it?

"Working at the oyster plant, I hear."

"That and mushroom picking."

"I didn't know you went shrooming. Did you find a good spot?"

"Yeah, pretty good. Keeps me busy."

"Well, if you run out, give me a call. I've got several good spots. I could show you if you're interested."

"I didn't know you were a fungus plucker." Might as well be one of the upper crust the way words escaped her when she needed them.

"There's a lot about me you don't know."

"Yeah." And a lot about you I've imagined, fantasized, dreamed and wanted.

"I wondered a couple of times if you were mad at me or something."

"No."

"Talking to you is a bit like pulling teeth, did anybody ever tell you that?"

"Usually what they tell me is that I could talk the ears off a field of corn. They say my entire family is like that. If they're trying to be nasty, they say we're gabby, and if they want to be truthful they say we're a pack of silver-tongued devils. I can't really explain why it is I'm wasting your time trying to be the mute. I didn't expect to see you, and I'm completely off balance."

"That's better." Dianne was laughing, flirting with those incredible eyes, knowing damn well why most of Dal's words were stuck in her throat and all of her brains were on hold. "Jesus, for a minute there I thought I was going to have to do all the talking."

"Oh, I'll be okay after a while. It's the thin air up here on this ledge. I mean all a person has to do is peek over the edge and you'll see just how far down everything else is. And at the bottom, hey, that water is deep. Gives a person a sort of a light-headed feeling."

"Yeah, the water's deep, but you know what they say, it's easier to swim in because you don't have to worry about skinning your toes on the gravel bottom when you kick."

How in hell was she going to figure out the logistics of what she knew was coming? A person could hardly find enough privacy in this pack to brush her teeth in peace, and now she had to figure out how and where to answer the open invitation in those eyes, in that smile. Oh well, she could always try a wild weekend in a motel in Tofino.

"So—gonna take me out and show me Iris on the tractor?"

"Give you a ride on the tractor if you promise to be a good girl." The old woman raised her somewhat scarred head and grinned, sending goose bumps up Dal's back.

"Oh, I'm good, Dahlia Cassidy. I'm damn good."